THE FAÇADE

THE
FAÇADE

M. N. O. P. Q.

Libuše Moníková

TRANSLATED FROM THE GERMAN BY
JOHN E. WOODS

ALFRED A. KNOPF

NEW YORK

1991

THIS IS A BORZOI BOOK
PUBLISHED BY ALFRED A. KNOPF, INC.

Copyright © 1991 by Alfred A. Knopf, Inc.
All rights reserved under International and Pan-American
Copyright Conventions. Published in the United States by Alfred A. Knopf,
Inc., New York, and simultaneously in Canada by Random House of
Canada Limited, Toronto. Distributed by Random House, Inc., New York.
Originally published in Germany as *Die Fassade* by Carl Hanser Verlag,
Munich in 1987. Copyright © 1987 by Carl Hanser Verlag

Library of Congress Cataloging-in-Publication Data
Moníková, Libuše.
[Fassade. English]
The façade : M.N.O.P.Q. / Libuše Moníková : translated from the
German by John E. Woods.—1st American ed.
p.   cm.
Translation of: Die Fassade.
ISBN 0-394-57250-5
I. Title.
PT2673.O4693F313   1991
833'.914—dc20   90-28717
CIP

Manufactured in the United States of America
First American Edition

Part One

INNER BOHEMIA

ONE

Orten lies on the scaffold at the castle's north façade, drawing the Allegory of Justice in the sweep of the projecting gable. The wet plaster splatters under the edge of his spatula; he squinches his eyes and mouth, holding his head to one side and trying to breathe through his nose. He hardly notices the dust anymore, smearing away the larger crumbs with the back of his hand. The figure is still missing one hand, but all the rest, her outline and attributes, is finished in the gable's central panel.

Whitish-gray lime has dried on his face, neck, and forearms, has crusted on his hands and floured his brows and lashes. The way he tenses his eyes results in a tic so uncontrollable and impersonal that it seems not to be his, but rather to token some mistake of phylogenetic development, a delayed response to feeble pecks inside the seven-shelled eggs of baby dinosaurs unable to exit the casing; the heavy plates provided the clutch too much security, were the wrong evolutionary path. The future belonged to small, agile species.

Primal lizards, trilobites—out of sympathy for petrifactions, for the dead ends of evolution, Orten carves an insect in the frieze.

Off to one side, two levels below him, Podol is working on the main sgraffito. Sixty-year-old Patera helps him by smoothing the whitewashed plaster, unfolding the cartoons and attaching them to the façade above the windows. Podol traces the cartoon's lines with his spatula, presses them into the moist wall. Once the cartoon is removed, he corrects the sketch and they begin to scratch away, filling out the design.

On the first level are two symmetrically arranged battle scenes, separated in the middle by a sundial. The left one depicts the conquest of the town, the right is a detail of the battle on the Ponte Milvio, freely adapted from a copy of a tapestry by Giulio Romano in the papal gallery. Between the windows is the tale of Samson and Delilah, which is to be restored using the original sketches. The classical motifs under the cornice on the second level, hunting scenes and a flat panorama of the landscape, have already been restored.

They use both old techniques and old permeable paints; the walls have to breathe. Capillary water in the mortar can't evaporate under modern paints, which are more weatherproof and form a skin. When they first began the sgraffiti, the layers of paint adhered poorly because the plaster was too wet. They have learned by experience.

They also know that since they are using traditional techniques their work has a limited life span, particularly on the exterior walls. In the past the north and west sides were the first to show signs of weathering. Nowadays the disintegration is more even and rapid.

Patera keeps pace, but Podol notices that he would like to take a break but is afraid to ask. He mentally curses Maltzahn, who is off to the Landmarks Office for the second time this month to present the committee in charge with documentation for yet another extension of their contract. The two years approved for the original pilot program were barely enough for half the exterior façades, and they had not touched the inner courtyard. They had presented a convincing case that twice the time would be needed, but now the problem is to secure the next four-year cycle already in view. No sooner will they have worked their way once around than the first façade, begun four years ago, will already be so corroded that they can start all over again. The effect of nitrates and sulfates on the lime mortar, accelerated by industrial pollution, has kept pace with their work; assuming that their provisional contract will last till the turn of the century, they are assured a secure income. Once the inevitable bureaucratic delays are behind them—or so Maltzahn theorizes—the Landmarks Office, well aware of the importance of the project, is sure to prove magnanimous. After years of time-consuming odd jobs—record and book jackets, movie posters, embarrassed entries in competitions for which they were much too old—this would mean financial stability seven months a year, and in winter they can work for themselves, without a care. Even Patera with his four unmarried daughters, one a widow, two engaged.

They look forward to their work like Sisyphus watching the stone roll back downhill.

"Let's take a break," Podol suggests.

"Whatever." Patera pretends not to care.

Orten connects the raised hands of Justice with the scale she is supposed to balance. He hatches the contours of her breast, the folds in her robe, the skew of her sword, applies a few strokes to indicate the mass of the scale beam, draws two lines to frame the panel, and scratches a window reveal in the layers of painted plaster. Scratching a form out of the applied plaster is not all that different from sculpturing. He values plaster as a medium, for the many ways it can be worked; its plasticity allows it to be layered or sculpted, but it cannot be worked as long as clay—it demands a more resolute hand.

Orten's sculptures have become fragmentary in the last few years, have lost volume, are more surface, the form generally discernible only as an outline, with roughened texture and dark patina, like stone, with no smooth gypsum white—simplified, aloof totem poles. The sgraffiti he scratches each day from the plaster here are hardly less plastic. Representational and ornamental, they recall bygone carefree days.

The work of the four men—two painters, two sculptors—proves more effective than the kind of standard restoration intended at first; Podol sets no restraints on his imagination when repairing the destroyed frescoes, his is the only method worthy of the boldness of the original designs.

Orten inspects the figure, checks her proportions. He often has the feeling that the wall narrows, that the curvature contracts while he works, that he has begun on too grand a scale and won't have enough room. Podol has no such worries; he used to do sign painting, and that gives him his self-assurance for these façades. "INN OF THE TWO DOVES," "SPIDER TAVERN"—he has yet to realize his designs for "Inn of the Three Cocks," "Cheeks & Crack Bar," "Show Your I.D. Saloon."

He knows that perspective and time are on their side. From thirty feet below a sgraffito is seen only as a serial impression, and not even that after three years. From up close Orten can see the inconsistencies of his allegory. The figure needs composure and concentration to hold her scale, strength and vigor to wield her sword, and above all, open eyes for both. He draws a third eye on the brow of blind Justice; it casts its beam down over the approach road. A three-eyed Justitia—if anyone on the next tour should happen to notice it, Hanna will have to come up with something. She can use it for the topic of her master's thesis, too: "Contamination of Classical Motifs by Christian Elements on the Renaissance Façade at Friedland." The four of them could provide her enough material for a doctoral dissertation from this wall alone.

He rinses his trowels and spatula in what water he has left and dumps the bucket. Pushed by the wind, the water falls sideways in the direction of Patera and Podol, and slaps against the star design in the courtyard pavement. Podol lifts his head and calls up to him, "Done already?"

"Yes," his answer is hoarse, almost inaudible, and Orten clears his throat to free his voice, but says nothing more. As if anyone ever could be done here. Working alone like this, he has got out of the habit of talking. He used to end up stammering if he spoke too fast or too slow; after hours of silence up on the scaffold, he has an aversion to speech. Whenever one of the other three asks for information, his dry throat constricts, and he usually doesn't bother to answer. Podol's chatter, his jokes, annoy him, his laughter irritates him, because it's so loud and because he is afraid friendship will demand he join in, and then Podol will have to explain the joke to him. Patera, who works with Podol, doesn't stand a chance—he has to laugh at everything. Orten doesn't want to be torn out of this dull inertia, which allows him to do good work and think of other things at the same time. The greatest satisfaction comes from thinking about nothing at all.

He gathers up his things and climbs down. His pointing trowel is dull and the handle of his spatula is loose. They will both have to be repaired before they start on the exterior façades, where they work side by side, applying sgraffiti to relief-coffers, which goes much faster. The thought calms him, as well as the fact that the spilled sand has been swept up and the scaffold removed. He doesn't want worries more complicated than that.

As he climbs down he can feel the tension in the back of his neck and a sharp pain in his shoulder. Now that he has left the gable, he realizes what an effort it is to work from the horizontal. He has difficulty focusing his eyes to normal at first and gropes uncertainly for the rungs before climbing down the next ladder.

Shoving his hat back, Podol gazes with satisfaction at a skewered warrior lying on the ground.

"Lots of blood! Red works well, even way up." He is glad to have someone besides Patera within hearing distance.

Orten wearily balances his way down. "We playing cards tonight, or are you going to the movies?" Orten shakes his head without turning around. "Hell, it's about time you knock off that crap for today. Laying down up there always gives me a stiff neck!" Orten hears Patera join in the laughter. "Next week we'll tackle the coffers, then we'll have this drudgery behind us!"

Podol tries to cheer him up, even though he has scraped off the first pediment practically by himself and has done the work of two men the whole time. They would all be up a creek if it weren't for him, especially Maltzahn with his calculations. The guy is a finagler who gets on all their nerves. All he does is talk big and scheme, and hasn't achieved a thing so far, except making them do his work as well. They can't put it all off on Patera. If Maltzahn isn't up on the scaffold tomorrow, they should think about recalculating his share; that would make him take notice. Or even better, just give him the boot.

Where are those towels again?

Orten scrubs his hands—he can never get all the lime off his nails—washes his face, and sinks down into his sagging bed. It is Friday, four in the afternoon; he can sleep till Monday.

He wakes up when in the next room Podol bangs his cards on the table and shouts, "Slam!" The door is so warped it cannot be closed. The damp is not so bad in summer, but from September on the nights are clammy. Once Patera's coughing spells start, it is high time to talk to the custodian about heat. The negotiations depend on Podol's mood. The custodian was born in the castle and runs the place exactly as he did before the war, when he was still directly answerable to its last owner. He still secretly waits for the old man's return and in the meantime skimps on publicly owned energy. People also say that the days of the Protectorate, when the local Gestapo was housed in the west wing of the castle, come closest to his notion of law and order. That was the period when, under dubious circumstances, he was promoted from stable boy with private duties to custodian. In the final days of the war he took part in an overdue and badly organized uprising, during which a great many partisans unexpectedly fell into German hands. He was left a cripple and stayed on as custodian. He is also a member of the Party, so he can't be touched. The last director quit because of him, and the new one, a thirty-year-old "milksop" as Podol calls him, who never finished his degree in art history, stays clear of him. The organs of the state had even less success managing the site than the three of them did.

He comes stomping along the wing and appears under the arcade outside their grated window on the ground floor, but Podol is already at the door.

"Evening, Mr. Jirse, what's the leg doing in this weather?"

"What's it supposed to do, a new one's not going to grow in its place, haha. Can't complain about the weather though."

"But we can, Mr. Jirse."

"No, can't complain. It's still summer, right warm."

"Summer yes, warm no. We need some heat at night."

"Nope, I don't heat in summer. No, no. That'd be some joke. What am I supposed to do in winter then?"

"You can save on coke come winter when we're not here."

Jirse is about to hobble away; Podol stops him. "Have you had a look at the walls lately? Come with me."

"No, I know all the rooms. The workers have been here already, checked everything out, it's okay."

"They were here for the theater, and backstage is shipshape, but we aren't. Our rooms are all mildewed."

"You young folks today can't take it. We didn't have heat, and couldn't get it installed, either. And there was no complaining."

"You know very well there were stoves in here, but they were ripped out for the central heating, that you don't even know how to operate! It's never on; we have to remind you every time. And I'd like to know who you mean by finicky young folks. I'm fifty-two, Patera is sixty. We stand out on that scaffold all day, while you're lounging around inside, and Patera coughs the night away, what with the damp in here!"

"If he can't handle it anymore, then he should give it up. Standing on scaffolds all day is not for everybody. You can end up catching something."

"Mostly he catches something in bed, breathing the damp air, along with the rest of us. We need heat, now!"

"Nope, there ain't none. He should give it up if he can't handle it anymore. At his age. If he can't even get warm in summer. Take me, for example, I'm warm now, breaking into a regular sweat."

Podol has restrained himself until now.

"I can well believe you're sweating, you rat. Out of fear, and rightly so. The next time we'll heat with your leg!" He grabs Jirse by his padded smock, but Orten, who has joined them, jumps between the two and holds him back before he can get violent. He just shakes Jirse and lets him go. Jirse staggers impressively, catching himself at the last moment on a column of the arcade, a postwar faun, loses the rubber cap from his wooden leg and lurches off, hissing something about defenseless cripple, criminal extortion, and consequences.

Variation, the following spring.

Orten is too slow. In this phase of negotiations Podol already has a tight grip on Jirse's lapel and flings him with full force down the arcade before anyone can intervene. Jirse's leg gets stuck in the unrepaired flooring and splinters as he falls. That same afternoon Podol fetches an iron stove from the neighborhood, knocks open the plastered-over vent and starts a fire with Jirse's leg for kindling. It is a solemn moment. While repeatedly shouting, "Didn't I tell you that we'd use that rat's leg for heat? Jan, you are a witness!" he fires it up and almost burns his fingers. Orten is uneasy, not only as a witness—he just has to look at a handicapped person and he feels blackmailed. Podol's triumph seems too flippant, and premature.

And a half hour later the police are there, with dogs that sniff at the door and the spot where Jirse says he fell, unable to get up again until he was helped by the archivist and the plumber, who was there because of water in the cellars. Podol was led away and detained overnight, the first time this year he had been able to fall asleep without shivering. The next day he was transferred back to their damp room in the castle. The investigation was suspended, since the splintered leg, the only piece of evidence that would support Jirse's charge, could not be found. They stated that they had seen no splinters; the altercation had not gone beyond the custodian's usual verbal insinuations. Any violent

9

attack was out of the question—given the differences in age and intel-
lect of the two. Granted, the custodian was pushing things to the point
where it would not be a wonder if someone lost all patience, especially
when there was no heat at night after a day of exhausting work on
the scaffold. Jirse's claim that he would look after it was a lie, unless
he happened to heat by mistake, Maltzahn added for the record. These
proceedings should serve him as a warning to remember his duties
instead of making mischief.

This was not the place, so the official arbitrator ruled, for protracted
internal disputes. The ultimate responsibility for housing the artists
adequately lay with the director of the enterprise; burdening the custodian with that kind of responsibility, particularly in consideration of
his condition, would lead to confusion of authority.

The archivist, whose fear of Jirse usually made him a leaky faucet,
testified truthfully that he had seen no splinters. The break might be a
recent one, but how recent he did not know. It was perfectly possible
that Mr. Jirse had come to grief even before his argument with Mr.
Podolský, as a result of the heavy blows fate had dealt him, so to
speak, but even if Mr. Jirse did drink, which in fact happened on
occasion, but never while on duty, at least never when he was in
charge, one could not claim that Mr. Jirse was an alcoholic. But he
also should have known from experience, given Mr. Podolský's im-
petuosity—and sincerity, too, he might add—just who it was he was
dealing with or would be dealing with if he did not heat for all too
long a period, conscientiously trying for too long a period to save on
state energy resources, on the other hand, if everyone would do the
same, gentlemen, our energy crisis would not be half as bad, we would
not have to import so much foreign fuel, we would save on naphtha,
with its high political costs, and on reactors, too. Yes, but what he,
Qvietone, really wanted to say—and he was amazed himself that he
was suddenly talking so much, pure nonsense some would say perhaps,
and some might also say that Mr. Jirse had now and then served the
Gestapo as an informer, but that was sometimes exaggerated, too. As
far as he, Qvietone, knew, only two Jewish families in the vicinity had
been taken away on the basis of Mr. Jirse's information, and they were
probably more like Zionists in today's terms. He had always been
impressed by Mr. Jirse's directness, his frankness, why, he had often
joked with him, saying, "Hey, Qvietone, you Huguenot bastard, just

be glad you aren't a Jew, and that I let you spend the winter here with me." Old Jirse would never leave a man in the lurch.

Quite unexpectedly, the results of a test showed that the alcohol level in Jirse's blood was very high. Jirse swore he had had nothing to drink before his argument with Podolský, spoke again of criminal extortion and how he wouldn't allow things to come to such a pass, that he knew other methods, but he sounded somewhat crestfallen. He had no problems with his past, but all those foreign words had confused him. The next day he appeared in the courtyard with a solid hinge and a new rubber cap on his wooden leg, and a sterner note of heavy fate about the mouth.

Qvietone gave notice and to his surprise quickly found a position at the local museum. On several occasions he has drunk at the Ram with the four artists, and if he sees them on the street he gives a friendly wave.

That same winter Maltzahn admitted that he had tried to bribe Jirse with a bottle of whiskey to keep him from filing charges. The other three were about to lay into him for this act of betrayal, when it occurred to Patera that that same bottle of whiskey had corroborated the suspicion that Jirse was drunk beforehand and had slipped with no assistance from Podol.

The iron stove remained, but when they returned the next year the vent had been cemented over and secured behind a hall stand screwed to the wall, in place of the requisite wardrobe. The tussle over heat began anew.

An electric heater was supposed to offer a temporary solution—the director had it installed, remarking conspiratorially: But not a word to Jirse.

Jirse has learned about it in the meantime, but pretends not to see it. It is really no help, is little better than a stage prop, given the high ceilings. The elegant parlor stored out in the hallway along with the rest of the surviving papier-mâché sets gives off more warmth than their living quarters.

They take various remedial measures. Maltzahn visits the director's wife in her imitation Louis XVI bed in the blue room of the posh and dry south wing; they will not be disturbed behind the wall of canopy curtains and braid trimmings. Podol sleeps with Hanna in her room above the stalls, formerly a changing room for livery servants. It is small and dark, but warm. Wrapped in three blankets, Patera hacks away beside the director's electric coil. Orten warms himself with tea or the late show at the movies, before creeping into his lumpy featherbed.

This is now the fifth year, the ninth season, of an impending round with Jirse over heat. Before they leave Friedland at the end of October, they will experience a few rare days on which Jirse orders the furnace stoked.

"Did I wake you?" Podol can hear Orten turn over. "You coming to the Ram?" Orten realizes there is no point in staying in bed. He reluctantly gets up and comes out. It is still bright outside. But a light is on because the arcades cast shadows and the windows in the thick walls don't let in enough sunlight. A streak of cigarette smoke rises to the bulb. Orten shudders. What a hole.

"Oh, there you are. We've played three hands already."

"I'm coming," Orten says quickly, afraid that Podol will demand they all play another hand. Patera gets up, obviously relieved.

"Sit down, Václav, we'll play one more until Jan gets dressed."

"No, I'm ready now." Orten decides it is up to him to extricate Patera.

They cross the courtyard under the façade, where canvas protecting Podol's sgraffito swells in the wind. "Just two more days and I'll be done with that gimcrackery," Podol says with satisfaction.

"I'll help," Orten offers. "Václav can take it easy."

"Thanks, Jan, I'll manage," Patera objects, not very convincingly.

"You can change off," Podol suggests. "I can't wait for that shyster Olbram to get back."

"Just don't send him chasing all over the scaffold again like last time, otherwise we'll never get done," Orten says. "Besides, all that diplomacy has fattened him up and he could slip and fall. And then you'll get hauled into court on charges of grievous bodily harm a second time. Just remember Jirse."

"I don't want to think about that rat. Now if I kick this tree trunk here, I'm happy to apologize. But a lot more wood is going to crack if I do that guy grievous bodily harm, and when I beat him about the head and shoulders—next time—the chips will fly!"

. . .

They are across from what was once the castle brewery, where the Smetana Centennial Exhibition is being installed, including a section to be titled "Prague Artists Restore Friedland Castle." Hanna steps out and calls to them.

"Go on ahead," Podol says, hanging back. Patera and Orten walk on.

"Jan, I don't know if that's such a good idea. Why, she could be his daughter."

"No, his daughter is older." Orten doesn't want to get into this again.

"I'm a father myself, I'm a reasonable man, but if an old geezer like that came along, I'd kick him down the stairs."

"Václav, don't kid yourself. You can't even know what's going on with your four daughters. You're not home seven months out of the year."

"All the same, admit it, you wouldn't allow it with your own kids."

"I just have two sons. They're still too young and green for girls. I can't imagine, either, that an older grown woman would be taken by them. And if she were, it'd save me those embarrassing explanations their mother has been nagging me about for some time now."

"Don't play the cynic. But I'm serious, you ought to have a word with Stanislav. He'll listen to you. If I say anything to him he'll explode. And it's not fair to his wife, either."

"Václav, please, you shouldn't fret so much about us all. You've got enough to worry about with your cough, and so do the rest of us. We're all just trying to survive here. Including Stanislav."

"Jan, you're an upstanding fellow. Sometimes I wonder—seems to me that Hanna first gave you the eye, and the director's wife, too."

"Well, you're wrong. They have a lot more fun with those two."

"No, Jan, don't joke. Are you really so respectable, or just covering up?"

"I'll tell you a secret. I'm not interested. I'm not interested in much of anything. And when I see you kowtowing to Stanislav, at sixty! You don't have to put up with that!"

"Oh, Jan, I know you're right, but that's not going to change much. Not with Stanislav. I know well enough that he's the best man of us here."

"Yes, he's the best. And it's okay to follow his suggestions about work, but you need to change the way you talk with him. Don't be so humble. I can't even listen to it. Sometimes it seems to me you're kow-towing to me, too, and I'm fifteen years younger than you."

"You see, Jan, when it comes to using his hands or to art, Stanislav's the best. You've got it all up there in your head, but it just doesn't come out. And you don't want it to, either. I've been watching you the whole time. You don't belong here, but I don't feel so inadequate around you."

"Václav, I haven't accomplished anything for three years now; you're better off sticking with Stanislav."

"Stanislav's self-confidence is great, but you draw people to you, with your self-doubts. And you can't change that."

"Bull."

Svoboda, a local artist, is already sitting at their table in the Ram. He has kept pace with the change to bleak abstraction in the landscape of northern Bohemia by switching from studied *paysages* to "industrial polychromism," as he calls it. He is waiting for Podol, for their usual evening of boasts, insults, and one-upmanship.

Podol comes in with Hanna. The director, who has been sitting at the corner table with the girl who helps out at the town library, gets up and pays at the bar, greets them vaguely, and leaves. "They're always at least the age of consent, he makes sure of that," Svoboda says.

"He'd be better off not to show his face in here," Podol remarks. "Jan, what're you having?"

Orten can't decide and orders soup for now. Patera has the same—he ate a big meal for lunch with Podol and only wants a snack. Podol orders trotters and kraut; Hanna decides on calf's liver. Having sent the director on his way, the manager takes their orders with an eager, friendly smile, but regrets to say that they are out of liver and kid-neys, but the cook could fix some breaded mushrooms, nice fresh ones. Hanna is agreeable. Patera decides to join her. Orten orders a steak. Svo-boda, who has been infected by Podol's gluttony, orders trotters as well.

As they eat they are constantly interrupted by people coming over to greet them, some of the newcomers, who only wanted to drink at the bar, but now pull up a chair and ask how they're doing and how the plaster is drying in this weather. Podol is happy to dispense an-swers. All the attention and bustle at their table arouses the curiosity of the people who aren't locals, and from the manager they learn about how the castle is being renovated. One of the artists wasn't here, though, she said, a handsome fellow by the way, who was off dealing with the ministry of culture, did a lot of traveling, organizing the whole operation, she knew them all well, after all they had been eating here every day now for five years.

Qvietone appears at the door and looks around for an empty table. He gives a decidedly dignified greeting, without his usual expansive wave of recognition. A woman has come in with him, hard to figure, presumably older than he, but there's something girlish about her, the way she stands there crumpling a handkerchief in her hand. Qvietone hangs back. When he makes a move toward the director's empty table, she notices a party leaving the table next to Podol and Orten, and she heads for it without looking back. Orten makes a note of her figure: Maillol, Bourdelle, Renoir.

She sits down at the uncleared table, and Qvietone hastily comes over. She pulls a chair out for him. She talks loudly, laughs for no reason, and watches herself in the window reflection behind Orten's head. Her dress, of some heavy, dusty-rose fabric, is buttoned up to her neck, and the broad belt accentuates her pelvis. Qvietone orders rosé wine to match; she downs it quickly.

Her long neck and the way she has her hair pinned up remind Orten of the giggling doll-like geishas that had so disconcerted him in Osaka. They hadn't flirted in the European sense, the total artificiality made them that much more natural, maybe because total nudity was somehow normal in the bathing tubs. Pubic triangles and breasts were of no importance when you could see the whole body; their breasts were generally very small in any case, and the way the legs met the hips was all wrong, dachshund legs—that was not his description, but Maltzahn's, who had played VIP along with him. They were charming as long as they wore their ceremonial garb with the carefully arranged bows and the little pillows on their backs, needles sticking out of their hairdos, white stockings, their toes unnaturally forced through the straps of the high sandals, making them take those little mincing steps. But once they undressed, the magic, the girlishness, was gone, they were like planks, too broad and flat, nothing for sculpture. He understood why they said the height of eroticism came from the hollow of the knee or the curve of the neck, or the eyebrows, barely noticeable, just fine lines. Their obsequious attentiveness embarrassed him, made him uneasy, he hadn't felt comfortable for a single moment.

The professional entertainers had the sense of humor of little girls. They had been hired for the birthday party of another sculptor attending the exposition. As the evening progressed their jokes got more and more daring. One crooked her fingers into a fist, shortening two knuckles by laying an index finger across them, which was supposed to represent the top of female thighs, and showed this to the birthday boy and Orten, who had been sitting next to him, but he caught on only after lengthy explanations interrupted by bursts of girlish laughter. Whereas they were all business afterward, or so the other fellow reported. Not that any of them had slept with him, but two of them had done such a clever job of soaping him up that he hadn't missed out on anything. Then they rinsed him off and cleared things away, bowed and left the room, like two schoolgirls who still had homework to do.

The woman at the next table reminded him of them. She had that same look with clothes on. She was heavier, more European. But she had that strange naïveté, coupled with lasciviousness, which she perhaps didn't even realize—the way she kept opening buttons in the course of the evening.

To match her dress and wine, Qvietone bought a salmon-colored rose from a woman selling flowers, who left everyone embarrassed at each table she passed. He asked for a vase; but he made do with a beer glass filled with water, arranging it on the table, shoving the ashtray and salted almonds to one side—his companion watching and smiling indulgently the whole time. It was not clear what exactly was wrong, the woman was probably the source of it, but whatever it was, it stuck to Qvietone. Orten started to light his cigarette, and she held one up to her mouth, too. He held out the burning match while Qvietone was still fumbling for one.

Orten left when Podol and Svoboda began grappling in their third, and still undecided, match of arm wrestling and Hanna, accompanied by Patera's quivery voice, started to sing "Boleráz." It was cool outside. The empty square, with its monument to the composer born in the local brewery, looked exactly as it had on that long-ago day when a naïve group of people had met here to rediscover and renew their native language. He walked past Augusta Printers, where Božena Němcová had had her story "The Grandmother" published, and where she had later stood begging, handing out little slips of paper: "Won't you please share a little of God's gifts?"—she meant bread. She died of mental exhaustion and hunger, age forty-two. Compared to her, George Sand is a writer of no importance.

Seven people have gathered to watch the film club's late movie. The upside-down economics of cultural life hits him in the eye, but it is one of the greatest advantages of socialism.

The film starts.

A boat sets out from an island in the early dawn. At first it is a dark dot jerking along against the gray horizon. The mainland grows at the left side of the screen as the boat approaches. A man and a child are sitting in the boat, they don't speak, you can hear the splash of oars. When they reach the shore the sun rises over the sea. The boy heads off to school with his book bag, the man takes an empty bucket from the boat and fills it with fresh water near the shore. His wife is waiting back on the island. When he arrives they each hang two pails on a yoke over one shoulder and cautiously carry them up the steep hill. Once up top they start dipping the water with a wooden ladle and pouring it in tiny doses over the plants in their field, a few drops for each sprout. The work is silent and endless; the water seeps immediately into the dry earth. When the boy comes home from school, after being picked up in the boat along with more water from the mainland, he and his younger brother help irrigate.

A few things happen. They harvest. One plant after the other is reaped, bound with others, the large sheaves carried on their backs to the boat. The whole island is their field, their hut in the middle.

They bow and scrape before their landlord. He sits on a raised chair, gazes at the bales, shakes his head, samples and feels, pays. The man appears to object, the landlord silences him with one cutting gesture. They leave the house with more bows. They go to the market. Buy dishes, supplies, candy for the boys. Ride a merry-go-round. The children laugh. They row back home that same evening. Before leaving they take the buckets from the boat and fetch water. They return with a full load.

The irrigation goes on.

A child takes sick. The mother leaves her work in the field, makes tea, lays compresses on the child's brow, the father rows to get a doctor. He has to wait a long time.

When the doctor arrives the child is dead. They have to pay the doctor and take him back. The man brings buckets of water with him.

The woman sits motionless, even after the child has been buried. This goes on for several days. Then she gets up, picks up a full bucket and flings it away, starts ripping up plants. The man watches her, waits, goes over to her, and strikes her. She falls, lies there on the ground, smearing her tears with dirt. The man stands beside her. She sobs more softly, grows calmer, stands up, dries her face, picks up a ladle and begins to water plants from the bucket she spilled.

We must assume Sisyphus is happy.

An acquaintance who designed the poster told him about the film. He understood what little dialogue there was, in Japanese.

Orten no longer finds scratching on the castle walls quite so futile.

That night, by chance, Podol is sleeping in his own bed; they are awakened by a racket—upended chairs, shattering glass—and lights. In the front room, where Patera sleeps, stands Maltzahn leaning against a table and making no attempt to be any less noisy than usual when he returns from one of his excursions.

Podol leaps into the room, in his long underwear. "We've been waiting for you!" He tries to go for Maltzahn's throat, who dodges nimbly and importantly flourishes a bundle of papers. "Come, Podol, come, give me a hug, Stanislav my boy, your prodigal son has come home to you again!"

"Yes, well, you're just in time!" Podol looks around for the best thing to throw, but Maltzahn doesn't bother to take cover, comes even closer. "Well, what do you suppose I have here? For you too, you bastard, even if all you do is mistreat everybody around here. And you thought that rat Maltzahn wasn't good for anything. Always just shirking his job, right?"

"Damn right, you idiot."

Orten and Patera have meanwhile managed to make some sense of the situation. It gradually becomes clear even to Podol that Maltzahn has a reason for carrying on like this.

"Give it here." He rips the papers out of Maltzahn's hand.

"Slow down, slow down, sweetheart."

"Don't call me sweetheart, you imbecile! Drink a little less next time if you can't handle it. And cut the comedy! What's up?" He glances at the papers, but doesn't read them. Maltzahn grows restless, grabs them back.

"Just be careful you don't screw up your future! Messieurs, all rise please! It is my great pleasure to inform you that the National Office of Landmarks and Monuments, the nourishing mother of us all, has entered into a contract for renovating the National Castle Friedland/ Litomyšl, a national monument of first rank, with the painter and member of the Academy Stanislav Podolský"—he bows to Podol and hands him two sheets of paper—

"with the painter and member of the Academy Václav Patera,

"with the sculptor and member of the Academy Jan Orten,

"and with the sculptor and member of the Academy Olbram Maltzahn"—he bows and keeps the last copy for himself—

"for a period of ten years.

"And this is for you all!" Maltzahn pulls a bottle of Egyptian brandy from his coat and raises it. "Long live the façade!"

Podol snatches the bottle from his hand, takes a long pull and claps him on the shoulder. "Olbram, you lazy skunk, I never would have thought it."

"And they implied that it does not preclude an extension."

"Oh please, not that," Orten remarks.

"Why not?" Patera laughs happily, and in that moment overestimates himself.

"Absolutely, Václav, right you are!" Podol rejoices with him.

Maltzahn fills them in, tells about all the trouble he had, explains the tricks he used, several times, is happy to accept Patera's admiration for his cunning, Podol's shoulder clapping, Orten's toleration, enjoys his triumph, doesn't let anyone else get a word in, not even Podol. They don't begrudge him his joy, he will have to be up on the scaffold in the morning.

TWO

They move from the courtyard to the castle's exterior walls. The scaffold is set up first on the south side, where there are large surfaces that do not require sgraffiti—because of the galleried arcades in the two upper stories, the high Gothic windows of the chapel on the right, and the wide diamond bossage of the central stone portal. They are under no illusions. The four hundred masonry relief-coffers in the projection on the left must be repaired or scraped clean, and that alone will require months of work; the frieze along the attic, the cornices, and pediments will mean another season.

They inspect the better-preserved upper section. About a third of the sgraffiti are missing, another part must be restored, what facing is still in good condition must be brightened. Finely ground marble has to be mixed in with the lime mortar to make it whiter, but it will take three coats—the old lime, which had longer to dry, is more brilliant. Large areas of the gable frescoes will have to be filled in. Podol wipes a rag dipped in powdered graphite across a cartoon stretched over the sgraffito, giving him a negative of the drawing. While still up on the façade, he makes provisional corrections, marking off proportions and trying at least to get the niche's borders right, because on this side there is a constant wind that is blowing stronger now and rips the cartoon's edges from his hands. The drawing will be completed later.

For that they need a dry, well-lighted wall that is large enough. Podol has already checked the rooms on the second floor of the brewery above the ground-floor apartment of the Smetana family, where they have stored their frottages—a complete documentation of all phases of the restoration will ensure that the castle, the most important Renaissance structure north of the Alps, can be reconstructed at any time in case of devastation or flood.

Where frescoes are missing and no frottage is possible, Podol creates new ones. They are supposed to conform to the spirit of the originals, but that in no way limits him. Along with the customary ornamentation, they have already found a profiled figure with a naked behind, hands twisted wrong, and a bald head. In time they have come to know the moods of their Renaissance predecessors—the irregularities of their cross-hatching, their use of the spatula—and can differentiate it from later changes made on the façades. The artists of the Secession scratched in semicircles that looped like watch springs, whereas the earlier work is conic and drawn with nails, the same horseshoe nails used to establish the distance between the rows of coffers. These aren't mistakes or a lack of talent, of that they are sure.

"He screwed it up here again," Podol used to say when they found coffers, usually above the windows, where the shading was reversed, and erased a portion of the sgraffito. Until he realized that as they had worked these small segments the craftsmen kept a view of the whole façade in mind: when in doubt use white, enhance the plasticity. They were fellow artists, who drew their figures freehand; no master builder could have failed to notice the endless variation of their motifs, or have restricted them: the farces of fauns at play, whose bald heads and buttocks counteract the innocuous effect created by the filigree of the whole.

After long research, Hanna found the significance of the hands twisted around on the buttocks. But the Indian, who lies on the ground with his hands chopped off, guards his secret.

They also found a collapsed chimney whose front side had survived and was shaped like a tulip. One of the masons, who used to be a stove fitter, wants to restore it.

The coffers in the lower half of the façade have been destroyed for the most part. While Maltzahn and Patera remeasure them, marking the rows and applying the stencils, Podol and Orten begin scratching the newly plastered sections under the cornice. An image has to be set in the center of each hewn stone, chiefly plant motifs. Variety is demanded, and the inventory of fruits and vegetables, leaves and tendrils is limited. After a few apples, ears of grain, and shrubs, Orten departs from the originals and for his next sgraffito scratches four wooden matches with sulfur tips. Podol strews *uccelli,* which his wrist remembers from the last sign he painted, across the stones: doves, in profile and frontal views with heads ducked, colonies of jackdaws nesting

noisily on gables, until a kestrel dives among them and they fall silent
or fly away, and even those that stay and begin to set up a racket again
are finally silenced by the kestrel's return; he draws the kestrel with
affection. There were four eggs in a nest behind the tulip chimney, but
ten days after setting up the scaffold, only one is left. They are now
trying to keep the weasel off the roof with a sheet-metal barrier.

Podol used the same method in his own atelier to keep out a cat that
used to leap through the dormer onto his table and, in revenge for
being roughly tossed out, made a real cat's mess of his drawings. His
house is five stories tall, the cat has not fallen off yet. Podol laughs
when he tells the story, and Orten, a country boy himself, laughs along.
Podol likes to talk about animals, knows all the latest rabbit-and-bear
jokes, the ones that keep the nation's head above water these days.

He tells how he drove an orangutan crazy at the zoo. It was playing
in the sand and he started talking to it very softly: " 'You stupid ape,
a strong fellow like you, and you're playing in the sand. You should
be hauling bricks.' It took two keepers to quiet it down again. I ran
away, they love to hide shit in their armpits, you know, and toss it at
the visitors."

They all laugh. This encourages Podol to recall another ape he read
about in the paper. "It kept getting out for a high time on the town and
they were forever having to find it again. They checked the fence—no
holes. The moat along the front was wide enough, couldn't have got out
there. So they set up a watch. Along toward morning the ape walks to
the moat, pulls out a banana, and waves. And what do you suppose
happens? Here comes an elk. Wades in to get the banana, and the ape
jumps onto its back. A taxi! And he's been doing it right along!"

General applause. Encore: "Or the thief poaching in a river for little
fish. What do the fish do?"

"They dart away."

"Hah, wrong. They get together and form a crocodile! And come
swimming along like that. The poacher takes off without ever looking
back."

What zoo was that? What river? Makes no difference, there are millions of examples. And the fact that bananas aren't the usual diet of
elks? That's the point, must be quite a delicacy for them, otherwise it
wouldn't have come to get one. How is it that elks are running free
and swimming around in a zoo? They're everywhere in Scandinavia,

on the roads, even in the subways, crawl into parked cars, not long ago one took a bath in a fountain in Moscow. A bath must be fun for them, and a banana besides!

By now they are all working on the upper third. Patera uses variations on plant ornaments, plus tried and true figures: chubby faces—moon, sun—heraldic mailed fists, Prague's coat-of-arms. Maltzahn, being a motorcyclist, resorts to traffic signs, turns one-way-street arrows into wavy horizontals and calls them yin and yang, joins flattened and stretched St. Andrew's crosses from railroad crossings, draws a circle around them and scratches on four wings: a windmill.

Podol takes a fancy to Mardi Gras: in the cleanly scraped coffers he draws impaled pig's heads, frogs and basilisks with human features, the Liar with no head and a face in his chest, pots and pans with legs, a tree-man taking root, a ship on wheels, *carrus navalis,* grimacing masks and the open jaws of Bomarzo's hell—the tail end of the carnival parade.

Later, when they are removing the scaffold, Orten will discover Podol's images. Shocked, he will feel sadness and rage at the transiency of their work.

He has now moved on to the signs of the zodiac and alchemy, makes an alloy of gold, a solar symbol, using copper, antimony, and mercury.

Podol notices in passing that Maltzahn has changed to plain numerals. "You have to leave more white, make the horizontals thicker. Besides, you can do more with those," he suggests amiably—his jokes depend on Maltzahn's laughter, too. "If you lay that sixty-nine on its side, you have the sign of Cancer, and give that four a little curlicue at the top, and you've got Jupiter."

"I know that." Maltzahn feels edgy and unsure of himself up on the scaffold next to him.

On the plank above them, Orten notices that his motifs are repeating themselves too often, and searches for new ones. He draws the bucket beside him and a yoke joining it with a second, next to it a blade of Japanese millet. He presses his trowel in the plaster and draws its outline, and beside it a compass. That looks too damned Masonic, so a post horn goes in the next one, with a mute—no secret society without its Tristero.

Patera has finished his third coffer for the day and concludes his series of edibles with a pretzel. "Václav's hungry," Orten remarks and draws himself a ham, Maltzahn adds a half liter of beer to his "infinity."

They take a break.

In the lower rows, where objects are recognizable, they have to keep closer to the old designs. Vegetables, mushrooms, and game are seldom represented in the originals. Even innocent plants and fruits can be tricky. "When do you first find bananas in still lifes?" Podol asks. "Never? It's the same as in socialism."

"After the Saxons left," Patera adds.

"And the elks."—Orten.

"Or take those turkeys in the Gothic frescoes in Lübeck. They were even used on postage stamps. Until somebody took a closer look and found those gobblers—long before Columbus! The restorer was just making use of all his resources," Podol says merrily.

"Wonder if that flatiron will ever appear on stamps?" Maltzahn teases.

"What flatiron?"

"The one there on the left, next to my pear."

"That's a ship."

"Looks like a submarine with a handle," Orten remarks.

"You guys' pears have all got phimosis! And that upended garbage can, what's that supposed to be?"

"That's a cornucopia!" Patera is hurt.

"Now he's offended!" Podol takes his beer and vanishes under the scaffold in the middle of the façade.

Below them Hanna is steering a group of visitors into the castle. They are from Stadice, members of the October Twenty-eighth Collective Farm, which in the last six months has increased its beet and potato harvest by a total of seventeen percent and produced double its quota in eggs and chickens. Their shortfall in beef and pork is as good as forgotten.

The name October Twenty-eighth brings various obligations with it, although the members of the collective are not always quite sure which of those several obligations are incumbent upon them. Are they to keep alive the memory of the founding of the republic in 1918? Or the nationalization of farms thirty years later? The most recent graft onto that date is presumably the federalization that followed the events of August 1968, which, although of a more exhortatory nature, makes sense to the Slovaks among them—one is no longer forced to speak Czech in Prague.

The name of their town, however, is unambiguous and carries no obligation of internal contradictions. It was from Stadice that Princess Libuše had them bring her future spouse, the plowman Přemysl, thereby putting an end to male gossip about unnatural petticoat government.

With the historically authenticated house of Přemysl began the Christianization of Bohemia and with it the epoch of national insignificance; the mythic War of the Maidens that followed the marriage was the last flash of revolutionary potential—until Hussites, male and female, stirred up history once again.

The collective farmers are aware of the patriotic significance of the town. They have already done the Smetana memorial in the brewery across the way, they all know his opera *Libuše* by name. One of them had had the honor of joining personages of highest rank for one of the solemn occasions on which it is ceremonially presented. That was ten years ago.

In the castle's concert hall Hanna explains to the group the events surrounding the artist's first public performance. Pichota, the collective's bookkeeper and cultural adviser, responsible in the latter capacity for excursions, takes notes, while behind Hanna's back the others are busy touching the furnishings on the other side of the ropes. Women do more of the touching. The most favored object is the polished hickory piano on which the six-year-old Smetana had dazzled, without any pedal work from his dangling legs. The warning sign in four languages looks worn, too: *"Nedotýkejte se*—Please do not touch"; Czechs are known for following requests made of foreigners.

The group glide in felt slippers across the rhombi of the parquet floor; stare at the tapestries, the oversize wall paintings, hunting scenes and landscapes, at the porcelain, the exquisite uncomfortable furniture; smile at the short beds, the enameled utensils for personal hygiene, the murano glass and inlaid tortoiseshell in the bedrooms. The high point is a small door hidden behind one of the huge tiled stoves and equipped with a spring bolt that can be operated from the bed. Hanna makes a pause here—for little jokes, the comparing of notes among the women, the testing of the mechanism. She can spare herself and the group the library, which usually follows.

On this floor there is still the cabinet of automata and clockwork toys, some of them duplicates of the vast collection of Rudolf II, all made in secret at great risk, but later almost completely plundered and taken to Vienna; both the copies and what originals were left are behind glass now, some of them still operational.

A trumpeter stands there, not dissimilar to the one by Kauffmann, but with a second arm and hair, though missing its crank; a full-bosomed woman who plays chess and, if need be, can also play the zither; a czarist drummer who bangs away when you give him a kick in the rear, the same stupidly enthusiastic look on his face as on the "Enigmarelle" later built by Ireland, but that one could write.

Around 1800 Vaucanson's duck is said to have briefly been part of the collection, before it was last seen in Helmstedt, along with his flute player, both already in deplorable condition. "The flutist no longer fluted, the duck, its feathers gone, was a mere skeleton, but it ate its oats quite cheerfully still, though no longer digested them"—to quote Goethe.

It is not known if prior to this, Beiries—polymath and *hofrat* in Helmstedt, subscriber to Schroether's *Selenology,* and learned eccentric with kleptomaniacal tendencies—made a brief stopover in Friedland.

The last room to be visited in this wing is the armory on the ground floor, where Friedland displays more in common with Frýdlant and Wallenstein than with Litomyšl and Smetana.

The felt slippers remain upstairs, stored in a large Renaissance chest near the stairs.

Outside, the other cohort of collective farmers comes sauntering from the brewery tavern. One of the men stops in front of the main portal and watches Podol, who is working on the curious coat-of-arms of the Trauttmansdorffs, the chief beneficiaries of re-Catholicization after 1620. He merrily bastardizes it with a bar sinister.

"What are you doing there?"

Podol turns around to him in surprise; usually they are left in peace. The question is very superfluous.

"I'm restoring the castle coat-of-arms, if you have no objection."

"You're desecrating it!" The man's voice trembles. "Besides which, it's the wrong one!"

Podol wonders if he may be dealing with some inspector from the Landmarks Office, but the man is too emotional for that. Maybe one of the descendants of the deposed petty aristocracy who refused to be proletarianized in town and work instead as laborers on collective farms, where they maintain a kind of residual supervision over their former estates.

"You're just full of useless information. Is your name Trauttmansdorff maybe?"

"Of course not!" The man is gravely offended.

"Or maybe even Pernštejn?"

Wounded silence.

"What concern is it of yours, then?"

"Back in the thirties we financed the last restoration here, not without help from the state. In case you know some Latin, it's recorded there on the façade. The work was done quite differently, each ornament exactly like the next, meticulous work. The restorer was a professor from the Academy. You've bungled the job! I have inspected it, gone clear around."

"And what a diligent scholar he was. Your professor didn't have the vaguest, the execution is so scholastic it's enough to peeve a person. Have you ever seen the old frescoes up top? Those weren't done by a fussbudget, every coffer is cockeyed! With butts and hands twisted around, bald heads, that's your meticulous for you!"

"You mean the Allegory of Chance. I'm aware the frescoes at the top are not so badly damaged. But you should keep to the originals in every case!"

"There was nothing down here, nothing of the old work. A few boring, wispy frills, with some building-block towers in between. It's all coming off! Down to the bricks!"

"Those towers are part of the coat-of-arms, and get rid of that bar sinister!" the man below shouts.

The brewery group stand around and cannot make up their minds whether to go through the portal—culture or more beer—but then Bullak, the leader of the cadre, staggers over to fetch the stray. "Thurn, stop chewing the leg off these bricklayers here, we're heading back into town." Even in his drunken, chummy state, he notices Podol's grim looks and hastens to add in a schoolmarmish tone, "The comrade has got better things to do. . . ."

"Right, like bricklaying!" A lump of mortar flies from Podol's trowel and lands on the cadre leader's jacket. A surprised and delighted Thurn, whose noble family has been taxed with dispossession, sizes up the lucky shot, and gets the next one right in the eye. "Who did you bribe back in the thirties? Those towers go, along with your stupid pig Latin!" Podol shouts at him.

Blind with rage, Thurn races to the cement mixer out on the lawn and starts hurling handfuls of gravel at the scaffold. Bullak is still trying to straighten the matter out when the second trowelful plugs his mouth. Podol's aim is getting more and more precise. Political oratory is of no use in this situation. Bullak grabs a loose stone from the pavement and flings it, just missing Patera, who has clambered over, anxious to find out what is wrong. "Duck!" Podol slams another trowel load in the direction of the collective farm. Svidnická, a lady honored for her hog breeding and Bullak's close companion ever since the bus ride, gets in its path. Her scream mobilizes the rest of the collective. Scrambling down from the coffers, Orten and Maltzahn find themselves in a hail of gravel, whereupon Orten dumps an open sack of sand on the soil expert immediately below him.

Urged on by Bullak, two comrades from the repair shop are about to scale the scaffold, but Maltzahn, who is suddenly nimble and sure of himself on the planks, pulls the ladder up just in time, and while they continue to search for a way up he drenches them with water, followed by unslaked lime.

The fiercest battle is between Podol up on the scaffold and Otto Zeta, decorated as a Hero of Socialist Labor for his tractor driving, who is trying to get up to him, flanked by Thurn, whose goal is the coat-of-arms. The inseminator has hated Maltzahn from the very first moment and furiously pelts him with loose pieces of the historic cobblestones. But Maltzahn is everywhere and hard to hit. Windows shatter behind him. He moves about, covering their weak spots, and is so successful at drawing fire away from Podol that the latter is able to land a decisive shot. Orten economically uses what little water they have, pouring it on anyone who gets too close. The stubborn agronomist is now so wet that he abandons his attempt to climb up and takes up gravel throwing instead. Patera hands out ammo and cheers them on in a hoarse voice—when he is not leaning against the wall to catch his breath.

The main body of collective farmers, who are elbowing their way out of the armory, see stones flying, hear the noise of battle, and are overcome with solidarity. They forgo the concluding tour of the theater and rush to help their comrades. Until now the four men on the scaffold have had a certain advantage, but they haven't a chance against seventeen more farmers.

Jirse makes himself scarce. For one brief moment Podol pictures that face in the line of fire, but then contents himself with Bullak, who recalls his first skirmishes as a partisan, shouts, "For the Fatherland! For Stalin!" and slips on a new volley of mortar. Next month's supplies are gradually running out. The sacks of lime and sand are empty or lie spilled and wasted down below. Sticky lumps of gravel, stones, mortar, tools, sticks of wood from splintered planks fly back and forth, but fewer of them now, with most of them piled behind the scaffold. Searching for new ammunition, Maltzahn casts an eye through the broken window and it falls on the heavy folios in the library. He hesitates briefly, he reaches for the bolt, but Orten stops him from climbing through. The window to the sacristy is ajar, and there lie the tools of the workers who are repairing the interior. He would rather not steal the bread from their mouths, but there is a pile of damp sawdust in one corner—there is no toilet on this floor—and that might do. Maltzahn takes a bronze bowl from the chapel and shovels the sawdust out the window. It sticks to the mortar and gives the attackers gooey hairdos, tars and feathers them cap-à-pie.

Patera is blinded by part of a drifting cloud of sawdust, steps into a hole where a plank has been ripped up, and there he hangs, while the farmers try to grab for his feet from below. But Orten takes hold of him under the arms just in time. For a while the battle is concentrated on tugging Patera in one direction or the other. The scaffold party manages to hold on to Patera; the populace of Stadice have only a shoe.

In his zeal, Podol picks up his last bottle of beer, thinks better of it and takes a drink, passes it on to Patera, who is gasping and wiping the filth from his brow. "Boys, it's a quite a shindig, but I'm running out of steam."

Their goal now is merely to maintain their position on the scaffold. They can hear the suggestions from below now: dismantle it, set it on fire, smoke 'em out, douse 'em with pitch! The women, who are now in the majority, are for setting it on fire.

The last trowelful hits a man they have not noticed until now, a tardy warrior who was the only person to have a look at the theater and has just now emerged from under the portal. For lack of other ammunition, Podol has used mortar scraped from the bar sinister of the Trauttmansdorffs. This final shot appears to calm the warriors, and on the verge of victory they beat a surprising retreat.

The man wipes his eyes, brushes the golden plaster from his hair and cap, looks up at Podol, and grins. He is the collective farm's assistant bookkeeper, who bears a startling resemblance to the former first secretary of the Central Committee. "I've seen you somewhere before," Podol says with a bow. "Without the cap," he adds, wiping off his trowel. "You can wash your face there at the well."

Watching him walk away, Maltzahn remarks to Podol, "At least he's still alive. All that's left of Palach is the death mask I was able to make."

"Have you ever known a politician who would set fire to himself?" Podol is too old a hand to be impressed by a deposed party functionary.

The farmers gather up their wounded. Svidnická lets herself be carried away by Bullak and Pichota; her chief concern, expressed in moans and twitches, seems to be that Maltzahn is watching her. A good portion of the freshly restored coffers will have to be redone, but Patera says he wouldn't have missed this battle and eloquently fingers the lump on his forehead. Podol and Maltzahn are also of the opinion that it was worth it. Podol's eye is swelling shut and turning dark, which gives him an insolent look, a one-eyed desperado—Žižka, Nelson, Moshe Dayan. Orten's lip is split and swollen, sparing him any commentary. He merely asks if they will ever get finished now. Maltzahn has no wounds. He pays considerable attention to his scraped hands, but the others are worse off in that regard, too.

In the meantime, the collective farm has regrouped by the well. The men laugh as they splash each other with water, the women prissily remove their soiled Sunday blouses. The men do not shrink from doing the same with their jackets and shirts; the first pair of red underwear glimmers under the arcade. A quick jog around the courtyard degenerates into a mad chase of the women around the well.

Hanna, who considers her tour ended, decides to flip the switch for the fountains before she goes, something normally reserved only for foreign delegations. Given the state of the pumps, they cannot be left on for more than five minutes; she has no intention of returning again today. At the sight of the first spurting fountain, Svidnická, who used to love to go to the movies, throws herself into the pool, an even more prodigious Anita Ekberg. Praxena T., captain of the sugar-beet brigade, follows her, giving it her all. Maltzahn, who is nearby searching for the tools they flung, catches their eyes. During his student days he worked in films as a walk-on—"young lad" or "German." Those same good looks also make an impression today.

He finds Patera's shoe.

That evening the entire collective gather at the Ram, spreading themselves out over the whole place so that all the strategically important positions are taken and trading stories about the day's high points, everybody at once.

They recognize the four artists when they appear, and the racket increases to the point where the historical structure itself is endangered. Bullak, Svidnická, and Thurn are sitting together, their arms around one another, and they enthusiastically wave for the artists to join them. The manager, with four half liters of beer in each hand, hurries by and smiles an apology, "I'm sorry, Mr. Podolský, they said they were leaving two hours ago." Podol steers by the light of his Cyclops eye for a table to himself. Bullak jumps up and grabs the manager's arm before she can set the beer down. The others will have to wait. Svidnická reserves the chair beside her for Maltzahn; Orten and Patera quickly occupy the other two, so that he cannot edge away from her.

Thurn stares at Orten for a long time, finally remarking with a heavy tongue, "You're an intelligent man." Orten is not up to getting involved in any further provocations today and waves this off, but Thurn has got his confidence up now. He wants to explain his relationship to the current regime, he says. He was in basic agreement with it because of the anthem. *Kde domov můj*, "Where is my homeland?"—that was a universal question. Where did we come from? Where were we? He could ask that question anywhere. And he could answer it anywhere: Where I have always been—"Do you know Wagner? So vast the realm / of worlds by night. That's a shame. Now in our family . . . Oh well, it doesn't matter." He was in basic agreement, he repeats, but what they had done with the national emblem, that he didn't like. That crude simplification of the lion, those out-of-proportion Slovak mountains on its chest, and that flame—used to be a cross there—and especially the five-pointed star, that was impossible.

"Just look at our money," Orten says, "that's even worse."

"It's of no value anyway and fortunately can't be converted, so it's never seen outside the country."

Orten ponders the fact that this little man's penchant for heraldry will cost him an extra three weeks on the scaffold.

At the next table, Juraj B., a Slovak whom fate has stranded in Stadice, explains the relationship between Slovaks and Czechs. From the very start the Czechs had pursued a policy of colonialism in Slovakia. Bohemia and Moravia had always been industrialized, whereas Slovakia had remained an agricultural nation.

"But there have been new investments there in recent years," Pichota says.

"Right, there are plenty of factories now, and they've smoked out all the beehives." They knew all they needed to know about Czechs, and he wasn't the only one here who knew the score. Juraj gives a meaningful nod toward the assistant bookkeeper, who is gazing silently into his beer glass.

"Yes, there were mistakes made in Slovakia," Bullak interjects from his table. "According to the latest resolutions of the party . . ."

"Shut your mouth!" Zeta abruptly interrupts, and Pichota concurs with him: "Yes indeed! Here in Bohemia people don't even know what a bee looks like anymore." He is already rather drunk. When he is sober he manages, along with some of the others, to keep an eye on their assistant bookkeeper. But when they get drunk—and Pichota drinks a lot when he's around his helper, to whom he is also supposed to be giving orders—they forget that at some point between the impressive dedication of their tractor station, when they had greeted him solemnly with bread and salt as their guest of honor, and his taking his current job as a bookkeeper, Russian tanks had rolled. No one, not even he, knows what authority he actually has. The bureaucrats display various reactions to his signature. Some of them take care of his requests and reminders immediately and with special consideration; others freeze and demand instructions from their superiors. He cannot, however, be fired.

"Why not?" Podol asks.

"They took him out of the forestry office in Slovakia, and now the trees are starting to die like flies around here," Bullak explains.

"So what?"

"Why get excited about the Ruhr or Leuna, when we may be dealing with revisionist plots?"

Podol looks at him with curiosity. "Tell me, are you really so cynical or just three sheets to the wind?"

"Don't misunderstand me, I don't have any influence on all that. He's no worse off with us than he would be somewhere else. And people leave him in peace. They can foist this sort of thing off on us just as they please." Bullak lowers his voice. "In the fifties there was a general in our neighborhood, worked in the office of our farm. He did a good job, was even a Hero of the Soviet Union, till one day he was made president. Then there was Tomášek, he worked as a clerk, two villages down the road. But pretty soon he ups and leaves for Moravia, as a pastor. Now he's a cardinal."

"Don't know him." Podol is not impressed.

33

"Whoever starts out in Stadice," Patera says, "has a career ahead of him."

"Or behind him." Podol gazes at that lime-smeared grin across from him, and appraises Bullak. "You already look like a plaster bust at party headquarters. They could exhibit you as a heroic people's farmer."

"Did you hear that?" Bullak claps Thurn on the shoulder. "Like my own plaster bust, that's good! Fellows, you're alright!" He's rolling now and no one is going to stop him. "Quiet! Listen up, everybody! We're going to be the patrons of these four artists here, and their brewery too! Every time we slaughter, you guys get a package of sausages!" He toasts them formally, amid the enthusiastic approval of his comrades. They all come over to shake their hands, stand in clusters around them, pound their shoulders, the castle had really been pretty silly, what with that piano and such, but it turned out really good afterward, and they would definitely be coming back. They wanted to send them a picture of the whole collective, the one with their Red Banner trophy that was in the newspaper, but only if in return they could have a snapshot of the four of them on the scaffold.

When they finally give in to the bus driver's nagging and depart, the restaurant seems very empty. It is too quiet for Podol, who sets up a racket of his own, weighs the pros and cons of having a patron and discusses the contents of the sausage package with Patera and Maltzahn. "Let's hope they put plenty of caraway in the country loaf." "Real black pudding, fresh from the slaughter," Patera says yearningly.

Maltzahn, for whom all that is much too fat, ponders, "What do they want with the brewery, a monopoly on the beer or Smetana's cradle?"

"They want to drink it dry, of course."—Podol.

After forty-five minutes the collective farmers have lost their charm. The manager has heard it all for the third time now. Podol changes topics.

"The rabbit walks past the bears' den, where the cubs are playing outside. Boys, is your mother home? No? Then you better watch out!— and shows them his fist." Laughter.

Two: "The rabbit is sitting outside its hole and shouts: I'll sharpen my claws on that bear! I'll sharpen my claws on that bear! Quiet down, the other animals warn him. I want everybody to hear, the rabbit shouts, I'll sharpen my claws on that bear! The bear arrives. Rabbit, what're you doing? Just sharpening my claws, and chattering away to myself."

Podol, Patera, and Maltzahn buckle over with laughter.

"Those are old," Orten says.

"And this one? The bunnies come home all dirty and stinky, and their mother asks them: Children, what have you been doing? Oh, we were just playing, and then the bear came along and wiped his ass with us!"

The three of them fight for air, while Orten asks himself what he is doing here really. This national defeatism is slowly getting on his nerves, and he has had enough of these three for a long time now.

"Stanislav, stop pushing it, why don't you," he remarks wearily.

"What're you talking about?" Podol erupts. "You don't say a single word yourself, just pull a sour face, nothing suits you, and we have to apologize to you for every joke!"

"The ones you tell you do. It's always the same old stuff: you're the big, bad gorilla drumming on his chest. Don't you get tired of that sometimes, at fifty?"

"Fifty-two! And not nearly so tired as you at fifty-four it seems. You were a good sculptor at one time. For three years now you've just been piddling around and spoiling everybody's good mood. If I ever get that old, I'll be sure and tell you right off, so you can go find somebody else to pick a fight with!"

"Jan didn't mean it that way." Patera is unhappy, but Maltzahn is watching his friends with curiosity.

"The hell I didn't mean it!" Orten looks at their faces, at this room that never changes, at the homely tables. He has had enough.

They are showing a Soviet film that he has seen twice now; the first time he got there too late, the second time he left before it was over.

The best thing would be to take off—new supplies wouldn't arrive for at least two weeks, that was Maltzahn's concern—but the last bus for Prague has already left. The bistro outside the bus station looks as if it's still open. They are turning the stools up on the tables when he enters, he nods to the waitress, he is thirsty, but she goes on working and is not going to serve him, it seems. He could visit Svoboda, but he will want to show his paintings again.

On the way out of town, he sees a couple standing indecisively at the door of the singles' dormitory—a prefab building with sacks of food hanging from the windows; the titmice will pick at them tomorrow morning, but refrigerators are not provided. As Orten crosses to the far side of the street, and walks along the fence of the athletic field, the light goes out in the stairwell. He is not sure whether it was Qvietone, but it could have been that woman. They are still hesitating in the dark, then they go upstairs. Orten waits to see where the light goes on, and is surprised at himself. At the same time he is annoyed with Qvietone—clumsy as he is, he still has success with the ladies.

The light is out in the bookstore on Market Square; the latest books should be in stock on Thursday, but there is nothing to see. For four months now, the butcher shop has displayed a red cardboard sign in its window, along with the potted flowers and dummy sausages: LONG LIVE FEBRUARY, MONTH OF VICTORY!

After several pointless detours, he arrives at the castle.

Jirse still has a light on, and comes out the moment he hears Orten in the hall. He has made a note of the polluted well, busted pumps, broken windows.

"Not tonight, Mr. Jirse."

Only Patera is home; he has left the lamp on and gone to bed. Orten looks at him: he looks old; how long will he be able to keep on working? Patera turns over in his sleep, wakes up briefly. "You left so early, must be hungry. There are still some sardines there."

Orten turns out the lamp. "Sleep well."

Endless hallways that merge into one another, corridors with empty niches, pedestals without statues; plaster flaking from the ceilings, decaying foliage that meanders, runs in circles.

Grand open rooms, with blistered mirrors, barred windows, fireplaces, plunder spread out before them. Other rooms, darkened, crammed with broken furniture, curtains billowing wearily in the draft; more hallways, cold stairwells, oppressive, but one can still breathe.

And on out under the rustling night sky, and through the air, approaching glistening stars and dark planets, undiscovered, visible only in their borrowed light, by their weak albedo. They are bloated, menacing, and then they are gone, saving the collision for the next giant of unimaginable size already rolling toward them—and now it releases me from its stony embrace.

I fly on, the next stars await me, open and close behind me, duck back into the silence of stellar dust, from Jupiter to the Clouds of Magellan, past Epsilon Aurigae, into the night—toward which I e'er shall wander. Worlds open up: volcanoes, magma, stones. Stones with all their indescribable properties, their lonely forms, not one of which remembers man.

A planet captures me, I am trapped in an air bubble inside, surrounded by gloomy walls of rock. I lie on my face, my mouth wrenched wide. I can feel the cold of the stone on my gums; a boulder on my back presses me against the floor, under the weight of my body and the stone, the chisel is being forced into my belly.

I have to make more space, change my position, stand erect, so that I can find out what this wall that I shall be working on is made of.

I leave my stony hole—a trap for a hollow man. But only after I have left behind a compact figure to replace my crumpled hollow form—a statue of the first level.

Outside, the façade becomes visible in the dawn.

THREE

"The hollow men live in hollow chambers, they build movable caverns in the stone, at night they are air bubbles dancing in the ice under the full moon. They would burst in the sun." Qvietone lifts his lamp: "Careful here." The rock wall dips, and they have to duck to get through.

"Kissee the magician has two sons, Mo and Ho, twins, whom even their mother cannot tell apart. But the older one is to be his successor. How is he to determine which that is? He sends them out to find the Bitter Rose—if someone tells a lie, it will burn his tongue when he tastes of it. It can be found only on the highest mountain peak and looks like a large lichen of many colors or like a swarm of butterflies. If anyone who is afraid approaches, it takes fright and locks itself inside the rocks. Nor does it help to desire it, for whoever desires it is always a little afraid of obtaining it, and suddenly it is not there."

Qvietone looks at his girlfriend, who has only been half listening until now. She turns around: "How does the story end?"

"The first son had almost reached it, but then he drove his piton through the chamber of a hollow man and slew him. He was horrified, and the rose vanished. He was now pursued by hollow men seeking revenge. At dawn the next day they found his clothes and gear at the foot of the mountain, but no trace of him.

"His brother Ho now set out. After a long climb he found Mo encased in the ice, just as Kissee had foretold, a victim of the hollow men's revenge. 'Do not be afraid to slay a dead man'—he struck the head deep inside the ice with his axe, opening his brother's hollow form, and slipped into it. And learned where the Bitter Rose grows. He brought it to his father, was made heir to his vast knowledge, and lived on, united with his brother, as Moho."

"Is that a Nordic saga?"

"No, it is set in high mountains, the Himalayas or the Pamir. But the name is universal. The thinnest part of the earth's crust, the ocean floor, as analog to the highest mountains, is called the Mohole mantle, abbreviated Moho."

"It reminded me more of *homo*. They say it takes both hollow and compact forms to create a whole human being. Besides which, every fetus begins as twins."

"That's the student of medicine speaking," Qvietone says in admiration. "But *homo* would work, it fits the general tone, I hadn't thought of that."

"What kind of saga is it?"

"It's a story from a novel about mountain climbers."

"Mountain climbers?" Her fleeting interest, which Qvietone has tried to hold by balancing suspense, flattery, and catchwords, has abated again.

The passage opens into the first large chamber. When they look back, blue daylight still shines in through the entrance, now grown very small. The height of the creviced ceiling varies; the carbide lamp reveals the galleries diverging from the asphalt path to be blind niches. Water drips from projecting rocks.

"Are there stalagmites here?"

"Further on, in the Cathedral there are the beginnings of mountain milk, but no real formations."

"Mountain milk?"

"That's a whitish mass, porous lime deposits that can form stalagmites, but usually just builds along the walls. If they dry out they decompose into lime dust and are washed away by rain. There are other kinds of formations, too." Qvietone wants to talk about calcite deposits and curtains, about how stalactites are generated when fossilized sinter breaks down and the decomposed piles of it are overgrown with new formations, about cave pearls with kernels of sand or gravel encased inside them, how even bat skulls can be a crystallizing core that is then transformed into sinter—solitaires in the darkness of caves. About eccentrics, distorted stalactites, which defy gravity and send out thin, crippled fingers into the surrounding air, attaching themselves like thin branches—neg-entropic arrests of gravity.

"It smells like garlic in here," Marie-Mercedes says. She doesn't want him expatiating on some topic; he is supposed to feel she has come here with him to forgive him, not use this as an opportunity to toot his own horn.

Surrounded by these formations, Qvietone keeps forgetting how ticklish his situation really is. He keeps getting carried away by associations and his own enthusiasm, and at such moments doesn't stop to think of the problems of their relationship.

He was dumbfounded when she telephoned him after three weeks of silence and suggested that they go on this outing. Several months before he had gone on and on about these caverns, but she was not interested then.

When he first heard her laughter—it was at a champagne breakfast in his mother's office—he felt fascinated by a woman for the first time in his life. Although fourteen years older than he, she had asked so many questions, and he had not attributed this to her friendship with his mother, but rather to his precise answers. She was about to take over the position of head of orthopedics in Friedland, to replace a doctor who was being sent to Kuwait for three years. Qvietone promptly broke off his graduate work in entomology and headed off to Friedland to look for a job.

No one had any use for his specialty, but the castle archives needed someone. He got the job that very afternoon, although it would be two months before Marie's new position was open. To bridge the gap, he worked overtime and used his accumulated hours for trips to Prague in hopes of seeing her. His mother had never seen him in her office so frequently and was delighted by the change in him. She confided to her colleagues that she had started to worry about Erik, but he had changed so much she thought he must have a girlfriend.

Spurred on by his libido, he even completed his abandoned doctoral thesis: "Mating and Pairing of the Monogamous Desert Sow Bug *Hemilepistus reaumuri* Mercedes," which he had discovered at age seventeen while on a vacation with his mother in Tunisia. The dissertation consisted chiefly of descriptions and drawings of this harassed crustacean's *posizioni,* with the phylogenetic classification crammed into an appendix (the chief result of which was that it earned him the enmity of Linsenmair—but given his urges, that had not bothered him much).

Her first task in her new position was to render a forensic opinion regarding the state of Jirse's stump following Podol's attack. She was unable to determine any further malformations or injuries.

Qvietone, who did not know that she was already in town, went into raptures when he spotted her; his words began to flow in a delirious monologue—I sing of thee, Democracy, I sing of thee, Mercedes—but he was the first person in forty years to confront Party member Jirse with his anti-Semitism.

He had never been afraid of that old Nazi, only disgusted by him, the way he was by some particularly repulsive species, the fluke *Leucochloridium macrostomum,* for instance, whose sporocysts penetrate the feelers of amber snails like thick worms and lie there pulsating, waiting for their next host, or by the larvae of the botfly under the hide of cattle. Like everyone else, he let himself be intimidated by Jirse's prosthesis at first; the stump was an organ of fascination—the tip of a cobra's tail distracting the rabbit before it strikes. But as Podol remarked after the hearing, Qvietone was the sort of rabbit that suddenly spins around and turns into a mongoose.

Jirse was not a problem, but the four men on the scaffold were. He compared his own honest toil in the archives with their sorties on the wall—Podol's loud laughter and pleasure in his work, Patera's bleats of approval and the toll the work took on him, Orten's silence behind the open windows and his sudden outbursts. He even corrected Podol sometimes, apparently knew a lot. When Qvietone quit, he left all such comparisons behind him.

The surprising turn of events at Jirse's hearing made Marie take a closer look at Qvietone for the first time. Until then she had thought of him as a spoiled boy with an overprotective mother; and she felt closer to her colleague than to the son. She invited him to the party welcoming her to her department; he dropped by often after that. He brought his dissertation to her office, too. She said, "Leave it on the desk." When a month had passed and she still had said nothing about it, he bashfully showed her the dedication. She was embarrassed by the Mercedes part of the bug's name. "Can it still be changed?" she asked.

"The name of the species is already registered in Paris and is now part of the internationally accepted taxonomy," he answered with self-assurance.

A little cocky for twenty-four, she thought.

"It smells like garlic in here."

"That's from the lamp, the acetylene from the carbide is never totally free of arsine, it smells like that."

"To my knowledge it's poisonous."

"Not at these concentrations. Although there is such a thing as arsenic addiction, used to be common among mountain climbers. They used it to give themselves robust complexions and increased muscle strength, as a way of promoting business. It was especially popular in Bohemia, before the Alps were opened to tourists. But once the dosage was stopped, rapid deterioration ensued. And the dose had to be constantly increased, until all of a sudden it was too much. It was called mountain sugar, arsenic trioxide, and causes cramping of the smooth intestinal muscles that leads to fatal vomiting."

"Madame Bovary," Marie says.

"Yes, whereas pure arsenic is not toxic at all; it's insoluble, you see. It's also called shard cobalt, because it looks like the shards from a clay pot, reddish-brown lumps that can be broken off in layers. The derivation is from the miners' word *kobold,* useless stone in a vein of ore. We should be able to find some here actually. It is also of interest how close the word *arsenic* is to *asafetida,* a medicinal gum that also smells like garlic. It is sometimes called devil's dung as well. I would be more inclined to say 'the stench of the fetus.' It has therapeutical applications."

Marie has already moved away, turning blindly into the next gallery. Qvietone hurries after her with his lamp. He has a flashlight in his pocket and considers giving it to her, but decides he would rather light her way himself.

"This formation is called the Great Sofa," he explains. It is a boulder with rounded-off flanks and a longish chairlike indentation, worn and polished smooth by tourists—burnished by bear bottoms, bare bottoms.

"Is there another exit?" she asks irritably.

"We're almost at the other end, but there's something I have to show you."

She is strangely tired, feels awkward and ridiculously athletic in these heavy boots, as if she were one of her own friends, a woman about her age. Walking over the uneven floor is an exertion; she is only too aware of the difference in their ages, and for the first time it annoys her. She sits down on the Sofa.

It was her idea to come here. He had stopped pressing her. He had given up pressing her about anything, especially since his last visit, when she had yielded to him so surprisingly, and improperly. After that, she had blocked all contact from one moment to the next, said not a word to him, played dead, like a beetle lying on its back. Besides which, there had been that spot of smeared blood on the sheet. She had stared at it, and he first thought it was a nosebleed, and although he noticed her panic, he didn't understand and apologized at once; he didn't know how it could have happened—she knew, she had started it. He had barely been aware of all the hopes that had come to fruition. She didn't want to hear another word, wouldn't let him touch her, wouldn't look at him. He was devastated.

She didn't answer his letters. When he risked a phone call two weeks later, he had heard her tell a woman she shared a hall phone with that she was not there. Two weeks later, when she returned home from a birthday party in her department, she found him sleeping on the mat outside the shower room on her floor, and did not wake him. The next morning, when she checked, he was gone. She called the museum, not so much to speak with him as to see how things stood with his mother, who had been upset at first when she realized who it was that Erik had picked, and then was offended once it became apparent that Marie was not the least bit interested in him.

She could find no neutral spot anywhere in Friedland, some quiet place where she could explain her situation. She didn't want to invite him to her apartment, she wouldn't go to his, neither place of work was suitable, the Ram even less so.

She first thought of the castle, but couldn't imagine a conversation in the middle of tours and that to-do up on the façade. Then she remembered the caverns; Erik could get the key for them from the museum. Inadequate safety precautions had kept them closed to tourists for two years now—the rooms near the entrance had been used as a brewery warehouse for a while, and wagon ruts were still visible, with lots of broken glass strewn about. The caverns were now reserved for research. Qvietone had made friends with the taxidermist in the prehistory department, and he now knew the caverns better than the former guide.

He wanted to fit her out in full gear, but she insisted she wasn't going spelunking, just visiting the cave. She also refused to bring along a basket of "refreshments," for which he had bought two different kinds of red wine—this wasn't supposed to be a picnic. When he picked her up, he had a tin of cookies with him, three-layered imitation petits fours, his own Alsatian recipe, which much to his landlady's annoyance he had baked in her oven the night before.

"You know I don't like sweets." She threw the one she had bitten into back in with the others she had already nibbled the icing and nuts off of. He remembered the salmon-colored blouse his mother had bought for her in France with what little cash currency regulations allowed her. Marie ripped it trying it on, because she hadn't unbuttoned it completely, and then spilled red wine on it besides. The blouse had lain in a drawer ever since.

She made a habit of belittling gifts. Although this disappointed and saddened him every time, it also impressed him—she couldn't be bribed.

They went on foot, were dressed too warmly for the hot June day, and had no choice but to tramp along the road in the dust raised by the traffic. They checked behind them each time, but there were no taxis out here in the country. It was almost two miles, the first half along this dreary stretch of road. Qvietone had wanted to rent bikes, but she thought that was a bit much for such a short distance. Just when they were about to hitch a ride back into town, there was a turn-off into the woods, and then another mile and a half uphill. He carried her jacket for her, then her sunglasses, even her wristwatch. She was sweating, while he climbed on ahead of her at much too fast a pace and with no apparent difficulty. He stopped often, offering to lend her a hand, which she huffily declined. She let him help her just once over a slippery spot—how embarrassing; she was very aware of her own weight and that he could be under no illusions, either.

Once in the cave, he flicked the lime dust off the bottom tray of the lamp, refilled it from the drum of carbide beside the entrance, and added water to the cylinder. He enjoyed showing all this to her.

· · ·

It was a mistake to take this job, but if she had stayed in Prague, with its patronage system and all those extra qualifications, she would have remained a staff physician, despite her second diploma. This could happen to her only here—suddenly to find herself half engaged to this boy. There wasn't even a real movie theater in Friedland. She had seen three films so far, and each time that grumpy sculptor or restorer had been sitting there, the one Qvietone was always enthusing about for being so well read, another stray from Prague.

"There's a wall with sgraffiti here," Qvietone says.

She slips down off the stone.

He leads her around the corner to a setback wall and lifts his lamp. He takes her hand and pulls it up to the rough surface. Only now does she see a hand, a human hand, and she jerks back. The little finger is missing, but not because the wall has flaked away—it even has a stump.

"A painter of the naturalist school," she remarks.

"No, a cripple, it's an impression. The wall was soft clay at one time, then crusted over."

"Rather large." In amazement she lays her hand in the print, the four fingers are much longer than her own, her little finger is almost the same length as the stump. She shudders as she touches the stone, notices how cold the cave is. Qvietone promptly lays his jacket around her shoulders, giving her a shy hug and kissing her hair. The lamp, which he has placed on a ledge, casts her shadow against the wall, next to the maimed hand. She watches as a gigantic troglodyte strangles her from behind, and for a moment she is paralyzed by the thought that she is totally at this man's mercy. She cautiously pulls away from Qvietone's embrace—only now does it occur to her how dependent she is on him in here.

"And that's not all," he says, illuminating more of the wall. "You see those scratches, those lines there? That's a leg."

"Where?"

"You have to see the whole thing; it goes clear to the ceiling. This arched ridge is the back of the neck, and if you follow it you can see where it joins the head, see? And here," he points to another corner of the wall, "are the tail and the hind legs. Prehistoric cattle were over twelve feet high! Thousands of years lie between those two images."

"Which is older, the hand?"

"Yes, imprints are the oldest traces. Art, the first carvings, come later."

"Isn't it possible that both images are by the same person?"

"No, if only because of the different nature of the background materials, but that would be lovely—the hand imprint as a kind of signature. Which would mean the artist was a maimed paleolithic lefty. That wasn't so rare at the time; there were about equal numbers of left- and right-handed people, with the right dominating only after the emergence of handcrafts, specialization. This wall is a palimpsest, who knows what's hidden under that layer of lime. See the horns on the ceiling? No one else knows about this carving, and it's at least three thousand years old. That is my bison, my Altamira, and from now on it will be called Altamira-Mercedes!"

She is dumbfounded by so much devotion, Qvietone's effusions embarrass her, she has no choice but to react inappropriately. "Is that as irrevocable as your desert bug?" she tries to joke.

"It's a crustacean!" He picks up the lamp and walks off.

She hurries to stay in a lighted area. She hears gravel rolling behind her; the cave is making her nervous; she has been here too long. "Are there any animals in here?" She wants him to stay close to her.

Qvietone moves on ahead and says nothing.

She stumbles, and he immediately stops. "Need help?"

"No thanks, it's okay," she says in a frail voice.

"Of course there are animals here," he quickly resumes, "some that live permanently in caves, others sporadically, especially near the entrance, and have adapted to the twilight state. Most of them are arthropods, arachnids for example—ticks, spiders, millipedes, false scorpions."

"Scorpions?"

"False scorpions. They have no stingers, but they do have pincers. They're only a few millimeters long, though. The *Neobisium aueri* Beier, for example, measures a mere four millimeters, but it's very rare, a survivor from before the ice age."

"Where?"

"In the Alps. They've not been found further north than that, don't extend as far as Bohemia, mostly at home in karst around the Mediterranean. Some troglobiontic isopods as well, unfortunately."

"What are those?"

"Sow bugs."

She goes ahead without replying.

"There are also cave butterflies." He gives it another try. "The inchworms *Triphosa dubitata* and *Triphosa sabaudiata,* they live near entrances. And the cave locust in southern Austria, of the genus *Troglophilus,* is considered a relic of an earlier warming period."

Marie, who has deferred until now, is increasingly suspicious.

"The genus *Troglophilus?* That just means cave-loving. Why should it be used in particular for a locust?"

"That's not so rare. Among the Neuroptera, or lacewings, there is a corresponding suborder called Neuroptera as well, that is, the true lacewings—though none of them are cave dwellers. And the whole taxonomy is purely a matter of taking the ending *-wing* and coupling it with some general, but in no way specific, characteristic. Among the families in this order, there are shinywings, dustywings, spoonwings, threadwings—but ant lions and owlflies as well—which means one can never deduce the larger order from the names of the families, because, for instance, the related order Mecoptera also contains families of *-wings,* but scorpionflies as well."

"The systematists are not systematic, then," Marie concludes. "Either they do sloppy work or their linguistic resources are very limited."

"Of course. I would not, however, wish to imply any malicious intent on their part. Just look at me. I'm a harmless young fellow, except that if someone teases or underestimates me, I throw myself into my work, the rest of the time I'm docile and devoted, even if you do think I'm a mama's boy—discounting the fact that that term, too, suggests a linguistic deficiency, if only because it fails to take all the metaphorical possibilities into account—but I didn't mean to get carried away. Maybe it's purely some basic disinclination of yours to take up with me, which, granted, I would find devastating. I would, therefore, prefer to attribute it to a certain chronic weariness and general irritability on your part, having more to do with the prevailing provincial climate than with me in particular, at least I would hope so, although I can only wish that when you are in town Friedland will be as stimulating a place of infinite variety for you as this cave is for me. But as to your criticism. The systematists have indeed only inadequate linguistic resources at their disposal for creating new concepts, or naming new species and families. The term *wing* is apparently a late term, a stopgap by which to establish connections after the fact within a system that already stands fixed. It's the same linguistic perplexity that at one time divided the periodic table into metals and metalloids, the latter term being applied to nonmetals. It's also a matter of economy. More termini mean a system with fewer interconnections and demand greater feats of memory. In the case of *wing,* however, the snake bites its own tail."

She gazes at him in silence.

"What's interesting, by the way, is how animals have adapted themselves to life in caves," he continues. "The loss of pigmentation, for example, or the involution of the eyes, the flattening of the body and lengthening of antennae and feelers, not in all species but in a great many."

She has heard enough.

"I am not unfamiliar with all that, we had comparative anatomy in our fourth semester," she says testily. "I am also aware of the effects of arsenic, and as to general observations concerning the linguistic inadequacies of systems and systematists, we can pursue those outside as well."

"I'm sorry," Qvietone quickly replies. But all the same, he is certain that she hasn't had Comparative Entomology.

"I was really asking about higher animals." She is amazed at her own patience.

"Do you mean vertebrates? There are stygobiontic fish that live in subterranean waters—from the River Styx—and then there's the olm of Yugoslavia, which even in the larval stage . . ."

"Yes, and the axolotl in Mexico, too." But she is not going to let him get started on the subject of neoteny. "I was thinking more of mammals."

"Bats, the gray long-eared bat *Plecotus austriacus,* is found all over Central Europe, and the small horseshoe bat."

"Larger animals!"

"An occasional fox or badger, smaller rodents, but no permanent cave dwellers. They have their own dens."

"And nothing else?"

"You probably would have liked the Pleistocene cave bear. *Ursus spelaeus* was really very large. One would hardly have fit in here."

She looks around. "What would you do if one suddenly did show up?"

"I doubt if I'd have much free choice. I would have to leave it up to him. Maybe he'd keep us here for his own amusement—bears are very playful."

"He wouldn't put up with a chatterbox like you for very long."

"I would try to divert him from you, survival of the dearest." He kisses her hand.

Now he's playing the buffoon again, she thinks. Has no more than pulled himself together, and he starts playing the buffoon.

"Women are of greater biological value," he can't help remarking.

"Messieurs-'dames, we are nearing the end of our subterranean journey. This is the last and largest room of the caverns, the Cathedral. Please note the architectural flow, and how the static, elliptical profile, with a two-to-one ratio between width and height, works to its advantage, providing a maximum of stability that has protected the cave from shifting or collapsing over the ages. Which is also the reason why the pristine beauty of this chamber has been preserved. This row of mountain-milk stalactites, together with their matching stalagmites extending in parallel to the edges, form the mouth of a large shark, which we call Jaws—many of you I'm sure have seen the American film. And we have Jaws II as well, somewhat smaller, the vault is less sweeping here, which accounts for its other name, the Horse's Mane. A third interesting formation is the stairlike arrangement of stalagmites on your left, the three tiers creating what is called the Great Organ, and here, at your feet, we have the corresponding *positif,* unfortunately rather the worse for wear. May I remind you of the warning posted at the entrance, which states that it is forbidden to damage, write on, break off, or remove any of the caverns' contents, including stalactites, stalagmites, eccentrics, concretions, and ice."

Marie gazes at the dirty-white growth along the ceiling, but can discover neither an organ nor shark jaws, Qvietone's fantasies are not catching. She sizes up the cave's elliptical profile and thinks about the word "collapse." "So these are your stalagmites," she says, still preoccupied.

"What you're pointing at are stalactites. Stalagmites are located at your feet, which is to say would be if impetuous visitors had not taken the majority of them along as souvenirs."

"You mean these humps? I never could remember the difference."

"Notice, please, that stalagmites grow from below, *m* as in magma from the earth, mollusks on the ground, mussels in riverbeds."

"Mollusks? Snails can creep along walls and across the ceiling, too. I'll do better remembering it by Mother Earth."

"That's lovely! And the mythical component fits caves better, too, although there are troglobiontic mollusks, the land snails of the family Zonitidiae, for instance," he mutters to himself.

"What?"

"Nothing. It is amazing how many myths refer to caves; most monsters live in caves. The Minotaur, for instance."

"Have you ever seen *The Testament of Orpheus* by Cocteau?" she interrupts. "A minotaur is walking along a country road in broad daylight, with not a cave in sight for him to hide in. Or was that in *The Blood of a Poet*? I'm not sure anymore. What's fascinating about the figure is the way he walks, so erect and solemn; the creature is so lonely without his labyrinth. Until now he could only grope at his victims in the dark, has never known anything else."

Qvietone looks at her in amazement.

"A mythological Kaspar Hauser," he says.

"It's the combination, you see; the human gait makes him so tragic," Marie goes on. "He is part of neither the human nor the animal world. There's no lonely figure like that in Nordic myths."

"Fafnir."

"He's got his treasure hoard. Besides, he's a dragon, a lindworm, there's nothing human about him."

"Only his greed."

"Are there any Central European cave myths? All I know is the saga of the Sleeping Knights of Blaník."

"Who till now have slept through all the disasters they're supposed to save us from," Qvietone adds.

"And the one about the treasures that are supposed to be hidden in rocks that open on Good Friday."

"Not just at Eastertide," he protests. "Counterfeiters work a full five-day week; they did a booming business in these caves during the fifteenth century; five thousand coins were found in the Golden Horse alone, struck in 1649, the Bohemian groschen was still worth counterfeiting in those days. Unfortunately, man's alienation from caves has proceeded ineluctably since Neolithic times, much to the regret of the speleologists. Treasure hunting doesn't pay anymore, not when you take into account the cheap prefab houses, paper money, and inflation."

"And now we're leaving, my alienation has reached its limits," she says.

"In a moment, but as to your myths. This side gallery here is the Tristan and Isolde Cave. You see that curtain of sinter where the ceiling gets lower and the folds in the lime are draped like a canopy? Those two hollows in the floor look like impressions of human bodies. That's the lovers' resting place, hence the name. A sword was found at this spot, too."

She lets herself be held back once more.

"The sword that King Mark found in the bed," she says. "Have they determined what epoch it comes from?"

"From the period of the migration of Germanic tribes, it's of Nordic manufacture, from Jutland or Seeland, to judge by the technique used for the incrustation and the style of the pommel, although the rivets are missing in the hilt. The pommel is broken and only three pieces of the blade are left, but it is still identifiable by the lenticulation and grooves, and the damascene work, too."

"Damascene work?"

"A sword blade is not wrought from a single piece of steel, several rods are welded together. Those are the Damascus bars, thirteen or more of them, always arranged with an eye to the various stresses different portions of the sword will undergo. The tang and the upper part of the blade must be especially flexible so they won't break, whereas the lower blade and point, used for the stroke and thrust, must be hard. That is achieved by regulating the temperature of the weld, the rate at which it is cooled, and the composition of the steel. In the lower portions, for instance, there is a higher carbon content, though the phosphorus content varies as well in damascene welds. Damascus bars were placed with their grain running counter to each other and welded in a braid, achieving an aesthetic effect as well as increasing the durability. The sword found here is decorated with an N-shaped pattern on the blade. From the cross cuts of ship masts we can also observe the great number of pieces used in such manufacture: the tempered wood was of various hardnesses, colors, and lengths, making it both stable and flexible enough to assume an elliptical shape against the force of the wind—those are long-lost arts!"

"I didn't know that," she says almost in envy. "Is that part of your field, too? Do you examine the blades for bronze age microbes?"

"You mean iron age. No, I was there the last time they took a sample. We have a young metallographer at the museum who did his doc-

torate on swords discovered in southern Moravia. He did a comparative analysis for us."

"Is he allowed to alter the sword?"

"It isn't intact in any case, and badly corroded besides. He simply
removes thin sections with a diamond cutter, two to three millimeters
thick, which are then ground and polished for the analysis, embedded
in plastic, and labeled. I'll show it to you, when you come by. Or
better, I'll have him explain it to you, I've read two of his articles and
am almost tempted to study it myself."

"Metallography sounds masculine."

"Do you think?" He is uneasy; he recalls that for her "masculine" is
not a term of praise. She uses it frequently for Hollywood stars, although she does like Richard Harris—he has been to see *Camelot* with
her three times now. She seldom talks about real men, or refers to
them only sarcastically. He never quite knows how he stands with her.
He has read that the man should know a great deal so that the woman
is never bored with him, but it's difficult with Marie, because she knows
a great deal herself and wants to be bored, even in her own field. She
is not easily impressed; his knowledge doesn't interest her.

"The sword could have belonged to Tristan at any rate; swords from
Seeland and Jutland were definitely known in Cornwall," he concludes.

"Maybe he forged it himself," Marie says. "Thomas de Bretagne
relates that Tristan was a worker of metals, with a special love for
mechanical toys. He invented the hinge and a never-failing bow that
was triggered by the game itself; he had trained his dog to be a regular
hunting machine, forbade it to make a single sound. He loved lifeless
things most of all! His father conceived him on his deathbed, only then
allowing his wife to approach, just as was the case later with Isolde
the physician, who in that regard was a mere nurse! After she has
saved his life, he kidnaps her to be the bride for one of her own vassals
and even allows his servant to insult her! He avoids all responsibility,
first as the vassal of old Mark, then as an invalid; he is not even
responsible for falling in love, it only happens by accident—the only
thing he was devoted to was that lethal potion! He is a narcissist, who
leads everyone into death, sucking them in with his disease, observing
his own reflection in it, although most of them die before he does. The

paragon of a fawning courtier, something for other people to look at, just like his father Rivalîn, with his 'imperial legs' that set everyone in transports. The only thing he felt pity for was his sword: 'Ah sword, what shall become of thee now? Thy honor has flown!'—you can find that in Marie de France."

"I don't know any of those versions, only the Wagner."

"There are at least ten others. In one of them Isolde is given away as a whore for lepers. And of all things you claim you've found his sword here? I'll have a look at those scraps!"

"I'll make the arrangements," he replies politely.

"I don't care about your damascene work, by the way, or where the sword comes from. I merely find Tristan insufferable. He is no mythological Kaspar Hauser, only a social moron, particularly when it comes to women!"

Qvietone has never seen her in such a rage. He is intimidated and vaguely aware that he is expected to act, to take a clear stand, he walks over to her, tries to embrace her.

She pulls away. "What's that?" she says, pointing at the wooden guardrail at the end of the gallery.

"There's a drop-off there, a ravine, with water at the bottom, from a spring, the Virgin Spring. The story goes that a girl fell into it, fleeing from a rapist."

"Have you seen the Bergman film?" She walks over to the barricade; the gravel path slopes off steeply.

"No." He hurries after her with the lamp. "Be careful!"

He illuminates the Cathedral once again, the sinter drapery and stalactites, efflorescences and scourings. "That wooden barrier is the only foreign object in the caverns," he says and puts his free arm around her shoulder, kisses her on the neck.

She doesn't move a muscle.

"Look there, the Bitter Rose." She is pointing at a limestone flower on the far side.

"A breccia," he says and hands her the lamp. He knows what is expected of him. He leaps over the barrier.

FOUR

She reached out with her arm almost simultaneously and just missed touching Qvietone's head as it dropped away ceremoniously before her. He was attempting to hold it high, to gain a foothold in the rolling gravel, but slipped slowly downward, as if after having shown her the cave's beauties he were now demonstrating its dangers. She held her hand out to him, but he was already too far below her; she could see him hugging a chunk of rock, watched the whole outcrop pull loose, break off—he was still holding on—and disappear under a wake of rubble. In the same moment she stumbled forward, the barrier gave way with her, and there she dangled with one foot caught in the planks. She worked her way free, tore a board loose and held it out over the ravine, but could see nothing—the light from the lamp bounced off the cave's ceiling, illuminating the Great Organ and the Horse's Mane, but darkness reigned below.

She did not hear the board hit bottom. The only sound was the ground crumbling beneath her as it continued to break away. She groped about and used the planks to pull herself back up, grabbing the lamp just before it rolled off. The barrier slid away, plunged. She lay there on the edge, staring into the ravine—"Erik!" Her screams got tangled in the caverns, returned to Tristan's Cave, were swallowed by the chasm. Qvietone didn't hear them.

She still had his leather jacket draped around her, buttoned at the top but with empty sleeves. Something angular weighed down one pocket, his flashlight. She turned it on. If she had had a light of her own, he wouldn't have fallen. She put it back in the pocket, zippered it up, and tossed the jacket in his direction—just in case.

· · ·

She immediately felt chilled, like a crustacean without its shell, *m* as in mollusk. She started to run.

She stumbled over stones and rubble, she bumped against sharp edges, kept running into dead ends, suddenly she was standing face to face with a crippled hand—Altamira Mercedes! He had been too eager, but it was her fault.

Her lamp banged against the Great Sofa, the chimney broke off, the flame crumpled, died in the draft. She hurried along in the darkness, her hands splayed before her, she gashed her head on a jutting ledge, and immediately took a sprawling fall into a void. She turned over on her side, but it was all the same whether she closed her eyes or tried to see. She crept cautiously forward on her knees and by groping ahead of her found a sharp turn-off. She couldn't remember having come this way. She could smell the earthy moisture hidden in the dust, she thought she felt something trotting past her—a cave weasel? She quickly stood up and turned around. Behind her, from a totally un-expected direction, she could see the exit shining like a pale blue lens in the distance. It was evening outside now.

Marie lurched down the wooded slope, staggered along the road, forcing drivers returning from their day trips to swerve out of her way, though no one stopped, and all the while her thoughts forged a chain of self-justifications and fantasies of Qvietone's rescue or escape, con-stantly interrupted by dire warnings that insisted on her guilt—she plumbed them, relished them.

"Verily, verily, I say unto you, Except a corn of wheat fall into the ground and die, it abideth alone: but if it die, it bringeth forth much fruit." It was not clear what this motto from Dostoyevsky had to do with her, but of one thing she was certain: she was alone now, and Qvietone was already multiplying—she had never thought about him so intensely.

She saw her hand stretched out to him; sometimes it was his hand, and sometimes it was Vilma's hand vainly trying to grab her husband's hand in the swamps of Byelorussia, until there was nothing more to grab.

Vilma, a distant relative.

In 1917, as the Austrians and Germans advance, her father's cousin, Vilma Janská, age twenty-one, flees from Tarnopol, along with other

Czechs from the colony there, in the direction of Kiev. Adding to the unrest and danger are drunken deserters from Russian regiments, who raid their own supply depots, plundering them for sugar, underwear, and tobacco. The only soldiers still engaged in Kerensky's widely dispersed offensive against the Triple Alliance is the Czech Legion, made up of poorly equipped deserters and prisoners-of-war, whose Pan-Slavic sympathies have made them an easily tapped source of auxiliary troops for Russian strategists, but who are no better than disloyal subjects of their kaiser in the eyes of the officers of the erstwhile Russian czar. Their initial enthusiasm—they are fighting the Austrians for an independent Czechoslovakia—makes them surprisingly effective soldiers, but they are left in the lurch by Russians deserting en masse.

The Peace of Brest-Litovsk, which to many of them represents a betrayal of their revolution, leaves the Ukraine open to pillaging Germans, who are joined by Ukrainian separatists. The Czechs withdraw to the interior, where they are deployed as part of the French army in the Entente's campaign of intervention. They seize the Trans-Siberian Railroad and now have in their hands the most strategic artery in the interior. Once they arrive in Vladivostok and secure the adjoining area for Kolchak's government in Omsk as a counterbalance against the advancing Japanese, they use the confiscated trunk line for the trip home to Prague—now that the war in Europe is over, the soldiers refuse to stay on as cannon fodder in Russia's Civil War.

Some of them defected earlier, however, and have joined the Reds in their struggle.

Arriving in Kiev, Vilma notices a lance corporal among the volunteers, a plump, harmless-looking fellow who drags passersby into the nearest tavern to buy them beers and tell endless jokes. His military blouse is too tight for him and its shoulder insignia are missing; he wears these as patches on his trousers. He makes fiery appeals in four languages for an independent Czechoslovakian army. She learns that his name is Jaroslav Hašek.

This orderly's notoriously civilian attitude is a constant source of irritation to the Russian officers, who from the start have regarded the Legion with distrust. When Hašek enters a café and sits down uninvited at an ensign's table, the Russian politely asks him to leave, whereupon he asks the officer if he knows who Jan Žižka von Trocnov was. The officer draws his saber, and Hašek hits him over the head with a bottle of wine. The Czech authorities have had constant problems keeping him out of the hands of the Russian military police.

Through her work at the military hospital, Vilma has gotten to know Johannes Herzog, a medical student from Dresden, who gives her an old issue of the *Čechoslovan* to read. From the description in Hašek's editorials and articles, she learns of a homeland—which she herself barely remembers—entirely different from the sentimental glorifications available in the club library. She likes some things about the monarchy: the aged monarch, *Old Procházka,* who loves to go for walks on the bridges when he visits Prague, and delights in how they lead to the far side—"My jubsects are boheming themselves I see." And the attitude of A. Mašek, a police informer, who, after being exposed and thrashed a second time by those subversives Hašek & Co., has them provide him a document stating that they have unmasked him several times now and he need no longer respond.

Hašek's account tells of how the informer was caught on the Ukrainian front and executed without benefit of trial.

The Czech Legion has already left Kiev by now, and in April 1918 is to be sent down the Volga and on to the negotiations in Paris, where it is to serve as a detachment in support of Masaryk's program for a Czechoslovakian republic. Hašek is opposed to the Legion's official policy and argues for a continuation of the struggle in Russia. Only when the Whites are defeated can the revolution succeed at home.

The legionnaire Hašek becomes Gašek, a comrade in the Red Army, political commissar of the 5th Siberian Army and commandant of the Tartar city of Bugulma. One of his official acts is an order issued to Citizen Igumenna, the prioress of the local cloister, to immediately dispatch thirty nuns to clean the regimental quarters. This order can be found in the archives of the Red Army. His administration establishes a literacy campaign. Under the threat of severe punishment, all residents are instructed to register in People's Instruction Courses within ten days. "*Batyushka* Commissar, better then to shoot us now," the terrified old country women wail, holding the sinister *azbuka* slates out before them. Enlightenment concerning the necessity of the new system proves of no avail among these grandmothers.

One month later Hašek is recalled and takes up editing and agitating

again as the publisher of the quadilingual weekly *Krasnaya Yevropa*
(Red Europe) and the military newspaper *Nash Put'* (Our Way).

The printing presses move with the army from town to town, and
the newspapers appear under various names and in various languages.
The last station is Irkutsk on Lake Baikal, the last paper appears in
Buryat-Mongolian: *Ör* (The Dawn).

His last home is a cottage on the banks of the Angara, where he
lives with a German, a Chinese, and his Russian wife. He spends his
days agitating among the Chinese, Koreans, and Mongols and his
nights alone with his fishing rod, staring at the river and humming
Czech folk melodies.

Vilma will meet him one more time, in Prague, in January 1921.

Johannes Herzog comes down with typhoid in Samara and is unable
to join the departing Czech Legion. Vilma stays with him. The city
seethes with revolutionary fervor—rallies, ad hoc committees, procla-
mations, and edicts mark the daily routine. In early June 1918, the
Legion sets out from Penza on an expedition of intervention—its route
to France has been blocked, the railroad system destroyed—and having
taken Kuzneck and Syzran, approaches Samara. The city's Defense
Council mobilizes the workers and farmers, but they cannot hold back
an organized army. A truce between the Czechoslovakian Red Army
and the Czech Legion collapses, and the Reds must evacuate. The
interventionists are a bomb that shatters the city's short-lived unity,
and individual units of power are flung in all directions: Hašek's operation is relocated to the southeast in Buzuluk; Vilma and Herzog
head southwest in a wagon. Hašek takes off again northeastward on
his own, to Simbirsk, passing himself off as the "idiot son of a German
colonist from Turkestan"—a last reminiscence as he gazes back over
the days of the monarchy.

Outside of Volsk their horse will go no further. Vilma unharnesses it,
and the animal, for which they paid dearly, takes a few steps into the
fallow bottoms at the roadside and then collapses amid withered, half-
grown stalks. Blinded by rage and the flies, she scratches at the hard
ground—she learned at home to respect horses—until a passing farmer

and his family convince her that this is sinful in the middle of a famine. She leaves the cadaver to them.

They spend four days on the banks of the Volga. Herzog is delirious, she forces him to eat the roots of reeds and wild onions, tries to keep the mosquitoes away from his blistered face. Then his fever breaks. They move on and are amazed at the hospitality shown them by the people along the Volga, already battered by war and hunger. They listen to their songs and stories about Stenka Razin and Yemelyan Pugachev, whom old folks fondly call Yemelka. The rebellion that he led, and that their great-grandfathers took part in, means more to these farmers than this revolution with its decrees.

At mention of the name Pugachev, the frail, apathetic Herzog sits up on his cot in the low room they share with the five members of their host family, and for the first time since they fled Samara he speaks a few coherent sentences. It is the Kalmyk fable of the eagle and the long-lived raven, which Pugachev tells his companion in Pushkin's *The Captain's Daughter*.

"Tell me, Raven, you bird, why is it that you live in the great world for three hundred years, and I but thirty-three summers? Because, old father, I live on carrion and you drink the blood of living things. They come upon a dead horse. Let us try it, they say. The eagle takes a peck, then another, flaps its wings and says: Rather than live on carrion for three hundred years, I shall have yet another drink of the blood of living things—it's worth the risk!" *Chem trista lyet pitat'sya padal'yu, luchshye raz napit'sya zhivoi krov'yu, a tam chto bog dast!*

It was the first book in Russian that Herzog read in Kiev.

"*A tam chto bog dast!*" cries the senile grandfather, whose reason was flogged out of him by Cossacks twenty years before. The young peasant woman leaves and comes back bringing a chicken and half the village with her. She cooks soup for the sick man and will not let him be until he finishes it. He has to tell the fable again; they all know it, but are amazed that a foreigner knows it, too, and can repeat it in poetic language. They learn that their experiences have been written down, that their life can be found in literature. They make it their concern to see that he recovers.

The barge towers on the Volga, the *burlaki* who live in the village and have heard the story, sneak the couple on board a ship headed downstream loaded with furs. Each is disguised as a *sorok* of furs, forty hides of fox or sable, and they slip by the shore police. Once on the river they are free. Vilma happily dips her hands in the warm, murky water, feels its fast current and the grip of its undertow; she does not think of the war.

In Saratov they are smuggled back on land, the ship glides on down toward Astrakhan, and the refugees resume their westward journey. They reach Kharkov by year's end.

The Ukraine has been plowed and replowed by civil war, and they do not know in which furrow they are running—behind Denikin's troops or in front of Frunze's Red units. They make a detour to the south around the city, but the road west is blocked. Given the contradictory rumors, they cannot be sure by whom. Where the river loops at Yekaterinoslav they hear about Makhno for the first time, about farm collectives being formed along the Dnepr, without any commissar's decrees, and about how the collectives have effectively turned back attacks by both armies of liberation, even at harvest time. Their infantry ride in farm wagons and are as mobile as the Hussites in their day; they have no equipment, only captured weapons that they bury after each battle in order to have them ready at hand for the next occasion. Nestor Makhno, a run-away teacher, is the strategic stroke of luck the peasant anarchists needed. He defeats his countryman Denikin and conquers Yekaterinoslav, controlled by Ukrainian nationalists, by putting his troops on a train and transporting them into the city as workers for the Pulitov mills—workers as the Trojan horse of the revolution. Symon Petlyura does not recover from the defeat and disappointment he has met at the hands of the man he hoped would be his ally.

Once he has defeated the Austrians, the Whites, and the Yellow-Blues for them, the Red commissars rid themselves of their "Makhnovchina"—this seems a safer course for the Revolution, although Trotsky and Lenin did for a while consider an autonomous territory for the rebellious peasants. The communes are razed and new cooperatives created by decree. Makhno escapes; is detained in Rumania, Poland, Danzig; dies a common laborer in Paris in 1935. His urn is placed in Père Lachaise cemetery. At about the same time in Barcelona, Durruti leads the anarchist International to its second high point.

. . .

Vilma and Herzog meet *batko* Makhno when his division, on its way back from Gulyai Polye, stops to rest in their village. They sit around the fire of their meager bivouac—most of the houses have been burned to the ground—drink, crack jokes about the Reds, about Denikin and Petlyura's shopkeeper soul, wax enthusiastic for Taras Bulba. "Just outside of Alexandrovsk, not twenty versts west of here, he lost his pipe, and prior to that his three sons. He killed Andrei with his bare hands for betraying their cause to a beautiful Polish woman, the Poles burned Ostap before his eyes in Warsaw—'Do you hear me, father?' he cried. 'Yes, I hear you, my son!' the ataman answered, encircled by their spears. He returned home, gathered his men, advanced against the foe once more. Then he lost his pipe—'We may have to leave the country, but they'll not have my pipe!' A whole battalion of Poles attacked, his comrades were able to flee. Bound to the stake atop a hill, he called out the route of escape for them. And died a martyr's death, my little dove. *Da razve naidutsya na svete takiye ogni, muki i takaya sila, kotoraya by peresilila russkuyu silu!*—'Will the world ever find fire, martyrs, and strength enough to conquer Russian power?' " Vilma and Herzog look at each other: "Gogol." An old soldier among Makhno's followers turns around. "And what sort are you?" he asks, checking Herzog over, especially the thick glasses. Vilma is always quick to answer risky questions; her Russian betrays no accent, but this time Herzog wants to reply. In a solemn voice he repeats the quote and adds: *"Ot Gogolya."*

"Bah, a teacher!" The Makhnovite spits and asks no more questions.

They find shelter in a commune the anarchists have named after Rosa Luxemburg. For the first time Herzog can admit without shame that he is a German. They can use a doctor. Vilma looks after the children and helps him with clamps and bandages when wounded peasant soldiers come to the commune; they have been told to bring their own dressings. Word of this problem spreads among the troops, and one day a horse-drawn wagon pulls up and two soldiers unload the equipment from a doctor's confiscated office, plus several bales of bleached cotton from a textile factory and a canister of chloroform—all of it is wrapped in an infirmary tent. They are very proud of the dentist's chair.

For the first time since he deserted to the Czech Legion near Zborov two years before, only to watch it fall apart, Herzog once again experiences a sense of community. He is amazed at the organized freedom of these peasants, at their anarchic discipline. Now that he is needed and respected, he risks the suggestion that they marry. Vilma laughs at his prerevolutionary notions, but he is stubborn, he wants to be sure that she will be taken care of in case something happens to him. He frequently has to drive to the front lines now. The Makhno soldiers have to protect themselves against three armies, and there are a great many wounded. With some embarrassment he mentions his family's property in Saxony, in case they should ever go back there.

"If we go back, then to Prague," she says, frustrating his well-meaning plans.

In June 1919, Pokrovskoye is occupied by the Reds, and the commune, barns and equipment included, is burned to the ground.

"I don't care about your family's factories; I hope they don't even have them anymore. My one wish is that they at least stand us against the same wall instead of dragging each to a different corner," she says as they flee. In Mirgorod the only priest they can locate, a Pole, demands that they be baptized before he will marry them. "From the font into the fire," she says to him in German, and calls him Jan. They couldn't simply register the marriage at the local soviet in Poltava, they would have been shot as spies working for the Germans or Wrangel.

In the muck of October they reach Kiev.

The Czech quarter of the city has been destroyed. Out of a settlement of twenty thousand, only a handful of old-timers are left who didn't get sucked up in the wake of the Legion or feel the pull to the newly established republic. They are taken in with some hesitancy by the family of the former apothecary, who had twice contributed large amounts of iodine and bromine to their infirmary. He doesn't want to hear anything about Makhno; they talk about the old days when the Czech Society sponsored cultural events—nothing political—but times have changed considerably. "And old Hašek is a Red now, they say he's agitating for the Bolsheviks somewhere in Mongolia. He certainly knew how to make a speech. What a shame. I liked the man."

"So did we," Herzog is about to reply when Vilma gives his hand a squeeze under the table and asks how things are going for the Czechs here.

He cannot take them in for more than a few days, the only foreigners allowed by the city commandant are those just passing through. Without papers, they don't dare risk being found near the train station. They decide to try to catch a ride on a wagon outside the city, but once they are on the road, Vilma is in a lot of pain and they have to turn back. They reach the suburb of Podolsk after dark, and after knocking for a long time, they are let in by a shopkeeper's widow. She asks a great many questions and complains about the risks she is taking—one night's lodging costs them half the money the apothecary has given them for the trip. The old woman makes them pay extra for some watery broth for Vilma.

They sleep in a shed on some straw that has been raked up, Vilma bundled up in her coat, but still shivering with chills and anger.

"If it would pay to denounce us, she would be off to the police by now! The Makhnovites would have made short work of her—slit her throat or burned down her house!" The idea warms her some. "You should never have paid for that broth, she ought to have had to choke it down herself. Why do such people live? Do you remember the two old women on the Chop'or, who threw stones at us because we wanted to sleep behind their fence without paying? They had pigs in their stall! Kulaks and usurers!" She sits back down. "Given what Gogol had seen and described, and considering his satires and the irony with which he viewed Great Russian pretensions, do you really think he means the ending of *Taras Bulba* to be taken seriously? Or is he in fact asking for some other power that could stop Russia—the Ukrainians maybe?"

"No, it's unambiguous—he's talking about fire and martyrs after all—it's the same pathos you find at the end of *Dead Souls:* the Russian troika flies like a bird, hurtling onward, and other people and nations will have to get out of its way."

"Right, nothing but dead souls, spooks at the reins!"

Vilma has a fever. Herzog tries to keep her warm, cushions her legs higher.

"The worst thing I know," she goes on, "is the story of Akulka in *The House of the Dead*. The way she was beaten because that good-for-nothing Filka had sullied her reputation—and the only reason her husband married her was for the money, he had the horse whip ready at hand on their wedding night, and then it turned out she was innocent. He begged her forgiveness, but Filka kept right on causing trouble—'They got you drunk, that's all. Akulka gave away her favors long before you.' So he beat her daily, from morning till night: 'If I don't use the whip, I'm bored.' Then Filka was called up. As he rides by her, he leaps from the wagon and bows to the ground before her. 'Forgive me, dear girl, pure soul, for the sins I have committed against you. I have loved you for two years now, my sweet strawberry, and now the band plays and they are making a soldier of me.' And she bows deep, to her waist: 'You must forgive me, too, good youth, I know nothing evil of you.' At home she tells her husband: 'Now I love him more than anything in the world.' 'Akulina, I am going to kill you.' He awakens her early the next morning: 'Get up, wife, we're driving out to the fields.' On the way he makes her climb down, plunges his knife in her neck, her blood spurts over him, he falls to the earth with her, embraces her, screams, then runs away. They found her a hundred paces from where he left her; she wanted to return home, to him, where else was she supposed to go."

Vilma sits up and shudders as she sobs.

The door creaks open; a poor excuse for a kerosene lamp appears; its light falls on the mistrustful face of the old woman. "Are the lady and gentleman comfortable, my little doves?"

"*Ubyu!*"

"*Verschwinden Sie!*" Herzog shouts in German, but the old woman has already slammed the door. He has to hold Vilma back to keep her from running after her.

"Don't cry for Akulka."

"I'm not crying, but I feel so dreadfully sorry for her." She stops thinking about the old woman.

He lies back, but it is too cold. How long will he still be able to feel this passion lying beside him here? He is not Dimitri, the Karamazov she loves the best; he knows that he is more like Ivan, who thinks and doubts. Alyosha—too transparent, pure altruism. And then there's the cheated Smerdyakov—no, I don't feel sorry for him. "Dmitri, yes, your Mitka, I know, who takes the guilt of the crime on himself. Ivan?— as ambiguous as Stavrogin in *The Possessed,* and just as sterile. Lures others into crime and afterward bores himself with his own logic. A Tristan, who draws everyone into his doom, a vain and deadly mask."

"Sure! Lise dies for him, his idiot wife Marya and her brother are killed, and he doesn't even look their way! Shatov is the best!" she says.

They lie here in their expensive chilly hole and mourn for a poor cheated man, for life lived in literature.

In the Rakitno swamps, Herzog comes down with typhoid for the second time. Under a low, drizzling sky, they drag their way over the spongy ground. Among the stunted willows, prickly dogwoods, and faded grass, Vilma scrapes a bed together each night, a nestlike affair filled with leaves, sedge, and feathers she has gathered along the way. She envies the quick foxes who can snatch birds. At one point she stumbles over a root and as she falls finds herself holding a water rail in her hands. In her fright she lets it go, but immediately thinks better of it and makes a dive for it, the bird is under her, she can feel its heart beating in her fingers, she looks away and squeezes until the quivering and kicking stop; she hears something crack in her hands— she doesn't throw up, but only because she has not eaten for three days. Her fits of nausea seem a normal state of affairs now, she hardly notices them, they are also the source of a distant joy—but one she will not allow herself yet—at the end of a dark, mysterious tunnel.

They can make a fire; she is proud of herself as the bird roasts on its skewer; even with no salt it tastes marvelous. After the meal she lays Jan's head in her lap and sings. From there he can look up into the abiding surprise of the contrast: her pale eyes and dark hair. She will manage it; in three days she can make it to the Polish border.

The cold and emptiness wake her at dawn, she gropes about her, only his coat is still there. She calls out softly, waits for an answer, but she leaps up now and runs, following the swatches of drifting fog. She doesn't want to go too far; he might be frightened if he doesn't find her at their campsite, and she might lose her way, too. She calls more loudly, stumbles in the mud, waterfowl fly up ahead of her; she is glad to see anything move, follows everything that does. Then she sees the two little protrusions, she has run right past them once; now she can distinguish his blond head from his shoulders. She jumps into the swampy pool without a moment's hesitation.

He is too far away, she flails and calls, tries to swim, to pull her feet out of the muck, for one moment she touches his hand, but cannot grab onto it. His head sinks; she stares at the spot, where nothing moves now, she tastes the marshy water on her lips.

She uses a clump of grass to pull herself out, creeps up onto a wobbly strip of land, and lies there with her face in the profusion of boggy moss. She never wants to get up again; she knows she has lost them both in the water, her husband and her baby.

As if he only wanted to ease his fever—that's how he lay there. It was no accident. She is furious and dismayed that he could have underestimated her like this; she searches for some motive, something she said or did that could have made him think he was a burden.

She can picture his head, the near-sighted blue eyes, the sparse curly hair, almost bald now after two bouts of typhoid, how he was always looking for his glasses—you're as much trouble as peace, she said.

He stroked her temples for hours, until she finally fell asleep there in that mud hut, he had never needed much to eat; there was almost always half a potato left for her. At night, when she would start up out of a light sleep or wake up grinding her teeth, he would be awake already and soothe her in Czech, with a soft, childlike accent. Why do people say German sounds hard? His *l*, his *ich,* his *a*—she could never speak that gently.

She sits there in his coat and dries her clothes in the radiant October sun. He once told her that she had to survive, it was the only imperative. He also said that she was very beautiful.

Yes, she was very beautiful. She made it out.

During the twenties people spotted her in officers' casinos of the "Little Entente," in Warsaw and Prague. It was also known that she loved kid-leather undergarments, which she wore in public. She had plump calves that looked younger as they approached the knee; her thighs were long and slender. She had stood with the Legion beside the cradle of the republic, veterans remembered her work in the infirmary, and despite her showing too much leg she was still considered marriageable, even if there was some truth to her reputation. Sometimes she would borrow a tray from one of the cigarette girls and stroll among the tables, made a game of raking in the money, and returned the tray with three and four times the usual take before starting to dance—a kind of Cossack tap dance that showed off her legs and leather. This was during her days in Bucharest and Belgrade.

In Prague she concentrated on the milieu of the Živno Bank, the financial backbone of the First Republic. Its general director, Jaroslav Preiss, sat on all the important boards of directors of major industries, including steel foundries and oil refineries, heavy machinery—Škoda, Kolben-Daněk and Ringhoffer—paper and textile factories in Slovakia, northern Bohemia, and Prague, and Czechoslovak Elbe-Shipping, Inc. The bank founded by the Czech Legion in Siberia in 1919 was one of the few over which he had no influence. Vilma burst into his well-ordered life. She had a throaty voice that she used to sing *dumki;* also working in her favor were her hipless figure and the Russophilia prevalent throughout the nation. (It can still be found among intellectuals today, though it never had anything to do with politics, only with literature.)

She gets him to invest in Thonet Productions, because she likes the light, airy quality of its café furniture. She is not surprised to learn that Schneider-Creuzot is to merge with Škoda, she remembers that the Legion was equipped with weapons made by Schneider-Creuzot. Remington wants to invest in the Czechoslovak Republic; she watches as German and Hungarian capital is successfully kept out, as Austrian-Jewish concerns are steadily bought up by Czechoslovaks, but then there is also the support given Luxembourgian steel and coal corporations—the republic is reestablishing its historical ties.

Preiss greets with amusement Vilma's question whether it might be possible to create a system of worker-managed factories—a witty provocation, Vilma all over, fitted right in with her Red past. For the moment Vilma ignores not being taken seriously; she wants to explain to him the difference between Makhno and Lenin, but that is not an issue for the executive director—for him they are both the same, except that Lenin was the more clever, "a wholesaler in revolution, whereas Makhno is only a peddler without a license. You shouldn't fly off the handle like this, we provide social safeguards for our workers, regulated hours, workers' compensation insurance."

"Are you covered by that?"

"I'm insured by the Sugar Industry Underwriters of Prague, by the

Assicurazioni Generali Trieste and by three other large insurance companies. Surely that ought to suffice."

She moves on from Preiss to an entrepreneur she met through him; his finances are more transparent, and have their limits. That becomes clear when Vilma takes up aviation. With the establishment of regular commercial flights by French-Romanian Airlines, she frequently flies to Paris by way of Strasbourg, then to Warsaw once that route is opened. She always waits for the moment when she can spot PRAHA in thirty-foot-high letters next to the little hanger at Kbely Airport.

She talks her friend into joining the Aviation Club, organized the same year as the Second Aeronautic Exhibition, where one can see Czech planes made by Avia and Šmolík as well as the new Blériot-Spad and Fiat-Monoplane. But when Karl von Habsburg makes a second try at ascending the throne of Hungary in October 1921, overnight all the Czech military planes are withdrawn from the exhibition. Mr. Habsburg is deported to Madeira. That same year, Oehmichen, a Frenchman, demonstrates a new product made by Peugeot and capable of hovering twenty to seventy inches aboveground for one minute; he calls it a helicopter.

Within a very short span of time, three pilots she knows crash; she takes flying lessons.

She no longer has time to read, but attends the theater on social occasions, and one evening she hears *Taras Bulba, a Slavic Rhapsody*. It takes her back to 1918.

For her the only reality besides the fear she feels when flying is Janáček's music. She hears everything, finds everything there—Akulka in *The House of the Dead*, Káťa Kabanová and Jenůfa; at age twenty-nine she hears *The Makropulos Case* and is three hundred years old, a wanderer through time like Emilie Marty, who is regarded as an impostor and a heartless thief. She understands; her people are dead, too: Herzog, Hašek.

They met after the war, at the Red Seven. Hašek had been dispatched from Irkutsk to mobilize the workers in Kladno, but the revolt had already been put down before he arrived; all he had left was his commissar's nimbus.

Friends persuaded him to use his Russian experiences for a cabaret act, it would provide him a living at least.

She saw him sitting and drinking at the next table—hollow-eyed, exhausted, endlessly weary. *"Svoloch',"* he babbled to himself, and his head dropped to the table.

She knew the word—riffraff. She had heard it as a Czech, a Russian, the wife of a German—from kulaks, Mensheviks, Essers, Bolsheviks. She left.

What might he have been thinking about?

About the guards in the barracks for typhoid cases in Totzkoye or the ones in the Rumanian prison—of the sixteen thousand men who were recruited into the czar's army, six hundred survived. The train conductor, a German, had taken one look at him and joked, "Male or female?"

About the taunts that had greeted him in the Prague press—a bigamist, even though the bourgeois republic did not recognize marriages performed in Soviet fashion.

About the repeated announcements of his death, the obituaries, the warrants for his arrest as a traitor?

Several months after his arrival a mob of angry ex-legionnaires and patriots surrounded him and were about to hang him from a streetlamp. The police rescued him, that was the humiliating part. He slipped away to a one-horse town in southern Bohemia, drank, and wrote great literature.

When he died, barely forty, his friends thought the obituary was a joke. Not even his brother came to the burial.

She began dancing again, paying no attention until the general mobilization of 1938 caught up with her. The soldiers were sent home, howling with rage and shame, because France and England had already come to terms over Czechoslovakia with Hitler in Munich.

"THE REPUBLIC OF CZECHOSLOVAKIA HAS PRESERVED PEACE IN EUROPE," read the comforting headlines.

Vilma stops wasting her time in casinos.

She puts her entrepreneur friends in harness and helps German socialists from areas near the border find jobs. She knows almost all the air force officers and organizes Polish and Czech pilots for an airlift of exiles to England. One young Pole reminds her of Jan; he is one of

many who will be shot down over the Channel. England will fight to
the end for Poland and Czechoslovakia. She thinks of how the French
let the Czechs fight for them in Russia. She would have liked to meet
the RAF officer in charge, but he probably never set foot on the continent, anymore than the organizers of the Heydrich assassination did.
Jan Kubiš and Jozef Gabčík were caught, and then drowned like rats
in the Church of Cyril and Methodius; Lidice and Ležáky were leveled;
detailed information about the preparations for the assassination is not
available to the public, either in England or in Prague.

The police discovered her in the course of the sweep that followed. A
photograph fell out of the stack of papers the Gestapo was rummaging
through, and they could only get it away from her after repeated
blows—Jan and her among the children of Pokrovskoye.

The Gestapo agent is more interested in the reverse side, which
has a wedding license stapled to it; the Polish priest in Mirgorod had
only German-Latin forms in 1919. "Herzog, Dresden? Is the address
correct?"

She says nothing.

"Precision optical instruments," he mutters. "It may be possible for
me to intervene on your behalf. You knew Preiss, the banker, did you
not?" He looks at her with interest.

Other agents drag her through the corridors of the Pečka Palace to
another interrogation. She wipes the blood off her teeth.

"You're a reasonable woman. Of course he can be a Jew, with that
name."

He examines the photo: Herzog with hollow cheeks, stubble beard,
Russian peasant's shirt, thick glasses. "He doesn't look like a German
of the Reich."

"That he doesn't," she says.

"So he was a Jew?"

"Yes, of course." The numbness of those empty years falls away
from her; she looks out the window, it is June, there must be straw-
berries out there now.

Further whereabouts unknown; her relatives were not notified. Vilma
would have attached no importance to that.

. . .

Marie had not known her, she wasn't even born yet. Her father had fallen in love with his cousin when she returned from the Ukraine in early 1920, accompanied by a Polish officer. He was fourteen then; she was ten years older. Vilma avoided the family; they learned more about her from the newspapers.

After the overthrow in 1948, her having died in a concentration camp helped the authorities overlook her contacts with anarchist and bourgeois elements.

They were not penalized on her account.

Obeying her father's wishes, Marie studied medicine—"because doctors don't get shot in war."

While she was studying she got to know a young sculptor, who struck up a conversation with her on the bridge where she was sitting and staring into the water, instead of attending a lecture. He took her along to the Academy of Arts, showed her his atelier and the things he was working on, which he kept under wet sheets. Even as she entered the room, she was aware of her desperate envy. "Doctors don't get shot in war"—she knew she had been lied to. Instead of going to lectures, she went to galleries and ateliers and, if she had the money, to the movies, several a day sometimes. The rest of the time, she read. She was always short of money, her scholarship was never enough for the whole month. At one point she took off to find an office job at a construction site. She knew she wasn't up to the physical labor, but it had to be a construction site.

"How much do you think you'll earn?" the department registrar asked her when she came in to withdraw from school—she had been admitted to medical school, she would never again have such an opportunity. "I don't know, maybe fourteen hundred korunas," Marie said doubtfully. "That should be no problem!"—there was no arguing with someone that easily satisfied. The next morning Marie returned, after having spent the night on a train. The tracks were blocked by snow and the train had barely left the station. Her father was able to cancel her withdrawal; the registrar had been slow to process it.

She passed her exams on the third try—quite a contrast to the majority of her ambitious fellow students, who wouldn't have had the nerve.

She was surprised that not only Andrei, the sculptor, but also his friends wanted to use her as a model. Ever since she had come home from summer camp twenty pounds overweight she had had no real self-confidence. Her weight had balanced out, but the insecurity remained.

Dostoyevsky's hysterical heroines, supple beauties in paintings made her feel uneasy—she had no desire to be a "Pomona," until she discovered herself in Arletty in *Les Enfants du Paradis*. After finishing their studies, the artists scattered, married fellow students, to whom they had only been condescending until then—while Marie remained their vague muse. That suited her fine; they could keep their noncommittal distance.

Apart from Qvietone there had only been her tennis partner, an unmarried colonel in counterintelligence, who as a teenager had taken part in the Slovak uprising against the Fascists. He always wore civvies. There might have been something in the fact that he was fourteen years older than she, that she was right in the middle between the two of them.

Before Qvietone, if she was in the mood, she liked to sing Soviet songs, the ones about uplift and soldiers, her favorites were *My za mir* ("We Are for Peace"); *Shiroka strana moya rodnaya,* the theme song of Radio Moscow; and *Put' dorozhka, frontovaya* ("The Song of the Driver on the Frontlines"). Qvietone was confused at first, tried to sing along, but didn't know the words, he was too young for them. But for her friend from counterintelligence, who knew all those songs and could sing them with great conviction, she would break into the kitsch from American movie musicals, and he would hum along amiably.

She felt uncomfortable with them both. They were a substitute for her former friends, who now only talked about their work, about commissions and deluded critics. Occasionally she would hear from them—they felt confined by their families. She could see herself as the confidante of married men in American films. She saw Billy Wilder's *The Apartment* five times. She lived her life in imitation of movie kitsch, with a splash of self-mockery.

The night she met Orten, let him light her cigarette in the Ram, she recognized Richard Burton's porous skin, his weary pale eyes. She knew what sort of couple they would make—she had always been somewhat embarrassed by her similarity to Liz Taylor.

But first the affair with Qvietone had to be straightened out.

FIVE

In the middle of the night Orten is awakened by knocking at the window. He first thinks Patera is back from Prague—one of his daughters had a birthday—and has forgotten his key, but the knocks are too loud for Patera. He can see nothing through the barred windows. He goes to the entry and opens the heavy door.

He steps outside, a drenched figure staggers into his arms. He doesn't recognize Qvietone right off, the face is smeared with clay, there are dried blood and sticky hair from a gash at the back of his head. He hangs on to the doorframe, shivering with weakness. "Come inside!" Orten helps him over the threshold; Qvietone drags one leg behind him and groans. Orten shoves a chair under him, helps him sit down, pours him a brandy. "What happened to you?"

Qvietone is shaking so hard he cannot speak. "You've got to get out of those wet clothes." Orten unties his shoes, left, right—Qvietone sucks air through his teeth. Orten puts on tea, gets some dry clothes from his cupboard, looks for the first-aid kit, tries to think of a telephone he can use at this hour.

Podol comes back from the john. "What have you done, my boy?"

"I slipped and sprained my leg."

Podol tries to feel along the leg under the wet trousers. "It's broken; you've got to get to the hospital."

"I'm not going."

"We'll drive you. Let me see your head first." He cuts the hair away from the wound, pours iodine on a cotton ball. "This is going to burn a little." He puts a bandage over it.

"He needs a tetanus shot," Orten suggests.

"No, my booster's still good." Qvietone's shivering is worse now;

they pull off his jacket and shirt despite his protests. He puts on Orten's. Getting the pants off is more complicated. At first he wants to keep them on, then insists he'll take them off himself. They cut the pants legs away so that he can get his leg out, then wrap him in a blanket and lead him to the nearest bed—Maltzahn's. He is still shivering.

Podol lays a hand to his brow; Orten notices that he has more trust in Podol. "You need a doctor, I'll go get one."

"But no hospital!"

"Now listen, Erik—that is your name, right? Even if we splint your leg and put it in a cast, and we can do that much better than any doctor—just imagine, you'd have an original Orten on your leg, made of the finest sculpturing plaster—you'd still have to deal with the pneumonia that you're sure to come down with. How long were you running around wet like that out there?"

"I don't know. I just lay there for a long while."

"Where?"

"In the cave."

"Up in the woods? I thought the caves were closed because there was danger of someone falling. How did you even get in?"

"I had the key, from the museum."

"What were you doing in there?"

"I was looking for troglobionts."

Podol looks at him. "I don't know what that is, but from the looks of you I seriously doubt it was worth it."

Qvietone keeps sullen silence.

"And how did it happen?"

"I wandered behind the barrier, the ground started slipping, and there was nothing for me to hold on to."

"How far did you fall?"

"I got wedged in a smaller crevice, that's how I must have sprained my leg, it was fifteen feet down maybe. I tried to climb back up, but just kept slipping farther, then the barrier came tumbling down and took me with it. I just lay there, hurt my head too, but I don't know for how long."

"How did you get back out again?"

"There's a stream at the bottom, or a subterranean river. I was lying in a little pool next to the main basin. I don't know how deep it was— I couldn't touch bottom. At first I thought I could swim it, that the river would take me out, but the water was very cold."

"Could you see anything?"

"I could hear the current. And I could feel the wind each time there was a turn; that's how I oriented myself. There are cracks in the ceiling, it's not the same thickness everywhere, and it gets lighter the closer you are to the exit. Besides, I had a flashlight, but I didn't know that."

"Why not?" Podol tries to imagine this.

"It was in my jacket, which I had left up top, and then suddenly it was lying beside me, I stumbled right over it. I had taken it off before, and it slid down with the barrier."

"Well, that was lucky. Did anyone know about your little excursion?"

Qvietone is silent for a moment. "No."

"Well, you didn't plan ahead very well. And that's not like you. You look like you're athletic, I've seen you jogging in the evenings, and you go canoeing, too, right? But this thing with the cave was pretty childish."

Qvietone creeps under his blanket, shivering.

"You'll be alright." Podol takes hold of his shoulder. "Here, have another swallow. Should I warm up some soup for you?"

Orten goes over to use the director's telephone; he saw the car outside, but he has to knock for a long time. He knows that they don't want to let him in. "Olbram, open up; it's urgent!" A woman appears at the door, Maltzahn is getting dressed in the background, he comes out.

"We need your husband's car, there's been an accident."

"Patera?" she asks.

"Podol?" Maltzahn asks, with a certain hope in his voice.

"Qvietone. The kid from the archives, you remember him."

"Sure, he's the one who got Podol out of that mess with Jirse. Where is he?"

"In your bed. Get a move on." Orten goes back. Maltzahn hurries after him with the keys to the director's car.

Qvietone has fallen into restless sleep, arguing with himself—Linsenmair, Tristan—they can't understand the rest. Podol looks at him worriedly.

"We've wasted too much time. Let's go!"

They lift Qvietone and carry him in the blanket to the car, which Maltzahn has driven up to the door. They lay him on the backseat, prop the leg up. Podol sits beside him and holds his head. Orten fetches the wet things from the room and adds the brandy bottle. Qvietone comes to briefly, sees Podol and drifts back off again.

Not until two hospital aides try to put him on the stretcher does he start struggling again. He clings to Podol, grabs hold of Orten, until they resolutely pull him off. They have to promise to come check on him the next day.

"I didn't know the kid was so attached to us," Maltzahn says, amazed.

"He's scared shitless," Podol says. "We just don't know what of. Jan, you'll have to go by yourself tomorrow. I've got an appointment with the mason about that chimney."

"He'll be very disappointed, it's you he's expecting most of all."

"I'll come by later, in the afternoon, but somebody ought to get there earlier, considering how scared he is."

"I could go," Maltzahn offers.

"I'm afraid you'd be no great help; besides you can do some work on the scaffold for once, seeing as Patera isn't here."

"Oh, I'll go," Orten says.

When he asks for the number of Qvietone's hospital room, he sees the woman in her white smock and white pants. She hesitates when she sees him, but walks on.

On her way back, she catches up with him.

"I wanted to thank you."

"For what?"

"You know I was with Erik in the cave when he fell."

"No, I didn't know that."

"I had no hope that he had survived. I spent the whole night calling around before I finally got hold of the rescue service. . . ."

"You needn't apologize to me."

"I'm not apologizing."

"Why are you telling me this then?"

"Beg your pardon. But you did bring him in. I don't know, he's so strange, he's had a shock of course. I don't know what he may have told you. . . ."

"He didn't tell me anything, and I don't want to know, either."

"Then you'll excuse me." She puts on an "I'm-busy" face and starts to leave.

"The only thing was that he put up strong resistance to being brought to the hospital," Orten says with some emphasis.

She looks at him. "You're suggesting he didn't realize how serious his condition was?"

"That I don't know, but at any rate he asked us to keep an eye on him. And that's what we're going to do." He surprises himself with his silly dramatics.

"Very kind of you. Again, my thanks for everything you've done for him."

"Now you're talking like his mother." She was riling him more and more.

"Yes, I'm also older. His mother was a colleague of mine in Prague. I feel some responsibility to her, too."

"Spare yourself the trouble," he says, interrupting. "Why is that kid so afraid of you? What game is it you're playing with him? This wasn't the first time he'd been to that cave. But when you're along, what do you know—he falls into the ravine!"

"So you think so, too, that I had something to do with it?"

"That you had something to do with it is quite clear, you were there, you know!"

"Go ahead and say it, say that I pushed him!"

"No, you didn't push him."

"But?"

He looks at her in silence.

The kid bothers you, makes a nuisance of himself, who knows if he didn't go a step too far in your apartment that night. You keep your curtains pulled even though there are no houses across the street. Leave him alone, you with your bittersweet, anxious face! You're only scared stiff that it will all come out!

"Leave him alone," he says.

Patera is back, unpacking, stuffing underwear into his cupboard. "Well, how'd it go, anything new?"

Orten realizes that the three days at home were important to Patera.

Patera discovers Podol's soup. "Ah, Standa cooked." He puts it on the stove, balancing the pot on the little heating coil. "He was planning to buy a stove, wasn't he? Otherwise we could give him a double hot plate for his birthday."

"We can buy it in any case. I don't think it would be quite the thing for a gift. Besides, he doesn't cook often."

"But when he does, it's good." Patera sucks at a marrowbone that has strands of parsley and leek dripping from it. Orten looks away.

"I thought they would at least have given you something to eat."

"That they did! There was a roast, a good three-pounder, they've been stuffing me. But my wife can't make soup, she rices everything, sieves the gravies and soups, as if I were an old geezer. I like solid food between my teeth, to gnaw the marrow from the bones, but she thinks that's unappetizing. They have adjusted completely to my not being there, I feel like a fifth wheel. I don't know if you can understand."

"I know the feeling. When I come home from my atelier and my family happens still to be up, my sons watch eagerly to see when the old man will finally stumble over the threshold and break his neck."

"How old are they now?" Patera asks, interested.

"Thirteen and eleven."

"Jan, aren't you exaggerating just a bit? You shouldn't take it that way. My daughters are glad to see me come home. But then glad to see me leave, too. Pavlína packed up the rest of the cake she baked for me, I ate it all on the bus. That's why I had to have some soup now, but I am feeling a little queasy."

"Wait, we just had some . . . oh right, the bottle is in Qvietone's jacket, and he doesn't even know. We had an exciting time last night. He had to be taken to the hospital."

"What's wrong with him?"

"Leg in a cast, five stitches in his head, pneumonia—just as I predicted—and they've put him on intravenous," Podol reports from the door.

"You were just there?"

"Yes, on my lunch hour. But he seems pretty cheerful, a little off his head though. Did he make you swear not to let anyone in the room, too?"

"Yes, he means the staff."

"He explicitly told me, doctors."

"I can understand that," Orten says.

"What?"

"Nothing."

"Let's hope he's on the mend soon. A nice kid," Patera says anxiously.

"I took him a couple of books, to get his mind off things," Orten says.

"Yes, he was glad you came by, was so proud to tell me about it."

"But it was you he was waiting for, he doesn't trust me as much. Did he eat anything? He wasn't hungry earlier."

"The soup was excellent," it occurs to Patera to say.

"I'm happy to hear that, Václav, you're the only one around here who doesn't turn his nose up at it."

"That's not true," Orten protests. "I'm just not hungry."

"Would you like some roast beef? They packed that up for me, too," Patera offers.

"Let's see." Podol cuts himself a piece. "Even Olbram would eat that."

"Where is he by the way? Wasn't he going to see about lime?"

"That's what he was going to do, but we sent him up onto the scaffold. He is the only one working at the moment. A rare sight; we should take a picture. Have you two seen our new chimney? What a shame the rest of them are still intact, otherwise we could plant a bed of blooming chimneys up on the roof. Maybe on the west side, one of those was cracked. If that crack gets any bigger, we'll have to regrout it next summer anyway."

"It's bound to get bigger," Orten remarks.

"I think I'll try a rose," Podol continues. "It has more petals than a tulip and rounder edges. And the whole thing is pink instead of yellow. Just picture it: this gigantic, strictly geometric box—with chimneys blooming on top!" He doesn't let Orten's skepticism bother him.

Max Linder's antics. Orten at the four-o'clock show: he is not in the mood to start another new row of ashlars; he has wasted too much of the day already with other matters. The copy is in amazingly good condition, has not been shown often. More people really do show up for slapstick; he tries to count them, at least forty, mostly teenagers and kids; he enjoys the commotion, the kids' screeches. Maltzahn likes to razz him about it.

What a great scene—where Linder fights himself, stages an assault with two pairs of shoes behind a curtain, trampling on each other, fists landing blows in the fabric, takes a punch, and comes tumbling into the room and finally chases the intruder away to the delight of his fiancée. A lighter hand than Chaplin's, who learned from him, no pretensions yet of creating art, technically perfect, but not stilted, fewer clichés. After the chase scenes of his early years, Chaplin gets slower and more sentimental; there's only a fine line between his beggars and millionaires. Can be a real rat, too: the way he jumps out of his limousine for a cigarette butt and snatches it out from under the poor bastard's nose, or turns informer and lets himself be waited on by his guards in a luxury cell—a man with no social conscience, with an incurable weakness for the private idyllic life, sentimental and cunning.

The snack bar in the corridor has opened, and Orten gets himself a cup of coffee and a *laskonka,* a meringue pastry with nut-cream filling, which has cost the same one koruna for twenty years now. He carefully nudges his way among children's heads, all about the level of his stomach and maneuvering toward their Nanuk and Polárka ice-cream treats.

The last scene—Max goes courting. The fortune-teller has warned him about a white dog. His sweetheart has a miniature white poodle. When she leaves the room, he removes a bouquet from a vase and stuffs the dog into it. The girl returns, calls for her dog, searches, and finally pulls her soggy pet from its hiding place. His courting has gone awry—the fortune-teller was right.

"You told me I should leave him alone." He looks up, the doctor from this morning is standing there with a glass of red wine.

"Good evening."

"Yes, good evening," she says impatiently; she is not about to be put in her place. "This morning you said . . ."

"Yes, I did," he interrupts her; it bothers him that she has caught him with a pastry.

She says nothing for a while. "You've got it all wrong. I would love to leave Qvietone alone. He sent word to me three times this afternoon that he wasn't doing well, had trouble breathing, fever, chills, bruises. When I arrived—I had to go through two wards—he pretended to be asleep, and watched to see if I didn't pour something in his tea or fidget with his I.V., and was disappointed when nothing happened. A morbid need to feel anxiety . . ." She shrugs. "But woke up as I was leaving, moaned softly as if trying to suppress dreadful pain. I know, he was suffering from hypothermia, the cold water and all, but he hasn't any fever now. . . . What was your impression?"

"Normal, he's in some pain, he's not putting it on. Podol thought so too."

She looks at him. "I think he keeps himself under better control for you; he respects you. You've lent him books, too, haven't you?"

"A few times."

"There's one that interests me, about hollow people, in a novel about mountain climbing."

He mulls it over. "Do you mean Daumal, the *Analog*? It's not about hollow people, but about an expedition to the highest mountain on earth, which it is believed must exist in analog to the deepest ocean trench on the opposite side of the globe, but is somehow sheltered from view. While they wait for the fog to lift so that they can move on through the surging clouds, one member of the expedition tells about hollow men and the Bitter Rose."

"Yes, that's it," she says with a little shudder.

"I'll bring it to you."

Gongs announce the next show, she buys her ticket and is about to go in.

"Wait." He takes her arm. "I'll join you."

Yojimbo. Toshiro Mifune's unmistakable walk: the springy gait from the hips, with almost straight knees, the decisiveness of his movements, made in no obvious direction. The grass flutters in the wind on the plateau, the willows imitate the vagabond indifference of a samurai with no lord; he decides his direction by tossing a stick into the air, chooses his name from the straws on the wind.

He skews his shoulders, shakes, and scratches himself as he walks. He keeps one hand on the hilt of his sword; when he pulls it out you forget he has fleas. The movement fills the whole screen.

For the first few minutes, the camera focuses on his back, the tight knot of hair on his head, the folds of the sleeves, the sandals; the stones on the path. Not a word is spoken.

At a fork in the road two figures emerge out of the swirling dust and sand, the wind drowns all other sounds, then the high, wailing voice of the old man becomes audible; he begs his son to stay—the only thing that awaits him in the city is chaos and destruction. And what have I got here, the son asks, pointing to his parents' hovel; the father watches him go.

The samurai asks for water.

Closeup: he drinks from a bamboo bowl at the well, the abandoned old couple pressed against the wall in the background. "It's because of people like you that others are never left in peace to make a living from their fields." The samurai wipes his mouth and walks on.

The city: a few plank huts raised on posts and crossbeams, the streets and square swept empty by fear and suspicion—the first living creature is a dog trotting off with a human hand in its mouth.

The sullen, evasive landlord at the inn explains: there is a standoff between armed gangs hired by the sake distillers and the owners of the gambling dens, who are both trying to control the town. The landlord offers the stranger free sake and rice, if only he will move on. "I like your town," the samurai says.

He walks out onto the square, followed by eyes peering through the planks, throws back the sliding doors of the gambling halls, checks out the faces of the guards waiting inside. One of them is a giant, with distorted acromegalic features and an idiotic delight in violence written on his face. With the self-assurance of a trained killer, the samurai provokes the hired thugs—an arm hacked off with a lightning quick blow and an impaled goon increase his value on the bodyguard market. He stays on with his distraught landlord and waits for offers. Both parties are ruined in the attempt to secure his services. He plays them against each other, organizes a bloodbath, and leaves. People can breathe easier here now, he tells his landlord and the coffinmaker, the last two just men in town. The peasant boy, who left his parents at the start of the film and hired himself out to one of the gangs, is spared: "Go home, there is plenty for you to do there."

A yellowed, flickering copy with parallel Polish and Czech subtitles separated by a bar. The annoyance quickly fades.

Every gesture is a ritual: the preparation for battle, the warming of the sake, even the wolfing down of the rice.

In a dingy room cut off by a bamboo screen, a plot is hatched against the men who rule the town. At any moment the shutters can be raised, the doors shoved aside—corruption and justice are cheek by jowl; the confining room merges with the repressive town.

There is an odor of another, older earth.

The sake bottles recall still lifes by Morandi.

"The simplicity of old cultures," Orten remarks.

Released from the initial tension of the film, they sense a moment of agreement, almost of happiness, the film was so beautiful.

Intermission is over, they finish their juice spiked with vodka.

Toshiro Mifune's shoulders are itching again; the wind blows hard across the grass. There is something feminine about the figure of the samurai—the hair knot set high above the nape, with single hairs sticking out, the folds in the sleeves rippling the herringbone pattern of his robe, the same stone beneath his sandals; then the film is stopped, it was the wrong reel.

Sanjuro is a loose sequel to *Yojimbo,* more ingratiating, with comic elements; the two films are connected by a sense of confinement, by an enemy who is always close at hand—and the figure of the vagabond samurai.

Much to the disappointment of the audience, the film is dubbed.

"What barbarism!" Marie is indignant.

"The first time I saw the film, it was still subtitled," Orten recalls. "But *Yojimbo* hadn't been released yet."

"I'd never seen it before either, it may be his finest work, that and *Throne of Blood.* I've only seen double subtitles before at the Ponrepo, when they show old archive films. *Queen Christina* had Serbian and Hungarian subtitles, the volume on the German soundtrack was turned down low, and the interpreter sat in a booth translating from the English text in front of her, you could hear her papers rustling. At times she would lose the thread and the audience would shout the translation from the German to her."

"I've seen that version myself." Orten laughs. "You get hit with 'I love you' five more times after the couple on the screen have stopped talking. Or with a 'yes.' It does have one advantage, it increases your knowledge of Hungarian: *igen!*"

"The most impressive thing about Toshiro Mifune is his *hai!*" Marie says. "He always talks as if he is furious, in that throaty, barking voice, and then it turns out that he's only making fun of someone or telling a joke. I wouldn't want to take it in any faster, the delay is part of the strangeness you feel, and then it resolves. The only thing that really bothers me is dubbing. Do you go see films at the Ponrepo often?"

"If I have time, almost every day. It's only two blocks from my atelier."

They are standing outside a newly opened wine cellar, the Oriole, across from the old high school, where *The Philosophical Story* by Alois Jirásek is on the boards, and today there's *Secondary Education in Friedland;* the wine cellar is open.

The chairs smell of new fake leather; it is clean and almost empty. Marie takes a look around. "How long have they been open?"

"A couple of days, I haven't been here yet either. Svodoba told me about it, he says they have Moravian wines."

She realizes that if she had known about it she could have spared herself the caverns. That was yesterday.

"What do you want to drink?"

The waiter is all helpfulness. In Prague he would be changing money on the black market at some Interhotel, and keeping the police posted. Lacking any such opportunities here, he is polite even for Czech cash.

They sit at the open window and gaze into the garden, where the tables have already been cleared. Closing time is eleven; they have an hour yet.

From up in the trees come rustlings and twitterings; as darkness falls the bats begin to flutter in search of orts. *Plecotus austriacus*—no, small horseshoe bats.

She pictures a scene in *Sanjuro* again—the chamberlain's garden, where a fleet of white camellias drifts downstream, signaling the attack. Qvietone resembles the young, zealous samurai. The film would have been better without the comic relief.

The Moravian wines are dry and pure, not the doctored stuff they market as Prague Vintage or Golden Blossom; Orten is not sure if she can tell the difference, not at the rate she is knocking it back.

"They call this place the Oriole?" She leans back, looks around. "I haven't seen an oriole in a long time." She refills her glass. "They don't keep their promises, we've been cheated, even if the wine is alright. I'm for circumventing the lack of orioles and renaming the place, in the Japanese fashion maybe: Pavilion for Better Listening to the Song of the Tanager. That doesn't promise much—if a tanager or an oriole was actually in the vicinity, you would hear it better here than on Lenin Square. And if they'd use that sort of precious nomenclature, maybe we'd have linen instead of paper napkins."

"Rectification of terms—Master Kung. That's more in the Chinese line," Orten says. "Among the Japanese, nomenclature is oriented more on the arrangement than on the purpose of the place. All their tea-houses, for instance. The tea-ceremonial rooms in Kyoto are named after a stone or a mound of moss at the door, or after the view. Koho-an Temple has a garden inspired by a famous series of Chinese land-scapes, the "Eight Views of Hsiang River." And the look of the interior is precisely proportioned; the shutters are set so low that your view is of just a portion of the garden, as if you were sitting in a boat. I hung a kind of *shoji,* one of their blinds, at my window, and now the water tower behind the wall is cut off and all I can see is the courtyard with my plaster sculptures set against it, all in white."

"In your atelier? What did you use to make it?"

"Tissue paper, framed with wooden slats, very thin."

"Doesn't it tear?"

"The paper is glued on in layers, and has cross-slats, too. A pretty violent wind would have to be blowing for it to rip. The window can't be opened anyway; it's a shop window, very large, with a transom. I air the room through the door, so there's seldom a draft."

"Isn't it a pity to cut off the view?"

"The Japanese know that you concentrate better that way. Although they do something more useful than I: they meditate. Sometimes they even let their eyes roam, gathering up the objects. Ryoan-ji Garden, for example, has fifteen rocks of varying size, to be read from left to right, in twos or threes, plus a few solitary ones, all carefully arranged on a field of raked white gravel. It's a 'dry landscape', as they call it. Only a little moss as a bed for the stones or to form islands in the gravel. The garden is closed off from the outside by a half-roofed wall. I sat there for a long time. Each of those fifteen brutes has been lying in just the right spot for five hundred years. Stones in general. There's a 'stone waterfall' there, too, made from weathered blocks of quartz with a slate trickle falling down the middle of the riverbed, silver-blue scales."

"No plants?"

"Most gardens in Kyoto are combinations of stones and plants—trees, hedges, bushes; there's a lot of water, too—fountains, brooks, ponds with islands and miniature temples, narrow footbridges or stepping stones connect them with the shore, so only one person can go out at a time. There is also what is called the 'borrowed view,' when the panorama is determined by the landscape outside the garden, like the famous one in Entsu-ji Garden. Behind the hedge rises Mount Hiei, in the foreground are trees and boulders. You have the impression it belongs to the arrangement of the landscape, as if Mount Hiei were part of the garden. I don't think a single piece of gravel in the whole grounds is there by accident. The landscape is subordinated to the garden, artifice has greater value than chaotic nature. The important thing is touch—they have to take hold of the stones, move them around until they lie in perfect harmony, and are never budged again, for centuries."

"Except by earthquakes," Marie adds. "Then they have to work a long time getting all that gravel back in the same order. And those crippled bonsai trees? Or the Japanese cock with the ten-foot-long tail? All wretched creatures. I wouldn't be surprised if the monks would rescue their decorative stones before they would people buried in the rubble!" She doesn't know why she is suddenly so upset. Oh, right: "buried in the rubble."

He laughs. "I think earthquakes are the reason for the attention to detail, the inventory of even the smallest plants and stones, and human life as part of it."

"You talk about stones a lot."

"I like stones. I was a stonemason before I started working as a sculptor. I have plenty of role models in the vicinity—Gutfreund, Wagner, Stefan."

"You said before that you work in plaster."

"Stone costs money, there's a two hundred percent luxury tax on it. And as for casting in bronze, even a very small piece, I can afford that only every five years. But, then, there's not all that much I want to preserve. Plaster has the advantage of not lasting so long."

Another monomaniac, she thinks. Whereas Qvietone tries to flaunt his knowledge, this guy stresses his incompetence—even though he knows a lot. She is jealous: of the stones, and of his apparent obsession with his work. She has never felt so inadequate about her profession before; she is above average in diagnosis, enjoys weighing the possibilities, speculating, but not the treatment—she doesn't like to touch people. And she doesn't want to exchange professional know-how right now.

"You were in Japan? When?"

"For the world exposition in Osaka, in sixty-nine, and then again the next year. We were called home from one day to the next, because of the troubled situation here. That was hard, because we had started work—I had to leave the Japanese to complete my mural on their own, dropped everything and booked a flight. You can't imagine what it's like dealing with Soviet travel agencies. The first time we flew to Japan we missed our connection in Moscow. We landed at Sheremetyevo, and then had to drive clear across town to Domodedovo, the airport for Siberian flights. First the flight couldn't take off because the pilot was out finding melons for his family, then they couldn't find the co-pilot, who had got drunk in the meantime and was sleeping it off in the canteen. From Chabarovsk it was another two days by train to Nachodka. We spent a night on a siding because we weren't supposed to see a military train heading out for Vladivostok. The delay meant that we missed our ship in Nachodka and had to wait four days for the next one. Nachodka is not a place for a four-day stopover—I can understand why people drink. When we finally docked in Yokohama, what a drastic difference. From gray barracks plastered with uplifting slogans and papier-mâché Lenins, to the gaudy colors of Japan, hundreds of banners and streamers on the dock, people waving and laughing till you couldn't hear yourself think. The delay meant I missed all my connections, of course; my flight from Tokyo to Osaka had departed two days before. After four days in Nachodka, I looked at the crowd of laughing Japanese and felt like an idiot. People were packed along the railing beside me, shouting and waving—I was the only one who wasn't. And something was bothering me as I stood there staring morosely at the throngs; the first people were already going ashore, hugging and greeting one another, while I just stared—until I realized that the whole time a huge sign was hovering above their heads: Orten."

"They had sent someone to meet you?"

"Yes, the Japanese engineer from the project knew the score. He had met the Czechs who preceded me, too. They knew all about Russian ships."

"And how did things go from then on?"

"From then on it was all Japanese efficiency. On to Tokyo by high-speed train, a hundred miles an hour even on that short stretch, we could have used that on the Trans-Siberian. From Tokyo to Osaka and a brand-new apartment they had arranged for us. Across the hall lived a physician, who met her husband at the door every evening, helped him out of his clothes right there on the threshold, and led him off to the shower to scrub him down. She greeted us with a bouquet of flowers and invited us in for tea."

"Who was there with you?"

"Kolář was already in the apartment—his collage apples were a great hit. Then it was off to the construction site the next day; to get onto the exposition grounds you had to have a pass, all ranked according to color. I had about twenty Japanese working for me, half of whom had nothing to do. They were all ranked, too. The interesting thing was that the 'upper echelon' was always the first to set to work. My engineer was the hardest working—it was a great honor for them to work on a world exposition, and for an artist no less. One day a fellow without overalls showed up, just stood around solemn and smiling, the others smiling back, spent the whole day there without pushing himself forward in any way. The engineer whispered momentously to me that this was his first day of vacation."

"And he spent it all at the construction site?"

"No, the next day he came in his overalls."

"So he didn't take a vacation."

"Well, yes, in some sense. It wasn't a matter of taking a vacation, but of knowing that he could take one if he wanted. The mural was poured concrete. First we built the frame, which went well enough. Although they were constantly competing with one another to work, there were simply too many of them. Once the form was finally done, we were supposed to pour the concrete. That would normally be no problem, goes fast with a cement mixer. But for some reason—my guess is the Czechs were trying to save money again—no one had ordered a mixer, so it had to be poured by hand. You've got enough men, our pavilion's commissar said. So we started. They wore white gloves and some of them poured from little buckets, while others jabbed and stirred with thin bamboo poles—where we would use a tamper. I tried to explain to them that they couldn't stop, that the wall had to be applied in one smooth pouring, but the concrete was hardening so fast that they could hardly move their bamboo rods, and when those started breaking off we had to quit in the middle of the job. And the concrete set. Then came the telegram saying that a few of us had to return home at once. I wanted to finish the wall, but since at the time we were all on the steering committee of our union, we had to come at once. We had to get in touch with the commissar of the Soviet pavilion; it would have taken two weeks with the travel agency. He had invited us to visit him several times, but we had never gone, now we needed him. He wasn't there, we left a message saying we would try again later. When we got back he was already waiting for us at our construction site. A white-haired old man, rather reserved. The first thing he did was apologize for '68. Then he made some calls. We had our papers the next day, and the co-pilot in Chabarovsk wasn't even drunk."

"Why did you go back a second time?"

"Because they had botched the job—the Japanese and their pecking order! Apparently they squabbled so long on the job that the first pour dried out completely before they applied the second, which caused the mural to buckle and start flaking off.

"Then came the letter, written by a Japanese who had studied music in Prague for three years. The salutation was: Most Honored Artist Sculptor of the Academy Mr. Orten! Then followed four pages of small-talk about weather and health and the beauties of Czech music, with excerpts from Janáček's sinfonietta. The Czech was a little clumsy, but the music looked fantastic—tiny black dots with pennants, all on brown paper with a blue floral print, red exclamation marks in the margins. It reminded me of the manuscripts in the calligraphy collection in Kyoto, some of them are a thousand years old. He later conducted the premieres of both the sinfonietta and *Taras Bulba* in Osaka. He wrote that he hoped to be able to come back soon and that we might see one another in Osaka sometime. And concluded by saying that such an opportunity had now presented itself, since the mural had to be redone, they had taken it down, destroying the form in the process, and were awaiting the arrival of the most honored artist in two weeks, which would give them just enough time to complete it before the exposition opened."

"And they let you go?"

"Of course, that sixty-yard mural had to adorn the front of the pavilion. Besides which, the Japanese were footing the bill."

"By way of Chabarovsk and Nachodka again?"

"Yes. This time we waited only two days; I'm a good friend of the canteen manager now. We drank to our eternal friendship, *nerushimaya druzhba,* just like always."

" 'Friends with the Soviets for All Eternity—But Not One Day More.' Did you say anything to him about the occupation?"

"He was overjoyed that they had been able to rescue us in time, had tears in his eyes. I couldn't explain anything to him. They are convinced they did the right thing. Besides, he claimed they wanted peace for themselves and the whole world. I believed him. He was a veteran of the Great Patriotic War and a heavy drinker. Our guide, a girl from the local university, asked us if we had ever seen a more beautiful city."

"Than Nachodka? What did you tell her?"

"Yes, Moscow—their Lenins were in stone there—and Ordzhonikidze."

Marie grins, but then turns thoughtful. "Wouldn't you rather have done a sculpture than a mural in Osaka?"

Orten looks at her. "Kolář was in Auschwitz after the war. There are no words for it, he said when he came back, and since then he has been trying to find a metaphor. He slashes canvases and pastes them back together again, crushes faces and reglues them—the logic of his collages are testimony to the same sense of order that governed each day in a concentration camp; there was a time for everything, wake-up call and workday schedules, only the killing occurred at random, at any time of day." Orten drinks. "It's different with me. My distortions are the result of a lack of talent, not of intent. Take sculpture. The human form at rest is the first, the highest level of the art. To capture something in motion is to constrain it, distort it. It is only believable if you are master of the first level. So far I have only managed the second—figures turning aside, sitting, lying. Not statues, objects." He takes another drink. "Michelangelo chiseled a 'Madonna of the Stairs' at age fourteen. I can never catch up with him." He grins. "Sometimes I see him in my dreams, hammering away at the Horsehead Nebula in Orion."

Marie orders another glass. The waiter, who is discreetly breaking down setups in one corner, brings the wine without objection, even places a second bowl of salted almonds next to the empty one. She immediately starts poking them into her mouth. Orten smokes. She ought to feel sure of herself next to him, but is still tense, as if everything he has said has a second meaning that applies to her. "What did you like most about Japan?" She doesn't want to leave yet.

"I liked a lot of things. The interiors. The way they use wood. They don't have that much wood. But most? The children maybe. Young Japanese are so beautiful that at first I just stood there on the street looking at them. They would turn around, too. Adults are used to Europeans by now—mostly Americans—or act as if they are, but they don't like them. But the children are still curious. I was sitting with a lot of schoolchildren on a train, midgets with big schoolbags, and it was one of those superfast trains, so they had to be very careful. I looked for someone in charge, but there wasn't anyone. Seven- or eight-year-old kids alone on a train, but very quiet and self-reliant. Nothing can surprise these kids, I thought. Then they discovered me. They stopped in their tracks and stared at me. A little boy was apparently totally overwhelmed by my big nose and round eyes. I think they must have thought I was very ugly. I winked at him, he got very excited. But I couldn't leave it at that, so I tickled his knee. He froze, looked to see how I had intended it, I smiled, he stayed very serious, he almost shuddered. He held his knee out as if to say I should do it again. I didn't risk it, however. I don't know how they are treated at home, I assume better than in Europe. I never saw an adult strike a child. But I don't know how they show affection to them either. The little boy almost missed his stop, the others were heading for the door, one came back and pulled him along, then they all ran off and didn't turn back again."

"You like children?"

"Not really, I'm more afraid of them, I think."

"Have you any of your own?"

"Yes, two sons, thirteen and eleven." It occurs to him that he's said this once already today.

"Are you afraid of them, too?"

"Certainly more than they are of me." Orten laughs.

Marie pours herself another glass. "Did you go to the movies in Japan?"

"Often, but they don't show Kurosawa. Samurai films, usually very brutal. In one, the samurai commits hara-kiri with a dull wooden sword, the guts burble out of the slit, it takes a long time before he dies. They make him pay for not having meant it in earnest, until finally someone chops off his head."

"Hara-kiri—I saw that one."

"It's possible, but there are lots of movies on the subject, and always about how the rules cannot be broken. Moral defeat is worse than death. I remember a film where two men are fighting at the end. I thought it was a draw, but then one fellow tears out his own eye and throws it at the other one's feet, and so the second one slits open his own belly."

"And who won?"

"The one with the eye, of course, that fixed the other guy."

"Were there any other kinds of movies?"

"Oh sure, pornography—the hero is preferably a blind masseur."

Marie laughs. "As a girl I presented flowers to the Chinese delegation at a film festival in Karlsbad. The film was called *Red Flag on Green Mountain,* and the female lead won a prize. But maybe that was for the other film, *The Girl with White Hair.* Her name was Si-Ku-Minh. There was also a Mongolian film that people expected to win, *They Called Him Suche Bator,* and a Korean one, too, *Back to the Front.* Ten years old, and I was roaming the fields of East Asian cinematography. The Chinese were so excited the whole delegation was speaking Czech inside of two weeks and began making plans to open a studio in Karlsbad as the first step into the European market. They didn't want to bring more than a few hundred people, they said, they knew that Czechoslovakia was a small country. That was before the chopstick jokes started."

"I remember," Orten says. "A lot of them were studying in Prague in those days, but no more than a million of them were supposed to come, for the same reason." He laughs. "Then suddenly they vanished. But the crowds on the streets of Tokyo are worse. There's always a mob, even in the karate films that are mass-produced in Hong Kong and play on every street corner."

"Do they show European films, too?"

"Very few, and then mostly American. Wait, I did see a Godard, with Eddie Constantine and Anna Karina. With dreamlike sequences of Paris—you can't recognize anything—just suburbs, no buildings that would identify the city, overexposed, sort of science fiction. I didn't understand a lot of it, it was dubbed in Japanese. It's about a chase, someone gets executed—a man in a pond, beautiful women with knives jump in after him and stab at him. I don't even know what the title was."

"Alphaville."

"That's what you get if you travel!" Orten laughs. "Next time I'll take you along and let you explain it all to me."

"But at least you heard Eddie Constantine speaking Japanese."

"I prefer Toshiro Mifune."

This reminds them both what an awful thing dubbing is and that it means the end of cinema, and they decide to send a petition to Czechoslovakian Central Film Distribution and the Film Library of the Prague Institute—Orten as the designer of several film posters, Marie as a long-time member of the Ponrepo Film Club. They agree to meet again soon to carry out their project.

At the door of her singles' dorm, Marie turns around: "What's your name?"

Orten pulls up short, this could be some departing reprimand; he feels as if he has been babbling away, boasting about his trips; she has hardly said a word.

"Orten."

"I know that. I want to know your first name."

SIX

Theater of Friedland/Litomyšl Castle. Period middle-class interior, one of the sixteen remaining Late Baroque sets painted by the renowned stage designer Josef Platzer—of the Prague Platzers, a family of sculptors—who also created the set for the première of *Don Giovanni* at the Stände Theater. He likewise designed both proscenium curtains, although the theater's other fittings were done by local artists: the mechanisms for set changes by Václav Bonaventura, a master cabinetmaker; the décor of the auditorium by the woodcarver Bartoš and the painter Dominik Dvořák, who used the castle's courtyard frescoes as a model. On the table, a bowl of steaming cabbage.

"Golden hands, madam!" MALTZAHN, as historian and dramatist ALOIS JIRÁSEK, wearing a pince-nez, calls to the open pantry door.

In the left corner, a piano; PATERA, as BEDŘICH SMETANA, plays the opening passage from *Bohemia's Meadows and Forests*.

At the open window, ORTEN, as Piarist father and scholar JAN EVANGELISTA PURKYNĚ, bent over a microscope, mutters to himself and takes notes.

"My good father, dinner is served!" PODOL enters, as the advocate of national renewal, MAGDALENA DOBROMILA RETTIGOVÁ, bearing a fragrant roast before her, followed by four maids with other bowls of condiments, vegetables, sauces, desserts—looking rather like Patera's daughters (just as one cannot deny a certain resemblance between M. D. Rettigová and Mrs. Paterová).

"Golden hands, madam, as it was my pleasure to note once already," MALTZAHN / JIRÁSEK says, resuming his bachelor's effusion in anticipation of the joys of an opulent meal.

The dumplings are set by the window to cool (dangerously close to the physiologist's histological sections).

"Father, dinner is served, if you please!" M. D. RETTIGOVÁ does not wish to see her culinary skills overshadowed by science—Podol has had enough of Orten's forever drawing out the action, and is hungry besides.

JIRÁSEK: "I have finished *The Philosophical Story,* and my tale titled *Knight's Inn* as well. Which now leaves only you, my dear Magdalena, and then the monument to our town is complete."

RETTIGOVÁ: "My good Alois, I must do the cooking and supervise my Czech maidens in housekeeping and the proper use of their mother tongue, a poor subject for idle chatter."

"Dearest lady, but of course it would all be to your honor and done with greatest respect. People must understand the vital importance for the Czech palate of a cookbook written in Czech, and not only for Czech women and maidens—Czech men are the true beneficiaries of your patriotic spirit. I had in mind a comedy, a popular entertainment with oratory, song, and a sampling of your culinary art as the high point. There is nothing lovelier than home-style capon; every husband feels so totally in his element when that proud, plumed fowl lies crisply prepared before him, with a crust that makes his heart beat higher, a dressing of apples and almonds, the fragrant gravy steaming in its boat—why, my good Magdalena, I would attend classes under your tutelage myself, indeed I would."

"If not your classes, then surely your table," B. SMETANA interjects to tease him and plays a scherzo from *Two Widows.* "As an apéritif for your Czech capons!"

RETTIGOVÁ: "But, good father, you are not fasting, we hope."

PURKYNĚ: "Most assuredly not, madam. The cuisine of the Piarists, though nourishing and pleasing to God—particularly since we franchised the rights to distill our herbal extract [He pulls a clay bottle from his sleeve.]—cannot make me forget how earthly pleasures look, or how they taste. And so, dear madam, I am always an enthusiastic guest at your table."

"Fridays as well, good father?" SMETANA, the wag, again.

PURKYNĚ: "Not on Fridays, it's true, that is unless the good lady is kind enough to prepare a carp, or mock pike made from the breast of goose—crayfish have always met with my approval."

RETTIGOVÁ: "Enough of fuss, good gentlemen mine, the summer is so very fine." She skips off, disappearing backstage and returning as the painter/restorer PODOLSKÝ. "How was I?"

MALTZAHN: "That depends on what you cooked. I'll admit it, I'm hungry. Jan, isn't your Purkyně too gluttonous? I thought he was a natural scientist, not a friar. If he's always hanging around the kitchen nibbling on crayfish, how's he going to make great discoveries?"

"You'll get those, too." ORTEN casts a sidelong glance at the books beside his microscope. "Purkyně wasn't a monk, of course, but I didn't want to demoralize you all from the start. You're just afraid you won't get your share because Standa is cooking. By the way, your Jirásek is not exactly a dramatic breakthrough. The man was almost blind from all that writing!"

"And Smetana was deaf." MALTZAHN turns toward the piano.

"Then you play!" PATERA, miffed. "I'm the only person here who can read music."

PODOL/RETTIGOVÁ: "Václav is okay as Smetana, and you can keep polishing your Jirásek, Olbram. But now, gentlemen, dinner is served!"

The maidens pull back the chairs and invite the restorers to be seated. Patera/Smetana lets a fart escape and covers it up with a chord from *Dalibor,* but the fortissimo cannot deceive the noses of the physiologist and the cook. He rises with dignity and is led to the table by the maidens in their gala costumes.

Jirásek/Maltzahn is already seated.

Appetizers: Dumplings filled with cheese and chopped spinach; Bulgarian crayfish, grade B, with domestic mayonnaise, Majolka brand; old-fashioned giblets; Metternich salad, renamed Tyrš salad, after the gymnast and founder of the Sokol Society, and strewn with sautéed mushrooms from Oetz instead of truffles; deviled eggs, now called Prague eggs, but known as Russian eggs prior to 1968.

RETTIGOVÁ: "Rinse and brush thirty to forty freshly caught crayfish, taking care to scrub the tails, place them in boiling salt water, add caraway and parsley, and boil for thirty minutes. Remove them from the water, dry them, and serve them on napkins folded attractively across the platter. Garnish with finely shredded head lettuce and a spicy dressing. Carefully remove the meat from the tails and claws, dipping both it and the empty shells in melted herb butter."

"And enjoy the taste," MALTZAHN says, poking at the sticky crayfish.

PURKYNĚ: "Why should such care be given to the tails, dear lady? When, as is well known, the principal excretions of crustaceans, that is the liquids, are passed through glands on the antennae attached to the head, which is solidly joined to the thorax to form the *carapax dorsale*. The gland opening is clearly visible in the first joint of the second antenna. You know, too, that crayfish are fierce recluses and ardent retrogrades, and as a defense against their many enemies can suddenly flex the outstretched tail forward, clapping it against the abdomen. And their pincers are even more effective! By scrubbing the tail you could damage the valuable flesh of the muscles, not to mention your own fingers. The coconut crab can even cut through branches thick as a walking stick. But above all, this: these creatures need robust neurochords for the tail reflex; indeed the nervous system as a whole is highly developed. It has evolved from the ladderlike system of the worm, but the ganglia are much more complicated, in both the upper and lower gullets. Can you not imagine, dear lady, that these animals perceive pain? To throw live crayfish into boiling water, given the highly innervated sensory organs . . ."

"You innervate me."—PODOL.

PURKYNĚ: "And what do you say, madam?"

RETTIGOVÁ: "Enough of this, good doctor. Is it not true that for its own purposes science treats animals in much the same fashion? Dissects and mutilates them, snips off bits to place under microscopes and observes the pieces as they lie there twitching? How often have I seen such practices myself from closest proximity!" Pointedly: "And you are preaching sympathy with all God's creatures to us, good father, while carrying out massacres there beneath your lens?"

"Dear friend, calm yourself please!" the Piarist brother says with a smile. "There is a difference between your boiling thirty crayfish alive and my dissecting one of them. Besides which, I anesthetize them beforehand. Here, you see this cannula, or syringe? I use it to inject a decoction into the circulatory system, a synthesized extract that lames the nerves and causes the heart to cease beating, similar to the effect of curare. The crayfish falls into a coma and forgets to molt. Only then ought it be boiled, and/or dissected."

"Well, *bon appétit* in that case," the half-deaf SMETANA says innocently.

"Yes indeed, sir, you are quite right. Who knows what effect such a potion would have if one digested it!" RETTIGOVÁ says triumphantly.

"None at all in the stomach! Only in the circulatory system. I would be quite happy to drink down a glass of curare before your eyes, for example," PURKYNĚ says, laughing.

SMETANA: "Laced with a shot of your home brew, haha!"

RETTIGOVÁ: "Nothing personal, good father. You have your science, I have my Czech cookbook. Curare may do for your purposes; I use other spices in my recipes. And I am struck further, dear doctor, by the fact that you hardly use your mother tongue when speaking of your profession! Might there not be some redress there, with all those thoraxes, neurochords, decoctions, and cannulas?"

"For all I care you can call it an extract—infusion, maceration, and hypodermoclysis." PURKYNĚ, bored.

"And neurochords? I would like to have a Czech term for those! 'Feeling threads,' how does that sound?"

"Like shit."

"Jan, that's enough now!" PODOL rips the authentic bonnet of M. D. Rettigová from his head.

"Madam, as you can see, I also speak the vulgar tongue." PURKYNĚ/ORTEN dodges out the door.

Podol takes off after him, but stumbles over his skirts at the threshold. The clatter of toppling pots in the pantry. Jirásek and Smetana hurry to help.

JIRÁSEK: "Dearest lady, we all value your efforts to revive the Czech language after three hundred years of *Darkness*—that particular novel took a great deal out of me."

PODOL: "That's enough, Olbram, don't hog the spotlight unnecessarily. I cooked." He sulkily adjusts his bodice and smooths the pleats of his apron.

SMETANA/PATERA, to himself: " 'Feeling threads'—now that carries a real punch. . . ."

RETTIGOVÁ explodes: "Maestro, you had best not have commented, for it makes me sick at heart, as it does the entire nation, that you have never truly mastered the Czech language! Your diary is written in German, Wenzig wrote the libretto for your *Dalibor* in German. And even—to your greatest shame—even the original version of *Libuše*! Both had to be translated by Špindler. You should really show greater reserve in your judgments concerning language!"

Purkyně comes back and offers his aroused hostess a pull of his Piarist extract; Podol guzzles a third of the bottle.

"Be seated, everyone. The food is getting cold."

"Very kind of you, madam." ORTEN moves cautiously past him to his chair.

Patera eats with trepidation.

"Might I ask . . ." MALTZAHN/JIRÁSEK stares at the second course before him.

RETTIGOVÁ has collected herself. "One of my recipes for innards. Two pounds of calf lights are boiled in vinegar water, with bay leaf and thyme, then minced, mixed with two diced onions and chopped parsley, browned in hot fat, and then steamed for a few minutes. The lights—we Czechs also call them lungs—are then mixed with egg groats and seasoned."

JIRÁSEK: "Egg groats?"

RETTIGOVÁ: "*Tarhonya,* a Hungarian specialty."

JIRÁSEK: "Hash from Hungary? [Aside]: And she calls herself a patriot. [To Rettigová]: Even though the Magyars are constantly agitating against the Czechs in the parliament in Vienna?"

RETTIGOVÁ: "There'll be no more politics at the table, my dear Alois. You may have your lights in the Czech fashion as well; after being boiled, they are cut in fine, noodlelike slices, roasted in a lovely flour-butter glaze, to which some of the broth is then added to make a thick gravy, and finished off by stirring in lots of cream. Served with the roll dumplings there in the bowl."

"Many thanks, madam. I believe I shall pass."

"Then hand them to me." PATERA/SMETANA avails himself of Maltzahn's serving. "I never get this sort of thing at home."

RETTIGOVÁ, offended: "At least you do not disappoint me, maestro."

Orten/Purkyně pokes at the gray-white stuff on his plate.

RETTIGOVÁ: "You must recognize brains, my good professor. Boiled in vinegar water, sliced in half, garnished with parsley. Browned butter poured over, if you like. Just be sure the membrane is totally removed. A delicacy."

PURKYNĚ: "Fortunately all the membrane has not been removed." He pulls his microscope over. "One can still trace the efferent fibers. Here there's a break, then it continues. Please note, madam, how the structure of the cortex of the cerebellum differs considerably from that of the cerebrum. The surface of the former is regular and displays no histological segmentation."

Rettigová swallows.

PURKYNĚ: "And that's not all. Where do these fibers lead? Do you see those cells, with their giant dendritic ramifications, their countless axon collaterals and vast numbers of cross-connections? Those are my cells, the Purkyně cells, which I spent years researching, all boiled to mush! Do you not feel the shame of it!"

RETTIGOVÁ: "My good doctor, if it reminds you all too much of your research, you should try my brain pudding. The brain is first minced, then mixed with beaten egg white and boiled for half an hour. When it is tipped out of the pudding form, there's not a trace of your cells left!"

PURKYNĚ: "It reminds one of the severing of the corpus callosum in the cerebrum; when both halves are split in two, the patient quiets down. Granted, he continues to shit away down below, but doesn't care anymore. And when you snip at pieces of an animal's brain . . ."

Jirásek/Maltzahn puts a hand to his mouth and vanishes through the door.

PATERNA/SMETANA: "Good thing I'm deaf, and blind now, too."

RETTIGOVÁ as PODOL: "Jan, I have to hand it to you. Not only are you a chronic spoiler of everyone's mood, but now of their appetites, too. I spend the whole day over a stove, and now this! Where did you get all this learned garbage? From that high-strung kid who's not been all that right in the head since he fell?"

Orten prevents Podol from making a swipe at the books on the windowsill next to the microscope. "No."

"From who then? Ah, I know. Your lady doctor helped you out!"

ORTEN: "What was I supposed to do? I studied up. You spent hours yesterday rummaging around in moldy cookbooks. You can find those in the castle library. But you've got to go outside for physiology. In any case, madam, the Purkyně cells . . ."

"That's disgusting. I'm not going to play your game!" JIRÁSEK as MALTZAHN, back from the john, throws down his napkin. "Makes me sick at my stomach!"

SMETANA: "Then give it to me." Patera pulls the bowl over. "Here I am enjoying a real meal for once, and I'm constantly being interrupted."

PURKYNĚ/ORTEN: "That's right, Olbram, you're constantly try-ing to interrupt so that no one will notice how miscast you are as Jirásek. What have you ever read of his?"

MALTZAHN: "What's all this now? It was required reading in the fifth grade. Have you ever read any more than that?" And now that he thinks about it—"Who is the source of disruption here anyway?"

ORTEN/PURKYNĚ: "I still have the eye to go—Sanson's reflected images—and the heart. The auricle displays large vessels rich in fluid, which to my knowledge have never been described. I've turned my attention to those. Purkyně cells, Purkyně fibers . . ."

"The great physiologist should stay home if he wants to do research, and not spoil other people's dinners," MALTZAHN/JIRÁSEK mutters.

PURKYNĚ: "Histology will not be halted by envious men busily gorging themselves. If I don't discover my cells today, then Sperry will discover them tomorrow, and Eccles the day after, who compares the negative activity of the cerebellum to the work of a sculptor."

MALTZAHN: "Ah! That's why he's so obsessed with this."

"Negative activity of a sculptor, now there's something you know about."—PODOL.

PURKYNĚ/ORTEN, undaunted: ". . . whose chisel removes por-tions from a block of stone and thereby creates a form. My cells, you see, are inhibitory!"

Awkward silence.

. . .

RETTIGOVÁ: "My good Evangelista, I will have no equivocal expressions used here; there are innocent Czech maidens present."

PURKYNĚ, in a rage: "Who knows how your innocent Czech progeny spend their evenings, always gallivanting about, my good Rettigová. I often see them loitering on the corner waiting for high school boys. Jirásek here can confirm that; he was a teacher himself for quite some time. Lending out Czech books—don't give me that! I only hope that it brings the younger generation in contact with the natural sciences, instead of forever concocting botched verses for poetry albums!"

JIRÁSEK: "I take it what you have in mind are 'gynecological autodidacts,' my good colleague. There were swarms of young men doing that sort of research in my youth. Whereas good poets were indeed a rarity."

PURKYNĚ: "Are you saying that you're making up the deficit with your *Dog Heads, Here with Us, Against all the World, Between the Currents, F. L. Věk?*"

RETTIGOVÁ: "Gentlemen, I choose not to have heard or, above all, to have understood what has just been uttered here. The good doctor's small-mindedness in regard to our literature leaves me despondent. I ask myself what the world should think of a culture that has so little regard for itself. But I fear he will be proven correct. Who among us will still be a household name in the world of a hundred years hence?—Not I . . ."

"But your recipes!" JIRÁSEK flatteringly interjects.

". . . nor you, professor,' RETTIGOVÁ says, turning to the historian, who is still managing a smile. "As bitter as it may sound, Czech history, particularly novelized history, does not interest even the Czechs, as has just now been made evident! [With a sidelong glance at Purkyně.] You, of course, maestro [With a gracious nod to blind and deaf Smetana/Patera, humming away to himself] do not need to be translated! And as regards Purkyně, who has made himself so conspicuously unpleasant today, his name, too, will presumably abide, as a result of his unappetizing snip-snip-snips."

ORTEN: "In mutilated form, however, as Purkinje."

MALTZAHN/JIRÁSEK: "Better than nothing."

"But what grieves me most, my good doctor," RETTIGOVÁ resumes, "is your assessment of our younger generation. I have no illusions of immortality, yet I do flatter myself that I have found an open ear among today's youth for my campaign of enlightenment. Shall all that work have been in vain? My cookbook, my treatise *Advice to Young Housewives on Achieving Contentment for Their Spouses and Themselves,* 1840, my verses and dramatic pieces on patriotic themes, my *Discourse on Veal,* my idylls of everyday Czech life, published at my own expense by Augusta? I do not wish to live to see that day!" She pushes one tear from her eye.

SMETANA: "But dearest friend, do not be disheartened. Even if we Czechs should have only your lights and dumplings!—*Proč bychom se netěšili!* Why should we not rejoice if God grants us good health!"

They form a semicircle and sing the opening chorus from *The Bartered Bride, con vivacità.*

Pantry/Kitchen

M. C. Rettigová's four students are cleaning up the stove and countertops.

HANNA

KARLA, her fellow student, majoring in Bohemian studies and Romance languages, also a castle guide for the summer.

MARCELA, wife of the castle director, the same age as the first two and their sometime friend.

PEPI, sixteen, Jirse's granddaughter.

PEPI listens at the crack in the door: "Now they're singing."

HANNA: "Then we can serve the coffee."

KARLA: "If I know them, they'll want their beer first. Is there any?"

PEPI: "There's some in the jug, the tavern across the way just opened up. It would have taken longer to get some from town."

Hanna and Marcela pick up the jug and glasses and take them into the parlor.

"Ah, the young have not forgotten the thirst of their elders." The voices of PODOL and MALTZAHN can be heard from the next room.

HANNA returns: "Madam Rettigová is just the best cook. There is so much to learn from her."

KARLA: "I like coming here so much because real Czech, High Bohemian, is spoken and we can borrow books as well."

PEPI: "Yes, that's why I come, too. And our fellow students can come here for books, which always provides an opportunity to spend some time with them. At home you're watched as if it were a prison. I'm not even allowed to get together with you, pff! If the old man had his way he would bolt the doors, and we would have to do the cleaning here for nothing."

HANNA: "I've had enough of our fellow students. I like auntie the best."

MARCELA: "And I like Master Jirásek. Besides, he is an important author."

"Unfortunately, an unimportant sculptor."—KARLA, softly to Hanna.

PEPI: "What a shame about the handsome archivist. Is he still in the hospital?"

MARCELA: "No, he's out and on his feet, with a cast on his leg; I just saw him; but he looked so very downcast."

HANNA: "No wonder. His pudgy old girlfriend, the doctor, has been holding hands of late with Mr. Purkyně."

Maltzahn and Podol at the door:

JIRÁSEK, teasing: "Aha, the maids are waiting now for their admirers, but that is youth, madam, and we were young once, too."

RETTIGOVÁ: "There is no flirting in my house, good Alois. What notions you aesthetes do have! Here we have only intimate woman-to-woman talks [He presses Hanna to his chest], or better, patriot-to-patriot."

Both exit.

Back in the parlor:

The gentlemen make themselves comfortable on the sofa, with smoking utensils laid out on the table beside them; Purkyně is back working at his microscope.

JIRÁSEK watches affably as their hostess moves about with a tray and serves coffee. "Plump though you may be, madam, you're still an attractive lady."

"But my good Alois," RETTIGOVÁ menaces with a wagging finger, "don't forget I could be your mother."

"Oh yes, mommy." He snuggles his head to her chest.

PODOL: "Piss off, damnit. I mean really, Olbram, you're worse than Jan!"

MALTZAHN: "What did I do? You have no sense of humor at all!"

"It's this way. I like having you at my breast about as much as I would an asp!" In annoyance, PODOL pours himself another glass of heavy tavern beer. To Smetana: "Maestro, is the beer recipe your father's? I knew him personally."

SMETANA takes a contented deep draft. "Yes indeed, I composed the men's chorus in the second act in honor of our fourteen-percent brew. Sabina had the libretto finished after just a few jugfuls, and I had the score roughed out myself; the instrumentation was a mere bagatelle. I tell you, you can never go wrong with trombones and kettledrums for a men's chorus, and with beer as your theme—why, even the eunuchs chime in!"

PURKYNĚ looks up from his pathology studies: "Is there not something dubious about a renowned composer who selects a confidant of the Austrian secret police to be the librettist for his most beloved and patriotic opera?"

SMETANA, with dignity: "Karel Sabina was an upstanding fellow, at least as far as our collaboration was concerned. I was just starting out at the time, looking for a subject. Perhaps it was precisely his experience as—shall we say—an *informer* that helped make the work a success. He had a sixth sense for the life of the common folk. It was in fact the beer scene that won a broader public for musical theater in Czech, that showed that subjects and concerns of profound national interest could be incorporated in what was until then an elevated, classical genre. I am grateful to him. Besides, I knew nothing of his secondary employment at the time. It is also an open question just how deeply he really was involved."

PURKYNĚ: "We know enough. No one was going to call him a spy, however; when it came to the librettist of *The Bartered Bride,* they were dealing with—how unfortunate—a confidant."

SMETANA: "What do you want? It's a lovely libretto. Take da Ponte, for instance. In his old age he plundered European culture, peddling priceless Italian books on Broadway, and to whom?—to philistines so that he could build an Italian opera house in the New World. That's not for me; I'll leave that to Dvořák, always gadding about. I'm more for the fields of home—*From Bohemia's Meadows and Forests,*

The Moldau, Tábor. We are kindred souls, my good professor; you have written a great deal about the Hussites, too."

JIRÁSEK: "Very kind of you, maestro. But language is my nemesis, whereas you, as our dearest friend already noted, need no translators. All the same, can one not determine beforehand whether one has engaged a police spy to be one's librettist?"

PURKYNĚ: "Presumably he got all the information he needed about Smetana beforehand."

SMETANA: "Was I supposed to go to the police?"

JIRÁSEK: "Were you never tempted to set Shakespeare to music?"

SMETANA: "No. Musical settings of great literary works—*Othello, Faust*—are always overshadowed by the originals. Whereas people celebrate the stories of a Schikaneder, a Sabina, or a da Ponte once they are set to music. The more famous the composer, the less one has to worry about the librettist. Or take Schubert's *Winterreise*—who ever heard of Müller? The same thing happened when Wenzig wrote *Libuše* for me. But that wouldn't have worked out so well at the start with *The Bartered Bride*—my confidant was better. Casanova was more famous than da Ponte, but his libretto sketches for *Don Giovanni* remained a private pastime. It is of interest, however, that copies of them are found not only in Dux but here at the castle as well, at least the sextet from the second act, which I have seen in the archives. It seems the private correspondence of feudal lords is good for something other than exchanging recipes and gossip."

All three turn to look at each other in amazement.

RETTIGOVÁ: "What have you against recipes, maestro? I thought you liked my cooking."

SMETANA: "But of course I do, my dear, I am speaking merely of material to be set to music."

"Václav did his homework."—MALTZAHN, sotte voce to Orten.

"And all during intermission."—ORTEN.

"I have also done some research on Rettigová," MALTZAHN whispers; he wants to stick it to Podol, whom he has been wooing in vain the whole time. As JIRÁSEK: "Yes, with dramas one writes oneself dry. All that research I had to do for *Jan Hus* and *Jan Žižka,* and Smetana takes a Hussite chorale, picks it apart and stretches it a little, and *voilà, Tábor* is finished, naturally much more popular than my historical version. Or take Svatopluk Čech. His wonderful satire *Mr.*

Brouček's Excursion to the Fifteenth Century, in which a Czech phi-
listine falls among Hussites, is hardly known at all. Janáček's opera,
however . . ."

PURKYNĚ: "Isn't either, sad to say."

RETTIGOVÁ: "Your envy has led you to confuse eras, my good
historian. Janáček's operas are not under discussion here."

JIRÁSEK, increasingly testy: "Madam Rettigová, I wasn't going to
say anything, but since you have brought up the matter yourself, you
should know that you are a much greater anachronism here than Janáček, who at least was already alive. In order to be part of our circle
here, you would have to be at least a hundred years old!"

A baffled look appears on the face of the advocate of revival.

PURKYNĚ: "She's as much a part of the nineteenth century as you
are, Jirásek. Janáček is modern in comparison, though he is your contemporary. Which should give you food for thought."

JIRÁSEK: "You can keep still, you're dead anyway, too!"

SMETANA: "Let's not be picky now."

JIRÁSEK: "And you're deaf! [To Rettigová:] And something else,
madam, that I find irksome about you. It was my intention to use you
to create a positive figure. A comedy about the beginnings of our national revival should be light-hearted and gay. But given your prudery
and pretensions, the way you bully everyone here, just because your
skills allow you to serve up a few half-raw innards that only a deviant
snipper-snapper could enjoy! [a glance at Purkyně], I shall have to take
another look at my manuscript. I claimed, for example, that you are
a magnanimous and charming woman, a true mother to her students—
you lend out books in Czech, even write some yourself, and with refreshing ingenuousness see to it that the Czech language is spoken and
Czech food is cooked. You play hostess at garden parties with patriotic
oratory, avoid all intrigues, keep silent about the revolution in Bel-
gium, if not in fact affirming it. . . ."

RETTIGOVÁ: "How dare you! That insurrection? That wretched
riot, which I condemned in our May 1835 issue of *May Flowers*? I
warn you, my husband will have the last word in this matter in court!"

JIRÁSEK: "My heartfelt thanks, madam, I would have expected
nothing less of a patriot active from the very start. [To the others:]
But you need think only of the *Jacobin*—not fifty years after Rettigová,
and the Czechs are afraid of revolution."

SMETANA: "But that's an opera by Dvořák."

JIRÁSEK: "So what? You risked nothing with your heroic mythologizings and bucolic idylls."

PURKYNĔ: "Might I call your attention to the fact that you gathered heroic sagas yourself, my good Jirásek? How were people to know any better back then. It's very easy to judge a hundred years later."

JIRÁSEK: "Don't keep interrupting me; it's much easier for you to pretend impartiality. What great risks are you taking with your microscope?"

RETTIGOVÁ: "A great many, I would say."

JIRÁSEK: "Only if he gets a bad grip on some living subject matter. These natural scientists don't take any risks whatever! Unless right in the middle of an impartial dissection he discovers that both Metternich and his successor, Bach, had tumors that caused them to oppress the Czechs. And then uses that to excuse them. But as for you, madam. Your views about how young wives are to behave at home—better to keep silent than to contradict your husband no matter what you may be thinking—that's not exactly encouraging. And you call yourself a progressive educator of women, an awakener of women? Don't make me laugh! No one can hold a candle to you when it comes to gossiping and scheming, abusing your servants, exploiting the young women entrusted to you. And when Božena Němcová came to you . . ."

"What? Božena Němcová? Who came to see me?" RETTIGOVÁ explodes.

JIRÁSEK: "It's nothing, madam, nothing. It's alright."

RETTIGOVÁ: "Nothing is alright! Don't you dare say anything against that saintly woman! She came to me as to her mother, and I took her in as I would a daughter. She was a martyr, and what ugly things people said of her."

JIRÁSEK: "They must have heard it all from someone."

RETTIGOVÁ: "Not another word! When she knocked on this door [she points to it], I opened it and all of Friedland was open to her as well!"

JIRÁSEK: "Yes, at the start. When she was nineteen, a lovely, innocent thing. But what happened then, twenty years later, madam? Those same townsfolk—they all left her standing outside the door. The same patriotic publisher, Augusta—not one more advance! A woman, a mother with children, who preached free love, that was going too far for those progressive folks. Augusta allowed her to starve, instructed the innkeeper to refuse to give her further room and board. She should write something, and if it was good, he was prepared to continue to allow her to vegetate. On principle, Pospíšil, the publisher in Prague, advanced nothing for works in Czech—we know this publishing pack!"

RETTIGOVÁ sobs: "Yes, yes, my fellow citizens were guilty of a grave sin there."

PURKYNĚ to Jirásek: "The national patriotic revival doesn't seem to be quite the happy subject you intended."

SMETANA at the piano plunks out "Where Is My Homeland" with one finger. "Water bubbling through the meadows, forests murm'ring in the highlands . . ."

PURKYNĚ quickly: "Where else?"

RETTIGOVÁ: "That's even more depressing."

PATERA: "We'll move on to another subject. Wasn't there something more pleasant back then?"

ORTEN: " 'Twas evening now—the first of May,
          The eve of May—the time of love."

MALTZAHN: "No, not that!"

ORTEN: "*The outlaw speaks, addressing clouds on high:*
        Oh you whose wide-flung courses speed the sky
        And earth as if in mystic arms embrace,
        Sad molten stars, distraught by heaven's blue,
        Who in your mourning grieve your grief anew
        And melt in silent tears to wet my face,
        'Tis you I chose as messengers to bear
        My inmost thoughts whate'er your bourne may be,
        E'en unto shores of my nativity,
        And as you pass to greet that earth so fair.
        Ah, lovely earth, beloved earth, its clay
        My cradle, mother, and my grave one day,
        My homeland, heritage of priceless worth,
        But lent to me, this one, this widest earth!"

MALTZAHN (envious): "We learned that in school, too."

PODOL: "No, no Mácha, please. He was never in Friedland. We should at least hold to the unity of place."

PATERA: "You call that pleasant? Mácha made a habit of attending executions; he thought they were fun."

ORTEN: "What's pleasant is that there was anyone who could write like that back then. And who knows him? Ask a Frenchman or a German about the European romantics, and they'll come up with Byron or Novalis—even the very well-educated will only smile politely at the mention of Mácha and take you for an oddball with a penchant for native folklore."

PATERA: "But it's not easy to translate, either."

ORTEN: "But that goes for other languages, too, the Czechs give in too quickly. When will the *small nations* finally realize that it's the same distance from both sides across the gap of two languages? Why are there such excellent translations into Czech, and of poetry in particular—Čapek's *Modern French Poetry*, Saudek's Shakespeare, Sládek's *Hiawatha*, it's finer than the original—and who knows about Sládek in America? Or his own poems, *On Indian Graves*, that he brought back from America? The same thematic in music is part of standard American culture!—in every Western the wagon trains are obliged to conquer the land to the strains of Dvořák's *New World*, and Gary Cooper tootles *Humoresque* on the trumpet."

MALTZAHN: "That's something at least."

ORTEN: "I'm not talking about Czech music; it's easy to adopt that. At least it was easy during the monarchy. This is about language. And about the way every foreigner who shows up here assumes his own linguistic incompetence is the order of the day—can't even say 'thank you' or 'hello'—and he can be sure that the Czechs will step into the breach. Since they can't travel abroad, at least they can amortize the investment they've made in evening courses. Look at how the retirees lie in wait for tourists, hoping to give them helpful information in their old Austro-Imperial German. Just for the pleasure of it, while the tourists are feeling for their wallets—'He's going to want something for this!' [He snorts:] But they're not the ones who interest me. I'm talking about the ones who read. Czech is hard to learn? That doesn't excuse the fact that they don't know who Karel Hynek Mácha is!"

PODOL: "Or at least his diary. With his Lori on the window seat, three or four times, from the front, from the rear, with her on his lap if the family is sitting nearby. And she complains, in German: 'It hurts for chrissakes! You went deeper than usual.'—That's how a Czech patriot takes his revenge on the oppressors! We were once a gifted nation, even under the Habsburgs we got away with it."

MALTZAHN, quickly: "Do you have it?"

PODOL: "Ask Jan."

ORTEN: "The censored passages from his diary can be found in twenty privately published copies. Each of them typed, a kind of *samisdat*. These idiots and their prudery! Whether it's Havel or Mácha, they suppress them both as subversive.

MALTZAHN: "Where did you get one?"

ORTEN: "Kolář did the illustrations and they gave him two copies. We owe all this, by the way, to Sabina, who preserved both the coded passages and the key to the code. He wrote the first Mácha biography, too."

MALTZAHN: "He had access to the sources, it seems."

PATERA: "I'd like to read that, too."

ORTEN: "The biography?"

PATERA: "No, the diary."

ORTEN: "You mean the selected passages. The diary is available otherwise only as part of the collected works. But it's very exciting even in abridged form. Pages of excerpts from his own reading, in Polish, French, German, English. At twenty-five he knew European literature like no Czech does nowadays. And all the while he was traveling, on foot in Italy. . . ."

PATERA: "I want that copy of Kolář's."

ORTEN: "I knew there would be no point in trying to talk with you guys about books."

MALTZAHN: "Then don't keep trying."

PODOL: "How did Kolář get the job?"

ORTEN: "He knew the publisher. They worked together on a book by Klíma."

PODOL: "Do you mean Ladislav Klíma? I read his *Sorrows of the Young Count Sternenhoch*, it's a pretty crazy book."

ORTEN: "That it is. The school of Nietzsche, but nastier and more consistent—he doesn't give a shit about some professor of philosophy. And he lived it out, too: a slice of bread and half a liter of rum a day. He never accepted work unless he was starving. Then he would take a job as a watchman and drink the time away. He was constantly writing, but then would lose most of it, left scraps of paper behind in the brickyards where he spent his nights, he didn't even care. No matter what, a man must exist alone—he hated pity, love of one's fellow man, and with cruelties worthy of de Sade, but not so monotonous. One of the masters of black comedy, but unknown."

MALTZAHN: "Is this your new role, lecturer on unappreciated Czech geniuses?"

PODOL: "Your sarcasm is getting on my nerves, Olbram! Go on, Jan, I like this Klíma fellow."

PATERA: "I remember there was a little black pamphlet of his lying around our house for a while, *The World As Consciousness and Nothingness,* sort of aphorisms. My father always got a reverent look on his face whenever he picked it up. I didn't understand a word of it."

ORTEN: "It would be worth its weight in gold now in a rare-book store, and *Sternenhoch,* too."

PODOL: "I'll have to check. Although I wouldn't really want to sell it."

MALTZAHN, annoyed: "I don't know him."

PODOL: "That's no reason to rant and rave. You should be taking a few notes, so that the Landmarks Office can see how we cultivate tradition when they leave us hanging here without any lime!"

MALTZAHN: "I'm sure you as Rettigová in your bonnet and dress would make quite an impression on them. And what has happened to dessert, madam?"

PODOL/RETTIGOVÁ: "Oh yes, I can offer you queens' eggs."

MALTZAHN/JIRÁSEK: "Since when do queens . . ."

RETTIGOVÁ: "Mr. Jirásek, seeing as you invited yourself and we here in Friedland must reconcile ourselves to your presence, might I once again most emphatically request self-restraint on your part and that you not call unnecessary attention to yourself. What was it you were about to say?"

JIRÁSEK: "I was merely going to inquire as to the nature of your specialty?"

RETTIGOVÁ reads from her book: "Take six eggs, two and a half pounds of sugar, two and a half pounds of flour and work them into a pastry dough, which is then rolled out to the thickness of a finger on a greased cookie sheet; from the dough you then cut pretty little squares. I brush each square with homemade currant jelly and fold the square to a tri—"

MALTZAHN: "Yuckhhh! Kreplach!"

RETTIGOVÁ: "Not quite correct, professor. Kreplach is filled with chopped meats, not with currants."

PURKYNĚ: "It must taste ghastly all the same."

RETTIGOVÁ, confused. "Perhaps I forgot to say that there is sugar in the dough."

JIRÁSEK: "In any case, many thanks, madam, but I think I'll stick with black coffee."

RETTIGOVÁ: "You could also try the cocoa *frappé,* or the *sabayon.*"

JIRÁSEK: "It sounds like sabotage. Somewhat surprising for a language purist. Have you run out of Czech already?"

RETTIGOVÁ, modestly: "We've only just started, Professor Jirásek. Further development of the language is in the hands of coming generations. I had hoped that you might find a lovely word for *sabayon* yourself."

JIRÁSEK: "My Hussites were unfamiliar with *sabayon!* I'm afraid Czech will have to continue to be contaminated with such foreign words, that is unless Sabina were to write another successful libretto, using a popular theme—a thanksgiving dinner, with *sabayon* on the menu. Then, for all I care, it can be called 'wine foam.' "

SMETANA/PATERA: "What else is the poor fellow supposed to do now? I thought you wouldn't take so much as a cup of *sabayon* from a confidant, not even one disguised under a Czechism."

RETTIGOVÁ: "The steam dumplings should have cooled by now."

JIRÁSEK: "Steam dumplings? Now that's the right stuff! Little, tender dumplings with *šodó,* that will become the national dish someday."

SMETANA: "I don't like sweets; give me kreplach with chopped meat instead."

JIRÁSEK: "But what about our good physiologist; surely he won't say no."

ORTEN/PURKYNĚ: "Thanks, I've already taken care of it." He removes a *laskonka* from its wrapping and applies himself to his microscope—under its objective he had placed the hissian fibers from a pig's heart, to which are attached wires from a voltaic pile. He delivers electric shocks, then places litmus to it, all the while crumbling at the crust of his dessert.

RETTIGOVÁ: "You needn't eat *any* of it. The dumplings are for a garden party later this afternoon. There will be dancing and Czech oratory, after which the young people will have a hearty appetite. I hope, gentlemen, that you all will join us!"

Change of scene:

Landscape beside a lake, with grotto.

Smetana and Purkyně, rowing a boat.

SMETANA: "Plunk plunk plunk plunk. Can you hear it? That's the Moldau near the Vyšehrad, one of the few passages in all of musical literature that begins with a harp. The musical signature of Radio Prague."

PURKYNE: "Isn't that 'Forward left, forward left, and never a retreat'?"

SMETANA: "No, you're confusing it with the foreign service of Czechoslovak Broadcasting. But to return to the *Moldau*—

"It begins very softly. Two springs emerge in the Šumava Mountains and meander around stones and roots into the valley, each with its own voice and path. One has a long way to go—that is the Warm Moldau; the shorter Cold Moldau approaches, they join, still very slender, still trying to find how they fit together, grow even more slender in the first rapids, foam and beat against the 'Maiden Stone,' pulling the soil of the bank with them and turning dangerous. They probe their strength. On moonlit nights they are romantic and let water nymphs swim across, or grow very stern and mirror the weeping willows along the bank, the steeples on the hill, the pike lying below and watching over the souls of the drowned. But they dance the polka at a wedding, dance at many weddings. Near Hluboká, the 'Deeps,' they slacken the speed, take on more water, flow around fortresses and castles. They have devoured the Malše now, and later it will be the lovely Lužnice, which in its bed carries the Nežárka and the Kamenice and carp escaped from the ponds of Třeboň; at Zvíkov the sisters receive the Otava, at Davle the Sázava, and just before Prague the Berounka flows into them; each river is itself drenched with two, three other streams. The Cold and the Warm Moldau, our Vltava, has drunk its fill of the rivers of Bohemia, and now flows plump and placid to the north, until it is caught up in the Johannis Rapids. The river foams, slams against the boulders; its depths are white, seething fonts whose whirlpools bear trees and rafts that crack and split apart, rotating them faster and faster, until they are spat out in a jumble into the open riverbed beyond the narrows, like the happy dead in the Cataract of San Miguel. The river has relieved the miller of his labor. Majestically it rolls toward the city, past the Vyšehrad, rocking in its depths the cradle that will one day surface when Prague and the land are ours again."

The boat docks.

Night. Libuše conjures the linden trees and the people's spirit of resistance, Dalibor plays the violin, two widows whisper about a kiss that the bartered bride received under the Devil's Wall when the Brandenburgers were in Bohemia; it is to remain a secret—babbled and gone, murmured and gone.

Change of scene.

The parkway leading to the castle, to the left a pavilion in the style of a classical temple, bearing the motto SILENTIUM on its frieze.

Jirásek and Rettigová are strolling under the trees, whose foliage is already tinged with yellow. Dance music and the noise of happy voices can be heard from the party nearby.

RETTIGOVÁ takes out her handkerchief to fan herself and dab her brow: "And they are back dancing again, youth never has enough, they waited so long for this party."

JIRÁSEK: "Are you still angry with me, Madam Rettigová, for writing a comedy about you?"

RETTIGOVÁ: "Better than a tragedy, sir. Let us forgive and forget. Your approach suits the times. [She looks up at the prematurely yellowed treetops.] How did you like the oratory?"

JIRÁSEK: "The speeches probably have to sound like that, after three hundred years of Germanization."

RETTIGOVÁ, disconcerted: "Some of the verses were mine."

JIRÁSEK: "Your dancing made up for it. It is no small thing to keep pace with the young."

RETTIGOVÁ: "And our literary quadrille—were you even paying attention?"

JIRÁSEK: "Literary quadrille?"

RETTIGOVÁ: "Either for four single dancers or four couples. One may change one's place or one's partner only when one knows the name of a writer of our national revival."

JIRÁSEK: "A clever dance, which lends education some practical application, and any gentleman left behind has no cause to complain. I do recall now how people were constantly yelling Klicpera, Thám, Melantrich, Komenský—there was nary a slack in the quadrille, partners were changing so fast. And I heard your name, too, Madam Dobromila, and that moved them on quick as a wink. An arresting scene and a harmonious conclusion: I see them all dancing off into the wings with your name on their lips!"

Rettigová, old, looks at him with weary eyes.

Change of scene:

Middle-class interior, at the window Purkyně bent over his microscope; on the table, a voltmeter, ammeter, a homemade stereotactic apparatus bristling with wires, index cards, and along the walls his preserved specimens and slides.

PURKYNĚ mutters to himself: "Just as I thought, these fibers transmit the impulse to the chamber. And if I tap away in Morse, at some point . . . there. And again . . . the chamber twitches, possibly an elevated sympathicotonia caused by the irregular stimulation? Once again . . . Now it's quite relaxed. And how does the calf react?" He shoves the pig-heart sections aside and removes a calf heart from its physiological saline, pulls up short, removes another one: "Can't be helped, all of them with fatty degeneration, merely a race between the butcher's knife and a heart attack." He cuts the heart open, spreads it out, pinning it to the wax basin, and fixes one end to the stylus on the kymograph; the drum jams at first, then the quivering needle records the oscillations on smoked paper. He drips more Ringer's solution on the heart and connects the electrodes to the pile.

"There they are again, my fibers, rich in plasma, thin, elastic, about which the great Harvey knew nothing! *Initium sapientiae, timor dei.* Yes indeed! And even if I should go blind looking at these scraps of muscle, have to sit here on my bloody arse for years, go arthritic in the neck, the Almighty must be trembling even now!

"What did I say! The twitching stops if I send the impulses too rapidly, at most introduces an extra systole. Refractory! The heart cannot be tetanized!"

From stage left and right, Rettigová, Jirásek, Smetana.

JIRÁSEK: "We wish to provide a patriotic ending: The Czech heart will never be cramped and rigid!"

They all come downstage and bow to the empty auditorium.

PODOL: "If we shadows have offended—" He takes off his bonnet and walks down the stairs. "I'll go see if they've finally brought the lime."

PATERA: "And I'll go to bed at noon."

SEVEN

A Citroën 2CV is standing in the castle courtyard; a young man is tugging a dusty paper sack out of it. He turns around and gazes with interest at Podol's getup.

"Mr. Podolský, I presume."

"Were you expecting Livingstone? What's this?"

"I've brought you your supplies."

"So you *are* Stanley."

"My name is Nordanc, André Nordanc."

"All we needed. Where's the gravel?" Podol moves toward him, with such long strides that his pointy knees bang against his wide skirts.

"This is lime, if I'm not mistaken, and sand. Six sacks."

"Of each?"

"No, altogether."

"And you're bothering us with that? Work's been held up here for six weeks now—everything was supposed to be here yesterday, which is why we all came back from Prague—and our shovels were stolen in the meantime besides! They were supposed to bring two truckloads, and you come along now with your six puny sacks! You can head right back with them. You tell your office . . ."

"I couldn't get any more in."

"In that little cracker box? I'm not surprised. You should have tried a Trabant, at least they don't rust through. Has the Landmarks Office taken to saving on gas for trucks?"

"I'm the new archivist, this is my car. They loaded me up on the way, so at least you could get a start. The rest is supposed to arrive tomorrow. They told me about you at the office; I recognized you immediately."

Podol laughs. "So you're already well informed. Good, we'll unload right away; I've just got to get out of this garb. What did you say your name was?"

"Nordanc, but people call me Andy."

"You're French?" Podol asks, once he has returned.

"From Luxembourg, but I've been here nine years now."

"Why?"

"That's a long story."

Each heaves a sack onto his shoulder and carries it across the lawn to the scaffold, followed by Maltzahn and Orten, who carries one and a half, since one of the sand sacks is only half full.

"Václav, let it be, I'll do that." Podol takes the last one from Patera. "What's that?" He points to a large leather satchel still on the backseat, with a transistor radio, some books, and an overstuffed bag piled on top, and at the peak a round wicker animal cage pressed down into it all.

"That's Max. I should take a look at where I'll be staying. Is there a director around?"

"Yes, sad to say. Up there, second floor, on the left. In case he's not there, come on back down, you can leave your stuff with us."

"I can either live next to you guys, or above the carriage house."

"In that hole next door? The mildew's worse in there than it is here. He offered you that? The carriage house is dry at least, but I don't know what it looks like in there."

"It has to be plastered first. And there's no bed. He called into town."

"You'll have a long wait. Come on in."

A large reddish-gray tabby jumps out of the cage, looks around with interest and begins a systematic sniffing of the furniture, including Podol's legs. After it has got to know the room, it forces its way through the door that's ajar and leads to the back room. It is gone for a good while. When Podol and Nordanc go to look for it, they find it stretched out on Podol's bed in a cello player's position, licking its leg.

"Just so we understand one another, I've nothing against you, but . . ."

"She's housebroken."

"She'll have no chance to prove it around here." Podol lifts the blanket and the cat with it—it bounds off and into the front room.

"She can stay in here, I don't mind animals," Patera says, stretching out his hand. "Kitty kitty." The cat sniffs it, lets him scratch her head, but then with tail held high goes back to Podol and rubs his legs, purring loudly.

"That's going to be unrequited love." Podol is uneasy at this display of affection.

Orten laughs. "Don't make such a fuss, she's not going to shit on your papers. This is Václav's room."

"Then she should show her gratitude to him and leave me in peace."

"Max, come here. I didn't want to cause any trouble." Nordanc is about to go, but Podol holds him back. "Stay here, you can sleep in Olbram's bed if yours doesn't come by tonight."

"Who is Olbram?"

"You haven't met him yet. He normally sleeps here, but actually he's sleeping at the director's."

"And where does the director sleep?"

"In the singles' dorm."

"I don't get it."

"It's very simple. Just unpack. There's some tea and something to eat. If you need anything else—we'll be up on the façade."

In the castle library, Pepi, joined by Hanna and Karla, who have no tours on Mondays, is browsing in gilt-edged books, all of them eighteenth-century erotica.

"I didn't know there was so much of it here," Hanna says, opening a *Journal des Dames* from 1777. "Naturally, most of it's anonymous. Here for example, *Point de Lendemain* by a certain M.D.G.O.D.R."

"Monsieur Denon Gentilhomme Ordinaire du Roi." Karla opens a small volume next to it. "They have it in duplicate, it's not all that good. I had to read it for a seminar, because Balzac mentions it in his *Physiology of Marriage*. Vivant Denon, one of the harmless libertines, along with Dorat, and admired for his 'elegant' style'."

"You mean boring, then," Pepi concludes, "but the pictures aren't bad. Look at this!"

"Let me see! Well, of course, the English always were pigs. And those there, the Germans, a little wooden. No name of course."

"Here, it says 'Paphos.' " Pepi has dragged more of the books over.

"That's the publisher," Hanna remarks.

"What have you got there?" A curious Marcela has entered, after spotting them through the open door. "I've never looked at this old crap."

"Here, even in Italian."—Pepi.

"No pornography in 'High Bohemian'?" Karla asks.

"You thinking of Mácha's diary, maybe? Given the anti-Czech sentiments of the Thurn and Taxis family, not very likely. They even prevented a memorial plaque to Smetana from being put on the brewery."
—Information that Hanna usually reserves for party functionaries.

"They were very active collectors of erotica," Pepi observes. "I showed it to Qvietone. He was always sitting here looking at his beetle books, all hand-colored, but he wasn't interested. He did show me a drawing of a click beetle that wasn't quite correct. He finally worked his way up to human anatomy, to that two-volume *Anomalia* there, in color."

"That's why he's so attracted to the elderly doctor," Marcela suggests.

"If that's the case, he can go courting Jirse. Where is he anyway?" Hanna asks. "I haven't seen him all day. Won't he be looking for you, Pepi?"

"He'll have to find his leg first! Why do you think it's so quiet around here this morning? Otherwise, he'd have been here long ago!"

"You're quite a scamp yourself, it seems," Marcela remarks.

"Me? I'm on vacation! Do you think it's fun to have to look at him every day, from up close? Mother didn't have the nerve for it this time, and so I'm left holding the bag! Somebody has to tend to his needs once in a while, she says. No one can stand him, my brother is the worst when it comes to making fun of him, he would never come! Even though the old man gives him anything he wants—he has never got over that he only had a daughter. My brother was here once. Grandfather opened a bottle of whiskey—three hundred thirty korunas is a lot of money to him—and that evening he took him by the arm and was going to show him off. They went to the Ram, and my brother ducked out after the first beer, but not before he had hit gramps up for a hundred korunas—just in case. He even took money for playing a game of parcheesi with him. And was told to pick out a souvenir from the armory before he left."

"The castle armory?"

"My brother's a liar, I admit, but I've seen the pistols. With inlay work, at least two hundred years old. He was going to pawn them, for hard currency. He knows a money dealer in Prague, and has contacts in Karlsbad, too, where he worked as a waiter during the film festival, but my father told him he had to give them back at once, otherwise he might be found out. Mother insisted, too, and he told them he sent them back, but I know where he hid them, wrapped in a shirt at the bottom of his dresser, he's just waiting for the right opportunity. And now he's in collusion with the old man, who had to say that he'd got them back."

"What are we going to do about this?" Marcela wonders.

"Nothing," Hanna says. "It was before your time. Your husband wasn't director here yet. Officially he took over a complete inventory. Given the sloppy way records are kept around here, it's a wonder that we've held together as much of the collection as we have. We miss Qvietone in the archives, that's for sure, old Patočka can't manage all by himself."

"Jirse keeps a sharp eye out," Karla observes.

"It's a good thing to know at least, particularly if he starts kicking up a row around here again," Marcela says. "And what do you get for looking after him?"

"Me? I'm just standing in for my mother. Whenever she gets that thin voice—'You know, Pepi, I'm not feeling well at all'—I feel guilty right away and can be talked into anything. But I always like to come here, too. At least it's a town; there's nothing happening at home. I can go to the movies here whenever I want, or visit one of the rooms in the castle, especially on the other side, where nobody ever goes. I could spend days in the storage rooms or in the hallways on the top floor. Or here, in the library. And the theater!"

"Does your grandfather let you go anywhere you like?" Hanna asks.

"He doesn't know anything about it. I make sure he gets a warm meal, help him into his leg, he can't expect anything more. It's all I can handle when he goes to the toilet. He pisses like a horse with the stall door open, splashes urine everywhere, and never flushes. I look the other way when he puts his false teeth in a dirty mustard glass every night, with strands of meat that slowly dissolve in the gook."

"Stop!"

"But he's going to have a long search today! When he's had too much to drink he doesn't remember anything the next day. He's always got something to do in the evening, pecking out his denunciations and complaints with two fingers on that old typewriter of his that makes such a racket, or spends hours scouring pots if I've forgotten to leave them to soak. Once he's drunk enough courage, he wakes me up, bends over me, and breathes the rotgut in my face at three in the morning—'I've got a bone to pick with you, smarty pants!' I scream sometimes. Either he leaves on his own, or I drag him to his room and toss him into bed, with or without the leg."

"Yes, I hear a lot of noise coming from your place," Marcela comments.

"From yours, too." Pepi is fired up now. "I tear up his tattletale crap, he looks for it the next day and asks if I've seen any documents. I tell him no. He caught me at it once and was so furious that he swung at me with his crutch. Trouble is, he's so old and weak I don't dare touch him, he's disgusting. I can't even defend myself! I just said that there were things about the armory that the officials would like to know. He denied it, of course, but kept his peace for a while. Then started up again in the evening. Since then he's been rummaging in my stuff, looking for evidence. He's informed on me before."

"What?"

"I came home with a cup he hid in my suitcase, I didn't know any thing about it. I dropped it, mother glued her birthday present back together, you can still drink out of it. They think I'm clumsy now. All the same, they keep sending me back here. Maybe they hope that someday they'll inherit all that rotted furniture lying around in the cellar. Although my father is a total klutz. He can't even turn off the television, just pulls out the plug, he's never even noticed the buttons, although he falls asleep in front of it every night—that's if he's not at some beer-sodden meeting firing up the comrades. I've heard his speeches about the necessity of new technologies, too. But what he likes most is to recite his odes—to the Party, the Red Army, our liberators."

"Our twofold liberators?" Karla asks.

"No, not that, these are old poems, about forty-five or the October Revolution—he throws some new catchwords in, uses Kohout as his model, who wrote a smash hit about Russian rockets. Dad picked it up: 'Some have stars upon their banner, we have banners upon the stars.'"

"That was probably his ode to Gagarin. The ineffable poet of youth organizations was still required reading in my sister's school," Karla recalls.

"My father hasn't written anything about 1968," Pepi says. "But in any case, he doesn't know how to repair old furniture, he can't even nail up a shelf, and we can't take it to some co-op to be fixed, either. But I'm the thief. My grandfather can barely stand up some evenings, but starts in gleefully spouting about how there's always tomorrow, and that some ugly things are going to come to light, and he's going to do his duty, even if it involves members of his family! I kept the memo, it was the only one of his denunciations that he actually hid. He even provided the inventory number of the cup, and of course he hadn't known anything about it. I didn't rip that one up. I'm going to show it to my mother, and I won't be coming back! Except to visit you, of course."

"But surely he can't go to the police with it," Hanna reflects.

"No, not with any of his slanders. But it's his great joy in life, he's got piles of accusations just waiting for his signature. He sits there at night, filling them out and adding more complaints. Podolský is in every one. Patera, he writes, is so weak he can hardly hold on to the scaffold and is totally inefficient—he asked me how to spell it. Orten is arrogant, he looked that one up himself. He's more reserved about Maltzahn, he's got better connections. Sometimes he mentions you, Marcela, as a way of getting at your husband, but he just keeps repeating the same stuff. About the disorder in the archives, the smudges in Patočka's register, about how the masons drink beer in the morning—the recent battle took him five nights and almost all his paper. He spent three nights just for the part about 'Waste of Materials.' All addressed to the 'Administrators of the National Castle of Friedland in Litomyšl,' he doesn't write to anyone else."

"Shouldn't you tell your husband to stash the paper better, Marcela?" Hanna asks.

"No question. And as far as those pistols go, that's misappropriation of nationalized property; we'll nail him for that!"

That evening Nordanc is standing in Orten's doorway. Podol and Maltzahn are not there; Patera is sleeping.

"I wanted to thank you again for letting me stay the night here."

Orten looks up from his book. "You needn't thank me, it's Maltzahn's bed. Would you close the door, please, so Václav can sleep."

Nordanc comes in, the cat slips in behind him. He looks around. "How long have you been working here?"

"Five years." Orten tries to go back to his reading.

"That long? But most of the walls are still bare."

"We're aware of that." Orten is annoyed now.

"When are you planning to finish?"

"This job will never be finished. We're already on the second round in some sections."

Nordanc finally realizes that he will get nowhere with more questions in this vein. "I was in the archives today. What a mess. Old Patočka . . ."

"Old Patočka is seventy, he should have retired long ago. The only reason he's still working is because of the muddle in the bureaucracy, and because they can't get anyone to stay on full time." He looks at Nordanc. "How did you end up here, coming from Luxembourg? Just look how far they have to go these days to find skilled labor," he says, laughing.

Nordanc sits down. "I've been in Prague since '68. I came the first time in '67 and fell in love, at twenty-three. I wanted to move here. It took almost a year before all my papers were ready, in the meantime my grand passion had left for Switzerland."

"She ran out on you?"

"It was a he. We met in a bar in Prague, where he worked as a waiter. I had been going with a boxer in West Berlin, who knew the guy who had opened the bar. I got a part-time job there, while I studied history. So I was a waiter, too. We planned to live together."

"Why had you come to Prague? As a tourist?"

"No, I don't make a very good tourist, I always want to settle in somewhere. Berlin is very interesting, the best place in the West that I know of. But Prague is much more exciting, and more beautiful."

"Have you been to North City and South City, Hostivař, Prosek?"

"Sure, projects are dreadful everywhere."

"Not that dreadful."

"Sure they are. Gropiusstadt is the same thing."

"Why did you come to Friedland?"

"I had the choice of either going back to Berlin as a waiter—they don't need historians there—or staying here. I knew the castle from pictures, the sgraffiti are famous. I went looking for a position, but there was nothing for me in Prague. They wanted the archivist here to have a degree in library science, but I got the job anyway because I speak German and French. Most of the archives here are in German, some in French, too. The French card index hasn't been reorganized since before the war. It will take years to get the inventory lists in order. And then some of the objects may be missing."

"They already are."

"I originally intended to specialize in the fourteenth century, Charles IV. He's the reason I came to Prague in the first place, he's a relative, you might say."

"Ah, the Luxembourgers."

"I didn't learn anything here that I didn't already know, but I did get to see the buildings with my own eyes—the castle, the bridge, the university. I had an idea that somehow I could reunite Bohemia and Luxembourg. So that the history would never be forgotten, the buildings, the river. Take the work you're doing here, scratching away at one coffer after the other, I was watching you today—from down below there's hardly any visible progress, but even if you never do finish . . ."

"What are you here for, to lend us courage?"

"—I can't for the life of me imagine anything more important," Nordanc concludes. "No, of course, I'm sorry. You don't need encouragement—not the way Podolský works. He's your friend, isn't he? I liked him right off, too."

"You can talk history with him. He knows a lot."

The cat is circling the room, closer and closer, moves in on Orten's chair and rubs its cheeks on the edges. Orten passes a finger along its back, setting its hair and tail on end.

"And the friend you moved here for left without a word to you?"

"It was a week after the Russians arrived, he didn't have time to let me know." Nordanc pulls off a ring with a blue stone, on the inside it reads TVŮJ ZDENĚK. "It was a present from him."

Orten feels uncomfortable, as if he should apologize for the Czech. "Did he ever write?"

"A postcard addressed to the bar, the check-out girl stuck it behind the mirror—in color, from Davos. 'My best to you all!' "

"Where's this bar, in the Lesser Quarter?"

"No, four bridges further down, but on the same side of the river."

"Near the river? There aren't any bars there."

"It's a restaurant up on the slope, with a view over the Moldau."

"A round building made of glass, Expo '58?"

"Yes, they say it's modeled after the Czech pavilion in Brussels. Do you know it?"

"I know the original pavilion, we helped do some of the installations—a couple of us from the Academy. It worked out well for both parties: we were without any commissions, and all they had to pay for was our flight, room and board, and a little pocket money. Word must have got around, because I've been at every world exposition since. They knew they could depend on me." Orten grins.

"Have you ever considered just staying on somewhere?"

"Italy is beautiful, but I've always taken time out to see the museums—the sculptures and paintings. I'd like to see some of them again, but there's no rush. I wouldn't know any other reason."

"Have you always just installed?"

"They exhibited some of my work in Montreal and Osaka, but something always went wrong. And so you worked at Expo '58! That's five minutes from my atelier, across from Ponrepo Cinema, do you know it?"

"Why, sure."

"Did you know, too, that a few hundred yards further up in Letná Park, the tallest Stalin monument in Europe once stood? I helped erect it as a student, and then to cart it away again! The dismantling was expensive. The sculpture students helped with the stonemasonry. Beautiful hewn stones."

"Stone is expensive, isn't it?" Nordanc inquires. "I might know where you could get a block of granite cheap."

"Forget it. I can't even afford the freight on it."

"That could be arranged."

The cat is now standing on Orten's book, trying to climb into his lap.

"Max, get down."

Orten strokes its flank. "He's a really big tomcat."

"It's a she. They told me it was a tom when I bought it, but a spiteful vet broke the news to me when I took her in to be wormed. I hadn't even checked."

"So instead of Max, Maxine." Orten regards the cat with new eyes. "Or Maxime? Everything seems to be a little . . . inverted with you. Were you disappointed?"

Nordanc laughs. "I had already got used to her. She only hears the first syllable anyway. Only if I'm scolding her I say Maxine, and she doesn't like that, she knows something's wrong."

The cat jumps down and strolls back to the front room.

"Okay, Max, I'm coming too." Nordanc stands up. "I hope I haven't kept you from your reading too long."

As Orten is undressing for bed, he turns around to the door. It is ajar. The cat watches him through the crack.

EIGHT

At last everything was ready. Preparations for the Smetana Centennial Exhibition were in high gear. In addition to the other exhibits planned for the castle brewery, the original furniture from Smetana's years in Göteborg had arrived (the Swedish patrons wanted to remain anonymous, but had agreed to be present at the opening celebration). In the adjoining newly plastered tavern, the workers were taking a break, recovering from the hectic last-minute changes in plan. The main room of the exhibition, traditionally reserved as a concert hall for the competition of young pianists from "Smetana's Homeland," could not be used. So the furniture was put in the side rooms, along with the panels of biographical data, copies of letters and scores, a few libretti and diplomas; smaller autographs, compositions, and letters lay in the glass cases.

The planned parallel exhibition, "Prague Artists Restore Friedland Castle," had had to make way for the Göteborg antiques. The only things to be seen were a few before-and-after photographs of the façade that had been hung on the wall in one corner, behind the polished grand on which the six-year-old Smetana was said to have given his first concert. Nor was there a shortage of voices that considered the previous restoration more elegant and precise—"another lame-brained lie," Podol expounded.

The main part of the exhibition, with documentation of the various phases of restoration, plus original work by the artists, had been moved to the Municipal and District Museum in town. In the name of his colleagues Maltzahn protested against this expatriation—"for the sake of second-rate furniture, whose authenticity as regards Smetana cannot even be proved." The historical castle brewery had a direct relationship to their work, was also much more prestigious than the Municipal Museum, which was seldom frequented, except by school classes shooed through the dusty exhibits as part of their instructions! His outrage resulted in their being given two more rooms, so that the exhibition could be realized on a larger scale than at the brewery.

Meanwhile, inside the municipal office of culture, a faction had formed that hoped to expand the exhibition with work by local artists, so that the public could make comparisons with what was happening in the capital. The initiator was, as to be expected, Svoboda, who was looking for a suitable framework in which to display his industrial polychromes, and found it in "Open-Air Art," a title that he and a girlfriend of his, whose specialty was "ceramic walls for children's playgrounds," gladly furnished to the sponsors.

Bright, dry rooms, adequate space to present their work—thirty-four artists from Friedland and the surrounding area applied to be part of the comparison. Svoboda now had a powerful lobby inside the local national committee. But when the motion was approved, he relented, primarily because of the cost—the expense of transporting Maltzahn's oversized alloy sculptures would have to be kept within limits. A total of five Friedlanders would take part.

Declaring he would withdraw out of sympathy for the other twenty-nine, Podol was shouted down as if by one voice—without him the whole thing would be pointless. Maltzahn, who had fought against the extra rooms, threatened not to allow his work to be exhibited with eleven other artists. The dispute meant the installation had to be delayed until a compromise was found: two more of Maltzahn's heads would be accepted (middle period), but his recent objects, his bulkiest (and most innovative), would not be shown. Patera was disappointed that his pictures were to be placed on the third floor, where only the work of Friedland's ceramists and photographers was displayed. The core of the exhibition and its documentation were to be set up on the second floor. Orten reserved the right to exhibit his work on the third floor—if at all—and demanded that the extra space this provided be used for more of Podol's paintings.

One problem was the bronze bust of Klement Gottwald that stood on a concrete pedestal in the main room, the permanent home for the history of the workers' movement in Friedland, which over the next three weeks was to make way for the latest trends in the art of restoration. But the pedestal wouldn't budge.

The museum director resisted removing the republic's worker president. Things were bad enough, considering what all they had already had to shift out into the corridor: documentations of the exploitation of linen weavers in the region, of the smelters in the town of Lubná, of the workers at Adler Shoes and the women who did the packing for MichelstrÄdter Company, who had all taken part in strikes and class warfare over the years—though, granted, splintered into disorganized factions. But with the founding of the Czechoslovak Communist Party in the twenties came solidarity and strong resistance, and for that reason alone Gottwald should remain. As should the maquette of the town, even though the new high rises and the development behind the hill had been only partially realized thus far. One day, however, the model would be reality, and school classes loved to visit it even now. The kids could point out their own homes, and it would also contribute to the success of the exhibition—constructing such precise scale models was an art, too.

"Help me, Olbram." Without another word, Podol lifts the maquette and he and Maltzahn carry it out of the hall. Orten tries to explain to the director that his beloved model will hardly survive the installation work intact, but the director is outraged at the arrogance of these Praguers. "As if the artists of Friedland couldn't restore Friedland Castle! And mark my word, if you remove that bust, there will be consequences!" He slams the door.

"That wasn't especially clever of you," Orten says to Podol when he comes back.

"Am I supposed to be constantly tripping over it until I'm up to my ankles in debris? Besides, I can't stand those new boxes. And to think he's proud of them! We scratch away day in, day out, trying to preserve the façade, and they stab us in the back with their concrete housing projects! If he wants to look at them, let him play with building blocks in his office!"

They carry Gottwald out into the corridor to join the female workers of MichelstrÄdter Industries.

"They intended to erect Porkoný's monument in the Osaka entrance hall," Orten recalls. " 'Brotherhood': a Red Army man and a Czech partisan embracing; naturally the Czech stands lower and looks up to his brother. We wondered what the Japanese were supposed to make of it."

"Two gays," Podol says.

"Armed?" Patera queries.

"And behind them, the panorama of the Hradčany—a scene for Ginsberg, who had nothing better to write about in '68 than the pretty asses of Czech men. They put up a bust of Lenin instead."

"There's a life-size version of him now, in Dejvice, outside the subway station. He's looking up, as if leaves were drifting down on him: 'Lenin in October.' The next day someone hung a backpack on him." Patera giggles.

"So now the police help him gaze into the future."—Maltzahn.

"The citizens of Prague and their monuments!" Podol laughs. "By the time one of them is finished, the cult of personality is usually over."

"But they cling to their Saint Wenceslaus," Patera says.

"Because the statue is so beautiful! I've never seen a more beautiful equestrian monument. Myslbek used the face of his daughter. And the nag was a real pro. They had to enlarge the door to an atelier in the Academy for that horse, it had posing down to a regular routine. After it died, Myslbek refused ever to do another horse. It survived the war intact, both Wenceslaus's nose and the nag's tail—unscathed."

"It's tied in a knot," Patera says.

"What is?"

"His tail. It survived the fire from Russian tanks in '68—you know those 'pecks the sparrows left in the museum.' "

"And the restoration was done that fast, and cost more than we could ever dream of spending!" Maltzahn says. "They had at least twenty people."

"The pinnacles have been gold-leafed," Patera says wistfully.

Podol grins. "Are you jealous, Václav? You only have to compare that neoclassical junk with our splendor here! Besides, they should never have allowed that to be glossed over! And that idiot wants to dictate to us what has to stay!"

"Calm down. The idiot is capable of using that bust to throw his weight around," Orten says.

"So what? Look at these pictures here! 'Bathers,' 'Seated Figures,' 'Girls in the Rain,' or these two doves there, a jumping jack, pigs in a rye field—and the worker president right in the middle, huh? Even if we left him on his pedestal, what would we use to balance it out? My three sculptures—'The Coat,' 'The Hat,' and my wife's legs with her feet in the air? If we could at least put a hat on it! He'll get his comeuppance one day!" Podol remembers that he wants to lay the bricks for a second chimney today yet. "Should I put a Stetson up on the roof?"

"Stick to your flowers. Go on, leave us in the lurch, go grow your violets," Maltzahn says.

"Olbram, this exhibition was your idea, so you can worry about it. I've got things to do."

At the afternoon ceremonies opening the Smetana Centennial in the old brewery, there are speeches by two functionaries from Prague, the chairman of Friedland's National Committee, and the director of the site, who expands the theme to include the nurturing of tradition, as exemplified in the renovation of the castle. The artists sit in front of panels displaying Maltzahn's photos of the scaffold and one exposed wall. An enlargement shows Podol working on the Allegory of Chance; the Bomarzo is left untitled.

When the deputy minister of culture points in their direction at Smetana's piano—"where our beloved maestro . . ."—a woolgathering Patera stands up smiling and bows.

This is followed by *On the Overgrown Path*, a piano cycle by Leoš Janáček.

The solemnities are to be continued the next evening at the exhibition in the museum. The politicians have departed; the castle's director plans to give his speech a second time.

"Then we don't have to go," Podol declares.

"Oh yes you do, seeing as how the two largest rooms are devoted to your work," Maltzahn says caustically.

"And it's a fine thing, too," Orten interrupts. "Stanislav ought to have a one-man show. That would make more sense than the director rehashing his speech about 'productive cooperation'!"

"Then why don't you make a speech, somebody has to say something."

"That's right," Patera remarks. "If you want to know, I'm glad to get exhibited again for the first time in five years. Even if you did nudge me up onto the third floor. Don't interrupt. I know, that's just how it turned out. It was very kind of Stanislav to want three of my old paintings downstairs. But if it's supposed to be an art exhibition, then somebody should say something about art. And you're the most likely candidate, Jan."

"It looks like you have no choice," Podol remarks.

"How am I supposed to have anything ready by tomorrow night. That's nonsense!"

"You'll manage," Maltzahn says with a smile.

"Your sculptures don't bring anything to mind."

"Then write about Stanislav, he's more your thing!"

Orten is nowhere to be seen the rest of that day or the next. Podol, Patera, and Maltzahn, however, can be seen disappearing into their quarters with stacks of technical literature from the castle and town libraries, and coming right back out again. This is repeated in the afternoon when the library reopens after lunch. Mostly books about Czech landscape painting in the nineteenth century, twelve of them monographs dealing with the Moldau Basin alone. Orten grows increasingly nervous as the volumes grow larger and larger; every new folio provokes an allergic reaction. Finally he throws them all out, along with their art-history books.

At some point Podol comes up with his bright idea about the bottles. That night he conspicuously and thoughtfully straightens up the room where Orten has been working, drinking coffee and brandy, and staring at the paper in front of him. The next morning he tells them this is madness, that he was an imbecile to agree to it, and that they will have to content themselves with the director's speech; the guy wasn't all that bad, better than the minister of culture by a long shot, and they had even had some luck with him.

10 a.m.: Orten is shouted down by all three of them.

11 a.m.: When Podol cautiously inquires at the closed door, he is told to go to the devil (Czech: up his ass). He leaves the bottles.

1 p.m.: The bottles are gone.

2 p.m.: Patera, who's keeping lookout, notices Orten's "unnatural pallor" when he makes a dash for the john and shouts, "Leave me alone!"

3:30 p.m.: Orten staggers down the hall and grabs Maltzahn, who is now standing guard, by the throat: "I always did want to punch you in the face!"

4:30 p.m.: Orten has to pee and unbolts the door again.

The room contains billows of cigarette smoke and an ankle-deep layer of crumpled paper through which they wade, but next to the lighted desk lamp they find a few pages written full and as yet uncrumpled; Podol pockets them before Orten gets back, then opens the windows. Patera empties the ashtrays, carries out the empty bottles, and tries to make some order of the paper chaos. Maltzahn is curious about what Orten has written, but Podol won't hand it over. He thumbs through it, looking for a beginning, deciphers a few sentences. "There's something to it," he says uncertainly.

"I'm not totally unsatisfied myself," Orten remarks in the door, where he is holding on to both sides of the frame. "Give it to me. I have to go over it one more time."

"Read it to us." Podol is mistrustful, but hands over the papers. Orten stares awhile at page one, turns it over, goes to the window, trying to capture a little more light between the bars. "I can't see." He starts to giggle.

"There's really enough light." Maltzahn rolls his eyes and turns on the ceiling lamp. Patera picks up the desk lamp, the cord trailing behind him, and shines it over Orten's shoulder.

"Ouch, you're burning me." Orten laughs more loudly.

"Sit down." Podol pours what is left of the cold coffee into a cup. "Have a sip."

"I won't drink that." Giggles.

"I'll make some fresh."

Orten laughs louder and louder, until he crawls into bed exhausted, the blanket vibrating in sync with his merry mood. They let him sleep.

5:40 p.m.: Orten bolts from his room and runs off in the direction of town.

"He's going to chicken out," Maltzahn croaks from the scaffold.

"Bull!" Podol climbs down.

"Maybe he's going to the movies," Patera suggests.

6:30 p.m.: Orten drags a heavy box into his room and locks himself in.

"What do you suppose he's got there?"—Patera.

"Bottles."—Maltzahn.

Podol stares at him. "You never know when to stop."

7:20 p.m.: Podol knocks tentatively. "Jan, are you alright? It's about time for us to get going." Behind the door there is only the noise of a high, rapid, steady titter. Podol pulls the door open.

"Come on in, I just finished." Orten is calm, collected, friendly. "You guys can take that along with you," he says, pointing to a bulky tape recorder on the desk.

"Why? We don't want it."

"I've recorded it, it can be understood."

"What can be understood?"

"My speech. It took three takes. But it's okay now. Don't look at me like that. I can't possibly give a speech in front of people, you know how I stammer even when I'm supposed to talk at union meetings. I'm not going, I'm not sober, and besides I don't feel good! Don't stare at me like that!"

"You don't seriously believe everybody is going to stand around this machine listening devoutly to what the great artist has to say to us! A message from Orten the sculptor! Are you nuts?"

"Why is that nuts? I'm trying to spare you embarrassment. I picked it up at five till six; it was the only recorder they had."

"It looks like it."

"It works. The tone is a little distorted, but that's probably more because it sounds strange to me. This is the first time I've ever heard myself on tape. It's a shock, let me tell you."

"For me, too. Get dressed, we're going!"

"Well I'm not!"

7:50 p.m.: Maltzahn pulls up with the director's car. Podol drags a struggling Orten into the backseat with him. Despite several more motivating cocktails they have forced him to drink in the last half hour, Orten refuses to get in without his tape recorder. Patera arrives, carrying it in tow.

8 p.m.: Opening. Svoboda—in a white jacket and silk scarf, with white accents on the toes of his shoes—floats among the waiting guests, moving from group to group, spreading good cheer. The artists of Friedland who are not exhibiting are all present. Castle director Horský in a cashmere shirt, with his wife, Marcela, who has something shimmering and angular dangling at her neck and ears; he poses for the *Friedland Echo* in front of Maltzahn's cast pieces;

the museum director, sans wife, deep in conversation with the representatives from the Landmarks Office;

the castle's side wing—Patočka, Nordanc (archives); Hanna, Karla (public relations)—is grouped together; two of the masons, one of them the chimney setter, have already discovered the buffet; Jirse is missing; Pepi?;

the museum staff; Qvietone, pale, leg in a cast, makes a point of standing off to one side;

the younger public librarian steals glances at the castle director; the older is curious about Orten's lecture, given the masses of material she has lent out; the manager of the Ram, wearing a hat, waves excitedly to Podol as he appears on the stairs with the others.

Orten trips over a carpet rod on the stairs, but Podol catches him. Maltzahn also takes hold of him under the arm, which arouses the attention of everyone at the top. Patera, shlepping the tape recorder, is not noticed.

For one brief moment, Podol—who keeps having to shake one new hand after the other—lets go of Orten by mistake. Maltzahn finds him in the next room, trying to pull the lever on the emergency exit; this discovery does not do their friendship of many years any good. Orten is brought back and Podol thrusts the speech, which he has kept safe until now, into his hand: "Jan, you can do it."

Suddenly they let go of Orten, who holds on to the speech and tumbles backward, but manages to prop himself on Maltzahn's uncomfortable object "Tremor I"; the alloy holds.

The silly giggling, the search for the start of his speech, and the I-can't-see-anything game start all over again. The pages flutter to the floor, Podol and Maltzahn gather them up, try to put them in order; a slow process since they are not numbered. Now that he has his guards busy, Orten sees his chance. He elbows his way to the exit, past "Tremor III," presses the button on the tape recorder, which the considerate Patera has set up, and before anyone can stop him he vanishes with a bound down the stairs.

". . . from his diary: The tragedy of my life consists in my having been created in the likeness of my inner self. Raphael was right in castigating me on the stairs beside his *School of Athens,* saying that I look the misanthropic, gloomy doubter so that no one might mistake me. They do not disturb me in my loneliness. . . ."

Having shaken his pursuers, Orten can sleep it off.

". . . some of the frescoes I have painted thus far have changed their colors. At first I did not wish to believe my eyes. I thought the light was playing a trick on me, and decided to wait until the sun stood higher above the horizon. The morning sun was far too merciful; I had not even noticed most of the mildewed spots. . . . I am weary and exhausted. I began this work without enthusiasm and it proceeds only very slowly. It is not my craft to paint frescoes. When I think of the wall, my head swims and I feel chilled. I have never painted a wall before and I fear that I shall never be finished. When I think of how pointless my current task is, my throat constricts; I am afraid I shall suffocate in the murmuring night. My only hope is to return to sculpture. . . . In my coarse clothes, with unkempt hair and eyes stinging from the paint, I am not the man for any public position. People tell me I look half the fool, in tatters and living like an animal. My family . . .

"I feel as if my body were shrinking more each day. My neck has grown thicker at the front, as if I had a goiter. My right shoulder is higher than the left; my head is wrenched back. If I must speak to someone, I cannot keep my eyes in a normal position. People advise me to rest for a few days, to pause in my labors. I cannot, however, separate myself from my wall. Each day I hasten to my spatula and colors, and then feel immediately better. As soon as my body has taken its accustomed position on the scaffold, it no longer tortures me."

When Marie calls two days later—after years of waiting and without anyone's informing Jirse about it, the telephone in the hallway is the chief benefit of the centennial celebration—Orten picks up the receiver for the first time. "Oh, it's you? Do you want to know how I'm feeling, too?"

"Okay, how are you feeling?"

"I survived, thanks."

"You're welcome." She is about to hang up.

"Wait, you're not calling about the exhibition?"

"The Smetana Exhibition? I wasn't here last weekend. I was going to ask if you wanted to go to the movies, *Mr. Arne's Treasure*. But maybe you're tired, you sound like it."

"No, no, I'm feeling fantastic!"

The film's finale: Black against the white background, the procession behind the funeral bier, and six figures veiled in white who carry it, meanders toward the frozen lake. In the background the dark hull of the ship locked in the ice and waiting for thaw.

"I feel very good today, with you along, Marie."

She first has to get used to the light outside. "Because the end is so beautiful, so three-dimensional and sculptural, and because I wasn't there for your speech, Jan?" She switches to first names, too.

"No, you made me feel so awfully uneasy the first time; you were so sanctimonious." He takes her hand, in which she holds a crumpled handkerchief, kisses her knuckles, and smells the same faint odor of hospital he has noticed when she bends over to him and wants to comment about the pictures flickering on the screen. The waiter at the Oriole is pleased to observe the progress in their relationship. There's no quibbling with Moravian wines.

"You made quite an impression on me, too. Along with your loud friend who loves to laugh at his own jokes, and the show-off with the camera around his neck."

"He happened to be taking pictures."

"You all bully the little old man."

"He's not as feeble as he looks. He's kept pace for five years now, when others would have given up perhaps. You don't have to feel sorry for him."

"And how about you?"

"You can feel sorry for me," he says, leaning his head on her shoulder. "I'm a poor stammerer. I'm glad you weren't there."

"Don't get your spirits up too fast. I've read your speech. It's making the rounds of Friedland. Michelangelo's diary has become the hot tip. I borrowed a copy this afternoon after we talked on the phone."

"From whom?"

"The girl next door has a carbon copy."

"That must be Horský's girlfriend, he had her type it up. He's apparently never heard the word 'copyright.' "

"I liked it a lot."

"You should take a look at the exhibition, without the brouhaha. Mainly Stanislav's things; the rest isn't worth much. Let's go tomorrow, I'll pick you up."

"I'm working the night shift. I have to be there by five."

"Then we'll go in the morning, that way we won't run into anyone."

"I don't know, it's too mannered for me somehow." Marie is standing in front of Podolský's oil painting "In the Rain," where two girls are running through slanting strands of water, in a crouch, pinafores stuck to their bodies, big feet in the grass.

"Take a look around, it's the best thing here."

"Maybe here, but in terms of . . ."

"In terms of what? Don't start in with 'measuring it against international standards'! He definitely measures up, he's even better maybe."

"Somewhat too stylized, don't you think? A dash of naïve art, but with the perfect precision of Czech technique."

"No, that's a very superficial judgment. Stanislav is an artist, what you call his technique is a well-thought-out composition, not just a talent for painting and drawing. Look at the façade and you can immediately spot his work—it's bolder, grander, freer than the rest, including my own. He has a sure sense of proportion, of movement, color—and it's evident not just in the coffers. Come visit his atelier, and I'll show you a couple of paintings he did at sixteen. It's all there already—the light, the plasticity, the harmony. He has it, that's all, even if sometimes he carries on like an old peasant uncle. Take this drawing, for instance, those are legs you can grab hold of, you can feel in your fingers how round those calves are."

"The pasterns are too thick for my taste," she says, laughing, "but the drawing is beautiful. He seems obsessed with legs. This plaster sculpture here, sticking up in the air, always the same contours."

"Those are his wife's legs."

"Both these versions of 'Woman Combing Her Hair'—is that her, too?"

"Yes, they all are."

Marie thinks of the young tour guide she has often seen with Podol. "And where are your sculptures?"

"Don't bother. There's always something lacking when I do a figure. I plan them with the mistakes. I try to use the error I've made, that I've started with, to take the error and scratch it out, so it gets smaller and smaller. Not the error, not the mistake—but less and less mass, which creates more and more mistakes. Something is lacking, the right treatment of the mass. Michelangelo knows that a statue is waiting for him inside every stone, and it definitely is for him, but it evades me— he manages to take a stone someone has already spoiled and pull a David out of it! That's true creativity. But there is no form waiting for me, only miscarriages, because I don't know how I should take hold of it, I always approach it so clumsily. I know that it knows about me, and that it will do everything it can to escape me. I take an ashlar, a fine, undamaged stone, and it's there, locked up somewhere inside, but I miss the mark and let it elude me."

"Would you rather it were something like this?" She points to a female bust by Maltzahn; the neck and head are silver, balanced atop golden breasts; titled "Anita." "I'd like to see your absconded forms."

"I don't have any stone here, just plaster."

"Did they all elude you, too?"

"No, they weren't accepted in the show. The plasters are upstairs."

They walk past butterflies and deathwatch beetles, on through the mineralogy department, where Orten stops to look at stones; past fish and reptiles, which have been partly removed to make way for art. The last case contains a mummified crocodile with eggs in its abdominal cavity and about thirty babies; next to it hangs Patera's gouache "Plowing." Pink assemblages of ceramics alternate with Patera's early paintings, mostly in browns. Orten's bulging, hollow pedestals and bundles of iron rods pasted together with plaster complement the decay of the landscape apparent in the photographers' work. They divide the room into little niches of futility. "A cemetery of statues," the newspaper called it; the critic asked what had become of the gravity and sureness of Orten's earlier sculptures.

Marie is impressed, she had not imagined they would be so disquieting; the mayhem is anything but inept. "You do that intentionally," she says petulantly.

Orten gives a short laugh.

At the other end, where the mammals begin—with the marsupials—one of Orten's contorted planes marks the end of the exhibition. A mother is standing nearby with her child, who is looking at the animals, but the woman is disconcerted by the cumbersome plaster figure and is trying to understand art. The title "Wombat" is no help; maybe a friend, or did it have something to do with "Combat"—a petrified warrior, a gravestone erected for a fallen soldier?

The child asks about the stuffed creature next to it. The mother reads "Standing Figure," at the same time pointing at an opossum. Now she turns around doubtfully to look at Orten's gravestone, and reads aloud the small print: " 'The wombat looks clumsier than he is. Being a dull-witted and indolent fellow, he is not easily upset. In captivity, the stupid, passive fellow is quite content with a diet of greens, carrots, fruits, and grain, and if one gives him a little milk, he is particularly delighted.'

" 'In describing the wombat, the naturalist Brehm appears to have let the language of anthropomorphization run away with him.' " Marie reads this final sentence aloud. "Above all else, it's quite unfair—it applies much better to your sculpture than to the animal."

The woman realizes that Orten is responsible for both the art and the fact that the animals have been removed, and pulls the child on. He stops again in front of the platypus.

Orten is glad they have finally seen it all and wants to go, when Marie discovers little red dots trying to hold on to the sunlit head and shoulders of his giant female "Standing Figure": *Deviant dwarves stand, modal dwarves sit.* Looking more closely, she notices insects running up and down the back of the figure and then striking out across the hall to the offices of the department heads. Orten and Marie follow the path and find the insects scattered about on loose pages of foreign-language newspapers lying outside the door of the entomological department—one enclave has gathered on *Oggi,* others on *Pravda* and *Dagens Nyheter, Ogonyok* is covered with them, and on the *Financial Times* they are several layers thick. "They're crazy about it," Qvietone declares from behind his desk, stands up, and comes lurching over. This all strikes Marie as very weird, and he notices it, but goes on playing the poor invalid. "Would you help me a little here, please. Actually they're not supposed to be running around out in the hall." He bends down awkwardly and pulls the mess over the threshold into his room. "Someone always leaves the door open and the newspapers get blown into the hall, and then the cleaning lady complains."

"Only the cleaning lady?" Orten asks. "Your bugs are already trying to climb the sculptures on exhibit, quite successfully."

"They're firebugs, *Pyrrhocoris apterus*. That's interesting; which objects do they prefer?"

Marie and Orten look at one another.

"Well, okay. Actually they belong in their containers." Qvietone shakes the bugs back into their breeding jars; several cling to the backs of the newspapers, crawl along his hand, fall onto the desk, creep in among his papers. Marie looks away. "When are they taking off the cast?"

"Next week." Qvietone is concentrating on his firebugs. "Here, each glass is lined with a different newspaper. Most of them were very hard to get, they're all from different dates, but age doesn't play a role. Just look at these jars here. The same animals, but they look quite different. Much paler. And here the excrement is especially heavy: *World Literature Today*, Norman, Oklahoma. And these are completely stunted, stuck in the larval stage, although the same age as those on *Pravda*."

"What newspaper is that?" Orten asks.

"The *Boston Globe*, but they react the same way to the *New York Times, Science,* and *Scientific American*—to whom I'll be sending the results."

"So the inflammatory propaganda of the capitalist press prevents even firebugs from growing up healthy," Orten concludes.

"It's not all that simple, the *London Times* or *Nature* are inactive, but pink paper must be downright salutary, look at how splendidly they're doing on the *Financial Times,* they love it."

"Probably because of the color." Marie is determined not to let Qvietone belabor one of his theories, but Orten has begun to get interested.

"And how do they do with *Rudé Právo?*

"About the same as with the Slovak *Pravda,* or the *Mladá fronta.* Inactive. The same goes for *Lidová demokracie, Práce, Večerní Praha*. On some, the bugs do better, like *Život stranya—Life of the Party—* they multiply quickly, but not outside the standard norms. I have a Finnish paper, the *Turun Ylipisto*—an in-house organ of the University of Turku, it has the same effect on firebugs. Which is also true of other European and Japanese newspapers, although the bugs do make some differentiations—between *Osservatore Romano* and *Il Manifesto,* for instance.

"So there are red bugs and black clerical bugs," Orten observes.

"No, these are all the same reddish-black." Qvietone is not about to be deterred.

"And so what is the cause?" Marie is growing impatient.

"I have thought about it: paste, paper, or color? I think I have the answer now. Paper contains a chemical that has an effect similar to a juvenile hormone. The animals remain larvae or develop to a larvalike stage and die before sexual maturity. A kind of reverse neoteny. The active paper comes primarily from American balsam firs. In that sense, it can also affect the Communist press in America." (To Orten.)

"And the *Friedland Echo,* have you tried it?" Orten nods toward the open newspaper on the desk, where the bad review of his exhibit is underlined in red. He recalls the signs that were switched, his "Standing Figure" as a "Wombat"; he now understands why the firebugs ended up doing gymnastics on his sculptures in particular. As if it wouldn't have sufficed to leave well enough alone. "What did you smear on the plaster? Beer?" He takes Marie by the elbow. "Come on, we're leaving."

Qvietone stands forsaken amid his jars, watching them go. He feels like the deceived charlatan Hermann in the novel by his favorite lepidopterist, whom he admires as an expert on mimicry. Orten is Humbert Humbert perhaps: "Both are neurotic scoundrels, but there is a pleasant path in paradise where Humbert is allowed to walk in the twilight once a year; Hermann, however, will never be given a parole to leave hell."

NINE

In the castle courtyard, Pepi is petting Nordanc's cat, which stretches under her hand and presses against the hot stones of the portal, a purring heraldic beast. Karla watches the way it fits into the bossage, extending neck and tail—"As if she wanted to win the prize for longest cat in Friedland."

"She'd win, too," Pepi says. "I have a black one at home, with white paws and a white spot on her chest, she's about half this size. Look how thick her fur is, and the way it crackles—and the color. We had a white one once, Kopra, from Kopretina—holy cow, what a beast. She could leap seven feet and snatch a goose from the pantry shelf. Do you think this one could manage it, too?"

"Sure, any cat that big has a lot of strength."

The tabby draws itself up and disappears around the corner. A black cat that has been sitting on the other side of the gravel path slips under the carriage-house gate in pursuit.

Nordanc emerges from the doorway, holding one hand up against the sun and looking about blindly.

"Ah, Mr. New Archivist, settled in?"

"Yes, thanks, miss"—they're worst at that age, actually at any age; smart-alecky and loud. "Have you seen my cat perhaps?"

"A big tabby?" Pepi tries to make sure the cats have a good head start.

"Yes, that's Max."

"You needn't worry, your Max already has a playmate, Fousek, the tom from the brewery, they're getting along quite well."

"That's what I was afraid of. Where are they getting along?"

"In the carriage house at the moment."

Nordanc hurries around the corner; the delighted girls watch him go.

"The cat makes a perfectly normal impression," Karla says.

"But his Czech is very good, even if he sometimes gets the genders mixed up."—Pepi.

The carriage house smells of oil and hay. In one corner is Jirse's lawn mower, about half the size of a threshing machine, a rusty monster, that he uses every two weeks to ruin both the lawn and the hearing of the nondeaf in the neighborhood. He won't let anyone else drive it, mowing is his prerogative. Jirse has screwed a brace for his leg onto it, making it so easy for him to use that he usually circles around the façade in a drunken state, paying no attention to whether he missed any grass on the previous pass. So far there have been no casualties, and Podol has allowed himself to be restrained. "But not for much longer," he assures Orten. Next time he's going to strew sand in the motor or rip off the leg stirrup—"Then let him figure out how to get up on it."

"He'll manage even then," Orten says. "He's not going to let anyone take his toy away from him. If he can't find a hook for his leg, he'll drag it behind him and plow."

Nordanc, who has experienced Jirse's mowing once now already, considers what might be done here. He takes a closer look at the machine. Impressed by its size and the extent of the deterioration, he feels a certain respect for the designers who came up with such contraptions back in the thirties—a museum piece. He doesn't have the heart to experiment with sugar in the gas line.

He hears something rustling; he has learned to differentiate by now, and spots Max lurking against the wall at the far end, her ears perked up, her tail stropping the stone floor smooth; sees her give a tense shudder and spring up onto the wall—the high squeaks of a mouse. The cat jumps back down and lets its prey loose, crouches again, waits until the fleeing mouse is just far enough away and makes another pounce, grabbing it in both paws and tossing it in the air. The mouse tumbles through space, Max jumps and snags it in midair, plays a little catch, then lies down and licks her paws. The battered mouse recovers enough to make a run for its hole, where the cat is busy with personal hygiene. Without turning her head, she thrusts a paw in the opening and pulls the mouse back out, tosses it aside and goes on licking. The mouse has nowhere to flee and tries to reach its hole again. As long as it just runs about, Max pays it almost no attention, but the moment it tries to disappear into the hole, there is the cat's paw. The mouse can only drag itself painfully forward now; its squeaks have ceased. Max takes it carefully between her teeth and carries it to the hole, wants it to make another try. The mouse creeps slowly into the darkness, bleeding at the neck, one leg torn off; the cat pulls it back out.

Max waits, raps her prey a few times with a balled-up paw, shoves the victim of her deadly game into the crack and immediately pulls it out again. The mouse gets smaller and smaller, a bloody lump of fur.

"Max, come here!"

The cat first tries to shove her prey back into the hole, but as Nordanc approaches, she grabs the mouse and slinks back into a dark corner behind Jirse's lawn thresher. The brewery cat, who has been watching the whole time, crouched near the carriage-house door, runs after her.

"Felines are characterized by a crack instinct." Behind Nordanc stands a young man, tall, slender, with a crutch.

"What did you say?"

He looks even better in the light; and the cast looks sporty, too.

"I mean that cats like to fish for prey in holes, as you've just witnessed. They prefer to capture it in its hiding place, even with fat mice running free all around. But until now the serval was the only feline I knew of that stuffs its prey into a hole in order to pull it out again."

"Are you a biologist? Do you do research on cats?"

"My field is insects, cats have been rather thoroughly studied. If I were to specialize in them, I would be interested in their relationship with their prey, and vice versa."

"And vice versa?"

"Yes, there are variant behaviors among the animals preyed upon. There are some that survive their acquaintance with predators."

"Are they that good at hiding?"

"No, on the contrary. Only if they don't hide do they have a chance, slight though it is."

They walk out of the carriage house. "You'll have to explain that to me. Do you work here in town?"

"I used to work right here at the castle. I had the same job you now have. My name is Qvietone."

"Then I know you. Nordanc." He extends a hand. "Patočka told me about you. He thinks highly of you."

"He's probably the only person here who does."

"No, I think Podolský does as well."

"What has he said to you?"

"Nothing, he just laughs."

"Yes, he's always laughing." Qvietone is disappointed.

"I saw you at the opening," Nordanc says, giving it some thought. "You left in the middle of the speech, although it was good, the comparison worked."

"It seemed ridiculous, listening to a tape recorder."

"Yes, that was funny, but you soon forgot it was a tape."

"I didn't stick around that long," Qvietone says.

"Would you like to join me for a beer at the brewery? You could give me a few tips about the archives," Nordanc suggests.

"Don't you want to retrieve your cat?"

"No, I'll leave her to her—what did you call it?"

"Crack instinct."

Nordanc muses on the term as they cross the courtyard.

"He bears a nasty resemblance to Jirse," Podol declares, watching from the scaffold as Qvietone stomps past.

"Nordanc, too, just look at the way he walks," Maltzahn adds. "Sort of knock-kneed, and in tight jeans, but I found out he will exchange currency for you on the black market. All the same, I think we'd better keep a good watch on our young biologist."

"He can watch out for himself," Orten says. "Once he starts in with his theories and bugs, Nordanc will be looking for an exit real soon."

"Qvietone is a little crazy, but he's got stamina. And Andy is okay, even if you don't like his legs," Podol says.

"I don't know, is it true that he—I mean," Patera searches for words. "You see, next week my two youngest girls are going to visit, I've already invited them."

"I don't think you need to be worried about your daughters, Václav," Orten suggests. "They have nothing to fear there, but it might be a good idea to lock them away from Olbram."

Maltzahn, who has felt uneasy around Orten ever since the opening, puts up with it. "Go ahead and make your jokes."

"Well, you have to admit Václav is worried for nothing."

"But what does that have to do with me?"

"It would be more reasonable for him to be concerned about you."

"Well, he isn't."

"Not at all," Patera says.

"Not yet." Orten gives his bucket a meaningful stir.

"Jan, what is all this? I've known Olbram for twenty years now, we're friends, he can remember when Pavlína was born. Besides, he's forty-five himself already." Patera is getting himself in deeper and deeper.

"What are you talking about!" Maltzahn is upset now. "He makes a joke and you fall right into it! This job is turning us into complete idiots—staring at this wall day in, day out, daubing away, and going for each other's throats." He slams his spatula into the sand and climbs down. "I need a drink."

The snake on the sgraffito he has started still has no head. Podol interrupts what he is doing and puts the finishing scratches on the snake before the mortar can dry. Then he goes back to his dragon, modifies it into a kind of gecko, which saves him from having to give it scales.

"The rat hid at first, but ventured out more and more frequently, even nipping at the golden cat's heels. Over time a kind of bonding developed. It became a sort of pet rat, even joined the cat in eating the rats she had killed."

"That's disgusting."

"Yes, I notice that I, too, speak of the rat's brazen behavior, while sparing the cat any criticism whatever. And if the cat has a name—this golden cat was called Tilly, or think of your own cat with its mouse a while ago—one has yet a different view of the matter. What was your cat's name?"

"Max."

"So it's a tom."

"No, a female."

Qvietone looks at Nordanc. "Aha. A she-cat. At any rate, Tilly tolerated the rat, they slept together, the rat moved from its hole to Tilly's box and on occasion would even chase the cat away from her food bowl. If other rats were let into the cage, Tilly would resolutely hunt

149

them down, never confusing them with her own rat. The rat felt totally secure with her, would eat other rats she killed. . . ."

"You already mentioned that."

"Yes, and shared everything with the cat, who obviously differentiated between it and all the others, even if it was sitting right beside one that was given her to eat. It moved about quite freely in the cage, following the cat about—it chose her for its pal, rather than other rats. Perhaps the rat smelled different, too, more like cat, but the decisive factor was that it kept calm, showed no fear. And so was no longer prey in the cat's eyes."

"How did the experiment turn out?"

"They separated them. Then, three months later, the rat was put back in the cage. It had grown very large by then, and the cat no longer remembered it. All the same she showed some hesitancy at the start, did not immediately begin the hunt. Then the rat took refuge in the cat's box, and perhaps it remembered something, because it didn't try to defend itself when the cat attacked."

"How long were they together?"

"Four months."

"What were the scientists actually out to prove? Which had the longer memory? First prize—the winner gets eaten. And you went along with it?"

"I'm an entomologist. Interspecific behavior among insects is not very pronounced, only at the lowest levels—parasitism. Come by the museum and I'll show you a few of my specimens. And as far as the archive goes . . ."

"That can wait." Nordanc would like to have some other topic besides insects for their next meeting. "I told Patočka I was just going to fetch Max; he'll be waiting for me."

"Would you give this back to Orten? I don't want to disturb him." Qvietone pulls a tattered book from his jacket pocket. "He lent it to me when I was in the hospital."

Maltzahn is sitting at the door, staring into his beer. He looks weary and gives only a silent nod as they pass by.

As Podol is walking down the corridor to see Hanna that evening, he hears a couple of dull thuds coming from the room next to hers. He unlatches the door and sees Nordanc in boxing shorts and gloves, bare-chested, punching away at a leather bag filled with sand. Nordanc is slight of build, but quick.

"Good footwork."

Nordanc turns around, his red hair plastered to his forehead; he really is knock-kneed, but he has broad shoulders.

"I didn't even hear you." The sack, which is suspended from a ceiling beam, bumps against him lightly. Nordanc lands a right hook.

"Let me try."

Nordanc pulls off the gloves, Podol forces his hands into the small openings; the leather is damp and smells of sweat; after a couple of punches they feel right. "I haven't tried this for twenty years at least. Are they yours?" he asks, giving Nordanc his gloves back. "I have bigger hands, but the gloves work okay. Where did you get the bag?"

"From a friend, the gloves, too. He left it all behind when he moved out." Nordanc lays them on the table, next to his blue ring.

"Do you collect souvenirs each time someone leaves you? How old are you?"

"Thirty-five."

"Those are good gloves." Podol rubs the soft leather again and gives Nordanc a puzzled look. "What made you stay here, really?"

"At first only because it had taken so long to get the papers and it would have been a shame after all the trouble I had gone to." Nordanc grins.

"Did you get a resident's permit?"

"For one year, that was allowed in exceptional cases."

"What sort of an exception were you?"

"I don't really know. Zdeněk—that was my friend—he knew somebody. Nationality has nothing to do with it."

"Luxembourg? And you could stay a whole year without having to exchange a certain amount every day?"

"It was done as a lump sum. They wouldn't have paid any of it back if I had left before the year was out. I had to go into quite a bit of debt to do it. When I arrived and found out that Zdeněk was gone, I wanted to turn right around and head for Switzerland, to beat him up. He really hadn't intended to deceive me, things just turned out that way. A letter he had sent to West Berlin finally found its way back to me, saying I should wait for him there, because of the political situation, but I had already packed. Besides, the letter didn't reach me until three months later."

"Did you ever see him again?"

"No, he was no longer at the return address. I did hear that he had continued on to Canada."

"And you've been here ever since?"

"I was furious at first, wanted to leave right away, but then so much happened. We were all living on the street—the occupying troops on one side, the people on the other, very tense, but courteous and alert, cheerful even, because they stuck together. For one whole year. They had something like the privilege of fools, it was catching, I've never experienced anything like it in the West. The Russians suspicious, uncertain, worried—sixteen-year-olds, plugs of tobacco clenched in their teeth, when people would ask what they were doing here, they broke into tears. Most of them didn't even know where they were. And the Czechs, desperate as they were, felt sorry for them. I saw one woman give a kid's buzz-cut head a pat."

"Sure, the Czechs have always been patient with occupation troops. 'The Republic of Czechoslovakia Has Again Preserved Peace in Europe!' But after a year they ran out of jokes and came to their senses, wanted to look reality in the eye. It was in the newsreels, they had to smear it on their daily bread. And you stayed for that?"

"I received notice that part of the remaining money would be paid back if I left, and I thought about it, but by then it was no longer possible. I had been to the movies, in January of '69, it was cold and damp when I came out. *Onibaba,* a dreadful film, two women murder solitary warriors and trade the armor for rice; they even beat a dog to death out in a field and eat it. I started down Wenceslaus Square in a kind of daze, and a few steps ahead was a small group of people standing around a piece of paper nailed to a tree: 'A half hour ago a young man burned himself to death here; his name is unknown.'

"A few days later I was coming back from work; I worked as a waiter at a place up in Letná Park, where Zdeněk had worked; about forty people were walking down the street carrying a sign: Jan Palach Died of His Burns Today. Passersby silently joined them, we walked up the Letenská, past Powder Bridge, to the castle, about two hundred of us by that time. Near the wall of the castle gardens, a Russian tank turned its gun toward us, but not a soul was to be seen. We got as far as the barrier outside the riding school. A Czech soldier was standing there freezing, told us we couldn't go in. The people just stood there, they were all so still. We didn't want anything really, just for someone to read our sign, the government was back in place anyway. One fellow said he would go inside and get someone. The soldier let him pass. We waited. After half an hour, people started drifting away. Some other guy said he would check. Neither one came back. Probably they just went through to the other side, down past St. Nicholas Church and on home. What could they have said to us? We didn't even know if anyone was there, there were no lights on in the castle windows. It got dark, it was about fifteen degrees, not all that cold for Prague, but damp. It was so quiet up there, foggy, we had forgotten about the tank, too, that somebody was inside it. The soldier hadn't said a word to us, and was relieved by a new one. Then the cold and pointlessness of it all prevailed, and we scattered. I left with the last group—four guys and two girls, we went to a bar, we were all freezing. One of the guys came home with me then; we just sat there, couldn't get warm.

"I went to the funeral, too, hundreds of flowers, in winter, when you can never find any in the shops here—wreaths, from politicians, too, one from Smrkovský, I liked him. But they had decided to keep Kriegel, who was the best of the lot, in Moscow, he wouldn't sign; he died not long after. Then they dug him up, Palach I mean, stole the body one night, so that there'd be an end to all the candles and the silent crowds at the grave.

"Overnight, people started calling Red Soldier's Square, in front of the School of Philosophy, Jan Palach Square. The sign on the Umprum, the Academy of Arts, was changed, the tram drivers would call out the name; after a few weeks it all stopped again. But to this day, the most beautiful square in Luxembourg is called Jan Palach Square."

"I didn't know that. I don't know much about Luxembourg."

"I even have a picture of it. Wait, here it is." Nordanc pulls a color photo from his cupboard: he is leaning, slim and laughing, against a wall, above him the name Jan Palach.

Podol hands it back to him without comment.

"So then I got an extension of my resident's permit. First had to go to Berlin, worked odd jobs for six weeks to get the money. And ever since I spend two months out of the year there, so I can stay on here."

"And in between you exchange currency on the black market." Podol is not about to let himself be touched by the tale.

"You got that from Maltzahn. He asked me first, people come up

to you on every street corner. For foreigners, the official exchange rate
is one to four, which is realistic. But when Czechs want to travel, the
state will give them only twenty marks, at one to ten. That's where
the black market comes in. Some people will offer you thirteen or
fifteen, just so they'll have a little money to spend abroad. It's absurd.
I've always sold at one to eight, and then only if I was broke. I'm not
allowed to work full time here. Maltzahn was hoping to get it that
cheap, too, but with a guy like him, with all his deals in Prague, I'm
not about to play the altruist. That irked him. Besides, I don't want
to get started with that here in Friedland. If at all, then only in Prague,
on weekends, if I need something there. I don't need anything
here. Which isn't to say that anytime you want you can't slip me the
word, or Orten."

"I don't need that junk from the Tuzex," Podol says. "I don't like Nes-
café, even if the housewives do fight to get it. I'd rather drink my black
Turkish coffee, dregs and all. We'll have to go a couple of rounds next
time, each with one glove." He punches the leather bag with his bare
hand, and rubs his knuckles. "Now I know what happened to that
sand in the first shipment. I wondered why they would bother sending
us half-empty sacks if they were going to make us wait anyway."

Maltzahn knocks on the door of the director's apartment. The children
are already asleep. Marcela opens up; behind her is Horský, who sticks
a box of chocolates in the pocket of his coat as he pulls it on. "I'm
terribly sorry, Mr. Maltzahn, you've come a few minutes too early.
But I was just leaving." He puts his other arm through the sleeve and
smiles tactfully.

"More like a little late. I've been meaning to speak to you for some
time now." Maltzahn steps over the threshold. Marcela gives him a
worried look, she's never seen him like this.

"Last week Podolský's frottages mildewed, not to mention our personal items. It took him two days to make new ones, and two days
without him on the scaffold mean one week lost for us. And we have
a schedule to meet. We've reminded you about those rooms several
times now. And you promised to speed up the work. But nothing has
happened so far. And we've got some other things to take care of
besides." Maltzahn closes the door behind him.

. . .

Nordanc flexes his knees and jabs with his left: lands three blows to the peritoneum, spleen, and carotid artery, countered by one to the solar plexus; he covers himself, jumps back, gives the leather a chance and takes a hard blow to the shoulder, moves back in, an injured welterweight, presses and counters with one hand, gets it right between the eyes, staggers, catches himself, and strikes back; taut stomach, youthful—Qvietone, his fan behind the ropes—he wins.

Wonders if he should visit the museum tomorrow. Better to wait a day.

Most of the bugs have been caught. Small groups have congregated along the windows and on the flowerpots, but they're no longer running about. The museum director has dragged the maquette into his office—the opening ceremonies have left it looking disreputable, with wobbling high rises and broken-off model trees.

"He'll spend days now gluing it back together." Qvietone is wearing black corduroy slacks, so new they shimmer like satin, a thin burgundy sweater, and sneakers, on both feet. He is just giving Martin, the young metallographer, a demonstration of the bossa nova; two years ago he competed in the junior division of the Latin American dance finals.

"When did they take the cast off?"

"Yesterday. Six weeks of pure torture. I threw my old pants away."

Nordanc looks around. "So this is where you work? What's in those jars?"

Qvietone explains to him the results of his *Pyrrhocoris apterus* breeding program on foreign-language newspapers, the inhibitory effect of various kinds of paper on the growth of firebugs. Nordanc reads the names; the last one is *Berlingske Tidene.* "Have you tried German newspapers?"

"Yes, I've got more of those than anything else; they get left on the trains, even though they check at the border. But I've discontinued those experiments, I don't have enough jars, but here are my notes: *Spandauer Volksblatt, Falter, Neue Zürcher Zeitung*—inactive."

"*Neues Deutschland, Volksstimme, Luzerner Nachrichten, Der Spiegel*—bugs thrived.

"*Kronenzeitung, Die Welt, Frankfurter Allgemeine*—the paper obviously promotes the development of the Malpighian tubes, especially glossy magazine paper. That could then also influence the numbers of intestinal symbionts, especially among cicadas. One cannot call them parasites, since both parties profit, and there can be only a limited number of endosymbionts. The five-spotted cicada, with its six forms of ovosymbionts, deserves a special study; hexasymbiosis is rare. The problem is less the relationship with the host than the compatibility among the symbionts; when a new one is acquired, an old one may perish. Over time, the elimination and co-option of various candidates in this particular cicada has produced a stabile symbiotic stock, all in precise interactive proportions—no comparison to an invasion of parasitic bacteria or yeasts."

"You don't say."

"Polysymbionts are remarkable in general," Qvietone continues. "The surplus of guests produces superstructures—shields, knobby growths, pseudantennae, a lantern structure on the head of some fulgorids—living eccentrics, all without function, pure luxuriances."

"So it's a kind of zoological equilibration?" Nordanc asks. "At the bottom the heavy yeasts, above them the self-sufficient infusoria and atop the pyramid a green euglena, with eye spot and flagellar whip?" He is amazed that he has remembered the names.

"The symbionts do not themselves form the building blocks, but rather the plethora of excretions from the nutrients at the symbionts' disposal," Qvietone corrects him. "Life's abundance, if you will; they have simply too much available energy."

"Muscle-bound."

"So to speak, and that's why humpbacks form—growths, curiosities, heraldic markings. The older the host species, the more symbionts it nourishes and the greater the tendency to luxuriances. Indigent insects have to content themselves with stink glands."

"And what relevance does this have to your newspapers?"

"Newspapers have no relevance. Why do you ask?"

Nordanc looks at Qvietone. "You write your name with a *v?*" He pages through a reprint from the *Annotationes zoologicae et botanicae* of the National Museum in Bratislava. "I thought your name was Quitone, with a *Qu.*"

"It was at one time, at least when my ancestors arrived from France in the sixteenth century. In the course of the national revival, one of my great-great-grandfathers began to spell it Czech fashion, 'Kwie-tone.' Two generations later someone in the family applied to have the original spelling restored, but a bureaucrat made a mistake; the poor fellow didn't know French. Since then, my mother, who married into the family, has periodic fits of francophilia and talks about 'contamination,' despite the betrayal of '38 and the hangover from colonialism that she paid for dearly in Tunisia and Algeria. Sometimes she's a real racist. I annoy her by using the phonetic form 'Květoň' in my letters, or 'Kwietone' in Old Bohemian style, and by planning a project for combating bilharziasis at its place of origin."

"That worm disease in Egypt?"

"Not just in Egypt, it's endemic throughout Africa, wherever there is stagnant water. In Ghana it occurs in the dammed-up waters of Lake Volta. Ever since the construction of the Aswan Dam put an end to floods, which used to allow the banks of the Nile to dry out once they retreated, the snails that are washed up no longer perish. They are multiplying to such an extent that already two-thirds of the population of Egypt is infected with flukes. And how proud the Russians were of their miracle dam!"

"Do snails carry the flukes?"

"They are the mediating hosts, without them the schistosoma larva could not develop."

"Schistosoma?"

"Hermaphroditic flukes: the male carries the female in a fold of its stomach, which is why at one time they were described as having a 'divided body'; they are helminths, primitive trematodes, compared to which the cicada is highly evolved. I have given much thought to how the dry periods in the river's old cycle might be replaced—one can only attack the snails; the schistosomata are too small. Chemical control can be begun only after infection, as in the biltricide project, otherwise it does not have the required effect—copper sulfates or pentachloro-phenol, for instance, kills the snails, but also poisons the entire river-bed. Besides, chemical agents are always the last resort, it must be possible to find biological ones. Even though one can treat individuals infected with the flukes, most peasants go on shitting in the irrigation ditches. And the urban sewers, which empty untreated into the rivers, take care of the rest; the fluke eggs find their way to water one way or the other. First they had to put up those enamel signs—Spitting on the Floor Is Forbidden!—in all the railroad stations and public places, post offices for instance, before tuberculosis abated enough for antibiotics to have an effect. All efforts come to naught because of poor public hygiene. Schistosomiasis, that is bilharziasis, has been reduced as much as it has in Japan only because early on they began to treat peasant latrines with chloride of lime. But enough chemistry; it never works without education. Freud was still totally oblivious, he spat on the stairs just as he pleased, and let the cleaning women wipe up the oysters. But he thought he knew all about women: 'What does the female want?' "

"Your mother's racism apparently made its impression on you."

"She's right about that. But whenever she starts planning my future, I have to laugh."

"Do you have another solution then?"

"There are fish that specialize in snails for their diet: puffers, Tetraodontidae. Unfortunately, the African species live in brackish water, like the Nile puffer, which would be unable to live behind the dam, or they are too small to crack the hard mollusk shells, like the Congo puffer. It's much the same with the South American species. But the Southeast Asian puffers are good snail exterminators, and can live equally as well in sweet or brackish water. One need only determine which species are the easiest to breed and introduce."

"Wouldn't they disturb the river's ecological balance?"

"What ecological balance? No one paid attention to the effect Aswan would have. When it comes to showing off technology, there are no ecological scruples. The fish would have to be studied first, in tanks of about two cubic meters, for which one would have to consult with a lab team, or at least an engineer, to work out the technical setup—aeration, water temperature, warm in this case; variation of salinity, moving gradually toward sweet water. One problem lies in the fact that so far only a few species of puffer fish breed in captivity. Which would mean a second phase in small ponds or pools in Egypt. I have applied for a grant, the project should be sponsored within the framework of some economic development program. They don't have any better solution, but it will just be shelved for a while, until they finally manage to lose it. I still have a copy, and then I'll remind them. It wouldn't even be that expensive, compared with other things they've tried. If need be, the experiment could be financed with UNESCO money."

"If you still have a copy, I'll take it with me. I'm going to West Berlin next month and I'll submit it to the STC, the Society for Technical Cooperation. They might be interested."

"Private sector? I doubt that. But you can have the copy."

Nordanc almost regrets that Qvietone is no longer in a cast; he seems removed from him now. The metallographer, with equally little work space on the far side of the desk, comes back from the lab with a tray of new samples, splinters fixed in plastic. Qvietone immediately takes a look and starts to help sort them. Nordanc stands around, not wanting to watch over their shoulders.

"You want to join us for lunch?"

They walk across Toulovec Square. Nordanc stops in front of a plaque. "Who was Magdalena Dobromila Rettigová?"

"As an expert in gastronomy, you should know that. Didn't you take Bohemian studies in Prague, or history? She wrote the first Czech cookbook. Besides which, she emancipated women."

"Like Henriette Davidis."

"Who?"

"With her tract, *The Virgin's Profession.*"

Qvietone stares at him. "What's new at the castle?"

"The director has torn some ligaments in his knee, and Maltzahn has a swollen cheek. The two of them had a conversation. No sooner is your cast off than Horský is running around all taped up. Jirse gave him a good once-over today in the courtyard, wondering if he could get smart with him now, too. And got right back up on his mower, zooming around until he decapitated the last lilac bush. Ran into the Silentium Temple, too, made quite a racket."

"It's a shame I don't work there anymore, he doesn't do anything halfway."

The young metallographer, who can tell the difference between arsenic bronze and tin bronze, grins to himself.

TEN

The sgraffiti on the wall join now, the better-preserved rows of coffers above the second-floor windows meeting the refurbished ones below. The projection is finished and with it half the south façade. The shading of the ashlars in the last row varies from right to left, compensating for the vault of the overhang and the arches of the windows. The new finely ground marble is darker than what they were using before they wasted it in the battle with the collective farm. The stones in the middle, which were done last, cast a faint shadow on the shiny surface of the molding. Podol decides to use full, rounded motifs that will leave a lot of white showing—rosettes, plump-cheeked trumpeters, a carp—and rejects Orten's matchsticks and Maltzahn's pine trees. "Those skeletons belong further up, they're depressing down here." He has slowly become aware that many objects he has affixed to the façade are taken solely from memory: boletus mushrooms have become almost impossible to find in the last few years; an oriole is a rarity, great bustards, which as a child he had watched above the meadows of southern Bohemia, have vanished; he has set a displaying hen just under the frieze—"so that they're not completely forgotten."

He raises his head to look up at the three flowing segments of the gable, at the graceful figures leaning there, all with his wife's legs, a lute in one arm or a cupid above the shoulder, laurels in their hands and hair. They are larger than life and have a voracious look in their eyes, a man-devouring, time-devouring look, and often an animal in their laps—sodomy on the pediments. Or coupling horses and peafowl; he has no idea how many tangled liaisons he has already drawn.

A row of apples passes diagonally across the sgraffiti to the cornice above him; he can see its jagged irregularities from every direction, but always reappearing, sure and strong. He recognizes Patera's cautious scrapings, Maltzahn's and Orten's sculpted apples—Orten's with leaves, Maltzahn's naked—all set between the obligatory ornament of two wavy lines.

The endless pattern of sharply contrasting squares swims before his eyes and he feels slightly dizzy, for the first time in years. He makes a grab for the façade's moist mortar to steady himself. The tips of his fingers leave behind prints, which he then joins with two lines, adds a few more ovals: a cluster of peapods.

He compares adjacent motifs: plants—corn cockle, field scabious; mushrooms—puffball, parasol, chestnut; fish—carp, a pike, a sea horse; birds—a murre, a crested grebe with chicks on its back, to complete the series. Aren't there anything but endangered species?

Almost with relief, he recalls his two doves, his first house mural in the Old Town, on the "Bridge," where you squeeze through a narrow lane that leads from Coal Market to Wenceslaus Square—the press of people passing under the scaffold planks, at their own risk, no one looking up. He drew an oval coat-of-arms on the wall, darker than the stucco; around it the curlicues of a baroque frame with cherub heads and acanthus leaves, and then the oval itself, left clean and empty by the plasterers. To fill its space, he has to set the doves one above the other. They shine in white, blue and gold, but seem dainty beside the ponderous frame—his first commission in the city. He came by often over the next few days, from different directions, raising his eyes as if by accident, searching for his emblem. It was hard to find, too high up, the doves almost squashed by the cherubim, too pretty—he had misjudged the distance. People praise it, but he knows: larger surfaces next time, leave more white, not so fussy.

He watched the passersby, listened to what they were saying; hardly anyone looked up. The few tourists who did discover the doves were forced against the wall by the crowds when they tried to take pictures of them from the far side—no loitering allowed.

A difficult city for tourists. Only a few of the famous monuments they know from pictures are not covered over, and you have to hunt for those. The rest is a mass of scaffolds, all alike, and the objects under them look alike, too. It makes no difference which scaffold they photograph, the one hiding Strahov Monastery, Lobkovický Palace, the Týn Church, or the jutting façades of the baroque houses—the north side of the Old Town Ring is permanently boarded over. In the tree-shaded arcade—it, too, has a plank fence, but is temporarily accessible—they can buy postcards from the days before the scaffolds, when the Týn Church was still visible: its two steeples, fretwork arches, the interior as well, the transept with Tycho Brahe's grave. (But you cannot see the window through which Kafka peeked as a child from the entry of his own house.) People are eager to send the postcards.

The tourists are stubborn, keep coming back, but find new scaffolds, barbed brackets, a city in outline. If they are patient, ten years later they can witness an unveiling. The National Theater becomes visible. People had almost forgotten the building's original form and purpose amid the debris and traffic jams of the torn-up quay. Suddenly all of it is gone—the complicated network of protective passages, the corrugated tin fence, the cables dangling above the heads of scurrying crowds, who are forced to make the most complicated detours from here to get into the city. In their place are gilded lampposts, shiny mosaics, and a new marble staircase. The visitors from the country have their "chapel" back, but the residents of Prague are preparing themselves for the next set of hurdles in the neighborhood.

At the première that had celebrated its opening, the building burned to its foundations, the very stones of which had been donated, each bearing the name of a Bohemian or Moravian town. But in no time new collections were taken up, money to rebuild the National Theater poured in. Within three years, the new building was ready. A hundred years later, no one cracks jokes about the ten years it took to restore it. The people of Prague have so many construction sites, detours, torn-up streets, and traffic jams to deal with that they have given up such childish jokes. Construction of the subway was delayed much too long, but they are making up for it now, on every corner. People are exhausted and testy. Gigantic concrete pits, dust, noise—the center of town is one huge construction site. National Street is nothing but ditches, detours, and barricaded side streets, with here and there a sausage, vegetable, or beer stand.

In the twenties, once nationalistic pressures had ebbed with the founding of an independent republic, an apocryphal "Society to Demolish the National Theater" was organized for the purpose of restoring the architectural integrity of the capital. The theater was a gaudy flourish, the result of the patriotic fervor of the eighties, when the important thing was to defy the Habsburgs with a façade in folk costume—and an aesthetic thorn in the side of a few purists. The movement festered just below the surface; rejection of its neoclassical architecture was a token of newly won sovereignty—like Masaryk's disclosure that the Zelenohorský and Královédvorský manuscripts were the forgeries of two inventive Bohemians, who contributed to the enrichment of Old Czech literature by taking a cue from Ossian.

But had the quay been redeveloped *without* a National Theater, the instigator of such a project would not have been proclaimed president of the republic, and the constituent states would have got along quite well without Prague—though presumably civil war would have been averted. Now that socialist housing projects have run riot, however, people take unanimous delight in the sturdy ostentation of the past, are quite content to let this monument of national unity stand, more than happy to see it restored.

A new section of the Charles Bridge can now be revealed as well, one segment between two piers whose hewn stones are of a conspicuously lighter color. The popular consensus is that the old ones are already in America—whether they also mix eggs with their mortar there is another question entirely. Some people claim to have seen the original caroline stones in Norman/Clayton, at least in photographs— a rodeo landscape with castle, the Nature Theater of Oklahoma.

Podol rechecks the row behind him: he is done with this wall. Three stones farther on, Orten has finished his last sgraffito, and Maltzahn and Patera are already cleaning up.

Podol stretches, his shoulder blade cracks, he feels a pain worm its way through him, he grabs his side.

Orten looks up. "What's wrong?"

"Nothing, it's passed. A little stitch in my side of late. How long have we been at this? Since May, four months. Another five, six weeks."

"We can hang it up before then. That depends on you."

"No, let's go on with it. Who knows what it will look like next year. And how's your constipation?" He grins at Orten.

"They moved today. Not much, a little firm, angular, looked like one of Zadkine's torsos."

"No wonder, with a name like that. Or maybe it was one of Archipenko's."

"There's not much happening with me in that department, either," Patera joins in. "Although, when I do go, there's no end to it."

"Brancusi," Podol says. "His 'Endless Column,' I've always liked that. The contractions, though, would need a special peristalsis."

"Isn't your topic somewhat *outré?*" Maltzahn approaches.

"Why so? Everybody has created shit castles in the air at some point in life. How about you, Olbram? I would think your turds could only be those of the most respected artists."

"You'd be surprised. Once they looked like one of my wife's sculptures."

"Your asshole has good manners at least." They all know that his wife supported him before he established himself with his bimetallic castings.

"Rodin must be difficult," Patera says, cutting Podol's sarcasm short.

"Big if nothing else! I did shit a monument once, it was 'Balzac.' But you need a lot of material! A generous semidiarrhea is best for producing the required mass. Stinks like hell."

"You might as well go ahead and try the bronze eagle Calder's grandfather did."

"I don't have to go all the way to Philadelphia. The Hus Monument on the Old Town Ring will do."

"Looks about like it, too."—Orten.

"I must say your Zadkinean angularity surprises me, Jan. Given your sense of proportion, you ought to be shitting nothing but little Arps," Maltzahn digs. "Your plaster rods would be too unwieldy."

"Just imagine a mobile." Patera grins.

"Or Gutfreund," it strikes Podol to add. "His secretaries at their typewriters, millworkers, bureaucrats with hats and attaché cases—and all in color! Or at least tinted."

"Chiaroscuro in the chamber pot," Orten concludes. "So far, only Pointsman has been stuck in that rut. Until today, it was just eating that was elevated to action art; now the task is to move beyond Dali and think of defecation as an artistic act, and vice versa! And then—mark my word, goose down will be the softest of all."

. . .

They move their things around the corner to the side facing the approach road, where new scaffolding covers about a third of the wall. They have four hundred coffers behind them, and on the west façade, before which they now stand, there is hardly a single panel left. A fleeting spasm of futility—routinely ignored—but this wall is especially bleak.

"Have you fellows ever read anything that might advance our cause here? A snappy opening at least?" Podol shoves his hat back on his neck and gazes listlessly at the wall.

Orten stares at the flaking plaster, mildewed blisters against a decaying background, the hide of a pilot whale. "Call me Ishmael."

Podol looks at him. "How are you going to draw that? Am I supposed to scratch the letters in the wall? Besides, I wanted to keep clear of the Bible."

"It's *Moby Dick*."

"I read that as a boy. I don't remember there being any nice short sentences like that."

"It's the first and only one."

"Sorry, but I can't use it. But we'll keep the whale in mind. Leviathan." He glances up. "It could go on the gable, as a contrast to your Justitia. Any other ideas?"

Orten can feel the monotony of apples and cheeks creeping up on him. "Someone must have denounced Josef K."

"What?"

Podol spends the weekend in his adjustable barber's chair, U.S. Patent 256 308, reading, making notes, and drawing. The chair stands on a massive, smooth base, can be turned, tipped back, and raised hydraulically (the semiautomatic mechanism works in only one direction), has an adjustable back, arms, footrest and headrest, four positions for the latter—but it cannot be budged.

The original white enamel finish has flaked off and the stripped threads of the left-turning whitworth screws cannot be reproduced by continental machinery, but Podol loves it, despite the obvious resemblance to a dentist's chair.

It is a leftover from a museum of furniture that in its day was almost unique in its historical sweep, extending from multipurpose benches and chests of the Renaissance to Alexander Calder's mechanized hammock; but the most comprehensive collection, patented adjustable living machines, has almost entirely vanished. All that is left in the cellar is a warped desk safe, cracked long ago, but which originally contained a lazy susan of secret compartments and elegant drawers that could be opened with a touch of the mainspring to reveal two dozen file compartments divided by thin sheets of plywood, the whole thing covered by a rolltop of flexible teak slats. The crank that rolled it back has been broken off, the desk top inside has rotted. From what he has read recently, Podol is convinced that it was the model for the desk of the uncle in *Amerika*—particularly because Kafka passed through Friedland several times on his inspection trips to northern Bohemia. Orten once came upon Podol standing helplessly before this wreck with a bucket of glue in hand—he is very fond of it.

They have only heard of another showpiece of the collection. A piano-bed that could sleep four adults, while by day it served as a vanity, commode, linen cupboard, and musical instrument all in one. The swivel chair that once belonged with it has two drawers, a writing desk, a sewing table, and a mirror under the seat. According to Jirse, the piano had had an excellent sound.

The bed was not as large as the Great Bed of Ware, a seventeenth-century piece that could sleep up to twelve people. Nor as large as the Bed of Skye in *Tynset,* which was older and had room for seven sleepers—until the great plague of 1522, when a weary soldier returning home from the continent found rest in its inn. (So important was the bed, the inn was named after it.)

He was not the first to arrive. A monk preceded him, a mendicant who relied on charity—his only possession the rosary between his fingers. The wench Anne accosted him, and out of habit she let her poor catch have his way, but hoped to have the handsome young stranger later, a soldier's body as a reward for her selflessness with the monk. In the meantime a miller had arrived with his wife, a smug and sated fellow, who already had an eye on Anne and was waiting for his wife to fall asleep, whereas the wife was hoping to waylay an impoverished German nobleman's young companion, who, having arrived much later, moved to the edge of the bed, where he lay unnoticed and could return her attentions. There was also a knavish barber, who sold indulgences and had promised to bleed his landlady gratis, if she would let him work his will in bed.

And into this roundelay of anticipated pleasure and smoldering lust—Anne had had enough of the monk and was groping for the soldier, the miller for Anne, the miller's wife for the youth, the barber for the landlady—a scream of terror rang out in the night. Anne had found her soldier, had bared the young body for which she lusted—and dipped her fingers in purulent wounds, bursting black plague boils from her continent, while he gasped in agony, oblivious of this final human contact.

And from there, from the Great Bed of Skye, the horror of bubonic plague spread over the country, the Midlands, the island, clasping everyone in its embrace.

The piano-bed from Ohio was not as large, but not so long ago it was put to twofold use by the Gestapo in Friedland Castle—during the day by those with musical talent, and at night by those of a more inventive nature, who in their off-duty hours used it for games of discipline played to the jangling chords of the *Eroica*. For a while their playmates were two young half-Jewish girls, who were destined for Theresienstadt.

The bed disappeared. Whether the Germans took it with them when they fled or whether the Soviet liberators, overwhelmed by Western progress, also found use for it as a couch for Russian officers, its history is lost in the last days of the war. Jirse still mourns for it.

Only damaged remnants of the great collection are left; the furniture on display for visitors in the rooms was gathered chiefly from other castles and landmarks under official protection.

They have found a use for a few of the original and unrepaired pieces lying about, for the coil-spring "pouting couch" or *boudeuse,* where Maltzahn and Patera spend evenings back to back, reading and drinking beer—if Maltzahn is not bedded down on Finnish fixtures belonging to the director (who for his part is trying to get comfortable on the state-owned furniture in his young girlfriend's dorm room). Orten and Podol use their three-seated *confidente,* a contorted double-S sofa, for stacking clothes. The droll object makes an immediate impression on strangers, but no one can sit on it anymore, not even when the missing leg is replaced by the *Pannonian Legends*—in a transcription by the Bohemian monk Jan Avostalis—which was lost in the confusion of the Thirty Years' War and now rots away here, unreadable, but fulfilling this final purpose. Orten is content to do his reading on a homely wooden chair with a straight back and hard seat. Podol will yield his barber chair to no one.

He turns slowly back and forth as he reads, his head resting against the stained brown neckpiece, laughing to himself. "The old lady at the beginning, with the two voyeurs across the way, she's good!" He picks up his sketchpad and draws various openings for Kafka's *Trial*. "Someone must have denounced Josef K."

"Like this, do you think?" He shows Orten a long-nosed Kilroy climbing over the wall. "A spy."

"It's too general."

"Or like this?" Podol multiplies Munch's "The Cry" with concentric circles around the open mouth, like a bullhorn.

"It's not supposed to be a cry for help, but a denunciation," Orten objects.

They try other ways of illustrating a denunciation. Podol knows the somber visions of Kubin and A. Paul Weber's "Rumor," but both are too detailed for their purposes, inappropriate for an expansive realization on the façade. Finally Podol draws several scenes in comic-strip style: the two cops, Franz and Willem, planted at the door; Franz with a broad grin, his chin jutting out, eating K.'s breakfast: "Doesn't know the law and claims he is innocent"; Willem, hardly able to squelch his laughter, mimicking approval. Podol decides not to use dialogue balloons on the façade.

The officer, Frau Grubach's nephew, listening at the door, legs spread wide, wearing boots, his face hidden behind the bill of his uniform cap.

Fräulein Bürstner: blonde, pouty mouth, blouse filled to bursting, the blouse that Willem has freed from the window latch—Franz's brutal smile looks like Batman's triumphant grin.

Fräulein Montag's more delicate features indicate fragile health—a lame, stunted, no-nonsense woman; she bears a vague resemblance to Podol's wife.

Leni resembles Hanna—"Don't forget the webbed skin between the fingers."

"I'm not that far yet."

"And Titorelli? You can easily fill five coffers with his moor landscapes."

"That's nothing for the façade, we need variety. The brats on the steps to his apartment, I like them better, but it means a lot of work."

The most successful sketch is of Josef K., holding out his bicycle license in one hand.

"Do we ever learn when all this takes place?"

"On K.'s thirtieth birthday, but no date."

"Yes, I know that. What a shame, otherwise we could celebrate Josef K. Day."

"There already is one, whenever you're unexpectedly invited to visit a courtroom or the police."

"Since I've gotten to know Jirse, that no longer happens unexpectedly."

"You could use Jirse for your 'Denunciation.' "

"Too great an honor. I'm not putting him on the façade. I still want to sketch the judge, sitting under his portrait, a picture within a picture. Maybe with a book in his hand, with a cover showing a judge with a book in his hand, and so on. As a boy I was always taken by ads showing kids eating cookies from a box, or mommy serving soup from a package showing the same scene repeated, on to infinity. Sometimes I could make out a fifth or sixth kid, a fourth mother smiling and forcing soup down her family. I knew that it didn't end there— the factory could never bake that many cookies! I ask you: if every kid is holding a box with twenty cookies—and the whole thing is repeated infinitely, are there more kids or cookies, more mothers or bouillon cubes?"

"Cookies," Patera is quick to respond, "and bouillon cubes?"

Orten considers. "Infinity is infinity. It's like with twenty times zero or one times zero."

"Doesn't it have something to do with 'sets' and 'powers'?" Maltzahn asks. "Which would mean the bouillon cubes would be of a higher power than the mothers, I mean the set of soup packages is larger than the set of mothers. . . ." He is getting tangled up.

"The only thing for sure is: mothers have more power than kids," Podol says.

"Don't make things so easy for yourself." Maltzahn won't give up.

"There are in fact more numbers between one and two than between one and infinity."

"How's that?"

"You talking about fractions?" Orten asks.

"The rational numbers are countable. The irrational numbers are uncountable and have a greater exponential power than whole numbers!" Maltzahn is triumphant.

They give him hostile looks.

"But we're dealing with whole children and whole cookies, unless you break them into pieces before you count them," Orten remarks.

"They do arithmetic entirely differently nowadays," Maltzahn continues undaunted. "In second grade for instance: 'One little bird flew after the other little bird. How many little birds were there?' "

"An infinite number." Patera is fixed on infinity.

"Two," Podol says hesitantly.

Maltzahn smiles a meaningful smile, waits for what Orten will say, who just shrugs.

"Three."—Maltzahn, victorious.

"How's that?"

"The first, the second, and the one after the other makes three."

"There's something to that," Patera says tentatively.

"Olbram, you'll fall for anything, even a seven-year-old's joke! We're no better than horses weaving in front of a stall door. Here we sit and start doing arithmetic, with little birds!" Podol goes back to his infinite sketches.

"If you are going to carry out projects like that on the façade," Orten says, "just go ahead and scratch your way into the library."

Podol looks through his drawings. "I never would have thought that Kafka would be material for a comic strip. *The Trial* is the finest source you could ever imagine."

Maltzahn, who has been watching over Podol's shoulder, has realized in the meantime that they are dealing with a real discovery. He knows a small Swiss publisher whom he could interest in the project. "We'd only have to find the right printing shop here, maybe have to locate the paper, too, and it could be done."

"Then we don't need your little Swiss publisher. Or are you trying to save him having to invest any money? And then at the end defraud the artist of the rest, the way they do with children's films meant for export? Why not just drop our names, too, so that he can peddle it as his own idea?"

"What do you want? They'll pay you for it in hard currency."

"A couple of Tuzex coupons that aren't worth shit! From here on out, this idea is legally protected! With a copyright if you like, you know all about that stuff. Before I get involved in your shady deals, I'll stay right here and scratch plaster, for korunas, knowing full well nothing will be left after ten years!"

When they go to eat at the Ram on Monday—the manager was impressed by the exhibition, but she thought Orten looked sickly and ever since she has been serving him bland, unsalted food—Podol goes on drawing his comics on beer coasters and checks:

Leni throws Teller against the wall;

the uncle from the country puts his arm around K. to calm him;

the lawyer in bed;

Block, the shopkeeper, on all fours in front of the bedpost;

the clergyman bending down over his pulpit, with searching eyes;

the quarry, desolate and lonely;

in the distance, a slim man with arms flung wide between two window casements.

"Should I draw K. at the end with a dog's head?"

Orten has just salted his veal kidney. "No, it's fine as it is."

Podol glances through the series. "One's more repulsive than the next. The worst is the preacher, he works hand in hand with the hangman."

"It's what preachers are for. Prison chaplain—his job is to prepare the condemned man for the noose. Or the knife. Once K. has got tangled up in his parable he can never get out. He has exhausted all logic and offers no resistance when the executioners come to get him. He even trusted the chaplain!"

"I'll give him a hood, with a skull for a face, looking down from his pulpit."

"Keep the smile, two rows, with a cigar in his mouth. And Jirse as the janitor."

Maltzahn arrives late, with Svoboda; ever since the exhibition they have had important things to talk about—two art managers with more than just provincial influence. He greets them with a businesslike air, passing over Nordanc, who is sitting next to Podol and silently examining the drawings. Maltzahn claps Patera on the shoulder and loudly pulls a chair over, so that they finally all stand up. Podol gazes at Maltzahn's cheek; the swelling has not gone down. "You've looked spiffier, Olbram."

"You said it. What all don't I do for you guys." Maltzahn impressively tosses a key on the table. Patera asks in all innocence about the door it goes to. Podol keeps a stone face. "So it worked?"

"Yes. Starting tomorrow you can spread out your frottages directly above Smetana's cradle. Both rooms are vacant, the cleaning lady has already been there and a table is on its way."

"I'd really given up any hope of it. That's great! If only your cheek is back to normal soon, too."

"It's not so bad, just this one tooth wobbles a little."

"Hell, get yourself to a doctor."

Maltzahn dismisses this. He hasn't been the recipient of so much attention in a long time, he waits for more. He feels he deserves it as much as he did for his ten-year plan, for which they have long since stopped thanking him.

Patera suggests various home remedies for toothache, and the manager offers to make a vinegar compress. The least she can do is bring him a tender perch with juniper berries, which she has told everyone else she is out of.

ELEVEN

Karla walks with Pepi to the bus. But the bus is late and they have to wait. On the hill across the way, above the roofs of the houses and the steeples of the Piarist church, one pediment of the castle is visible, still bare, no sgraffiti—but below it are the top platforms of the half-constructed scaffold.

Pepi tries to make out who that is, climbing with a bucket in his hand. Orten? She would have liked to say goodbye to him. A second figure, hatless as well and wearing white mason's overalls joins him, points to a spot on the wall, gesticulates. They walk back and forth, assembling their tools. The darker figure hangs up his jacket; the gentle wind sets it swinging from the scaffold. They kneel down, only a little way apart from each other, and start to work.

"How much longer are you staying?" she asks Karla, almost enviously.

"Two weeks. And how about you? What are you going to do once you get home?"

"I still have ten days of vacation. I'll go swimming and maybe earn a little extra on the collective farm."

"Out in the fields?"

"No, with the cows. No one wants to do it in summer because of the flies. I can milk, too, with the machine or by hand. If calves are born, I rub them down with straw. They stay with their mothers at first, tied to the wall behind the gutter. I bring them over to drink. To get them to go back you have to stick a finger in their mouth, they hang on and suck, they have real rough tongues. I keep them clean, haul warm water over, and if the dried shit on their hocks doesn't come off with water, I scrape it off. Cows are clean animals; they only get dirty if they're kept too crowded."

"Do you like working in the barns?"

"Well, it's more fun than when our school class is sent out to pick hops. I like the odor, too, there's always a sour smell to the barns, only the hogs really stink. I like wild pigs, though, too. When I get home, my mother has something close to a bad conscience, I'm in the university-prep program at school. Not long ago somebody told her for the umpteenth time, 'Your Pepi isn't stuck-up at all, she'll do the dirtiest work'—people don't have any idea! She sets food down in front of me, but I'm never hungry. I just sit there stinking away, I don't want to wash up after I've been with the cows. Besides, I can read then without anyone disturbing me, they won't even come into the room."

She looks back across to the scaffold, but can't spot the two men right off. Then she sees Podol holding on to a rail next to Orten's jacket; he is bent over and Orten is supporting him. Someone is climbing up to them, a small man—Patera. Podol returns to the wall, Orten is talking to him now, gesticulating, Podol goes back to work. She guesses more at what these movements mean than she can actually make out. Podol's spatula strokes are smaller and more controlled than Orten's supple motions—how often has she noticed that over the last few weeks? Patera is up top now, the fourth man is not there yet.

"What did you say?"

"What do you read?" Karla asks again.

"At the moment stories by a woman named Rachilde. For years I just read Dostoyevsky, *The Possessed* three times. I was only thirteen the first time."

"How old are you, sixteen?"

"I'll turn seventeen soon. Rachilde wrote one story about a castle that, no matter how hard you try to reach it, is always the same distance away. Maybe Kafka read it, it had been translated by then."

"That's very interesting, but not very probable."

"Well, he read Němcová's *Grandmother,* and used the episode with Kristla and the Italian lackey in *The Castle.* Why not a French woman writer, too? I'm thinking about using it next year for my graduation thesis, but as usual my teachers probably won't understand any of it, and my father will have to pay a visit to the school again. They put up with me only because he's been in the Party longer than the principal."

"And your father? What does he say?"

"He'd love to yank me out of school, keeps talking about a factory job and how I'm going to have to learn about life, me with my fancy ideas. But brags about me to his drinking buddies, as if it were his doing. Him and his odes to the partisans! But in the Prague uprising in May of '45, they hardly dared show their heads over the barricades. He told me that himself."

"And your mother?"

"It was my mother who insisted that I stay in school. I'll always be grateful to her for that. And that she let me have a cat when I was little. But otherwise she's leery of me, too. When I got strep throat picking hops last year and had to go to the hospital, she didn't even believe me. The day before we had hitchhiked into Karlsbad—unauthorized leave they called it, even though we had finished the job—and I took a bad chill. I couldn't swallow or talk, couldn't even open my mouth. They took me to the infirmary and I just lay there, because the intern on duty was afraid to do anything. I lost so much weight that even the teachers got scared, as usual they had figured this was just another case of faking. When the agony wagon picked us up—kids who were green around the gills, from different schools and hop fields—the others were all laughing. No sooner had they slammed the door shut than somebody pulled out a guitar and they started singing. I was the only one who couldn't join in. And for forty miles heard nothing but 'Cut it out, we'll soon be there, don't be so silly!' By that time I was running a fever of a hundred and five and it was nothing to laugh about. The doctor at the hospital who was going to lance the abscess was pretty horrified, asked me how long I'd gone without treatment. They put me on an I.V. and gave me so much penicillin that I couldn't sit or lie down. They put me in the ward for infectious diseases—no visitors, they held kids up to the windows for kisses—and my mother showed up ten days later to ask me how I was doing! Because she was still pissed at me on account of the idiotic letter from my teachers. They evidently figured I had intentionally come down with strep throat to get out of picking hops!"

"And died on the rack, faking it—I know all about it. What did she have to say then?"

"I was feeling better by then, but when a patient came to tell me that somebody was asking for me, I bandaged up my head and staggered to the window, with mournful eyes and such a sickly voice that my mother really got scared. That didn't last long, unfortunately. Once I was back home, everything was status quo. Evidently you have to cash in your chips right in front of them every day before they'll come to their senses! And that would get stale pretty quick, too."

Karla laughs. "What are you going to do after you graduate?"

"Go to university, what else. Literature, languages. Even though my father has vaulting ambitions of my being a nurse. But I'll have to work very hard, he says."

"Will they let you go to university?"

"I'm not going to ask them. They haven't asked me what I want either! We can't get any poorer. They'll probably squawk at first, but then my father will feel flattered, and my mother herself remarked how important languages are—that was after she got a package of coffee from Haile Selassie, like everyone else at the military hospital, and she could only thank him in Czech. She found him so charming—'So little and so brown.' One day she came home with 'zdravstvuite, robata'; the department of psychiatry where she works had pledged to take a Russian course, for the Brigade of Socialist Labor. They only got a silver medal, probably because my mother flunked; at least she never spoke Russian again."

"So you'll be coming to Prague?"

"I'm not even sure yet that I can come up with the registration fee, but I'm a cadre kid; that'll be the first time it has ever paid off."

The bus comes around the curve in a cloud of dust and makes its first stop in front of the Liberation—a common name for postwar grocery stores, just like Brotherhood for general stores; you still see them sporadically out in the country.

Pepi looks across to the scaffold: all four of them are there now, Podol is working; nothing unusual.

Karla reaches into her purse and gives Pepi a package.

"A souvenir from the castle. Be careful!"

Pepi unwraps the tissue paper: glass, a small beaker with an irregular, undulating rim, smooth, with tiny cracks and air bubbles in its greenish base.

"It's beautiful!"

"Baroque industrial glass. These were used as candleholders for the lighting in the castle theater."

"Can you even drink from it?"

"But of course. The form is perfect for red wine—no stem, you warm it in your hand. You can see here on the bottom where it was broken off. It's very sharp."

Pepi reverently feels the rough edge. Saying goodbye has made her so tense that suddenly the glass shatters in her hand, literally turns to dust before her eyes. She stands there despondent, sees the splinters in her hand but not the blood, nor the approaching bus.

Karla gathers up her things, gives her a hug. "There are still two good glasses in there, that'll be enough for when I come to visit."

Only now does she realize Pepi is hurt, and she tries quickly to wipe away the blood, cuts herself doing it, their bleeding hands touch for a moment, they laugh, sisters and witches. Then the bus door bangs shut.

As Karla is leading a group of tourists through the Blue Room, showing them the huge fireplace—Italian, seventeenth-century, mantel decorated with lion heads and rising to a crown of pink marble—she notices Jirse's wooden leg lying among the artfully arranged ash logs.

Il grido. A man travels aimlessly through the Po Valley, searching for the woman he loves. He meets others who could love him, but he doesn't stay, he wants her. After months of wandering he finally finds her, with a child in her arms; she is living happily with another man. Summoning what strength he has left, he climbs a tower at the edge of the village, rising like a tree trunk from a swamp, and jumps off, with a loud scream.

They walk past the Oriole, not saying a word. "Come to my place." Marie takes Orten's hand.

The furnishings are dreary, singles' dorm décor with a few things to lend a personal touch, though equally standardized: handwoven tablecloth and lampshade, cotton-print curtains at the window and the glass panel in the door, a ceramic ashtray. The couches arranged in one corner are too narrow and low, the backs too short; the stove and sink display the usual carelessness of people who live alone; the bed is surrounded by open books and *Kino* magazines. She uncorks the wine bottle with an expert's strength and dexterity, a feminine skill that has always amazed him. They are much less adept with a screwdriver, often don't even have one.

"Žernoticer," he reads. "We wouldn't have found better at the Oriole."

Marie pulls the cork with her left hand, the same one she uses for sewing up wounds in the emergency room. "They broke me of using my left hand for writing or eating when I was a child; they couldn't keep track of the rest."

"So you're a frustrated lefty?"

"I'm ambidextrous." She remembers the paleolithic painter of the bison, the handprint in the cave.

"Have I upset you?"

"No. I was thinking of Aldo. He turned down Betsy Blair, and then Alida Valli didn't want him. I didn't expect him to jump off at the end."

"Actually he just sort of let himself fall, the parapet was too low."

"Isn't that the same thing?"

"No."

They smoke.

"Did you like Alida Valli better?" she asks. "She looks like my mother."

"She's a beautiful woman, but that wasn't the point. He had a picture in his mind, a dream. He had already made his decision, had chosen once and didn't want anyone else."

"Have you ever made a decision like that?"

"I was chosen once that way."

"How was that?"

Orten tells her about Alina Szapocznikova, the Polish sculptress, whom he met as a student, in the cafeteria. She was wearing a sweater that hung from her, so threadbare it provided no warmth. She was staring into her plate; she had already eaten her way through her chits for the month and could buy no more. He gave her two of his. Before he could finish his soup, she had devoured two bowls and was waiting to see what else he would get her. He saw that same hungry look everywhere—Poles, their country totally destroyed, Hungarians, the French, Germans, Russians—half of Europe was studying in Prague. The swollen ranks of students crowded into ateliers and lecture halls, took their notes on the back of whoever was standing in front of them.

She was older and more experienced than he. She had been taken to a concentration camp at age fourteen, was raped by the Germans, and then again by the Russians when it was liberated. She was one of the best students in the sculpture classes. She sought Orten out, and they lived together. Soon her sweater no longer fit. After the overthrow of the government in February 1948, she decided to leave Czechoslovakia for good. "We Jews can smell when a pogrom is coming." She wanted Orten to come with her, but he felt he was still too young and immature for Paris, promised her he would come later, but the borders were closed not long after. He went to Bulgaria for a semester, instead of Paris, and discovered what a fool he had been to hesitate. But he left the Communist Party within six months, while all his friends were required to stay in much longer.

Alina had done well in Paris, was married and divorced several times—she had had it with helping young men make their marks as artists. Finally she moved into a villa with her son, her maid, and a dog. She kept visitors at bay, Orten included.

Her last letter to him was a carbon copy of a description of her latest project, in English: a Rolls-Royce, six-fifths of actual size, with exact measurements and details to scale, in pink marble, as an outdoor sculpture. Below that, in Czech: "I hope to find enough big, rich snobs to implement this."

They met one more time, at a symposium for sculptors in the Tatras. She had to detour around Germany by way of Austria, her son was afraid of Germans. In the snapshots that Orten took—the only photographs of her other than those done for art magazines, showing her next to her oversized objects—she is scrambling around on a block of stone, hammer and chisel in hand, but graceful, in coarse linen trousers and a baggy sweater, her dark hair cut short and those same hungry eyes.

When she died at age forty-eight she was already included in lexicons of modern art. "The only person I know who is."

"She reminds me of Vilma." Marie tells him about the relative she never met. "And your wife?"

Orten doesn't reply; he doesn't want to force her to make comparisons. "What's with Qvietone?" he asks out of nowhere.

"Nothing." She is growing impatient. "The cast is off, and he's been cured in general, let's hope."

"I'm not so sure about that. The last time we saw him he was still pretty jealous. That bug trick was asinine."

"That bothers me less than how I respond," Marie says. "As if I were constantly trying to trick him. I'm either sarcastic or condescending, and then he thinks he has to show off and only piles it on that much more. When he really is quite clever and knows a lot, not just about bugs. But he's still so young."

"Now you're talking like his mother again. At twenty-five he should know what he's doing."

"Were you so adult at his age? When did you get married, at twenty-eight? You weren't all that much wiser," she says with annoyance.

"It was a different time. Everybody around me was getting married, there was an avalanche of people looking to connect, needing new responsibilities and wanting to test themselves—the postwar period. I felt lost without Alina. I knew men who had fought in Spain at sixteen and kept their cool. But what Franco and the Fascists hadn't been able to accomplish women in peacetime did. Beg your pardon. The men started spinning in place. I saw it everywhere around me. Szapocznikova was an exception. Most women needed someone for support, and wanted children. The men fell for it in droves. I saw all that and was jealous besides.

"I met her after graduation. We were restoring a monastery in Slovakia near the Ukrainian border. She was shlepping milk cans."

"Your wife?"

"I helped her, we talked. Her father came that same evening to find out what my intentions were. I had asked her if she didn't want to study. She would have agreed to anything. Mainly she wanted to get away from home. When we came back, three weeks later, she was standing there at our barracks, suitcase in hand.

"I went out into the fields with her, and after a half hour of shouting across the mountain, where her aunt heard us first, then shouted the message on to her mother, who passed it on to her sister, who then was supposed to ask her father on the next mountain. A positive answer came back. She left with us.

"In Prague I put her up at a friend's apartment, all I had was a room and was earning almost nothing, but she got along well with his wife, who worked as a tram conductor and helped her husband with his art, chiseling the backsides so that he could advance faster in his career."

"And that worked?"

"Not really, she hadn't the vaguest, but she was a very energetic woman and he a model family man. And a good sculptor to boot. He learned to put up with her help, the most important thing for him was peace and quiet at home. I had learned to handle the loneliness that had tormented me so badly, but their place was getting too small, what with the kids. Her parents in Slovakia were asking questions, she didn't want to study, and I felt responsible for her—we got married in an Orthodox church."

"In Prague?"

"Marriage was at least as much a shock for her as it was for me. I was hardly ever home. We lived in one room and had to share a bath with two other couples. When the woman who owned the apartment died, we inherited her room and her canary. The other family behind the plywood partition already had two kids, it was noisy. I left the house early, so did she. She was earning money in a lab, which took care of the rent. She took it into her head that she could help me sculpt—she had seen it done—but that didn't work out. I barely allowed her in my atelier. She started to have her suspicions. We already had one child, and she should have known better, but she didn't love him. Only our second, born out of crazy jealousy and an attempt to save our marriage. Of course it didn't work. He was our last one. She can have as many as she wants, I wouldn't begrudge her that, and there's money enough since I've had this restoration job here—but she lets me know she's miserable, is lonely and sick. She has asthma, so does our older boy—but as inhuman as it may sound, I'm not going to try to make up for it by going out and doing things with her, which is what she really wants. She doesn't have any friends here, but she has my old friends now, and their wives, and they all agree what a bastard I am. And I admit, I'd rather hunker down with my plaster than go home. I take care of the kids and then vanish to my atelier, don't get home till late."

"Do you work that hard?"

"Sometimes I just lie there for hours, smoking, listening to the radio, reading and staring at whatever I've started to work on. It's such a small space that I can't sort things out. I'm always looking at just one side, they all block each other, I hardly know which piece I was working on last. I can't let myself go, there's no room. I need some distance, but even if I'd get rid of the sofa—no lying down on the job—it wouldn't help. Actually I can only sit on it, there are bookcases on the wall above it, with my old pieces and books. I've put the largest figures out back in the courtyard, but there's still not enough room. Either I work hard, and then I can't fit in there anymore, or I stagnate, surrounded by half-finished plaster figures, worrying them over in my mind, which is even worse—and that's been the state of affairs for three years now."

"Can't you work at home, when no one is there during the day?"

"We have the whole floor now, there's space enough, but it's impossible. I want out. I've suggested various solutions, she can have everything, she's already found a summerhouse on Troja Island and taken it over, and I've turned it into an atelier, but that's not enough. She wants my bad conscience. And that I've got, lord knows, it's always with me, but I can't change anything, because she won't allow it."

Marie says nothing.

"And Stanislav?"

"His wife has trouble walking since she had polio, he carries her up and down four flights of stairs in the Lesser Quarter every day. His atelier is on the ground floor across the street. It's the best marriage I know."

"And when he's in Friedland?"

"His daughter helps out."

"And what about Maltzahn?"

"His wife is older than he and has been ill for years. She's a good sculptress, but has gone into seclusion. They haven't lived together for a long time now."

"Do they know their husbands have girlfriends here?"

"They probably have a good idea. Sure, they know, that's part of it."

"For you, too? Am I part of it?"

"You've got the wrong idea. Those are very solid relationships, we're tied down here for six months a year, in every sense. Maltzahn wants to marry Marcela, as soon as it's arranged that she gets the two little kids."

"Everything nice and proper, then." She forces a smile.

"For the others, yes. At least an attempt at it. I'd rather wipe the slate clean before letting you get involved with me."

"But I've already done that. You don't have to do any extra slate cleaning on my account."

Marie looks down on the main road below, at the dried mud along the shoulders; a truck rumbles past and shakes the windows; the bag of groceries she has hung there slips from the plastic handle. "The eggs!"

Orten picks it up, reaches inside. "You're right."

"Put it over there."

A second truck rattles past below, followed by a bulldozer. "How can anybody keep this place clean?" she asks, pointing at the swirling dust that rises to the window along with the exhaust.

Orten walks over to her. They both look down, then across to where a spear is flying through the sky above the stadium across the road—youngsters training for the local olympics. "Do you see that sea horse there? Now it's stretching out into a crocodile."

"Awfully skinny. And it's got a thorn in its back. An emaciated dragon. And behind it is a snake's head, or are those flames?"

"The Gorgon's head."

"Tell me, muse, of the man of many ways. What is love?"

"Being able to see the images in clouds," he says, bending down to her hair. "I even love your hospital smell now; that frightened me so much before."

"Were you afraid of me?"

"Still am, sometimes. When you're so quick and so certain about things. Or when you're silent for too long." He kisses her cowlick, runs his finger along the nape of her neck. "You were born in the wrong place, you belong in a kimono."

She turns around, makes slant eyes.

"I want to see all of Kurosawa's films with you, each at least three times."

"Any others?" she asks.

"Godard and Buñuel."

"Not all of Godard. Buñuel yes."

She picks up the grocery bag and rummages inside, stuffs ham and cheese into his mouth with her sticky fingers, decides to open another bottle of wine, to put water on for tea, to push the cupboard door closed. "Stay here."

Janáček's String Quartet No. 1. Marie has laid her head on Orten's shoulder, a distant look in her eyes, and clearly hears the convulsive inner tones embedded in the lyric passages, which are merely a less compelling dulcet background.

"He kills her at the end, where does that come in?"

"Don't be impatient, first they have to be happy."

"There's nothing about that in Tolstoy: the man is suspicious from the start. Isn't it strange? Beethoven wrote his *Kreutzer Sonata,* then Tolstoy wrote a novella, and then Janáček wrote a quartet based on Tolstoy's *Kreutzer Sonata.* "

"From the sound of it, it the woman ought to kill the man at the end," Orten says.

Marie looks at him. "Don't get all too cozy with your bad conscience. You accept all the guilt straight away, that way no one can come along with any other demands or expectations. And do you think it's right for her to kill him?"

"It's not a matter of right or wrong. They don't know any other way out of their misguided, wounded passions. Even if the man kills her at the end out of jealousy, the woman was already a partner to the crime."

"I'm going to miss you." She stands up and dresses. "I need some fresh air."

They cannot part just yet, although every word they say only deepens the misunderstanding—statements of position, overdrawn explanations, which are meant to put things right and only muddle them more. Orten stammers, Marie turns savage in her disappointment, constantly probing the spot that hurts the most. They keep trying to get back to the moment when they understood each other, when they assumed they understood each other, when they began to come closer. They take detours, trying to find the shortest path to each other, and become impatient with each other's insensitivity. They wander through settlements on the periphery of the small town, discover two taverns they didn't know existed, but don't go in. Marie is shaking, but won't let herself be warmed, either by his hands or his jacket, stubbornly walks right through muddy ditches, won't look up, won't say a word; for an hour now she hasn't answered him. Orten has asked all his questions, made all his suggestions—say goodbye now, take her home, separate for good, see each other tomorrow or the day after, take a trip together—he doesn't know what else he can say wrong.

It is growing light when, chilled and burning with tension, they arrive at the castle. The sgraffiti stand out from the wall, white rectangles shining in the morning fog, birds are calling now. She stands there, she hasn't seen the façade from up close for a good while. "You've got this much done already?" She brushes the stones with her hand, moving over grooves and hollows, feeling the contours, tracing the ornaments and animals, human heads, flowers, solitary figures, intertwined figures, reading their work on the wall with her fingers—thrilled, overwhelmed, and furious.

"And here I almost thought you weren't worth it!"

TWELVE

Four days after Nordanc's visit to the museum, there is a knock at his door. Martin, the metallographer, is standing outside. "I wanted to say goodbye."

Nordanc's first thought is that Qvietone has sent him with a message. With a mixture of disappointment and happy surprise, he bends down to keep Max from slipping out the door, and then opens up. "Come on in."

Jirse is standing outside his porter's lodge in the castle passageway; no one has seen him for a couple of days—not since the Turkoman delegation lit a fire in the Blue Room before Hanna could stop them. The leader of the *sovkhoz*, Jaqup Qulan, a Central Asian variation on Bullak from Stadice with a suitably tanned face and squinting slanted eyes, leaped back and forth across a shawl laid out before the fireplace and sang non-Russian songs. Jirse has a new plastic prosthesis under his rolled-up trouser leg; half the calf is visible, flesh-colored, molded to match the one he still has. He stalks over the cobblestones, testing a different sort of limp, using the whole sole of his foot instead of the rubber cap he is accustomed to, but the straps chafe him. Podol steps out from the arcade across the way, followed by Patera and Orten, while Maltzahn locks the door behind them.

Podol tries to ignore Jirse's wave. "Great way to start the day, it's been so nice and quiet around here," he grumbles.

"Mr. Podolský, c'mere a minute." Jirse waves conspiratorially and disappears into his office. Podol stays where he is.

"Go on, he probably has some mail for you," Orten says.

"First he leaves it lying there for four days and now he carries on like this." Podol stomps his cigarette out. Jirse is lugging a package, and Podol hurries over to relieve him of it—the unfamiliar calf has its effect.

"Sign here," Jirse says, moistening the pen with his tongue.

Podol tries to take his own from his pocket, but the package is too bulky. "Was there any charge?" he asks.

Jirse dismisses the question. "F'get it." But after a little wrangling Podol manages to get him to hand over the bill for delivery charges.

"To the Artists and Restorers of the National Castle of Friedland." They go back in again. Podol shifts the package around, shakes it at his ear.

"Is it ticking?" Orten asks.

"That would explain why Jirse didn't want to take any money," Maltzahn suggests. "But it's no reason to put it on my bed."

"It's the only free spot." Podol shoves the debris from breakfast—dishes, newspapers, books, and a pile of drawings—to one side of the table and cuts the twine. A photograph of a collective farm falls out. "The Stadice Collective Farm sends its greetings to the Artists of Friedland!" Bullak, in the middle of his compatriots, with a proud smile and a banner in one hand, next to him Svidnická, with a badge on her considerable breast. "Olbram, you missed something there."

"Let's see." Patera and Maltzahn both reach for the photograph at the same time.

"This fellow here is the one who cost us all our supplies, what was his name again? A strapping lad. I remember how out behind the john at the Ram he and that sugar-beet matron . . ."

"That's Otto Zeta, Hero of Socialist Labor," Orten says. "You see his medal? And he's combed his hair, too."

"That suit fits him about as well as it would a bull from the barn," Podol comments.

Maltzahn regards the photographs. "Her mouth is too wide." He gives it to Patera.

"But the blouse looks good on her." Patera is impressed. "And here's that little bookkeeper."

"Let me see!" Podol pulls it out of his hand. "That's not the one I mean. Where's the other guy?" They look for a face they know from posters—a fox face, a long nose, dimples when he smiles, straggly hair.

They can't remember what the farm's second bookkeeper looked like, hiding under his cap that day.

"This has to be him." Podol points to a man in the third row, who is just turning away from the camera, his face is blurred.

"I don't think he's even there," Orten says. "He would only be a disruption in a celebration like that. Maybe he's been sent back to the forestry office in Slovakia, for some crisis or other."

"The only one I remember is this guy, in the red underwear." Patera points to another face.

"That's the soil expert; he used up a lot of water."

Beneath several layers of increasingly greasy paper, there gradually appear: cracklings, blood sausage, country loaf, liverwurst, brawn, headcheese, and a mass of congealed blood with barley. Patera immediately lops off a piece of the latter for himself. "And now a beer." They sample their way through it all; there's enough caraway in the country loaf, the brawn is homemade, not too sour. Maltzahn just picks at it a little, with an eye to his figure—Orten is reminded of Marie's description of him, "squishy pretty boy."

"That's all." Podol turns the box upside down and shakes it over the largess. From a crack in the cardboard a gold-edged letter flutters down and lands between the blood sausage and the country loaf.

"That'll be the bill," Maltzahn says.

No one wants to pick it up, until finally Podol wipes his greasy hands off on his overalls. It bears no address, but on the back are the initials V. X. T. & T., in gold.

"Agriculture is paying off," Patera remarks. "I'm just not sure what that double T means."

"But the X is clear to you, right?" Orten asks with some interest.

In the meantime, Podol has ripped the envelope open.

Dear Gentlemen:

It were best, I presume, to have addressed you as "master painters," but the use of such a vigorous salutation in the plural goes against my sense of proportion. It would be no wonder if, given the current, and chronic, state of affairs, I had long since surrendered that particular sensibility, but one must live from something, must one not? I myself was constrained early on to abandon every form of proper address—you may wish to regard this as resentment on my part, but rest assured I would indeed address each of you individually as "master painter," despite all leveling tendencies of our time.—I am well aware of the power of appellation. But more of that later.

First, a few clarifications: I could have left the country—my relatives in Regensburg make periodic attempts to return me to the bosom of my family—to which I have no objection. I observe all this and rejoice in their regard for kinship, and indeed it would be quite lovely after so long a time to see all my cousins and the mannequins they have married, to shake their hands and to say that I am one of them. But it is precisely because I am not one of them—do not laugh, gentlemen—that I remain where I am.

Let us clear away all misunderstandings—the estate of Stadice never belonged to me, whereas our family did own, for some two centuries, your castle, by which I mean Friedland and Litomyšl, which explains my eagerness, my good restorers, to observe you at your labor. Moreover, the tower coat-of-arms and the "in hoc signo vinces" are part of the time-honored symbol of the Thurn and Taxis family, as you know from your study of heraldry. I do not wish to complain. I work in animal husbandry, an object of amusement if not outright derision to my fellow workers, most of whom have no idea who Anton Webern was, nor do I wish to hold that against them. They do know a great deal (or at least something) about melioration and the cultivation of sugar beets. If that sounds presumptuous, I beg you to put yourself in my position. But to the matter at hand.

The trip back to my roots was most beneficial for me, even though the castle was never mine—my uncle owned the estate in the thirties, during which period he ordered extensive repairs done. I was frequently there during holidays, and I recall it as a time of great freedom, probably because my uncle was a bachelor with a pronounced preference for young people and understood their ideals and problems (strangely enough I never met one of my numerous cousins there, about whom I was quite curious to begin with, but in the end my uncle proved the best of companions, particularly in later years). But I digress. I am writing to you because after so many years our encounter reawakened old memories, and to see the state showing some concern, however inadequate (my apologies!), touched me in a peculiar way, almost compensating, I must say, for many a bitter day here on the collective, where Comrade Bullack—who can barely sign his name with the aid of a stencil—determines the output. I do wish that you could visit me sometime. I have a collection of rare recordings, a library, and a gallery of ancestral portraits hung along a rather too narrow wall. As a bachelor, I can afford an enjoyable evening of reading and music, particularly since the closest house is across the road, a good twenty yards distant from the church. I live in one room of the local parsonage, which is otherwise unoccupied and unused, but they have chosen not to place more than one room at my disposal, despite the fact that there is no pastor.

I wanted to say something about "symbolic deception." Napoleon's son, Napoleon Bonaparte II, was bought off with the title Duke of Reichstadt, for which history regards him as a fool, dying at age fifteen, in a pandered liaison with a dancer. The power of appellation extends far beyond related matters of phonetics or syntax; the simplest syntax can result in very complicated semantics, as for instance in the game of go, two variants of which, the Venus shell and the black coral, are crown jewels in my collection. (You really must visit me sometime.)

Semantics—inspired by my studies of Roman Jakobson, who taught at the University of Brno before the war (Russian escapees are the best!), I was permitted to slink into the seminars in linguistics at that same university for two semesters, until upon registering for exams, the only student my age to do so, I was unmasked as an erstwhile exploiter and expelled.

It is "symbolic deception"—a daily occurrence with all values, analogous to the physical decay you have had to confront on your façade for years now—that led me to insist on your leaving our family coat-of-arms on the castle portal. It would not be of abiding permanence, as you well know, and there would still have been sufficient room for the Trauttmansdorffs and Pernsteiners, who admittedly were there before us.

I found our conversations extraordinarily instructive. In your own field you are all very distinguished, even if somewhat willful in dealing with the cultural treasures and historical precedence.

Let me thank you for the informative afternoon and for the care with which you tend my ancestral patrimony.

> With highest esteem, I remain,
> gentlemen, yours sincerely
> *Vincenc Xaver Count Thurn und Taxis*

P.S. Concerning your inquiries at the Ram Inn as to a certain janitor at the castle. That could well be—from my holidays there, I recall several grooms in my uncle's stables who competed for his favor, one of whom distinguished himself in zeal and devotion. On the other hand, I have on principle never concerned myself with domestics.

N.B. I hope you enjoy the package sent you by our doughty farmers, all of it from our own slaughter and prepared according to local recipe. The sausages enjoy high praise here. I personally do not eat such things.

> A bientôt

"I'll drink to that!" Maltzahn shouts.

"A pompous ass!" Podol is outraged. "Should I advise him that his ancestors ran a carriage and delivery service, opened other people's mail and got rich by blackmailing them? Two hundred years at Litomyšl my foot! They picked it up for a song in 1855, the castle and the estate! They plundered the most valuable furnishings and paintings, copper engravings and lithographs, and carted it all off to Regensburg. And he vouches for the fact that all of us here are very distinguished in our field! I think I'm going to be sick!"

"It's probably the sausage," Maltzahn suggests.

"He doesn't eat such things! A degenerate faggot with a pitchfork!"

"Not so loud." Orten has spotted Nordanc crossing the courtyard.

"Andy! Do you want some headcheese? And fresh blood sausage, straight from the slaughter?" Podol waves him over.

Nordanc pockets two liverwursts and cuts off a piece of the blood and barley for Max. The brewery is open by now, so they all drink a beer before starting work. It is going to be a hot day.

. . .

The nights have cooled noticeably now. Patera's cough is worse, and he's been having stomach pains of late. Podol's dizzy spells continue. Orten insists they stop early this year; they agree to the middle of September. Another two weeks.

The rows of sgraffiti and the cornice on the west façade will serve as a cushion next season. They are on schedule, and the drudgery of the large fresco in the courtyard is behind them—it wasn't a bad year.

Orten examines Josef K.'s bicycle license on the meandering ornamental frieze, wonders if years hence anyone will be able to figure out what it means. A new, fast-moving generation of restorers will come, who will attack the façade with spray-can acrylics, forever sealing the palimpsest of flaking images that have lasted for centuries now, a testament to the imagination of an age and to the artistic freedom of its creators.

The last meal at the Ram. Podol at midpoint of the oval table, between Patera and Hanna, who is talking with Karla, who is next to Orten, who is saving the next seat for Marie; Qvietone can figure that much out and takes the next chair over; Nordanc quickly sits down beside him, flanked by Patočka, who wants to talk shop about the archives, and so bends the ear of the director, who is keeping an eye on his wife, Marcela, and Maltzahn on his right; then come Svoboda and Patera, who are arguing about the colors of the horizon. Podol pours Patera another glass of wine. "To the façade!"

They all drink, Orten is the only one who hesitates. Even the manager joins in the toast. "We're going to miss you, Mr. Podolský, and all the rest of you gentlemen!" The next round is on the house.

Marie has arrived by this time, the hair at her temples sticky with sweat. Orten and Qvietone dive into her aseptic aura, each addicted in his own way. Marcela and Karla exchange a meaningful glance. "Sorry I'm late; there was a lot of stitching to do today," she says to Orten.

Qvietone feels a twinge in his convalescing knee and turns to ask a question of Nordanc, who provides a detailed answer.

The wine doesn't agree with Patera. He takes a deep breath and looks around the table. "There are thirteen of us."

Jirse appears at the door. "There, you see, number fourteen," Podol says.

The object of everyone's attention, Jirse hobbles over; half of those present have not seen his new leg and notice the change in his walk. He automatically heads for Podol, then stops and looks around until he spots Orten, who is busy at the moment with the jammed catch on Marie's purse.

"Here's a letter for you."

Orten glances at the envelope. Bright-colored stamps, a blue flower, two green fish, a gold pagoda—Nippon. He is a little surprised. "That can only mean something's gone wrong again."

In the familiar ceremonial style of his Japanese friend who is a friend of Czech music—he can't decide whether this is the same handwriting—he is informed that if he can accept its invitation within three months, a film studio in Kyoto has commissioned him to create a bas-relief wall outside its executive offices; all travel expenses will be borne by his employer; both his honorarium and a budget for materials will be determined upon discussions once he is there.

"How did they come up with you?" Maltzahn asks enviously.

"I don't know." Orten is less enthusiastic. "Apparently my porous wall that they screwed up last time reminded someone of perforated movie film."

"So it pays to screw up."

Orten ignores him and goes on reading, learns that he will take part in the cherry-blossom festival in spring and that in addition to the works of Leoš Janáček, the letter writer has now begun to study the quarter-tone compositions of Alois Hába, and sends greetings and best wishes to his friends at the Prague Conservatory.

"Well, you don't have to worry about what you're going to do this winter," Podol comments.

"Neither do you; they want two people. The wall is supposed to be a hundred and eight feet long, and I've been asked to suggest a second artist. Will you come along?"

"Let me see." Podol takes the letter. "What are all these musical notes? Have they got you confused with somebody else?"

"They've confused me with somebody else twice now, but that's the least of our problems. They are stingy. If they nitpick the way they did last time, we won't even need to start work."

"We'll have to tell them that right off. I was never in Japan and I'm not going to let them spoil it for me!" The trip becomes real for Podol only after difficulties arise.

"Jan, shouldn't another sculptor go along?" Maltzahn speaks up again. "Someone who knows the ropes?"

No one hears him amid the general tumult. The letter is passed around, and while some are reading it, others look at the stamps and the complicated but correct address.

"This has been a long time underway, and you're supposed to be there within three months? That leaves only six weeks for a visa and all the rest," Svoboda declares.

"He's been carrying it around with him all this time," Patočka says sotto voce and points to the bar, where Jirse is lapping up beer.

"You're right. He waited till your very last night, the mail doesn't come in the evening," Qvietone says.

"Isn't it an express letter?" Nordanc asks.

"An expressly slow one. I know him. He always takes his time with my mail, too. Once he's got something, he holds on to it. He's not very quick at handing it over."

"But it had to be forwarded first, and the local address is very abbreviated: Jan Orten, Friedland, Castle. That might have caused some confusion."

"Our sausages got here," Podol remarks. "But it doesn't matter where it's been all this while, we've both got to start packing, Jan. But it all depends on what they have to say about this at home. How about you?"

"No one is going to miss me at home." Orten looks at Marie, who has not said a word yet. "Maybe three of us could go."

"I could take a research sabbatical," Qvietone mutters. "If I can't get a visa for Japan, maybe I could come along part of the way, to Mongolia, to study the generic behavior of bumblebees. I've submitted a proposal once already. . . ."

Nordanc, who has listened to him with interest, quickly calculates that he has just enough German marks for a trip to Japan, though it is questionable whether he could get a visa for Mongolia.

"Then I'm coming along, too," Maltzahn says. "I know the owner of a gallery in Kyoto, he'll send me an invitation in time. I'm still due some money from my reserves, Italian lire I think. Although six weeks will be cutting it short." He stands up, as if he must go pack right now.

"Why, then, let's just go ahead and ask if they don't need some sgraffiti on a façade," Podol says. "Actually, I had a vacation in mind. Are you coming along, too, Václav?"

"No, you guys go ahead," Patera says. "It's nothing for me. Besides, who would invite me?"

"May I see it a moment?" The manager carefully takes the envelope, she is chiefly impressed by the pagoda stamp. She reads Orten's address, amazed at "how that Japanese fellow writes it so correct," and incensed at the sloppy way the post office has scratched it out and scribbled in the new address. "How can anyone be so crude, as if they get letters like this by the dozen every day!"

"They probably do," Orten says.

"But not as beautiful as this." She gazes proudly at Podol, although the letter is addressed to Orten: a man who takes such pains to restore the castle here in Friedland, who has been filling those bare walls with marvelous pictures for years now, is a great artist, in demand throughout the world.

Even Patočka is proud; he holds the envelope in trembling hands and has already catalogued it in his mind—a rudimentary stamp collection, most of it missing, is also part of the castle archives. "Congratulations," he says to Orten.

As the party breaks up, Orten casts a questioning look at Marie, who has still not said a word.

She makes slant eyes, pulling up their corners with her index fingers, and smiles.

Part Two

OUTER
SIBERIA

THIRTEEN

Praha-Ruzyně—Moskva-Sheremetyevo;
Moskva-Domodedovo—Siberia.

"The hell!" Podol fumes, upset by the unscheduled stopover in Sverdlovsk. The Russians and their everlasting *"seychas"* ("plenty of time") are getting on his nerves now, too. Their taxi from Sheremetyevo barely made it to Domodedovo, but these guys had it all arranged somehow, because the pilot hadn't even arrived yet. The stewardesses are all business; they are used to breakdowns and difficulties; they say there will be a stopover, but give no reasons. The Asian one has a smile like Marie's. Until now everything has gone as planned, but Podol, who has never flown in this direction before, is still fuming. Nordanc seems to have the greatest patience; this is just a grand adventure for him, and the pilot's melons rolling around in the cabin upset him less than passport checks and baggage searches at customs. Amazingly, it turns out that Svoboda's passport does the job; the resemblance is not all that great—the entry for color of eyes reads "blue," and Nordanc's definitely tend more to gray, and his hair is more auburn than dark blond—but it seems to be acceptable. He let his crew cut grow out and unscrewed his earring before they crossed the border, and the inch or so difference in height—Svoboda is a good five foot ten—can be explained as normal daily shrinkage, or if necessary as part of the aging process; the passport has been renewed once already. And luckily, even the first name works in his favor—Antonín/Andy; as far as the Russians are concerned, he is a Czech, a brother, and no one expects deserters from that direction. Besides, spies usually have Swiss passports and speak the language better.

They don't need visas. He struck a good bargain with his hundred marks, even though Podol said a Czech passport wasn't worth that much. And in case Qvietone did manage to meet up with them in Novosibirsk (something the others knew nothing about), he could even go along with him to Mongolia. Had a Luxembourger ever traveled so far in the socialist East? Svoboda had been pleasantly surprised by a hundred German marks, and hadn't seemed very uneasy about it, either. Are all these Slavs so devil-may-care?

Nordanc's Russian answers consist of amputated and "Russified" Czech, which grates on the others' ears. True, Maltzahn's mangled and driveled attempts at the language are not much better, but he does it with great verve, much to the delight of the female personnel on board. Orten says nothing, but he has the most efficacious papers; Nordanc hides in his shadow, snug in Orten's moribund speech.

"So what did he trade for the melons?" Podol wants to know.

"They're loading some sort of tin cans right now," Nordanc reports.

"Pomidori." Maltzahn can read it on the boxes being rolled in underneath them. "All we needed, they're probably still radioactive. Kyshtym is just down the road," Maltzahn adds, looking at his map.

"What you call just down the road in Russia is usually a good way off," Orten says. "Besides, that was twenty years ago."

"You never know. They didn't notice anything at first, either, not until the ornithologists started finding piles of dead migratory birds in England, with everybody trying to keep it a secret." He lowers his voice.

"You can speak normally. I doubt if the girl understands Czech." Podol nods toward the Yakut lass, who is smiling and watching Orten again.

Several of the local passengers leave the plane to stretch their legs. *"Na progulku?"* the stewardess asks.

"Nyet, kak dolgo yeshcho?" Orten has gathered up his few scraps of Russian, and to Nordanc's amazement the girl answers him with a shrug of the shoulders. So they wait.

They take off. The flight is less unsettling than before, when the melons were rolling down the aisle and between the passengers' legs. Not that it had seemed to upset the others. One big-boned man across the aisle, who had called the stewardess over, whispered something, and pressed money into her hand—she then picked up a melon and brought it to him.

"That takes care of one," Podol said. Maltzahn suggested they buy them all before the plane crashed, but no one knew what to do with them. They had already aroused suspicion by declining the dripping, juicy slices that the Buryat passed along the rows near him with a self-assurance that brooked no refusal. Nordanc, who tried to pay for his piece, only added fuel to the fire. The Russians and the Asians were delighted to take some—the young mother at the front, for instance, who simply beamed as she held out the tidbit to her child (after a few bites, the boy's mouth turned pink and sticky and stayed that way for the rest of the flight). The man wrapped the other half of the melon in his *Pravda* and put it in his briefcase. The dam was broken, the first piroshki appeared, were passed back and forth, each with a different filling, each a special recipe—potato or sauerkraut, mincemeat or jam (five homemade varieties)—and were traded for pears, plums, cucumbers. And here came the first bottle of vodka.

Nordanc begins to feel at home. The underlying tension of carrying Svoboda's passport buoys him up, sharpens his senses for the conspiratorial camaraderie. Western stinginess, efficiency, and prudence are embarrassing here—the meticulous Swiss, the Germans who are always too loud, and the English, who are the worst penny-pinchers of all. Was it not possible he was a Czech himself?

Orten would have been the first to disabuse him of the notion. Nordanc casts him a sidelong glance. Orten is the only one who has not dived into the pool of warmth. Podol is now singing along with the miner from Chita, Maltzahn is flirting with the Russian stewardess—blonde, well-groomed, a Marcela Horská type. As they emerge from the clouds, Orten stares out the window at the boundless forests of the taiga, a green ocean of lost chances, forever undiscovered and unexplored. It won't be long before Nordanc learns more about that, too.

Orten has to work hard not to get caught up in it; he has seen it all in the movies—the generosity, the great Russian soul. But he still mourns for Palach, for the crushed spirit of '68, for the desire, lost now, to get involved in the affairs of his country, to change it from the foundations up. He remembers the tanks, the exhausted, confused soldiers, their round heads, the buzz cuts—how old are you he asked one of them—sixteen. They were here to put down a counterrevolution, the boy said through his soggy plug of tobacco, a face smeared with snot and tears. Many of them didn't even know where they were—

France or Germany, somewhere in Europe. Those who did know didn't let on. Their dismay when people spoke Russian to them, their humiliation at having advanced with the Germans against their brothers. He could see the old women in District Six, where the Russian émigrés of 1917 had settled, who dragged themselves out onto the streets to ask, My boy, what are you doing here?—the faces of their own grandmothers. And they wept, their heads propped on the windshields of their *gaziks,* and the old women stroked the stubble—go home, lads, before something awful happens.

The holy patience of Russia is swaddled in these warm feelings—patience with Stalin, with Brezhnev. No thanks, no piroshki.

Nordanc discovers furry eyes peering from baskets—rabbits. He is aware of chickens, too, in hiding-places close by—peeps, social calls from handbags to covered cages. Enough to give a British customs agent ulcers—cheek by jowl with continental rabies. Pet rats smuggled into the country and gracing the shoulders of tourists strolling through Piccadilly—ferreted out and put to sleep, police caps as temporary holding tanks for transmitters of disease, burned after use—the sergeant ought to take his holidays here. Pet rats, crack instinct—when do we get to Novosibirsk?

First Omsk—the tomatoes have to be delivered. Orten wonders if they will ever be able to catch the next train from Chabarovsk to Nachodka, or if it hasn't already pulled out. There is one comfort: they won't have to wait longer than four days for the ship to Yokohama.

Podol remarks that Omsk is not a scheduled stop. Orten waves this aside. Some of the passengers who boarded in Sverdlovsk are taken off the plane, the rabbits, too. In their place, a goat in a wooden cage is placed on a platform at the rear. Podol and Maltzahn are beginning to wonder if they are on the right flight.

Two hours of pointless sitting around—it is dark when they take off.

Novosibirsk is to be their final destination for today. They are taken to a hotel reserved for foreigners, near the airport; the airline will assume the costs, but they will have to pay an extra Intourist fee. The other three are keeping a close eye on Podol now, ever since he almost came to blows with the Aeroflot dispatcher. Nordanc wants to avoid having another, and perhaps sharper-eyed, check of their passports. Orten is determined to keep this a one-night delay, for them all. It would most likely not be easy to get Podol out of a jail run by the local militia.

He flares up again at the reception desk when the punctilious desk clerk requires that all registration information be recorded exactly. Podol writes in Czech, and she asks him to fill it out again in printed letters. He slams down his passport, though he is particularly proud of it, but then picks it up again and says with a smile, "You cow, stupid, fill it out yourself." The postpositioned adjective is a concession to the tone of Russian fairy tales, like those he was once asked to illustrate, a spontaneous flourish of syntax to enhance the poetic function of the language, though detrimental to its appellative and connotative character. The young Communist is unsure of herself: on the one hand, the word *kráva* and the Russian *korova* are too alike to be misunderstood, on the other hand Podol's smile is simply too winning; she must have misheard him, or it means something else. She has fallen into the trap of Podol's amiability, a blend of foxy Moravian farmer and shrewd artist, and in her confusion she hands Podol the key to the luxury suite on the second floor, the one with wax flowers on the table and velvet curtains—until one of her cadre mates hastily explains that these comrades (the term apparently makes Czechs easier to deal with) need only emergency quarters for the night. Since there is no hard cash involved and the bill will be sent to Aeroflot, the two rooms at the back on the ground floor will do.

They are too weary for a long argument, not that anyone is listening. The girl leaves for home, the hotel is locked up for the night. Podol's suggestion that they go out for a drink—they can climb out the window—is greeted by Orten with a haggard smile. It is eleven-thirty, the workers of Novosibirsk are already asleep, there are no bars, people drink at work during the day, or on the street, behind garbage cans or boarded-up church doors.

They sit in Podol's room, which he is sharing with Nordanc—the low level of sympathy between Maltzahn and Nordanc precludes their spending nights together, and ever since Nordanc's project, A Charles-Bridge Ashlar for Art, which ended with his getting cheated by both the stonemason and the truck driver, Orten has had mixed feelings about Nordanc's proclivities in practical matters; although Nordanc swore with the saddest of faces that he had made a deal for the stone at half the price, including delivery charges. They drink Nordanc's brandy, which he managed to locate during their hasty switch of airports in Moscow, and try to recall occasions when things have gone even shittier.

"At the Venice Biennial they stuck us in a flophouse," Orten reminisces. "This place smells of disinfectant, but at least it's clean. That place smelled of everything imaginable. When Fábera pulled back the curtain, he almost wept. It was an air well facing a gray wall; he had been so excited about the roofs of Venice, the light, had been in a regular fever the last few months, even tried to shift from his brown tones to blues, to capture 'transalpine azure' as he called it. It was his first trip to Italy. They had stuck all six of us in one double, the whole 'artistic delegation.' Fábera ran down to the desk and set up one dreadful row, in Czech. The only words he knew in Italian were: *pittore, Praga, Venezia, biennale*. Then he vanished. We didn't know where to look for him. The moron from the union who had come along as our official leader didn't know from nothing, he was peeing in his pants, told us that Fábera had deeply disappointed him—his first chance to visit Venice and then carries on like this. He demanded a session where we each could criticize him. He wanted to apologize to the hotel for the incident, it was all we could do to stop him. He couldn't speak a word of Italian either, but he had managed to learn how to toady effectively in any language.

"Two days later Fábera came back, simply radiant, in the best of moods, elegantly dressed. Fellows, you have to come visit me. He had moved into a *palazzo* on the Grand Canal, where usually only Americans lived, with a suite all to himself, and went into raptures over Venice, and its magnificent women. Had already got to know a whole slew of gallery owners and could give us some good tips. The directors of the Biennial had been really quite embarrassed; they had put him in the wrong category. These holes were apparently reserved for socialist countries."

"And the rest of you?"

"We stayed where we belonged. Let some other guy go ahead and knock himself out trying to show off."

"And then apologize for playing the role of the idiot." Podol takes another swig. "We're going to have to lay in some supplies tomorrow. There is vodka to be had in the shops, isn't there?"

"Not to worry. If that runs out, they can expect an uprising, the first in sixty years."

The beds sag, are too soft, and too short. Podol lies with his legs drawn up, bouncing with every turn—footwork, left hook, he has

Nordanc tell him about the most recent boxing championships. By the time Nordanc starts talking about Max and his worries whether Svoboda will feed her regularly, Podol is already asleep.

After a bad night, they are not even especially surprised to find Qvietone in the breakfast room. The only comment is Maltzahn's muttered, "All we needed." Nordanc is obviously excited, close to blushing, but tries not to let them notice. He had wanted to make inquiries about Qvietone—there were not that many possibilities for foreigners to stay in Novosibirsk without being noticed, without registering; only two hotels were permitted to accept them—but he had not dared ask. Qvietone, who had arrived two days ago by the Trans-Siberian Railroad, inquired about their flight yesterday and learned that it had been delayed.

He is the least surprised of all, but keeps a distrustful, questioning eye on Orten. Might there not be a chance he could continue his trip in their company? Orten suspects that this is only a pretext for tailing Marie. "Is this everybody?" Qvietone asks as well, as nonchalantly as possible. "It's enough," Podol replies, but Orten says vaguely: "Not quite."

Their flight is scheduled to depart that evening, and faced with the bleak prospect of staying in a back room all day, they decide to take a stroll through town. The unctuous head desk clerk, who reeks of *dukhi* (perfume) and is definitely a bastard in Podol's opinion, keeps their passports. They let Qvietone play tour guide, he has been here twenty-four hours already; besides, he grew up under socialism and has an adequate knowledge of Russian.

Red Prospect extends gray and monotonous before them, hemmed in by concrete barracks and uplift billboards. The atmosphere of the center city is so depressing that they consider retreating to their hotel with the vodka they have bought. Qvietone remarks that there is supposed to be a monastery or church at the other end of town. They take a trolley, get lost, are given new directions by the passenger collective in their tram car, according to whom they are to ride to "Krestovka" and ask there again.

The apartment blocks disappear, the buildings are smaller now and more widely scattered, old frame houses with weathered gables and carved moldings, painted white and blue. The car empties out. As they round a curve below a hill, they spot church towers with wooden shingles. They get off without asking; there is only one old man, fast asleep, and they don't want to wake him. They walk through a grove of birch trees, until they reach the edge of a wide swampy *dolina,* from where they can see their tram making a wide loop around the church. "That must be Krestovka," Podol says. They had got off two stations too soon. They don't want to turn back now, so they wade across the bottoms, zigzagging around clumps of grass and hags, and arrive, close to collapse and with wet feet, at the main gate. It is locked. Podol sits down on what remains of a wall, removes his shoes and socks, and pulls the bottle out of the bag.

"But it's a lovely area," Qvietone remarks, trying to justify the excursion. The looks they give shut him up.

"That's true," Nordanc says softly.

Out of habit, Maltzahn perfunctorily takes a few pictures—broken windows, planks ripped from the sides of the chapel. "Our sgraffiti wouldn't hold up here."

"Eighty years old, and in this condition," Podol says.

"Eighty years is a long time around here." Orten has been hardened by his two visits to Nachodka.

An old peasant comes down the road and warily asks what they want. Podol points behind him with his vodka bottle. "We want to get in the church, what else. Is it ever open?"

All the peasant understands is that they are foreigners.

"Closed, forbidden," he says sternly. It is not clear what upsets him more: that the church is dilapidated and closed, or that foreigners, with vodka in hand, want to get into an Orthodox church.

Without giving them another glance, he hurries off, stooped and bent.

"He's off to fetch the local militia," Maltzahn says.

"You figure he lives in disguise here in the woods, waiting for lost tourists, to unmask them as spies?" Podol puts his socks and shoes on and walks along the wall. "Although there's nothing much left to wreck." He peeks through a crack in the chapel's planks. "Always the same damn thing, shards and shit."

Behind the church he spots an old woman wrapped in a shawl. She is kneeling beside a wooden cross in the ramshackle cemetery and

crossing herself with such grand, fervent gestures that Podol pulls back
in fright. But she has seen him and shrinks back, then hurries off across
the fields to the woods, to where there are three wooden shacks and a
well. "Wait!"

"Let's go," an edgy Orten says.

Podol gives a stone a kick, picks up his bag, and unscrews the cap
of his bottle. "This place would drive a man to drink!"

They troop along down the tracks, but can find no station. Qvietone, who didn't see the old woman and is gamboling along the woods'
edge, finds some small brown fungi in the underbrush. He gives them
a try. "A little leathery, but not bitter, about like horse mushrooms."

"Let me see." Podol takes one. "It's all dried out and shriveled." He
tosses the mushroom away.

Qvietone goes on chewing defiantly, nibbles some bilberries, too,
and washes it all down with a pull of vodka. He picks a handful of
the berries for Podol, who takes an angry bite—he can't stand bilberries. He thinks about the frightened old woman at prayer.

Birches, almost bare now, evergreens, rowans.

Concerned about how they will be able to get back, Orten and Maltzahn keep watch out for a tram, but Podol stops at every tenth tree
stump to pull the vodka from its bag; they had assumed that four
bottles would last them until Chabarovsk, but they will have to buy a
couple more on the way back now. Qvietone trots alongside, chewing,
stopping beside tree trunks to inspect mosses, peeled-off bark, leaves,
fungi, berries, and empty birds' nests; he fingers grasses and siliceous
sedges, scratching himself, runs his hand across the furry leaves of field
thistles and the clustered ciliate funnels of lady's mantle, *Alchemilla
conjuncta,* strokes quaking grass, removes the white, spongy marrow
from rushes, watches it curve erect like feather-light inchworms of the
cave butterfly, *Triphosa dubitata*—where is Marie? Nordanc stays close
by him, wants to see each new find, marvels at the names, hears terms
like "plant galls" and "owl castings" for the first time, is unable to
translate them.

They take a shortcut, which turns swampy again; crossing a ditch,
they climb the hill, find themselves on the main road, the smoky city
in the distance. Trucks pass, loud and stinking, but no trams, though

the rails are something of a comfort, but it is getting late, Maltzahn warns. And colder, too.

A truck stops. The driver, about thirty, shouts in Russian syntax above the roar of his motor: "What sort of sort are you?"

"From Czechoslovakia."

In contrast to Venice, that has some effect here; they are told to climb in. Podol, Orten, and Maltzahn scramble into the backseat, Qvietone, as their interpreter, joins the driver; Nordanc squeezes in between him and the door, both his knees jammed against the windshield, and one of Qvietone's thrust against his hip, its pressure easing or increasing with each maneuver of the gearshift. Nordanc's hips answer the secret messages. He watches Qvietone, who has apparently developed a taste for his fungi; he chews away, smiling a bemused smile, his legs half asleep, Nordanc's counterpressure is simply part of the tight quarters in the cab; at the moment he enjoys being squashed. The driver asks him what he does. Of late, Qvietone finds he is speaking Russian freely and almost flawlessly. He explains that he is a biologist, a scientist. "Research," he thinks to add. "Akademiya Nauk."

"*Ya ponimayu.*" The driver steps on the gas.

They sense they are driving in the wrong direction, but it's probably just a detour. For now, they are simply glad to be warm and sitting down. The cab smells of tobacco. Podol's bottle slips from its bag and bangs on the floor. "Vodka!" The driver is delighted, takes a pull, says "*Druzhba,*" and starts to sing. It is "The Song of the Driver on the Frontlines" (*Put' dorozhka, frontovaya*). Qvietone can see Marie waving to him from distant Friedland; he repeats the Russian refrain. Podol sings along in Czech behind him—dusty soldiers in their tanks and *gaziks,* the high-wheeled Russian jeeps, had brought the song to the villages and towns of Moravia in the spring of '45, and they were showered with bouquets of lilac by the jubilant crowds. By the dozens they climbed up onto the passing vehicles to embrace the soldiers, clung to the cannons, waved, laughed—clusters of human fruit in May. As they entered Prague, Podol had stood on the running board of a convoy truck, sharing the driver's *makhorka.* PILSEN IS DANCING THE BOOGIE-WOOGIE, the headlines read, but the Russians had the longer journey behind them—the battles in the High Tatras, the dead and wounded at Dukla Pass. They had the lovelier songs; they were the liberators. They should never have come in '68. Orten knows the words, too, and those of the next song as well, "The Moldau Girl"; the driver is from Kishinev, and regards the Czechs as neighbors. But Orten does not sing along. He watches the gravel road, hemmed in now on both sides by birches and firs, and parallel to it, the tracks of the suburban railway they had used to orient themselves.

The road takes a sharp left under a railroad bridge just as the freight train passes overhead. Orten tries to make out the slogans on the flags of the locomotive—SOVIET POWER PLUS ELECTRIFICATION . . . Lenin knew what was what, he liked to go to the movies himself. Assuming they are traveling in the right direction, Orten expects a view of the city once they have rounded the curve. Instead, the woods grow denser.

They start to feel uneasy. Qvietone is told to ask if this is the right road and how long it will take. The driver dismisses the question; of course it's the right road. They figure there must be a construction site at the edge of town and ask about the aerodrome. In Tolmatchyevo, right, he knows. He starts singing again, this time accompanied only by Qvietone, who hums along. Podol does not know the song, besides which it is clear to him that they are not in Novosibirsk but in the middle of the taiga. He taps the driver on the shoulder, *"Gorod,* town?" and points behind them. *"Gorod, da, gorodok,"* the driver smiles, pointing straight ahead. He takes another drink. A banner appears at the edge of the road—"RUSSIA'S POWER WILL GROW WITH SI-BERIA. M. V. LOMONOSOV." No signs for Novosibirsk.

"Tell him we want to go to Novosibirsk," Podol says to Qvietone.

"He told him already." Maltzahn is upset.

"Then let him tell him again." Orten would just as soon climb out and try to hitchhike back in the opposite direction.

"It can't be all that far. If worse comes to worse, we'll take a taxi," Maltzahn suggests.

"And if there aren't any taxis?"

"Then I don't know. Whose idea was this to begin with?" Maltzahn first throws Nordanc a hostile glance, then Qvietone, who is engrossed in the browns, reds, yellows, and greens of the passing trees, in the circling of birds as they take wing; he can predict their flight above the treetops. A rabbit tries to dodge them as they come around a curve, and his eyes follow it safely across to the other side. He understands the languages and gestures of animals, and the driver's increasingly obscene songs, too, which, much to the latter's delight, he sings along with, the taste of edifying fungi still on his lips.

Maltzahn is close to suspecting that Qvietone is in cahoots with the driver to kidnap them all (ransom: Czech passports)—with his knowledge of the language he must have figured out by now what's going on, and this definitely doesn't look like Novosibirsk. He demands that Qvietone "clear this up," but he doesn't react, just smiles to himself; he understands everything, but processes it so quickly that Maltzahn's words are no more than a small, insignificant disturbance, like the musty odor of wet socks that has gradually suffused the cab, a kind of unifying element.

As tension mounts, Nordanc suddenly says: "I see houses."

These are new buildings in the middle of the taiga, lower and more substantial than the apartment blocks they have seen thus far. "Were those guards?" Maltzahn asks.

"Where?"

"Back there, there were two of them, soldiers."

"I didn't see anything," Podol says.

The first buildings are on wooded lots among the trees; there are no streets. A squirrel is sitting on a windowsill, gnawing at nuts that have been laid out for it. An idyllic scene—winterized dachas, washlines stretched between birch trees, children's underwear fluttering in the sun. Old-style Russian frame houses are nowhere to be seen. Behind the buildings, a broad expanse of water glistens through the trees, a large lake.

"It ain't Novosibirsk," Podol says.

A fellow in sweats and a fur cap is jogging up ahead among the trees. He throws himself down on the grass and does push-ups. Their driver stops. The jogger looks up, does two more push-ups, and comes over. "*Vot delegatsiya,*" the driver says, and lets them climb out, but keeps the rest of the vodka for himself. He gives a friendly wave; he was glad to help out, he says, adding that the Czechs are brothers.

"You're from Czechoslovakia?" the young man, who is about Qvietone's age, asks, wiping his brow. "I'll take you to Anatoly Vasilyevich."

"Who's he taking us to?" Orten asks, but Qvietone is already walking on ahead with the jogger, out of earshot now. He makes some remark, the Russian laughs; Nordanc, who is right beside him, is apparently enjoying himself as well.

"I'd like to know what they're laughing about," Podol says angrily.

"And Nordanc's right in the thick of it, of course," Maltzahn remarks. "Doesn't understand a word, but is egging them on. I just hope he sticks with Qvietone from here on out."

"We'll all be sticking with him from here on out from the look of things," Orten comments. "We should at least find out where we are."

Qvietone and Nordanc are waiting outside one of the buildings, the one with the kids' underwear.

"Where's he off to? Did he go to get someone else?"

"He's changing," Qvietone explains.

"Why are we waiting here anyway?"

"Because without him we're not going anyplace."

"We don't want to go just anyplace, we want to go back. Where the hell are we?" Maltzahn wonders if he shouldn't take a few pictures, just in case.

The young man comes back out in gray flannel trousers, a dark blue turtleneck, over which he wears a gray sports coat, and buckskin moccasins. They don't recognize him at first, but he smiles and introduces himself. "Jakov Plotkin, doctoral candidate in mathematical sciences."

He has a round, childlike face, bright eyes, and fair hair; although he is still young, he is already slightly bald. He gives them all a firm handshake, they mutter their own names, only Qvietone replies clearly: "Dr. Erik Qvietone, zoologist, Prague."

"An honor." The Russian scientist bows. "Welcome to Akademgorodok."

Anatoly Vasilyevich Dobrodin is the deputy director of the Geological Institute at Academic Community—which has been erected south of Novosibirsk on the shores of Lake Ob as the home of the Siberian Academy of Sciences—and the secretary of its communications department, which coordinates services for all foreign delegations. As such, it is his task to decide how much attention will be shown to guests, and also what quantity of information they will be given, for the measurement of which his younger colleagues first came up with the jocular term "bitpers" (bits per person). But in light of Dobrodin's steadily increasing urge to communicate, an urge that has grown in proportion both to his age and to the noticeable drop in the number of Western experts who have visited Akademgorodok in recent years, they have since unanimously adopted the term "bytepers." On guided tours with persons to whom he has taken a liking, he manages several hundred megabytes (straight ASCII).

Inasmuch as Plotkin refused to call a taxi for them before they paid a call on Anatoly Vasilyevich, they try the direct approach with the influential functionary himself. When he hears that they want to fly to Chabarovsk today, and then continue on to Yokohama, he is taken aback and remarks that there's "plenty of time" (*seychas*), and that they first really must partake of a little *zakuska*. After all there would be another plane tomorrow. "And just among us, my friends, what does Yokohama have over Akademgorodok? Our town must surely have the highest average IQ of anywhere on earth, the truth of which you may confirm for yourselves right now." Linking arms with Orten, he is ready to accompany them into town. "Perhaps we can best begin there," he says, pointing to a pompous edifice. "The Institute for Nuclear Physics."

"I'm not going in there! Who knows what all you'd be exposed to, what with the lousy safety precautions. Any fool knows better!" Maltzahn looks all around, searching for the bus he would love to jump aboard.

"Don't get hysterical," Podol hisses. "They're not going to contaminate their whole scientific elite."

Dobrodin gazes at him quizzically. Qvietone offers some hasty explanation in Russian; the only word they understand is "elite," which arouses their suspicions; he has apparently been sabotaging their departure from the start. The Russian laughs, and claps Maltzahn on the shoulder. Nordanc, totally confused now, laughs with him. Podol and Orten exchange glances: Qvietone is gradually becoming a problem, they notice now that he is still chewing away, and apparently has no inhibitions about translating word for word; he's having simply a grand time playing the polyglot.

"You coming along?" Dobrodin takes a disconcerted Maltzahn by the arm.

"Excuse me," Orten stammers, "we're not scientists." Qvietone is most definitely high, so they will obviously have to depend on their own skills in Russian.

"Of course we are!" Qvietone interrupts and is off on a tirade that even the Russian has trouble following—his gaze shifts from Qvietone to Maltzahn, from Maltzahn to Podol, to Orten, resting somewhat longer only on Nordanc.

"What's he telling him?" Maltzahn watches Qvietone with growing distress.

Orten is busy collecting cumbersome words for an explanatory statement, while Qvietone is apparently continuing to amuse himself. Having discovered a squirrel in the park, he begins to pull fussbudget faces and hop about like a giddy little rodent.

"Stop nibbling on that crap!" Podol pulls the sack from his hand.

"Sciurus vulgaris," Qvietone says, taking offense.

Dobrodin looks at Podol in amazement. "Calm down," he declares in deep, sonorous Russian. "Why spoil the lad's (*malchik*'s) fun?" He reaches into the sack and pulls out a mushroom. "People here call it 'little scamp.' Siberia is full of marvelous plants and animals, the boundless treasures of nature. Do you know the Baikal *omul?*" He takes a bite of the mushroom.

"Sibir', ya ne boyus' tebya, ty tozhe russkaya zemlya!"

"What did he say?" Nordanc wants to know.

"Siberia, I fear you not, you too are Russian earth," Podol translates. "It's the same as in Czech."

"Except it's all on a somewhat grander scale," Orten remarks.

"Are we going to have to stay the night?" Maltzahn asks.

"I'm afraid so." Orten casts a glance at Qvietone.

A truck has pulled up to one of the large buildings on the other side of the road. Orten has the distinct impression he recognizes the driver.

"Six o'clock. If we hurry we can still make the eight-o'clock flight. It's less than twenty miles, we'd be there in half an hour."

"There'll be none of that, my little doves," Dobrodin says, laughing. "You're my guests today. And morning is always wiser than evening."

"And our plane tickets?"

"Those are good for two months. Besides, we can always give them a call."

He lays an arm around Qvietone's shoulder. "Psilocybin, we synthesize it in that building over there." He points to the Institute for Organic Chemistry further down Science Prospect.

"An ester of phosphoric acid, *Psilocybe semperviva,"* Qvietone replies, almost mechanically. *"Fungi magici*—I've read my Longo. And I own Cetto's great atlas of fungi, too." He smiles wanly.

"He's giving me the creeps," Maltzahn whispers.

Dobrodin stares at him. "You're a zoologist? But you have broad interests, I presume. Do you see those façades? Institutes, every one. Each different. We are careful about making sure the colors match, there has to be color, not like in Novosibirsk. Our young scientists must feel at home here. It is a great honor to work here. Thousands apply annually, but only the best are accepted. There are opportunities here, too, for young and talented foreign researchers to gain experience. I know the director of the Institute for Chemistry well. He is also a friend of Professor Heyrovský, your Nobel Prize medalist for holography."

"Polarography," Qvietone snorts.

"Now he's trying to lure away our up-and-coming scientists." Podol has understood Dobrodin's comments for the most part. "Erik, tell him you're not an addict, and that if need be you can synthesize the stuff at home."

There is no talking to Qvietone, who is now convulsed with laughter.

"We could make a trade," Maltzahn suggests. "He stays here and we go on our way. After all, he got himself into this."

"He's coming with us, at least as far as the next train," Podol says. "In exchange, we can give them a few suggestions for their façades."

Dobrodin picks up on the word "façade." Given the extremes of temperature, it had been difficult to find construction techniques that were not only absolutely durable but also aesthetically satisfying. Generations of enthusiastic scientists, artists, and planners had joined in the task, but in the end solutions had been found and tested here at Akademgorodok. And this was only the beginning. A similar concept had been developed for the oil refineries being constructed at Angarsk near Lake Baikal. People had to feel at home in Siberia, that was the watchword. Within ten days snow would be falling. Then they would see for themselves what sort of natural disasters had to be mastered.

"We won't be here for that," Podol replies.

"Let's hope not," Orten says.

Dobrodin looks at him. "You must excuse me; I didn't quite get your name."

"Orten."

"I mean your full name."

"Jan Orten."

"And what was your father's name?"

"Štěpán." Orten is confused.

"Are you in such a hurry to get away from us, Jan Styepanovich?" Maltzahn and Podol break into grins.

"I have to be on the job in Kyoto within ten days," Orten explains with some difficulty. "Stanislav Karlovich and Olbram Josefovich here can confirm that." He grins back.

"My father's name is Jiří," Maltzahn protests.

"Okay, Olbram Juryevich. Don't forget that we're all trying to get back on our way together."

"All of us?" Maltzahn glances at Qvietone, who is still laughing. Podol grabs him by the arm, dragging both him and Nordanc along behind Dobrodin, who is crossing the street. Qvietone pulls away once they are on the sidewalk. "The Institute for Hydrodynamics. I've always wanted to visit it."

"This is the first time he's ever seen it!" Maltzahn explodes.

"That's a wonderful idea," Dobrodin observes. "Are you coming along, Olbram Juryevich? You can leave that heavy camera with the doorman."

"I can or I must?" Maltzahn mutters. Podol shrugs.

"You'll have to tell me all about your work in Kyoto." Dobrodin links arms with Orten again. "And your restoration work in Bohemia. Our young friend here tells me it's quite unique."

Qvietone has been bragging again it seems. "There's restoration work wherever you go," Orten says, half in Czech. "It's a Renaissance castle. The only thing unique about it is the unusual size. We're restoring the . . . sgraffiti?"

"Yes, yes."

"On the façade." Orten is surprised how easy it is to make himself understood. He doesn't know if the Russian has latched onto him now because he's actually interested or to divert his attention or to have someone to help him up the stairs. He's overweight, so the third choice seems the most plausible.

"You're a sculptor?"

"Yes."

"Then we have a lot in common. An interest in stones! You want to alter them, and my job is to preserve and study them. We geologists all have our favorite stones, just as you sculptors must have. But whereas you bang away at a single slab with heart, head, and chisel, we bang away at continents. Europe, what is that? Speaking on a macro-geological scale, we are part of a tectonic plate. The political squabbles on its surface are laughable when compared to what is happening in the earth's mantle. I was part of a deep-bore project on the Kola Peninsula last year; it was enough to make you want to call all men your brothers on the spot. And it is pure luck that our plates have fused so tightly, forty miles thick. Apart from earthquake zones to the south and on the eastern rim of the Pacific, we are incredibly stabile. We Eurasians belong together. One might say that the Americans, with their thin crust, incite conflicts merely to improve their tectonic position. Look at their expansionist policies—they sense the trembling, the insecurity, and buy more cars; they stuff themselves with bananas from Central America, with meat from Australia, with drugs from India— they cram the whole world into their mouths, hoping to plug the hole of their fears.

"Their West Coast is nothing but an eggshell, and they know it. We can only stand back and watch. We could offer them assistance; we work on the same problems here at Akademgorodok, just ask Lavrentiev. We have a seismic belt ourselves, we have rumblings under Lake Baikal, too; there have been measurements of six, seven degrees magnitude on the Medvedyev scale in Georgia and Kirghiziya—all they would have to do is ask us, but their blockade is so total that they never even learn about our growing capabilities. True, there are some visiting delegations, like yourselves—don't interrupt me, you are artists, and perhaps here by mistake, but I don't really believe that; curiosity and creativity are part of your profession. You have come here from a fraternal country, and I'm not asking how you feel about '68, and please don't ask me, either. But our Western visitors are still keeping their distance. A few do come, some of them stay on for good in fact, but that's not enough. Perhaps we've not made sufficient progress for them, perhaps they know more than we in some areas, but that's why we are here, to learn. We are waiting for America, we want to help them when they botch the job, not just in terms of their tectonic crisis, not just along the San Andreas fault; we want to contribute to stabilization in a larger sense. The havoc wreaked by unemployment among their young people—send them here! We have deserts, mountains, tigers, and temperatures of fifty below, and more than enough work! Send Siberia a half million young Americans, or ten times that many, there's room for them to spread out. Whoever proves himself can stay. Of course it's hard, we have our rowdies and hooligans, too—though it's interesting that we've had to import foreign words for them—and in the present phase it's inevitable that the state must use a restrictive hand." Dobrodin smiles. "But I ask you, which is worse: for a bloodthirsty mob to shout 'Jump' to some desperate man who's lost his job and climbed a television tower, or for an officer of our militia to demand sternly that the fellow climb down at once because it is forbidden to trespass on socialist property?"

Dobrodin's expatiations are too complicated for Orten's knowledge of Russian. "You have a few too many men in your militia," he says—exhaustion has made him careless.

"In the second case, the man will probably live," Dobrodin replies. "Even if it is only because he has mobilized his inner resistance—perhaps against too many militiamen, as you put it."

Maltzahn has picked up on the fact that they are talking about the militia. He has a sixth sense for ticklish situations and comes over, smiling an asinine tourist smile, and asks in his most touching beginner's Russian about the photographs displayed in the cases along the corridor, evidence of all the successes achieved by socialist use of tectonics.

Dobrodin is more than happy to address his concerns, but there is one more thing he wants to know from Orten.

"Which do you prefer, Jan Styepanovich, gneiss or granite?"

"Gneiss is too expensive. Hard. But beautiful." Orten is somewhat bewildered, but relieved as well.

"Yes! Beautiful! Metamorphic stone heated twice inside the earth, hard. Fine as marble. We geologists can divide humanity into gneiss lovers and granite fans." He laughs at his use of the foreign word "fans." "I'm glad to know that you belong to the former!"

The pictures in the corridor document the planning and construction of various stages of the "Angara Stairway," the dams at Bratsk and

Krasnoyarsk, the projects for Ust'-Ilim, the reservoirs and canals; the variety and beauty of the wild rivers of Siberia.

"And probably intend a frontal attack on them all," Maltzahn comments.

"Not all of them," Dobrodin says to his surprise; comprehension is evidently mutual. "We don't need that much hydropower. And don't underestimate the labor involved. Bridging the ravines of the Angara demands almost superhuman efforts; it is impossible to build a three-thousand-foot pontoon bridge across its current. And don't forget the cataracts, the Pyanii and the Pokhmelnii alone are enough to discourage any reasonable man."

Orten translates the names: "The Drunk" and "The Guy with a Hangover." Those must be some nasty rapids in Russia.

"And how was it bridged?"

"Across the ice. When the river froze, the ice cover was used as a platform for the bridge. Although, given the gigantic boulders that had to be dumped into the river, no one knew if the ice would hold, no one had ever tried that construction method before. But we have a saying here in Siberia: 'Be nice to Father Frost.' In Yakutiya there are whole towns built on the permafrost, without any real foundations. In spring, when the thaw begins, they tend to tilt a bit, we have a good many 'tipsy' towns, but usually they stay on their feet. The permafrost is up to three thousand feet deep and only a thin layer at the surface actually thaws. People can protect themselves against winter in the holes they dig into it for cellars; it's only about twenty-eight degrees above zero down there when it's seventy-five below outside, and in summer, when it can get up over a hundred, the temperature stays the same. A refrigerator salesman would have a tough job up there."

There are already too many refrigerators, Nordanc reflects. He is reminded of the commune where he lived in West Berlin. If there's anything we don't need more of it's refrigerators, Ziploc bags, and bottles of Tabasco.

"And in our natural 'refrigerator,' our permafrost, there are treasures millions of years old. Ores, diamonds, coal, gold, oil . . ."

"And mammoths," Qvietone says.

"Those too," Dobrodin says, laughing, while regarding the next set of photos. "Dams of frozen earth, no cement at all—and they hold! We have to be very nice to Father Frost."

"Of course we build in other climatic zones as well," says the hydrogeologist who has joined them in the meantime, pointing casually to the display cases and moving on. "That way to the labs."

They try to figure out a way to avoid a further guided tour or at least to shorten it, but Dobrodin is already spouting the next set of statistics when Qvietone, who has remained more or less unnoticed until now and is standing beside the case with pictures of the Aswan Dam, turns to the engineer and asks, "How do you plan to wipe out schistosomiasis on the Nile?"

The hydrogeologist casts a surprised look at Dobrodin.

"Good question." Dobrodin claps Qvietone on the shoulder. "Even though one must admit the disease was present before we came on the scene. We're working on it. Do you have a solution?"

"I have." Qvietone is suddenly quite calm.

"That's true," Nordanc says. "Using fish that eat the snails."

They all look at him intently—for the first time.

"Then I'll arrange a meeting for you at the Zoological Institute tomorrow." Dobrodin laughs.

"Set it up for today, please," Qvietone says in all earnestness.

"Do you mean right now?" Dobrodin gives it some brief thought. "It's ten minutes from here, someone must still be there." He takes Qvietone by the arm and moves nimbly down the steps with him. Nordanc and the others bring up the rear.

"I told you he's talented," a smiling Dobrodin calls back over his shoulder to the hydrogeologist, who is still standing beside the display case.

They awaken with throbbing heads, queasy stomachs, and thirst—the celebration last night at Dobrodin's institute went on too long, a gathering of Czechs, Russians, Kirghiz, Evenks, Yakuts, Buryat-Mongols and one Luxembourger amid collections of stone samples and boring probes. Whenever you thought that at last you had spotted a Yakut, he turned out to be a Koryak or a Kamchadal. "Have we ever got it easy with just Slovaks," was Maltzahn's comment.

"They've got a Jewish republic tucked away somewhere, too," a hungover Maltzahn says, lowering his voice. "Completely cordoned off."

"There are scheduled flights to Birobidjan," they hear Qvietone re-mark from under his blanket. "And the Trans-Siberian passes right by. You could make a side trip from Chabarovsk."

"If we ever make it to Chabarovsk." Orten is getting dressed. "And if we do, we'll be happy to be sitting in the train for Nachodka." He bends down very slowly to his shoes.

"Besides, it's not a republic but an autonomous district," Qvietone con-cludes. "And in case you do make it to Chabarovsk by day, you'll have to wait till it gets dark anyway, no foreigners are allowed to make the trip to Nachodka along the Ussuri border by daylight." He gets up.

"We sat there on the tracks the whole night, too," Orten says.

"Did your fish impress anybody yesterday?" Qvietone's smart-ass airs are getting on Podol's nerves.

"The only person there was an ornithologist, an old man, whose first question was whether I knew which was the largest songbird."

"And did you know?" Maltzahn asks.

Qvietone glares at him in silence.

"The raven," Podol says. "I know all about those trick questions from school. The Russians love that sort of thing. Yesterday someone asked me . . ."

"What?"—Maltzahn.

"Oh, nothing, I'm just amazed how quick they all are to talk about rather private things, sensitive subjects they'd never talk about at home, including politics. The jokes are the same ones we were telling two years ago. . . . Damn, do I have a headache. What all did we drink toasts to? Wasn't there one to Dubček?"

"Right, to 'the likable idealist,' as Dobrodin put it," Orten says.

"And what's your opinion of Dobrodin?"

"The likable realist. Their loose tongues are not just a result of the vodka; it has more to do with our harmlessness. We've just dropped in, by accident, and they'll never see us again, we aren't very fluent in the language—you'd have to look far and wide for an audience like that."

Maltzahn nods meaningfully.

"So how does your fish story end?" Podol asks again.

"A couple of experts in the field are supposed to listen to it this afternoon." Qvietone is doing cautious knee bends.

"Ichthyologists?"

"Those too." He pays no attention to the ironic tone in Maltzahn's voice.

Nordanc is sparring with his reflection in the mirror, bouncing on his toes, seems to be in good shape. Maltzahn watches indignantly. "Get away from the window at least, they've taken us in here as their brothers."

"That's my point." Nordanc gives the air an uppercut. Judging by his expression, he landed it.

"We've got to get out of here by this afternoon," Podol says.

"I don't have to go to Chabarovsk." Qvietone is boxing now, too. "I'm on a research trip, and whether I spend half my time here or on Lake Baikal—"

"What in the world are you going to do here?"

"I have an official invitation from the University of Ulan . . ."

There is a knock at the door.

Plotkin asks how they slept. The dormitory was not up to hotel comfort standards, he knew, and there hadn't been any doubles available, but there was a shower down the hall, and they could get breakfast in the canteen.

Maltzahn pulls a face and grabs his stomach.

Plotkin laughs, yes, Anatoly Vasilyevich's parties were notorious. If they couldn't eat anything solid, they should have some kefir. It's a good tip.

Blinking and a little dizzy, they cross Science Prospect, following it past the various institutes to the center of town. Maltzahn wants to buy some film. The day is radiantly clear and frosty, just below freezing. Pushing baby carriages and carrying shopping bags, people on the street wear their coats open; they are enjoying the weather and the well-stocked stores—the lines for vegetables are shorter here than in Novosibirsk.

They are stopped several times by people asking them if they have any *Znachki*.

"*Znachki?* Badges? We aren't members of a kennel club." Podol gives one lad his ballpoint pen instead. "Did you see how happy he was?"

Orten inspects the posters at the movie theater: a monumental war epic, tanks and Katyusha rockets, the name Sergei Bondarchuk in large letters—when it comes to war movies, they are the experts. Orten thinks of *Destiny of a Man,* when black and white faces were enough.—"For us, film is the most important of the arts!"—For the Americans, too.

Coming attractions: a Hollywood production, a disaster film, Russians and Americans join to deflect a meteor, Sean Connery as an American scientist, Natalie Wood as the Russian assistant of his counterpart in Moscow, the focal points of détente. In Prague, the film was pulled after a very short run. It is being shown here all the same, but only after long discussions, in which Dobrodin pushed hard for it, Plotkin says. Orten can still recall the ending: a piece of the meteor grazes New York, and the population flees into the subway; after the impact, the tunnels are flooded—muck, debris, collapsing ceilings. "Our metro is much cleaner," the Russian says.

That may have been the scene that convinced Dobrodin he should let the film be shown. "Anatoly Vasilyevich likes comedies." People are already in line at the closed ticket booth.

Orten wonders if he should tell those who are waiting that the few lame jokes aren't worth it, but after the war movie they need to recover from all the solemnities. Their main motive is probably an immense curiosity to see what Americans look like. Plotkin already has his ticket.

They'll be annoyed at Natalie Wood, she's too self-effacing, that is unless they like to see themselves portrayed as poor relations. The hand-to-mouth workaday world of socialism in Western films, from Hitchcock to Costa-Gavras—the uniforms are always the wrong color of green, and the pictures of the dictators in the interrogating rooms are always a botch, they don't even bother to touch them up; antiquated cars, women in headscarves, a cowed populace teeming with would-be collaborators just waiting to be contacted by Westerners. Reality is much more prosaic than that; besides, the ketchup blood is always overdone.

"Our cinema is modeled after the Rossiya Film Palace in Moscow."

Orten finds it difficult to look at the façade of glittering glass and chrome. "Just a tad smaller."

"But in Novosibirsk we have the largest opera house in the Soviet Union. Did you see it?"

"You can't miss it."

"That plaster barn with columns?" Podol, ice cream in hand, joins them.

"Yes, it's wretched." Plotkin laughs.

Maltzahn comes back, without film for his camera. "They told me to try at the Beryoska Shop."

"What's that?"

"It's like our Tuzex, for foreign currency."

"You've got that crap here, too?" Podol breaks his wooden ice-cream stick and flicks it out into the road. They are on Pearl Street, the town's showcase, a row of brightly painted façades—red, pink, yellow, and ocher facing the green of the taiga on the other side. "Unspoiled" is the word they hear most frequently; the second most frequent is "develop."

They have reached the shore of Lake Ob, where the scientists come to relax all year round. A crust of ice has already formed at water's edge.

They return by way of Children's Lane, where Podol stops several times to inspect the statues of fairy-tale characters set out in front of the playgrounds and kindergartens—Beautiful Vasilisa, Baba Yaga, dragons, *bogatyri,* along with Kostei the Immortal, whose life lies hidden in a bird's egg. Plotkin points proudly to his own daughter among the children at play. Podol stifles his comments.

There is an auto race in progress outside one of the schools, ten-year-old boys steering noisy homemade minicars down a stretch of road buffered with tires and lined with cheering schoolmates and adults, who time them with stopwatches. One boy makes almost no noise at all, and at first they think: aha, batteries, he's fitted it out with an electric motor. Then Orten spots the feet. The kid may not be an engineer, but he has all the talent he'll need for the Moiseyev Ensemble—those imperceptible mincing steps that make it look as if he's gliding. He spots two more drivers using the same method. "OUR YOUTH IS OUR FUTURE" is inscribed above the school door, and he is reminded of Lem's *Futurological Congress,* where people sit in drug-induced ecstasy, sweating, empty-handed, proudly steering their hallucinated cars.—"What is socialism? Living better today than three years from now."

The walls and floors of the mathematicians' club, The Indeterminate Integral, are covered with equations, and to the accompaniment of

Glinka, Borodin, and the Rolling Stones, young men grab chalk out of each other's hand to prove lemmata, set up algorithms, and weigh their complexities, while from the far end two girls work their way toward them on their knees, erasing the chalk marks with rags. No sooner do they clear a spot than the mathematicians start scribbling away again.

"Aren't there any blackboards?" Qvietone asks out of real interest.

"They're too small."

"Aren't there any female mathematicians?"—Orten.

"Oh, sure." Plotkin laughs. "But women are rare in pure mathematics. We have a few in the applied sciences. My wife is a metallographer. They are researching techniques for expanding crystals to counteract extreme cold, which causes metals to contract and turn brittle."

"We have a metallographer at our museum, too, he's a specialist in old swords," Qvietone says. Nordanc throws him a quick glance.

"Our women are hard workers," Plotkin concludes.

"Those two included," Orten says, pointing to the girls on their knees.

"Yes indeed," Plotkin laughs. "The blonde, Vyerochka, sometimes corrects the equations before she wipes them off. Would you like to see the Metallographic Institute? We don't have any old swords, but our materials-analysis lab is interesting." He is not going to let Orten expand on his comments about the cleaning techniques being demonstrated.

"We don't have time for that," Podol says.

"I do."—Qvietone.

"Interesting—young guys, all under thirty, and most of them bald already." Maltzahn runs his hand through his hair. They are back outside now.

"It's a matter of hormones," replies Podol, who is half bald himself. "The difference is that while they romp through indeterminate integrals, you are intrigued by that fluff about birds flying in a row."

"Well, your arithmetical cleaning lady has some nice thick braids," Maltzahn says, taking offense.

"No wonder. In a town with the highest average IQ, even the common laborers must be geniuses. I'll bet the truck drivers here take evening courses in mechanical engineering, or French."

"That depends on how far they have to deliver," Orten remarks. "My guess would be more like Koryak."

"But testosterone also correlates with left-handedness, immunological deficiencies, and stammering," Qvietone says, and they all stare at his head. His silken locks are scientifically unconvincing. (All the same, Orten briefly reflects on his tendency to stammer, and he doesn't have all that much hair left, either.)

"Dyslexia and autism," Qvietone continues. "And high levels of prenatal testosterone can lead to idiocy," he ventures in conclusion.

"All we need is for Plotkin to blurt out that they're doing research on that here, too," Podol mutters.

"As far as I know hormone research is only of marginal interest here," Plotkin explains. These Sibiriaks have damn good ears.

The statement delights Qvietone.

"Anatoly Vasilyevich is waiting for us. We've planned a visit to our computer center for today."

"But we're leaving."

Plotkin stammers, "You don't mean you're saying goodbye?"

The computer center, originally only a wing of the Mathematical Institute, has grown to be one of the largest buildings on Science Prospect.

"Institute Street, Lake Prospect, Tourist Street, Children's Lane— everybody sure knows where he belongs around here," Podol says, and Plotkin laughs.

"With such a concentration of intelligence, the names are a little mundane," Orten says.

"What do you expect? We have no real tradition here, no history. The names are functional. In New York all they have is numbers." Plotkin views Orten with increasing acrimony.

"Is there a Chess Street here, too?" Maltzahn quickly asks.

"No, but we do have a Computer Lane, right through here, please."

On the walls of the second floor, between the closed doors, are fuzzy reproductions—Corot's *Lady with Hat,* Repin's *Burlaki,* a spotted dog that is hard to make out among the black and white daubs of a rolling landscape. "A dalmatian; we had one once," Qvietone says, coming to a halt.

The series concludes with a woman raising her fist in the style of a revolutionary poster and Vladimir Tatlin's monument to the Third International. They puzzle for some time over the last picture: a round head, almost bald, laughing, a wide brow; sort of Cubist in style, the squares of color thickening around the mouth and eyes; the lines lose their contours the nearer one gets.

"Picasso or Sacharov," Podol guesses.

At the mention of the second name Plotkin takes a surprised closer look, and then smiles in relief.

"Picasso," Maltzahn repeats.

"He looks more like Stanislav Lem," Orten says indecisively.

"It is Lem," says Qvietone, who has caught up with them now. "That perophthalmus is unmistakable. And the protruding ears. Otherwise it could be Picasso, too."

They stare at him. Podol runs an eye along the row of closed doors, wonders if it might not be possible to lock Qvietone in a john somewhere.

"Computer graphics," Plotkin says.

They walk along in silence, somewhat depressed.

An Asian engineer in a white smock is waiting for them at the end of the corridor; the doorman has called up with news of their arrival. He is honored, he says, and asks who the delegation's leader is. Plotkin offers some smiling explanation. When these guys don't want you to, you can't understand them, Podol realizes. The only word he can make out is Dobrodin.

Beyond a closed glass door they make a turn and arrive at an elevator, which opens after the engineer inserts his I.D. in a slot. They are going down. They make one stop, a second Asian in a white smock and carrying a folder gets on, I.D. in hand, and after the two have greeted each other, the new one makes a general appraisal: where do these strangers come from, their coats offer no clue, he checks their shoes, Nordanc's jeans and tennis shoes are obviously deemed inappropriate.

Passing through yet another closed door, they go through an I.D. check. A blue-eyed engineer, an energetic young fellow with the playful charm of a sharp technical mind, checks their names off the list that has been provided him. "You have been in the building eight minutes now," he says, smiling at Maltzahn, who, when asked his address at the main entrance, had hesitated about even entering the institute and has been keeping an eye out for traps the whole time. "May I know the name of your employer?"

Maltzahn turns around, facing the elevator, where their Asian escort stands smiling broadly.

"We don't have one," he answers sullenly.

"Just write 'Landmarks Office, Prague,' " Podol interjects.

"Landmarks Office, Prague," the engineer repeats in a flat voice, but makes a mistake writing 'Landmarks.'

"And you are Antonín Svoboda, a painter?" he asks, collecting himself.

Nordanc is lost in gazing at those long eyelashes; they make him think of Zdeněk, his fugitive Prague friend. He doesn't respond.

"Yes." Podol claps him on the shoulder.

They can go on.

Behind glass walls they see about thirty engineers sitting at computers, all of them very young, more than half of them Asians. One fellow, with long hair and an earring, is slouching in his chair and chewing. This is the Communist half-breed Roger Snafu, who two years before made his way across the ice of the Bering Strait from Little Diomede, Alaska, to Big Diomede, U.S.S.R., in order to "complete the bridge of language." Not long before his trip, anthropologists (all émigrés from Central Europe) had published the first conjectures about the close correlation between the syntax, vocabulary, and hunting methods of California Indians and those of Ostyaks and Voguls, Siberian peoples now living in the northern Urals, all of which indicated a wide dispersal of tribes after the breakup of the Asian-American land bridge. Snafu decided to initiate a migration in the opposite direction, to tribal origins. At the time he was already a highly regarded second-generation computer expert—his father, an upstanding WASP, had been part of the team that built the Whirlwind Computer at Livermore Laboratories in the fifties. On a departmental outing to the slopes of Tamalpais, a mountain north of San Francisco, he met a young Indian girl. Her dark, smooth hair and taciturn manner were a balm to him after all the noisy, bleached-blonde girlfriends of his colleagues. She showed him small animals he had never seen before, and gave him plants to eat that let him fly. She said that "pais" meant "mountain," and pointed to the clouds. When he returned to earth, she left for her reservation. Her name was Elea.

A year later—he had married one of the blondes by then—a baby was found on the laboratory grounds, a tiny, bawling Indian boy with a blue shimmer to his eyes. The blonde thought he was cute. By the time they adopted him, the name his colleagues had suggested as a joke had won out. "Roger," said his father, when asked if he really wanted the boy's name entered as "Snafu." His own name was Silbermann.

Roger Snafu was a gifted mathematician. On the occasion of his son's being awarded a Ph.D. at the tender age of twenty, the father was so filled with pride that he got carried away and told Roger about that afternoon in the California mountains two decades before. Now that he knew that his adoptive father was also his biological father, Roger felt free, felt he could leave without a word of thanks. He spent a week searching for his mother on the reservations along the West Coast, then headed east to make his career as a naval logistics specialist at Langley. Three years later, when, reading about the language bridge, he discovered that the name "tamalpais" was the same word used by Ural tribes for "mountain." He broke off his ballistic calculations and decided to speak with these Voguls himself—if he couldn't find his mother, he could at least seek out his distant brothers.

He knew he would have to come bearing gifts. Wrapped in blankets on his sled were three brand-new Apple I computers, which at once persuaded the Soviet border officials not to send him back. They allowed him onto the continent, but kept him under guard on the Chukota Peninsula. Two weeks later, an official finding arrived stating that, although the computers were indeed a windfall, the 6502 mother board was already obsolete even by Russian standards. Faced with the likelihood that he would continue to be kept under guard on Chukota, Snafu pulled three RCA 1802 chips from his fur cap, each with gold pins and stamped "MIL-specified," the only micro-processors unaffected by low-level gamma rays, making them applicable for use in space—a little gift he had intended for his relatives among the Ural Voguls. This magic trick got him his transfer from Chukota to the Ob and a nomination for admission into the Siberian Academy of Sciences, along with all the perks accorded Soviet computer experts.

All of which apparently left him unimpressed. On his evenings off, he reads journals of linguistics, Tynyanov or Jakobson, builds his language bridges and wigwams in the air, listens to music. They will let him travel to the Urals only under escort. For the time being he has given up his personal people-to-people campaign.

The chips were not the only surprise he had for the authorities. Along with the computers he had piled his sled high with complete sets of vintage comics, partly to protect the machines, partly for his personal use, or so he declared—something no one was willing to believe at first. Even his colleagues assumed this was an attempt at pro-American infiltration, with Pogo as the opossum of opposition to opportunists like Donald Duck and Mickey Mouse. Most of those who spoke perfect English had difficulty understanding these texts; they found the allusions to Russia ("them stole us our Georgia") confusing. By now, however, the comic books were a hot, if clandestine, item among Siberian mathematicians.

Snafu is leaning on his desk now, chewing cashews. He winks at Qvietone and holds out the bag to him. "What's your fuckin' business here?"

"I . . . I am an entomologist," Qvietone stammers in surprise. His English is considerably weaker than his French, or his Russian at the moment.

"A what—?"

"He is interested in . . . devoted to . . . bugs," Nordanc says, sensing he must jump in.

"So am I. Do a lot of debugging round here. These Russians sure need it bad." Snafu flashes his Russian colleague a grin and they both laugh.

"What did he say?" Qvietone asks.

"He gets rid of some sort of bugs," a confused Nordanc translates.

"You mean he delouses the place?" Podol grins.

"No, he gets rid of bugs or beetles." Maltzahn is looking around.

"Looks more like he brings them in," Orten says.

"I'm not going any farther," Maltzahn declares. "They're going to expose us to state secrets, and then we'll never be able to leave." He casts a hostile eye at Plotkin. He should not have told them anything about Snafu.

"Why did you leave the U.S.A.?" Orten asks. His two Russian escorts now regard him as an agent provocateur.

"I had my personal reasons," Snafu says, in very good Russian. "One was that I couldn't stomach Commander Grace Hopper."

"Grasshopper?" Nordanc translates.

"Is he allergic?" Qvietone has lost the thread. "Does he mean long-horned or short-horned grasshoppers? The taxonomists are constantly shifting the genus *Locusta* around."

"An awful bitch."

"A woman? Didn't you say 'commander'?" Orten is having trouble, too.

"The chief's squaw?" Podol asks.

"Something like that—in the navy. She knows her way around computers and ballistics, but that's all. She was my commanding officer. The three chips, the RCA 1802s—you've probably heard about those. I'm the star pupil around here," he says, flashing his grin again. "I lifted those from her desk. Damn happy I did, too."

"I am a sculptor," Orten says. "I can understand how you could dislike her. I don't know anything about your chips."

For one brief moment he almost has the feeling that Snafu is going to go for his throat—as if the idea that there could be someone who had no interest in his contraband has hurt him or made him jealous, as if his long, irrevocable journey has been in vain.

Snafu laughs and holds out the bag to him: "Have a nut."

Valery Login, the department head, comes toward them, arms spread wide. He hugs Podol and Orten but stops in his tracks when he notices Maltzahn back off with a frightened look on his face. He then merely offers a hand to Maltzahn, Qvietone, and Nordanc and asks them to have a seat.

"We've finished here already," Plotkin says. But Qvietone has recovered now, and to everyone's surprise he asks, "What do you mean by 'debugging'?"

Login pulls up short, then laughs. "Roger Yelenovich likes to make jokes. He is looking for errors. Although it is extraordinarily difficult to calculate errors exactly, as you know. As might be expected, the rounding errors increase proportionally to the number of sums added, and often the total can only be calculated to three or four places after the decimal instead of to our standard norms of accuracy of seven or eight decimal places."

They look at one another—their Russian has definitely given out now. Orten notes that Snafu has used his mother's name for his patronymic.

"You mean, then, the 'bugs' are errors?" Qvietone inquires.

"Yes. How does that go again, Roger?"

"At some point early on, someone found a squashed gnat on a magnetic tape," Snafu says while he chews, "and the binary numbers were unreadable. They've been called bugs ever since."

"But a gnat is not, properly speaking, a bug," Qvietone says. "Why didn't they call it a 'mosquito' or . . ."

"Midge?" Nordanc is amazed that he knows the word.

"Demidging?" Snafu considers the term. "It was probably something larger, a moth maybe." Qvietone's questions have begun to sound silly to him, too.

Qvietone is about to explain some things about Lepidoptera, but Login steals the march on him with a lecture on simple, double, and extended accuracy in arithmetical operations. He is the only one here who has not yet realized that the *delegatsiya* are not specialists.

"Let us apply Newton's method for rational approximation in calculating a zero integer in a polynomial," he says with a smile. "A common method of solution for centuries now. But as such it offers a mere approximation that can be precisely calculated by iteration to a given number of decimal places. But I don't want to bore you with the obvious. You can calculate as well as I the point where we will arrive at a stable value that cannot be extended by further iteration. We can also agree upon an adequate degree of accuracy. But with computers? The results can already differ beyond the sixth place after the decimal! You will object, of course," he says, laughing, "that by extending the arithmetical manipulation you can make the method more precise. And right you are! We can do that, too. Our young scientists are just as impatient as you Czechs," he assures them, dismissing their objections. "I know that. We have our contacts with Prague. And I can see just how impatient you are," he adds, as a playful admonition to Maltzahn. "You want to get at the computers, and I understand; we have hotheads like you here as well." He smiles again and runs his hand through the blue-eyed programmer's hair. "Am I right, Vasya? But our physicist colleagues are giving us trouble. For years now they've been using the standard numerical programs from the U.S.A., which allow for only conventional precision in the calculations. Which we then must revise. And that our physicists simply won't permit. My hands are tied!" Login displays his hands. "That is the reason we have been unable to overtake the Americans. We simply limp along in the track of their errors!" He claps Maltzahn on the shoulder. "But together we shall solve the problem. Our colleagues in Bulgaria have already . . . Aren't you feeling well, *golubchik?*"

Maltzahn's eyes in his pale face are searching for a door.

"Perhaps the comrades would like a breath of fresh air." A suggestion of their escort Vyacheslav Ptolemenko, who takes some satisfaction in his nickname "Logoff," the rival of Login.

"You are interested in chess, of course?" Login is about to invite them to his office to show off his Kaissa and Pioneer chess programs.

"They aren't mathematicians at all," Logoff/Ptolemenko says, laughing.

"There's no reason why they should be," Login replies, making a quick recovery. Ever since his friend Kortchnoy signed on with pirates in Manila, he can handle any disappointment.

"We have to say our goodbyes upstairs, too." Podol is standing in front of the Geological Institute. "And, of course, to you, too."

Plotkin brings them to the entrance. "Anatoly Vasilyevich is waiting for you." He diffidently shakes Podol's hand. "We'll see each other before you leave," he says as he waves to the others and jumps onto a passing trolley. Its door closes behind him.

"That was close." Nordanc points to the tip of coat fluttering from the rubber divider.

"Where's he going in such a hurry?" Maltzahn's suspicious eyes are still following the departing trolley.

"Probably getting reinforcements," Podol says. "You heard him—we'll see him again before we leave."

"Don't joke about it."

"Maybe he wants to drive us to the airport."—Nordanc.

"Judging from that meaningful smile, it must be a big surprise," Orten remarks.

"That's what I'm afraid of, too." Maltzahn suggests they find a taxi right now and take off without saying goodbye to Dobrodin.

"It's too late for that." Podol has already been recognized by the Tartar doorman, with whom he had danced the *kozachok* at last night's party. He gives them a friendly wave to come over.

"Where is Erik?" Nordanc has only now noticed that Qvietone is missing.

"With the zoologists, talking about his puffers."

"We should wait for him."

"He wasn't intending to come with us anyway," Maltzahn points out.

"Let's first go upstairs and say our goodbyes. Maybe Dobrodin can call a taxi for us." Podol pushes open the inside door. "These institutes all have the same musty smell."

"Ah, there you all are! How was your visit to the computers? Incredible machines! Did you see the new chess program? Even here in Akademgorodok there aren't many people who've beat Kaissa."

"We came to say goodbye," Podol says. "And to thank you. It was all very interesting. We'll have to add a few mathematical formulas to our façade. But we have to be on our way today, to Chabarovsk." Even as he speaks, he knows that he is talking too much. The look Dobrodin is giving them says he doesn't believe a good part of it. And that he'll get around to whatever part that is. Dobrodin smiles as if he isn't even listening, as if what Podol is talking about is of no concern, particularly the part about their trip, because whatever Podol may think, it doesn't really matter where they are going. What matters is that they are a delegation—a head count that was easy to keep track of, fleet neither of foot nor of language, without any expertise, which made it easy to slip them in and out of most anywhere, critical, but likable, slightly mistrustful, that was normal—a delegation of the sort you could only hope for from a fraternal state. Only Americans could have been better. Artists from Prague instead of American scientists. But one has to live with life's shortcomings. In light of all this, the fact that their plane and the one to Tura are scheduled for alternate days is a minor difficulty.

"You can't leave just like that, my little doves, not only because it would make us very sad, but also because there is no flight to Chabarovsk today."

"Didn't you tell us yesterday that there would be one today?"

"I did. It's all my fault," Dobrodin says with a smile. "And it left right on schedule. At seven this morning. The one at six this evening goes to Tura. The flight schedule for winter started today. Those two flights alternate from here on out. You can fly to Chabarovsk tomorrow and to Tura the day after. On even days in the morning, on odd days in the evening. You won't lose any time because . . ."

"Where is Tura?" Maltzahn asks.

"I wouldn't advise that."

"Is it in on our way?"

"Not exactly."

"Is it east of us?" Maltzahn persists.

"Somewhat. But mostly north." Dobrodin pulls out a map that shows the mineral treasures of Siberia. "Last year's, already obsolete," he chuckles. It is hard to make out any names of towns amid the dozens of shaded zones and symbols. Compared to the letters of "Kusbas," those of "Novosibirsk" are quite small. As far as Maltzahn can tell, Tura is a point where airplanes would never be able to land. "There's an airport there?" he asks incredulously.

"It is the capital of Tungusiya." Dobrodin chuckles again. "If you still wanted to fly today—it's about as far out of your way as from one end of Czechoslovakia to the other. Not all that far, I admit, but a connecting flight might then prove difficult."

They don't find any of this funny.

"Notice how you can see the adjoining topological regions quite clearly." Dobrodin points to his map. "Each region of color can be adjoined at most with three other regions, which is why only four colors are needed to mark them all. The famous four-color problem. And what would it look like with surfaces of a higher order? What do you think?"

"We want to go to Chabarovsk," Podol says.

"In a bit. A torus, for example, requires seven fields of color. The Möbius band, six. A surface with two handles needs all of eight; different laws apply for surfaces that cannot be oriented. The double helix, which ought to be of interest to you as countrymen of Mendel . . ."

"Are there any other flights this afternoon?" Maltzahn interrupts.

Dobrodin looks directly at him. "To Krasnoyarsk and Vilyusk. Connections from both places would be about as difficult as those from Tura. I would guess about a week to Chabarovsk."

"I have to begin work in Kyoto in a week," Orten says dejectedly.

"I know," Dobrodin says, touching his arm, "and I'm dreadfully sorry. But as I was about to say before I was interrupted"—he glances again at Maltzahn—"you won't lose any time if you wait until tomorrow, because you can depart that same evening from Chabarovsk for Nachodka. I've written down the times of the trains. But until your flight leaves, you are, of course, our guests."

"We would rather go back to Novosibirsk, just to be sure we make our flight tomorrow morning."

"That's probably the most sensible thing." Orten is wavering.

"Could you call a taxi for us?" Podol asks.

Dobrodin flings his massive hands wide. "You can't do that to our mathematicians. They have been practicing since early this morning for a concert of Czech music to be given in your honor this evening. Jakov Plotkin left the rehearsal only because he wanted to take you to the computer center. He feels responsible for you. After all, he did gather you up." Dobrodin laughs. "They will be practicing all afternoon. Our string quartet. They even took part in the All-Union competitions last year. You simply must attend," he says, turning to Orten.

"I don't know. We have nothing to wear. We've been running around in these clothes for two days now." Orten looks down at his muddy shoes.

"Not to worry. Petka is seeing to it that your luggage is brought here, I've already sent him word."

"Who is Petka?"

"Petka is our institute's chauffeur. A dependable fellow. He has a few errands to run in town and on the way back he'll pick up your things. Your luggage will be here by concert time. You have no need to worry. Pyotr Alexeyevich does like to keep his tonsils well oiled." Dobrodin laughs. "But he'll find his way home. And he's a careful driver. Anyone who's had an accident usually is. Once bitten, twice shy. Pyotr Alexeyevich hasn't got into trouble for a good eight months now."

"That's not a long time," Maltzahn confides softly to Nordanc.

"You'll probably object that that's not a long time." Dobrodin laughs. "Maybe not in Moscow or Prague, but it's a long time here. People often don't stay in Siberia longer than that. The climate's not to everyone's taste. But it's sunny today, hovering around freezing. Your tennis shoes may not be quite the right thing," he says, turning to Nordanc, "and you'll all need gloves pretty soon. It's just starting to turn cold. Give it a month. But then, of course, you're leaving. You need have no worries about Petka or your luggage."

"Wouldn't it have been better to ask us first?" There is a testy note in Orten's voice.

"Much better, my good man, of course! My calls have just missed you all morning. And when I finally got through to the computer center, Afanasyev told me you had just left. And Login didn't even want to speak to me, seemed upset. High-strung gentlemen, our cyberneticists are. I do admire them, but sometimes you have to ask yourself . . . Did you meet Snafu? I'm worried about that boy. At first, he and my son Matvey were friends—he's a chemist—but then they suddenly had a falling out. And all because of some rat, or mouse? Not Mickey Mouse, but something like that. Matvey forgot and left the thing somewhere. Well, yes, as his mother says, he is a slipshod fellow, but they were so childish, badly drawn, cheap paper, a sort of newspaper, like *Ogonyok,* but apparently meant for adults. I ask you now! If they need little pictures just to understand a few sentences, is it any wonder that they don't answer our letters! They already have twenty million illiterates, and they say even their teachers have trouble spelling. Can you imagine? And they're supposed to be ahead of us. I've drunk Coca-Cola; but their illiteracy problem is even worse, let me tell you. Just look at the bookcase in any truck driver's home here! Every Tuvinian, every Nivkh can read and write, except maybe for a few very old people. Take the Yukaghirs—only six hundred of them, but all literate! Even the hundred Oroks on Sakhalin. Do you know what literature means for people here? If some problem is exposed in the *Literaturnaya Gazeta,* the consequences are more serious than if it were in *Pravda."*

Particularly for the editors, Orten thinks.

"Snafu has had a difficult life, I know." Dobrodin looks up briefly and smiles. "But does he ever have a temper. Matvey came home with a bloody nose; we couldn't get anything out of him, but then Vasya told me that it was the talk of the computer center. If Petka gets into a brawl somewhere, that's his business. But two highly qualified scientists? Everybody knows about it. And what caused it all? An opossum in a comic book!"

"That was Pogo," Nordanc says.

"So you're familiar with it, too?" Dobrodin gives him the once-over for the first time—tennis shoes, jeans; and he's put his earring back in. "I told Matvey that hooligan manners weren't going to get him anywhere with me."

"If Plotkin knew our plane had left—the string quartet was already practicing—why didn't he tell us?" Orten wants to get back to the topic of their departure.

"He couldn't do that." Dobrodin laughs. "It wasn't his fault, anyway. Besides, he wanted to surprise you!"

"So that was his surprise!" After being dumbfounded in Russian for so long, Podol has found his tongue again. "Our Dobrodin is quite the benefactor! The *doprdelin* has the gall to mock the size of Czechoslovakia, and then talk about detours and connections! I should have asked him if he means the borders before or after '45, when they stole the Carpathian Ukraine from us! As repayment for their casualties on Dukla Pass. They could've detoured around that! But it was easier to blow a few thousand soldiers sky high, and then pocket their neighbor's territory, which we were only too willing to force on them. A gift of the grateful people of Czechoslovakia! And their sham of a plebiscite? And then '48, the defenestration? All the same, their little detour, teeny-weeny Czechoslovakia, was worth a jaunt in their tanks in '68! But the Oroks can read! The only question is, in what language?"

"Don't shout so loud," Maltzahn says.

"Unfortunately they can't understand me. Apart from a few phrases—'long live!' and 'many thanks'—Jan has to take care of the rest. Where did you learn your Russian by the way? We don't dare let Qvietone even get a word in edgewise. I feel like an idiot around here, in every respect!"

"Your 'mathematical formulas on the façade' was flawless," Orten says.

"That was just some icing on the cake. Finish off with a Russian flourish, and be done with it. Haven't you noticed how everything sounds like a lie in another language? Even 'What time is it?' or 'How do you do?' I feel like a hypocrite."

"A moment ago it was an idiot."—Maltzahn.

Podol glares at him. "Like an idiotic hypocrite. Everything is just recited. I can't manage a single sentence of my own, none that I really mean. What language do the Oroks on Sakhalin speak?"

"Definitely not Japanese," Nordanc says, and they stare sullenly at him.

"We won't be hearing that any too soon, either, at least not in Kyoto." Podol tries to stretch out on the stunted dormitory bed. He pulls a bottle of vodka from its brown paper bag. "Are they all midgets around here?" He takes a long pull and throws the blanket over him. "I want to get some sleep before they drag us off to their concert. Czech music! These scientists can wear you out more than a week up on the façade!"

Orten tries to dodge Maltzahn's questions and apprehensions; he doesn't know when the luggage will arrive either. They go their separate ways. Maltzahn heads down Tourist Street, he wants to buy a few postcards. Nordanc trots off in the direction of the Zoological Institute in hopes that Qvietone's lecture on bilharziasis will be over soon. Orten walks down Pearl Street, where buildings line just the one side; he wants to walk in the taiga. A sign on the House of Culture announces this evening's concert of Czech music by the Academy String Quartet. He is relieved to see that there is nothing about a "delegation," so they may still be able to get away, if their luggage arrives in time. Dobrodin—*dobroděj,* the benefactor.

A poster for an exhibition: "Soviet Architecture 1917 to 1932." The building is open.

In the vestibule, ineluctable Lenin—this time just a bust on the wall; his presence was much more disturbing as a guidepost on Soviet Square in Novosibirsk. The doorman is surprised to discover a visitor to the exhibition on a workday. Admission is free. A room on the second floor has been cleared as provisional space for the display. The original plans and photographs are only partly protected under glass; most are simply spread out on tables covered with green felt. On some of the items Orten can make out the stamp of the people's commissar for education. You could hardly call it an installation, but the projects are certainly as radical as the poems of Mayakovsky, whose "Marching Orders for the Army of Artists" is posted at the start of the exposition.

> *Dime-a-dozen thoughts and gushes—*
> *Pull those burrs out now, you weasels.*
> *The streets are our brushes.*
> *The squares are our easels.*

The easels of those days prove amazingly useful places to erect buildings. Between the edifices of Russian classicism and the wooden shacks of the suburbs rise buildings of glass and steel, like the airy, hyper-boloid broadcasting tower of Radio Komintern, which makes Eiffel's tower look clumsy and ponderous. All the same, they appeal to Eiffel, as their "French older brother" and model, to come to Moscow and lead the masses—Mayakovsky wants to harness architecture to the chariot of the revolution as well. Instead of Eiffel and his tower, Corbusier comes; his design for the Zentrosoyus is built without either heating or ventilation systems. The quality of construction is awful, but it is the first of his large projects ever to be realized. Tatlin's tower for the Third International, which they have already seen done by computer graphics, is a wooden model here, somewhat larger than the one Orten saw in Paris a year ago. He is reminded of the domes of Santa Maria del Fiore and Brunelleschi's wooden model in the cathedral museum in Florence, of Leonardo's flying machine. Tatlin's tower was never built, nor did they use his aesthetic design for an airplane, the "Letatlin."

The best example of constructivist architecture from the revolutionary period is the *Leningradskaya Pravda* Building by the Vesnin brothers, a five-story skyscraper kiosk, lighter and more urbane than El Lissitzky's skyscrapers. One projection of the Moscow Planetarium reminds Orten of a villa done by Adolf Loos in Prague's District Six—some friends of his live nearby. The similarities continue: the Suyevklub by Golosov, the *Izvestiya* building, the stage designs for Chesterton's *The Man Who Was Thursday*—Orten feels as if he were in Prague in the twenties. Now it strikes him where he knows Dobrodin from: the agile plumpness, the homely, Olympian humor, and the cunning—they all remind him of Chesterton's Sunday.

The exhibition ends with monumental structures: two designs for the hydroelectric project on the Dnepr with its 2,200-foot dam. The first is a tectonic mass, its transformer station a rough-hewn stairway with bunkerlike slits for windows; the second, in contrast, is a gently curved construction, rising almost weightless above its supports and lighted by ribbons of windows—the Dneproges, which did get built later. The most beautiful of these buildings is the boiler house for the Moscow power plant, MOGES; the photo shows modern glass-and-steel bay windows, but the ground in front is still bare. There stand a horse in a high, wooden Russian yoke and a boy in a billed cap, hands on his hips, who stares proudly into the camera—yesterday a farmer, today a worker helping build this industrial complex. Where did the élan of the Revolution go?

The Lenin Mausoleum on Red Square. A photo of a provisory wooden version built three days after Lenin's death. Stchusev completed his sketch overnight, and no sooner had it been approved by the funeral committee than the first explosives were blasting the frozen ground beside the wall of the Kremlin. "The painful news of the demise of mankind's greatest genius, of the champion of human freedom, has crushed with awful agony the hearts of our nation's citizens and those of working people throughout the world." After a few months the mausoleum was enlarged with a funereal grandstand, lending the edifice a more monumental look. Ornamental wrought-iron nails joined the pyramid's wooden planks. The government did not approve Mayakovsky's suggestion that, instead of erecting a funeral vault above Lenin's resting place, they build a true symbol of the movement, a factory. Five years later the mausoleum was rebuilt in stone: the stairs of the pyramid in red, gray, and black Labrador granite, the ceiling a single slab of red Karelian porphyry supported on granite columns; the interior gray and black, with porphyry pilasters and intarsia work of ruddy smalt. The mausoleum could not be higher than the wall of the Kremlin. The interior had to allow for a continuous stream of thronging masses, with no overcrowding or traffic jams. The whole edifice had to blend with the environment—the Spassky, Nokolsky, and Senat gates, the Cathedral of St. Basil, and the dome of the Supreme Soviet. It should incorporate both valor and the grief of their loss.

Orten reads Stchusev's description and tries to recall his first impressions of the walls of the Kremlin. Red Square was too small, the mausoleum a kind of bunker under siege. No crowding, two disciplined queues, the police saw to that. Foreigners in the shorter line. Both lines met inside the vault; traffic jams proved unavoidable. Someone in their group of students noted that Lenin was holding up better than Stalin. Orten had never visited it again. He did find the new plaque in the wall last time, but didn't want to get in line just to see a solitary Lenin. The lines had not grown any shorter, as if the Russians had found some additional link to the "workingman's greatest friend" now that their generalissimo had been removed from sight. Lenin, the workingman's great friend: "Trust is good, control is better." The crushed rebellion of sailors in Kronstadt, of Makhno's peasants in the Ukraine—he was lucky that artists like Gorky and Mayakovsky wrote about him; all Stalin had were the ones who survived each shift in politics; that went for architects, too.

Orten once had a dream in which the mausoleum was a leaden chamber, its ceiling collapsed so that you couldn't stand up straight; in one dark corner, lead coffins had broken open to reveal the bones of revolutionary bureaucrats—Dzerzhinsky, Trotsky—mummified faces, spider webs in the eye sockets.

In a second dream he had climbed the Kremlin wall and found his way to Stalin's open casket, hidden out of sight behind a high steel enclosure—there he lay, pale and old, while in the Hall of Trade Unions the masses continued to trudge stolidly past his stuffed uniform, a mask stuck on top.

The dream repeated again, he has to scale the Kremlin wall a third time, move down long corridors, past heavily curtained doors, Lenin's furniture draped with yellowed covers, locked bookcases—Orten forces his way into the last suite, into the last cubbyhole crammed with junk, where Brezhnev has crept to hide. He drags him out, slits open his chest, stabs—again and again!

Churches were founded above boneyards. Fake ribs, bloody cloths, wooden splinters have been grounds for war; Venetian merchants risked their lives to bring the corpse of St. Mark to Venice. How would one-sixth of the world react if its holiest corpse were suddenly missing?

My republic for a corpse! They would immediately give back the Carpathian Ukraine, and set Poland free. A neutral Europe for a corpse!

Orten examines the plans for the mausoleum more closely: the calculations for the thickness of the walls, the sketches for both doors. Assuming that it was the real thing lying there, and not a wax puppet. Then again, if the government was trying to cover up a fake, you could distribute fliers and call the population's attention to the fact. Then Gerasimov would have to be brought in, as in Weimar, where he verified that it was indeed Schiller's skull. Their own expert would confirm it for them: the original was in Friedland. But you would have to give serious thought to security.

Best thing would be to post Jirse as a guard.

On his way back out, Orten nods to Lenin's bust: We haven't seen the last of each other!

Smetana's string quartet *From My Life*. Plotkin and his colleagues play with an earnestness that transcends the occasion of honoring a "delegation."

"What a shame Patera isn't here," Podol says.

The hall is full of concertgoers in gala dress. Their own grubby traveling clothes are only too obvious, the luggage has not arrived. Dressed in an elegant, sleek black suit, looking almost slim despite his 220 pounds, Dobrodin consoles them—Petka would come through. "You Czechs are great musicians!" He circles around them—floating, greeting, tossing the tails of his tux like a ladybug on her honeymoon flight, or a euphoric moth.

After intermission, two young scientists behind them whisper guesses as to what will come next; the slant-eyed young woman says "Dvořák." Her unusual accent makes Orten turn around; she is very young and serious. He tries a fleeting smile, but does not risk looking directly at her; his pullover and face are no match for the solemn proceedings. He casts a sidelong glance toward Podol, who seems to be feeling equally uneasy in his flannel shirt. Nordanc stretches out his legs; his tennis shoes glow, nonchalant and ostentatious, in the festive darkness of the hall; Qvietone told him to get lost today. It is obvious that Maltzahn suspects every second concertgoer is a KGB agent in gala disguise, including the violinists on the stage, who are bowing to acknowledge the applause now. They discuss something, and then, without any announcement by Plotkin, they start to play. Orten feels pinned down, he doesn't go to concerts, doesn't even have a record player in his dusty, chalky atelier, and he is hardly ever home long enough to put on a record, either. Depending on how not-tired he is, he listens to whatever is on the radio. He struggles against being pressured into recognizing the piece—all these cultured types here are working hard at it. His only suit is gray, his working clothes are white with plaster, he relishes all these reverent faces about as much as he does Nordanc's incongruous tennis shoes. He wants to leave.

Then he recognizes the music. At first only as something familiarly "Czech"—he has prepared himself for Dvořák—but the lyric elements of this quartet are strained, they break off abruptly and are replaced by a new knot of dissonances that have been clustering behind them, swelling quickly to misunderstandings, to exploding tones that are ripped into the depths, only to culminate in a furious spasm. Tolstoy's *Kreutzer Sonata*, as interpreted by Janáček: Tolstoy set his story in a framework that slowly retards and relativizes the narrative, whereas the music ends in something like tonic chords of blood spurting from beneath Pozdnyshev's sword.

Marie had run from him because he had said that it actually ought to be the woman who kills the man. Their last evening together. But not because of that, no, there was something else. He sees her now, at the end of her silent flight, standing wet and shivering before the façade. As if he had ended up in this faraway place just so he could think of her without any feelings of guilt.

What is more, he seems to be the only person here who recognizes the piece. The solemn faces all around him look somewhat perplexed. He is not sure about Podol, who has closed his eyes, as if he had not napped long enough this afternoon. Dobrodin does not know the work either; he tries here and there to nod his head to the rhythm, but is forced to give up each time. He shouts "Bravo" and rises to applaud when the four young mathematicians take an unpracticed bow. Plotkin is blushing a little, he had not expected such a success.

Dobrodin goes over to them, gives each a hug and invites them to join in a *zakuska,* a snack. Naturally our Czech friends were coming, too. Maltzahn would rather go check on their luggage, but outside the House of Culture a fellow in a cap hails Dobrodin, who then laughs jovially and tells them that Petka first took their bags to the hotel by mistake, but that they were in their room now.

They return from Dobrodin's party a little fuddled. Maltzahn holds his head and complains that they must have put something in the piroshki, because there was no way he could feel this dizzy from the little bit of vodka he drank. Their suitcases are on the beds, apparently undisturbed, except for the one that Maltzahn opens. Nordanc's passport, his Luxembourg passport, is lying next to his camera and tape recorder—he had hidden it in the lining. Maltzahn begins to rummage through his own bag (which is on Qvietone's bed) and orders them all to make a thorough check of theirs. He is both relieved and disappointed to find the twenty dollars he had wadded up with some Czech bills and concealed inside his soap dish. He counts them, the Czech ones too, holding each up to the light, one after the other—you can't be too sure.

"Best thing would be to bite them." Podol is getting impatient. "How much funny money have you ever actually seen! I'd love to meet the idealist who would counterfeit Czech korunas."

"These are dollars."

"Yes, you wouldn't be hiding just korunas in your soap dish. You figure Russians never wash? How can you tell for sure anyway? All I know is that all American bills are the same size and color. I wouldn't want to be blind there."

"I wouldn't want to be blind anywhere." Qvietone giggles. He's having trouble keeping his balance, so he props himself against the bedpost while he makes a complicated attempt simultaneously to undress and locate his pajamas among the clothes he has dragged out of his suitcase. They watch him, unamused.

"Where are our passports?" it suddenly occurs to Maltzahn to ask.

That almost sobers them up. The strangest thing is that no one has thought of it until now; there must have been something in those piroshki. Orten peers into the darkness outside, as if expecting someone else.

"It's snowing."

The next morning Dobrodin is not available. He has had to drive into town on urgent business, they are asked to wait.

"But we have to leave," Orten says.

"He'll be here around noon." His secretary is polite, but no longer so charming as she was yesterday evening.

"Where are our passports?" Maltzahn asks.

She looks at him, but says nothing. "Comrades, I'll have to ask you to wait outside. You have another two hours. Perhaps you'd like to do some shopping?"

"What sort of shopping?" Nordanc asks once they are outside.

"Gloves and fur hats." Podol is pounding his hands to keep them warm.

"Dobrodin did say we would get a taste of the local disastrous snowstorms. I could use some boots."

"Don't exaggerate," Orten says.

"Who's exaggerating? He's right. We need to lay in some stores before they send us off somewhere, at least we can find everything we need here." Maltzahn pokes around in his wallet, checking to see how much money he has.

"What are you talking about?"

"You know very well what I'm talking about! Why do you think Dobrodin drove to Novosibirsk? They have our passports and they're holding us here. I knew it from the start. I'm going to buy some gloves, too!"

"So am I," Qvietone says.

Orten casts him a peevish look. "Don't you start in, too."

"I'm cold."

"Do what you want. And if there aren't any lines, you can always go see the architecture exhibition afterward. It's worth it."

"I'm not in the mood for art," Maltzahn says reproachfully. They turn to look back at Nordanc, who has been stopped by two young men just outside the dorm.

"After *snatchki* again, I guess, badges," Podol surmises.

"This time on the lapel." Maltzahn gives his collar a meaningful tap.

"You don't think spies introduce themselves here, do you?"

"I think I heard them asking him about rock records," Qvietone says.

"Or hard currency." Maltzahn is not about to be deterred. "They know very well that he's traveling under a false passport. Now they're trying to set a trap for him. We've got him to thank for this whole mess!" He is watching Nordanc across the street, as if expecting him to be arrested any second. Nordanc reaches into his pocket, gives the lads something and comes across the street now, all smiles.

"What was that?" Maltzahn asks.

"A cigarette lighter."

"From the West?"

"From Austria, a streamline, costs one mark. You can get them in Prague for ten korunas. What's going on here?"

"Nothing," Podol replies. "Come on, you could use some different shoes, too."

. . .

Dobrodin has not yet returned at noon. Two hours later the secretary is able to inform them that he has called and will be back at four. At four-thirty, they learn that their passports have been impounded and will be run through another check before they can continue their trip. Dobrodin looks exhausted and upset. He puts up with Podol's indignation, dismisses Maltzahn's angry outburst; he really can't tell them anything more at the moment. They will be staying on temporarily in Akademgorodok.

"Well, that probably takes care of Chabarovsk for today at least." Podol looks up and down the street. "I'm gradually getting to feel I know the place."

"I doubt if we ever get to Chabarovsk. We'll be lucky if we even get back home!" Maltzahn glares fiercely at Nordanc.

"I'm going to go and explain the whole thing," Nordanc says. "They can't keep you here just because I've got Svoboda's passport."

"And just where is it you think you're going? They'll come and get you when they need you," Podol replies. "Besides, I don't think it has to do just with you. They're sure to have concluded by now that we're alien intruders, camouflaged as a 'delegation,' and that they've let us in on their latest research. Dobrodin has nothing to laugh about, either, I'd say."

"That's absolute nonsense. They could see we didn't understand a thing."

"They'll think that was just especially clever of us."

"Cut the jokes." Maltzahn is getting worked up now. "Nordanc's comic books, Qvietone's questions—of course they suspect us! I wouldn't go anywhere right now!"

"So you think that just because Andy knows about a comic-book marsupial and Erik wants to control some disease, we're all doomed?"

"There's no point in trying to talk seriously with you!"

They spend the afternoon arguing and shopping. Later that evening they run into Plotkin, who is on his way to pick up his daughter from kindergarten. He seems taciturn and timid, and he's in a hurry to get her.

"Your concert was very lovely," Orten says.

Plotkin brightens briefly and shakes his hand. "Anatoly Vasilyevich has accomplished a lot here, believe me. You are our guests. Akademgorodok has its own special status. Up to a point." He smiles. "You won't have to go to Novosibirsk."

"But we want to go to Novosibirsk. We have to get on our way!"

Plotkin hesitates. "That's probably not advisable at the moment. You see, the committee . . . Dobrodin shouted at them," he says, laughing. "You have friends here. But the taxidermist in the zoology department reported that you said something against the intervention of the armies of the Warsaw Pact in '68."

"I remember now," Podol says. "There were several of us. We sang some songs and I was feeling chipper, so I asked them: Lads, have any of you ever been in Prague?—they were talking about how beautiful the buildings are here. And one guy nodded and declared proudly, 'Sixty-eight.' So we went outside and I punched him in the nose."

"That was the taxidermist." Plotkin really must go.

"So it's not because of Andy's passport that they're holding us here." Podol has turned pensive. "This could take some time."

"I wasn't all that careful with Dobrodin, either," Orten says.

"There's a difference between your not being careful with Dobrodin and my punching out a soldier of occupation. Let's not start in with self-criticism here. And Olbram, spare us your advice about how we should have been more careful."

Three days later Orten buys himself some gloves, too, his inner resistance has crumbled under Dobrodin's silence and the temperature outside. That same afternoon, after waiting for hours in the post office, they are finally able to get a call through to Kyoto. Amid global gurglings that explain their situation far better than the bad English spoken by both parties, a later date of arrival is agreed upon. They know the town inside out by now. Nordanc has new fur-lined boots and Maltzahn a fur hat that would be all the rage in Prague, or so he claims, even in Paris, but doesn't turn a single head here. "They've moved into a phase of covert observation," Podol explains to him. They are less and less conspicuous. The more it snows and the more they muffle up, the more they look like the rest of the population.

"With one major difference—we shiver worse," Orten says.

Hardly anyone speaks to them on the street; the teenagers know by

now that they don't have any *snatchki*. Except for Maltzahn's inces-
sant conjectures, these are quiet times. Since they are no longer regarded as a "delegation," but are nevertheless tolerated, they can go
their separate ways and pursue their separate interests, to the extent
that local conditions allow. Nordanc goes skiing on the nearby hills,
surrounded by young, muscular scientists, who are happy to have him
treat them to a glass of grog and turn tight-lipped only when they have
to pay for a second round. But the next day, a few solid sorts greet
him on the street, and that makes up for all the tensions with Maltzahn
and for Qvietone's obtuseness. Qvietone goes ice-skating on the lake,
with the children and teens, and enjoys himself. One day when Nordanc rented a pair of skates, he saw Qvietone zip by on cross-country
skis; since then he's been sticking close to Vasya from the computer
center. Orten takes Podol and Maltzahn along for a second look at
the architecture exhibition, which has since been expanded by the addition of "Contemporary Impulses from the Crimea." Podol comes to
a halt in front of one of the oils. "This is what they call contemporary
art? I know that stuff from the fifties!"

"But they weren't allowed to smear like that back then," Maltzahn
says.

A few yards further on: an issue of the architectural magazine *Aza-
nova,* plus some designs by students for a project in Sweden and the
sketch of a skyscraper from the twenties. "That was Soviet art once,
too!"

Orten has already seen both parts of the epic film about the Great
Patriotic War twice now, and he can't bring himself to go again. The
long wait for a ticket to the American disaster film begins. When he
asks one last time about the date, the kind-hearted woman selling
tickets whispers that a different American film is being shown at the
Youth, *Roman Holiday*—marvelous, it came around every year at New
Year's, but was earlier this time, because it had to be sent on to Novosibirsk, Berdsk, and Baryshevo. She had never missed it. "People
want to be happy," she says with tears in her eyes. "Your Highness!"
she whispers, imitating Gregory Peck—the sheer delight of undubbed
versions. Orten, who understands movie addicts of every sort, squeezes
her arm conspiratorially. "Where is the Youth?"

He trudges to the other end of town, through Golden Valley, where
kids are romping with sleds, then along the shore of the lake. He spots
Nordanc trying to execute a shaky spin. Qvietone comes skiing up

from behind in a flurry of snow. "Marvelous day!" he calls as he whizzes past. Orten wades back to town, rejoicing in his grim determination to pursue no sport whatever. His shoes are soggy, maybe boots did make sense. He has got the streets confused—it probably isn't Obskaya that he wants, but Obshchaya, "universal" street—his first etymological sortie in Russian. He asks, people shrug, there is no Obshchaya Street here. He is getting impatient, he was so looking forward to the movie, to Rome and the Colosseum, he can hardly wait to see buildings that are more than ten years old. Then he spots the Youth Cinema on the far side of the street.

"There is one advantage, though," Podol says after a week. "They haven't been constantly steering us through some institute or other." He listlessly takes a trick. Orten stares at his cards, then out the window. How long will this snow go on? The heating system isn't worth much. Smoke drifting along the ceiling, wet clothes draping the beds— he can distinguish between the odor of his socks and Podol's, his are worse. Maltzahn's aftershave hangs in the air, too, tinged with a cloying trace of Nordanc's and the acerbic herbal scent of Qvietone's. Even Friedland wasn't this pointless.

Maltzahn bolts into the room. "Some guy downstairs just asked me if we are coming to the reception at the institute."

"Of course not."

"Oh yes we are. We have to. It could be misinterpreted."

"We've been misinterpreted the whole time here. And don't forget, you don't want to be in possession of any secrets!" Podol picks his teeth with a card. "Which institute is having this reception?"

"I didn't quite get that. But at least somebody is finally talking to us."

"Was he soused? Drunkards speak to me every day on the street."

Maltzahn is getting impatient. "Just remember, we've been hanging around outside Dobrodin's office all week, and nobody will talk to us. His secretary has always got some sort of excuse, too. How long are we supposed to wait?"

"Well alright, looks as if they've been given some instructions. Let's just hope Dobrodin is even there."

"I spoke with Plotkin yesterday afternoon," Maltzahn says, lowering his voice. "Met him by accident when I was out sledding."

"You've taken to sports now, too?" Podol laughs.

"Am I supposed to sit around here all day playing cards and staring at your sourpusses? I was against sticking around here from the start! I didn't even want to get into that truck!" Maltzahn is going through a transition: at the moment he finds the Russians more bearable than the Czechs. "Plotkin indicated yesterday that it's now up to the municipal committee of Akademgorodok to decide . . . what to do about what may be regarded as our anti-Soviet attitudes."

"About what?"

"We have to prove that it isn't true."

"But it is true! I'd be happy to beat the tar out of that taxidermist again."

"And are obviously proud of it, too! Do you want to get out of here or not? We ought to be glad that Dobrodin has kept us from being interrogated in Novosibirsk. At least you can explain things here, these are intelligent people."

"Don't be under any illusions." Orten shrugs. "There are taxidermists everywhere. And janitors. Or ambitious comrades, scientists who keep their jobs by spying on others. Think of Prague—professors of philosophy selling vegetables or cleaning streets. Translators who collect old paper. They aren't allowed to work in the factories. And auxiliary cadres who can barely write their own names, but take over whole faculties! The main thing is that they sign their names at just the right moment!"

"And on the right documents." Podol brushes his game of solitaire aside. "And as far as this place goes? They don't seem all that intelligent to me. How did that go? Can a paralytic become a member of the Academy of Sciences? Yes, but only if he suffers from progressive paralysis."

Maltzahn pulls a wry face. Podol escalates: "Can an illiterate become a member of the Academy of Sciences?"

"Yes, but only a corresponding member."

They turn around. Dobrodin is standing in the door, laughing—it has been a week. "We were telling those jokes ten years ago, my little dove."

Podol realizes that he's not very good at demonstrating pro-Soviet attitudes.

"Hurry up, lads. Don't keep Comrade Goldansky waiting."

They look at one another. They hadn't expected to be summoned quite this soon.

The "conversation" turns out to be a tour of the Institute for Physical Chemistry, followed by a *zakuska* in honor of Vitaly I. Goldansky, a scientist from Moscow and an expert on the tunnel effect at very low temperatures. He draws a double curve and uses it to explain the motion of molecules between "potentiality troughs" as they pass across "activation barriers"—which in classical theory must be "climbed."

"But as we approach absolute zero, even at 4.2 degrees Kelvin"—he smiles and passes his foot through the impending wall—"quantum mechanical effects allow whole atoms to tunnel through these barriers of repulsing energies! Which leads us to assume that there are traces of life in the form of slowly occurring chemical reactions out in the cold of space, in the dark clouds of interstellar dust."

While Orten pictures the dark clouds of the Horsehead Nebula, imagining himself in his hollow form working his way toward it through the constellation of Orion, chisel in hand, Podol is wondering whether a quick, radical interrogation might not be better than this cordiality, this slow, persistent misunderstanding.

". . . should that indeed be possible, interstellar formaldehyde can become a polysaccharide only by means of the tunnel effect," Goldansky concludes. "In the matter of the possible significance of cold chemical reactions for the development of prebiological building blocks, let me quote Mayakovsky, who in addressing his colleague Pushkin says: 'Eternity is ours, why should we not spend a few hours together?' " Applause. Goldansky makes a slight bow. "In England, a year after our work, Vikram Singh and Hoyle . . ."

Orten has a coughing fit, the scientists clear a path as he elbows his way to the door, under the envious gaze of Maltzahn and Nordanc. Meanwhile, Qvietone has a question—where had they dug up those two? At the last moment Podol makes his move, grabbing Orten by the arm and leading him out the door. "That was a great idea." He pounds him on the back, Orten starts to gag. "Cut the nonsense!" Podol says, throwing open a window. The chemicals and models of apparatus are all under glass here in the corridor, but the air is just as stifling as inside. "It's high time we get out of here! Olbram would claim they're trying to poison us." Podol notices that he is a little dizzy himself.

The scientists come out. Goldansky walks over to Orten and inquires how he is feeling. "I don't know if I made myself clearly understood," he continues, turning to Podol. "Potentiality troughs are inner structures of the atoms in the molecule that are altered during chemical reactions."

Podol nods gloomily. He wants to say, "Don't overtax yourself," but he can't come up with that in Russian at the moment. He has spent the whole week leafing through Qvietone's dictionary and he understands everything, even, somewhat to his dismay, technical terms that out of context he would let flutter by him in Czech—but the exhaustion he has felt the past few days has slowed him down. "Troughs of potentiality," he repeats vacantly.

"Unfortunately, those have disappeared." Goldansky chuckles. "Tunnel procedures have one catch: as a result of the reactions passing through them—particularly at such extremely low temperatures—it is doubtful whether complex organisms can be restored to life after having been frozen for such a long time."

Podol translates this with difficulty: "Because some of the atoms can tunnel through, you can't achieve the hundred-percent standstill you're after?"

"Right!" Goldansky is pleased with Podol's progress. He waves over the lab assistant who is carrying the tray of drinks and toasts Podol. After his second glass, Podol begins to feel better. "So you mean it's not really worth having yourself hibernatized?" He amazes himself with the word.

Goldansky bursts into laughter. "Exactly!" He claps him on the shoulder. "But that's just between us. At least not until we can shield our chillees from certain 'events.' "

"What sort of events?"

"Sharp question!" Goldansky winks at him. "From the radiation, my good man!" he whispers.

Confused now, Podol says nothing.

"But then again, my tunnel procedures are not that hostile to life." The scientist snickers. "Above two hundred degrees Kelvin, even at physiological temperatures, they can play a significant role for biopolymeric molecules, proteins, or DNA. Given comfortable substructures, you see, they in fact make transferals possible."

Podol looks around for someone who might intervene here. Dobrodin has already pulled Orten aside for some amusing anecdote.

"Perhaps I've got ahead of you," Goldansky suddenly remarks. "Conformable substructures . . . now how shall I explain that to you?"

Podol spots Maltzahn, his face suffused with delight, walking toward Dobrodin—so all it takes to disconcert people is to withdraw the paternal affection you first force upon them, and suddenly they know what gratitude is. He watches the eager young researchers circling about the professors, notices Plotkin's lithe omnipresence, the old woman bending down diffidently over her bucket at the end of the corridor. "I think I know what you mean."

Maltzahn toasts with Dobrodin—to health, to science, to art. With thumb and index finger he estimates the distance between Dobrodin's nose and chin, brow and mouth; he has done portraits of important personages before. What counts is the gesture, not the measurement. The young scientists stand around them, laughing, have themselves measured, too. Jealousies flare up about the breadth of brows. Orten tries finally to bring Dobrodin around to their trip.

"I know, my dear," Dobrodin says wistfully. "We're going to have to come up with something."

"Who's supposed to come up with something?" Podol asks when they have returned for the night. He stretches out on his short bed, making both end boards creak. "What are these scientists researching anyway? My head feels like a potsherd."

Maltzahn has wormed a few things out of Plotkin. "We have to show our good will. They've put on a concert for us, with Czech music, and now we have to repay them, show them we know something about Russian art as well."

"I can tell them a few things about the Crimean kitsch they have hanging in their gallery," Podol suggests.

"No, not that. Something classical, beyond dispute. No criticism."

"Should we mount a production of *Swan Lake*?" Podol rises onto his toes and flails his arms.

"You'll run out of jokes soon enough if we're still hunkered down here in the snow six months from now."

"In May?"

"That's when the thaw sets in, and we'll be stuck in slush. What did

Dobrodin say? The buildings start leaning—they've already got people working in their tipsy towns."

"That was in Yakutiya; there's no permafrost here," Orten says.

"All the same, it must be one hell of a sight when the computer center here starts leaning, or the Nuclear Physics Institute."

"Are we going to think about coming up with something or not?" Maltzahn's patience is wearing thin. "Some sort of gesture. I thought maybe something literary, but I don't know much about that. I could do Dobrodin's portrait, but it has to demonstrate our collective point of view."

"We aren't a collective," Podol says wearily. "A pack of idiots who got lost. What good is 'good will' going to do here? Shall we put on a comedy?"

Orten gazes at the ceiling. "That's an idea. Something short. *A Cloud in Trousers,* for example—you can impress even these natural scientists here with Mayakovsky."

"I don't know him," Maltzahn says.

"We could dramatize *The Twelve Chairs.*" Podol weighs the possibility. He looks around. "But we don't have that many chairs."

"Gogol," Orten says. "We'll put on *The Inspector General.* We'll go to the library tomorrow and get a copy."

You're too tense for Khlestakov, Olbram," Podol says. "I know you're having trouble with the Russian, we all are, but you have to enjoy some speeches. Here: 'I don't stand on ceremony, I do my best to hide my rank and status. And yet as soon as I leave people say: "There he goes, don't you see him, there he goes!" And when I appear anywhere people say: "Here he comes, don't you see him, here he comes!" ' "

Maltzahn: "Here he comes, don't you see him, here he comes."

"Not so mechanically! You have to have fun with the idea that everyone thinks you're someone else!"

"Just like with us here, right? The role is too long. Give me a servant or a messenger who just delivers something without saying a word."

"You'll get that, too, we're going to have to double up on roles anyway. Erik, you're Marya, my daughter."

"Why a daughter?" Qvietone has arrived late and is looking for his copy.

"Because we need one. Or you could be my son, I suppose, except that Khlestakov isn't . . ." Podol's eyes come to rest on Nordanc. "I thought you'd been working on this. Besides, you're Bobchinsky. And Andy is Dobchinsky."

Nordanc pages through his copy, muttering.

"Andy, you'll have to play the welfare commissioner, or the judge. Both are short."

Nordanc pulls a face. "Couldn't we merge the welfare commissioner and the judge? Like with Dobchinsky and Bobchinsky? I can hardly keep them apart. I hope we're doing it as a reading. I couldn't get a word of it out on cue! I didn't grow up with Russian the way you did."

"I ought to punch you in the nose! Think we grew up with it voluntarily? I was already out of school. Just for that, you get the role of the waiter besides!"

Nordanc wraps himself in sullen silence. "Fine, I have no problem with the waiter. But the judge's role is too long. I can barely read the alphabet."

"Then it goes to Erik."

"But I'm already Marya and Bobchinsky," Qvietone protests.

"Then Jan will take it, he isn't anything yet." Podol turns to Orten. "It was your idea after all. And you're Osip, as well, Khlestakov's servant."

Orten scans the text. "That's too much."

"We still need someone for Mishka," Podol says. "Olbram, it's yours, a servant's role."

"The mayor's servant? So that you can keep kicking me in the butt! I'd rather have Osip instead."

"You can't play your own servant!"

"Haven't you got a messenger who doesn't say anything?"— Maltzahn.

"No, they all speak."

"We've forgotten the mayor's wife," Nordanc chimes in. They look at Podol.

"Okay. Then give her to me."

"How are you going to play your own wife at the same time?" Maltzahn asks.

"I'll manage. I'll just have to speak a couple of sentences offstage.

Most of the time she's on with Marya and Khlestakov when I'm not around."

"Husband and wife in one person, like schistosoma, the hermaphroditic fluke," Qvietone can't help remarking.

"Leave your bloodsuckers out of this! It's because of your schistozies that we're stuck here. Who was it that had to unload his leech project?"

"I haven't unloaded it yet."

"Why am I not surprised!"

"And the young widow and the locksmith's wife?" Nordanc has just managed to decode the list of characters.

"We'll leave them out," Orten says. "Streamline the roles of Dobchinsky and Bobchinsky, and the postmaster, too."

"We don't even have him yet," Maltzahn realizes. "Jan, maybe you . . ."

"I'm already the judge and Osip," Orten is quick to reply.

"Actually, you could take it on yourself. He never runs into Khlestakov."

"You got anything else for me to do? I'm already the welfare commissioner." Maltzahn is getting riled.

"We'll cut the welfare commissioner."

"Let's not argue," Podol says. "It all depends on the costumes. We'll have to ask Plotkin what they've got in the closets at the theater club."

"Are you serious? It's only supposed to be a show of our good will. There's no need to overdo this," Maltzahn objects.

"Our delivery will be so lousy that we should look good at least. Olbram, tell Plotkin we'll be ready in three days, and invite Dobrodin, of course."

"We won't have it together in three days." Nordanc is skeptical.

"It's not a matter of being perfect, but of being able to be on our way as soon as possible. Strictly speaking, we could give a performance tomorrow."

"To whet their appetites?" Maltzahn asks. "No, we shouldn't just reel it off. Day after tomorrow maybe?"

"If we can get some costumes, then the day after tomorrow. And don't forget to invite Goldansky, to even the score for his tunnel twaddle!"

. . .

About sixteen up-and-coming mathematicians, the ones that Plotkin could keep from pursuing winter sports this afternoon, are sitting in the Indeterminate Integral Club. Up on the makeshift stage, in the makeshift spotlight, stands Podol—the mayor, in a green pelerine and two-cornered hat. He peers out into the hall, looking for Dobrodin. A violin is hung on the wall behind him. At his side is Maltzahn as Khlestakov, in threadbare swallowtails. He points to the remains of a meal on the table and reads: "It's not my fault, I really am going to pay, but at the moment . . . The landlord is impossible! The tea stinks of fish, the soup, the meat! They're starving me!"

PODOL has equal difficulty reading, he holds his script closer to the light. "Mayor: Allow me to suggest you take other apartments."

KHLESTAKOV: "No I won't go! I know what you mean by other apartments: prison and the clink! How dare you. I am in the civil service, a civil servant from Petersburg!" Maltzahn checks his text, then balls his fist.

Podol casts his arms wide, flinging his book to the floor. He bends down for it, and loses his hat. Bravos from the mathematicians, who have been taking the reading seriously until now. Podol perspires, tries to find his place again.

"I mean no malice. It was only my ignorance! [Laughter] The state pays so badly. [Applause] My salary is hardly enough for tea and a little sugar. ["Same as ours!"] And bribes are as good as unknown here, and when, then nothing to speak of, trinkets, little gifts." The rest of the speech is drowned in the applause of the mathematicians. Podol bows in confusion.

Qvietone enters, dressed as Marya in red saffian. His blond braid slips with each affected, mincing step. He stops in front of Khlestakov and tries to blush in embarrassment. (Qvietone is not a good actor, but he is the only one who knows his role by heart.) "Oh!"

KHLESTAKOV (Maltzahn has quickly thumbed to the page): "Did I alarm you?"

MARYA: "No, but I thought Mamma was here."

KHLESTAKOV: "Et pourquoi pas?"

MARYA: "How sweet! I expect you know ever so many poems, too, verses in French?"

KHLESTAKOV: "J'ai la marotte / d'aimer Charlotte."

"There's many a subfunction with trivial ideals!" a mathematician shouts, and is greeted by stomping of feet and laughter from his colleagues, who would love to slip in something about braid theory, too. Cries of "Quiet!" from the other faction quickly carry the day.

MARYA coos for the third time: "Wonderful!" Qvietone gets tangled in his skirts, stumbles. Maltzahn catches him just in time.

KHLESTAKOV: "And you, mademoiselle? You have no songs to sing for me?"

"Oh, but I do." QVIETONE glances at his script. " 'The Pines.' No, wait, 'The Birches.' "

"Oh yes, dearest, do begin." Maltzahn is curious—there is no text for the song in his script. After hesitating briefly, Qvietone decides that any other plant will do just as well and begins to sing "Kalinka." Enthusiastic applause from the audience, who join in.

Nordanc, as DOBCHINSKY, appears at the other end of the stage: "He can inspect the courthouse!"

PODOL/MAYOR, incensed: "What about the geese in the corridor, the filth in the courtroom, the laundry hanging out to dry wherever you look?"

BOBCHINSKY, stammering: "Then the hospital of the municipal poorhouse."

MAYOR: "Go! Clean shirts, clean nightcaps, Latin mottoes above the beds!" Exeunt.

Enter Orten as OSIP, Khlestakov's servant. He paces back and forth silently in front of Podol, knocks on the walls, listens, looks toward the door where he thinks he can spot Dobrodin's shadow. "Is there no other way out?" Laughter.

MAYOR/PODOL: "Of course. We are free men here!" Applause.

Osip brushes some dust from the mayor's uniform and flicks the tassel on his two-cornered hat. The mayor smiles and shifts the hat around so that Osip can flick the tassel at the back as well. With lowered voice, toadying: "Tell me, is he strict, your master?"

Osip scratches his nose, bounces on his toes. The mayor slips a banknote into his jacket pocket. Osip pulls it out, examines it, goes on bouncing. The mayor slips him another.

OSIP: "Oh yes, he likes things done properly."

MAYOR: "And does he find fault and curse?"

OSIP starts to whistle, and gets a third banknote: "Does he ever! Everything must be just so."

QVIETONE/MARYA, from across the stage: "And counts come to visit you?"

OSIP thinks it over: "Counts? Yes!"

MARYA: "And he attends the opera?"

OSIP nods meaningfully: "Often!"

MARYA: "I shall sing for him, as soon as he wakes up!"

"Kalinka!" the mathematicians shout. "Katyushka! *'Shiroka strana moya rodnaya!'* " a deep voice booms from the door.

" 'The Song of the Driver on the Frontlines'!" PODOL shouts, and they all sing along.

"Put' dorozhka, frontovaya . . ." Some only hum; they have forgotten the words. The sonorous bass in the background supports the rest of them. Applause, shouts of "Go on!"

PODOL finds his place again: "Tell me, what does he like?"

OSIP: "Well now, different things, it all depends, for instance . . ."

MAYOR, eagerly: "What?"

OSIP: "He likes to eat well!"

Nordanc as Mishka makes a noisy entrance.

MAYOR: "Psst, be quiet, don't make such a racket!"

MISHKA: "I . . ."

The mayor claps his hand over Mishka's mouth. To Osip: "Go along now. Take anything you need! Enjoy yourself, have a fine time! We'll talk again soon!" He winks at him.

Exit Osip. Mishka, who is close to suffocating, tears himself away—and tips over his chair. He stands at attention. The mayor attempts to strike him. When Mishka sets the chair right again, the mayor kicks him in the rear.

"Go get Prokhorov and two more officers. Have them clear the area in front of the house. No petitioners, no mischief makers; nobody who even looks like one. The usual."

MISHKA: "The usual."

MAYOR: "Kicks him in the rear, like so. Understood?" He gives him a kick.

Mishka stands at attention.

"Like so. Understood?"

Mishka salutes.

"And like so!"

Mishka takes a header; the mayor helps him to his feet.

"I am like a father to you all!" He rubs a tear from his eye, grabs the violin from the wall, and with great fervor plunks out a Russian melody. *("Ochi chorniye"?)*

The mathematicians respond with a standing ovation. Before the curtain is raised again, the large shadow beside the door slips out of sight.

"Plotkin thinks that the last scene might be understood," Maltzahn says that evening.

"But he laughed, too." Podol wipes his damp face with his handkerchief. "And Dobrodin sang right along. It was Dobrodin, wasn't it?"

"He left in the middle, after you did your violin bit," Orten says. " 'I am like a father to you all!'—He could easily have thought that was intended for him. Where did you come up with that? That's not in Gogol."

"So what? 'The Song of the Driver on the Frontlines' isn't in Gogol, either! It was definitely a marked improvement over our stammerings. That was a good idea of yours, too, Erik, your 'Kalinka.' And you looked ravishing as Marya!"

"And as my mother, too," Qvietone says.

"Absolutely," Nordanc remarks softly.

"You were first rate, Andy. Dobchinsky and Bobchinsky rolled into one!"

"You asked a little too much of me in my role as Mishka," Nordanc replies, feeling his rear end. "Right in the sacroiliac."

"I'm sorry, I would much rather have kicked the truck driver who brought us here. You can still sit, I hope?"

"I think I'll stand for the rest of the day."

"So what happens now, can we leave or should we put on another farce maybe? But if we do, I'm going to kick your ass, Olbram, and your good friend Plotkin's! And above all, Dobrodin's, the damned *doprdelin* with that everlasting smile on his face!"

"I don't know," Maltzahn says. "Your references to how all men are free here, and poorly paid. That wasn't exactly a clever tactic."

"It's in the script! They've got at least twenty copies in their library. They should go read their own classics to find out what's what around here!"

. . .

"Dobrodin thinks we've moved a step closer," Maltzahn reports. Ever since Orten refused to get involved in any new discussions, he has become their go-between. Podol's lack of self-control and Qvietone's thirst for knowledge present too great a risk for them to negotiate with their hosts. "The committee only has to verify that we are really sculptors." Maltzahn casts Podol an uneasy glance.

"Do they think we're spies trying to smuggle their discoveries into Japan?" Podol slams his breakfast piroshki back on his plate. "First they force their progress down our throats and then they suspect us! The only scientist here is Erik, and he's gotten nowhere with his attempts to unload his discoveries. What did they tell you?"

"That I should apply to the Institute for Tropical Medicine in Azerbaijan," Qvietone says.

"Good, you can go to Azerbaijan and we'll go to Chabarovsk. We're done here!"

"Not quite," Maltzahn says. "They want us to leave some object behind."

"What?"

"Dobrodin would see to it that a block of gneiss is put at our disposal, that's no problem."

"Oh, but it is a problem. Do you know how long we'd have to stay on here then?" Orten asks.

"It shouldn't be anything too individualistic, either." Maltzahn is thinking fast. "Nothing objectionable. I know—we'll do a façade!"

"In the snow?"

"Just a couple of sgraffiti in the reception hall, as proof . . ."

"Renaissance sgraffiti in a research institute that's only ten years old?"

"It's sure to please them," Maltzahn declares.

"That's what I'm afraid of," Podol says. "We do three of them, and then they'll want a whole wallful, I know these guys too well. We won't get out of here before May!"

"I've got it!" Orten pours some vodka into his teacup. "Standa, you can do a coat-of-arms on the wall, like that sign you did in Prague."

Podol takes his bottle back. "What would you like best? 'Inn of the Indeterminate Integral'? 'Inn of the Three Cosmonauts,' 'Gagarin's Place,' 'Michurin's Pub,' 'Plekhanov's Tavern'? 'Pavlov's Bar'! 'The Salivating Dog'!—Do you know this one? But it has to be told in Russian." Podol gathers up all his scraps of language: "Comrade Pavlov had a flea. Comrade Pavlov took the flea, put it on a table, and went 'tap, tap, tap' with his pencil. The flea heard it and jumped three times: hop, hop, hop. Comrade Pavlov wrote in his notebook: 'When I put a flea on the table and tap my pencil, it jumps.' Then Comrade Pavlov took the flea, tore off all its legs, put it on the table and rapped 'tap, tap, tap' again. The flea: nothing. Comrade Pavlov picked up his notebook and wrote: 'When I take a flea, tear off all its legs and go "tap, tap, tap" with my pencil'—impressive pause—'the flea can't hear.' "

They all look at one another. Podol laughs. Maltzahn doesn't want to risk spoiling his good mood. "That was good. Especially your Russian. Do you think you can do a smaller one in your style . . . a sign, I mean?"

"I can slap my two doves on their wall, my two cooing Old Prague turtledoves in their ugly new Science Town. Jan, give me the cup!"

Orten considers: "Doves? That's it!"

"What do you mean?"

"Don't you remember 'Kdyby tisíc klarinetů,' where the kid runs away from the draft, they surround him, and he tries to take refuge under a monument to Beethoven: 'Help me, Beethoven!' and Beethoven helps him—all their weapons turn into musical instruments: the bullets they're firing at him turn into piccolos, the machine guns in their barracks into double basses, the rifles are violins, the whole battalion becomes an orchestra. Back in the sixties."

"I know, *The Thousand Clarinets*. Those were the days when it still made sense to cross your fingers for deserters. I don't go to see Czech films anymore. But what are you getting at? Am I supposed to chisel a Beethoven monument out of gneiss? Or call upon some higher artistic authority to help us out of this mess? An artist? What great artist wouldn't they be suspicious of around here!"

"There's only one! I've seen prints of his tiny slapdash hands—my plaster hands are meathooks in comparison—but no one is going to contest him as our choice! We'll use his dove of peace!"

"Great! We'll let Picasso open our scientific dovecote for us!" Podol fills his cup. "Olbram, tell Dobrodin we need some plaster!"

. . .

"*Zateilivo.*" Dobrodin is standing in the great lecture hall, gazing at Podol's dove of peace; beside him are Fyodor Nyetchayev, the director of the Institute for Nuclear Physics, and other important personages of Akademgorodok.

"*Da znachiel'no,*" the physicist says and nods gravely.

"What are they saying?" Podol has spent the week working on a scaffold, never hearing a word of Russian. "Interesting to significant," Orten translates with a grin.

Podol scrambles down. Orten, who has been working just below him, plastering over the steel rods that support the figure, follows. Maltzahn is likewise present on the scaffold, although of late he has been so busy making new friends in the Metallographic Institute that they have seen little of him. He gazes out over the assembled academics and runs a hand over one of the dove's wings, then he climbs down. Podol regards his work with satisfaction.

"Looks a little bit like a chicken," Orten says.

"Because it has legs!" Podol replies. "Picasso's dove just squats there, smug and fat-assed. This is the Czech version, lean and wiry."

"More like plucked," Orten replies.

The director of the institute is heading toward Podol with outstretched arms. Podol hastily wipes his hands on his jacket. It is stiff with dried lime, but he likes that grainy feeling.

"Comrade Podolský, your dove shall always be for us a treasured memento of the friendship between our peoples. It is the symbol of peace, to the preservation of which our research likewise contributes. May your beautiful dove both inspire us and remind us of our responsibilities." Applause.

Podol doesn't need a translation, he knows the sentences by heart. Thirty years of indestructible friendship, *nerushimaya druzhba*—now that sticks in your mind. Orten wonders what would happen if the bird fell from the wall now; the mortar is still wet. He admires Podol's self-assurance, the way he executed his concept of a dove without any regard for the obligatory symbolism. This cross-eyed bird transports him from this hall and its sterile insulation panels to Podol's atelier— brightly painted cupboards, out-of-plumb walls covered with his wife's lacework, the view to the Hradschin and the roofs of the Lesser Quarter, with nesting swallows and cats lying in ambush.

The director of the institute pins a badge on Podol's jacket, next to the trowel stuck in his pocket: Lenin in profile, flags fluttering behind him. Orten receives a profile without flags, Maltzahn a full-face view— Lenin as a boy. "Simple mementos, symbolic," the scientist declares.

"I thought maybe it was the Order of Lenin," Podol says.

"No, they are just *znachki,* badges, you can find them in any souvenir shop," the director says with a laugh. "But in plastic. Yours are enamel, from my private collection. But now let us really celebrate!"

A *zakuska* is standing at the ready in the social rooms: *Krymskoy shampanskoye,* caviar, sturgeon, a dozen brands of vodka. They simply must try the Balm of Riga. He pours out *sto* grams for each of them.

"Don't you have any smaller glasses?" Podol asks.

"What would be the point of that?" The physicist laughs, clapping him on the shoulder and sending up a cloud of lime.

Orten looks around for Dobrodin—he is talking with two older scientists. It doesn't appear as if anyone is worried about their departure.

Qvietone, Nordanc, Plotkin, and some others are gathered around a man of about sixty with a leathery face, whose broad gestures attract more and more listeners to the circle. He spots Podol and joins him.

"We're really quite alike," he says. "We're all putter-outers!"

"What?" Podol searches for Orten.

"But you put out art, and I put out fire. Haha!"

"Comrade Morosov is our guest of honor," the director says. "Commander of the Kiev Fire Brigade. He has been awarded the Order of Lenin." (This to Podol, with a smile.) "He is here to have a look at our Institute of Chemistry, our colleagues there are working on . . ." He falters and glances at Dobrodin. "In any case, he is here to further his knowledge of how fires are fought when the sources of the water supply are frozen over," he concludes resourcefully.

Morosov gives the director a surprised look. "Well yes, the Dnepr is not the Ob, as I always say. And if you have now developed a new substance for extinguishing fires . . . , fine, I shall say no more." He laughs and claps Plotkin on the shoulder. "You are my heroes!" Embarrassed pause.

"Is there a fire department here?" Podol asks.

"Of course," Plotkin replies. "But the main station is in Novosibirsk."

"It's almost as large as our extinguishing collective."—Morosov.

"Larger."—Nyetchayev.

"Certainly not," Morosov says heatedly. "We have many more fires to put out!"

"I can believe that," Nyetchayev snaps.

"But why argue, my little doves?" Dobrodin breaks in for the first time. "You should take an example from the dove of peace and the patience of our Czech friends." He laughs, putting an arm around Podol's shoulder. "Stanislav Karlovich, it makes me almost sad to think that your beautiful dove isn't hanging in our Geological Institute. They already have their model of an atom here in the entryway. It's enough to make a man jealous. But perhaps, if you should be so gracious, a second work of art . . ."

"But you see, *little dove,* our patience has its limits." Podol frees himself from Dobrodin's embrace. He has a strong urge to fling his *shampanskoye* in Dobrodin's laughing face, but controls himself, much to Orten's astonishment. *"Na zdorovye!"* he says, turning to Morosov, to whom, as the only nonscientist present, he has taken a liking. He pays no further mind to Dobrodin.

Hardly anyone has noticed the incident. The young scientists press in closer still around the fireman. "Please, go on, Pavel Arkadich."

Morosov lights his pipe. "As I was saying, our fire brigade and its two hundred sixteen vehicles had moved across to the eastern bank of the Dnepr in order to prevent the fascist hordes from seizing both men and vehicles. But when we looked behind us and saw Kiev in flames, we quickly reversed directions."

"Did you see any Germans?" Nyetchayev moves in closer again.

"They were there; they had set the city on fire. But we paid them no attention. Our job was to quench the flames."

"That sounds quite heroic," Nyetchayev says with a smile.

Morosov considers this. "The decisive factor was not ourselves but rather our heavy apparatus. Some of it was rather battered, I grant, but all of it could still move very fast. In a sense, we were only along for the ride. Besides, that is our job."

"And what about the Germans? When they saw two hundred sixteen heavy vehicles returning at high speed across the bridges, to a city they had already taken?"

"They were surprised, somewhat dumbfounded. They shouted as we passed, a few threw themselves in front of the vehicles and were run over. There was some shooting, too, but no serious attempts were made to stop us. Or to hinder us when we went to work putting out the fires."

"They probably even provided you with quarters." Nyetchayev chuckles.

Morosov stares at him. "It all happened too quickly for that. Such considerations played no role whatever. Later on, perhaps. I think, rather, that they understood that when confronted with such a fire, the experts and their machines had no choice but to do their professional duty. The population understood that as well."

"The population understood that you are heroes!" Plotkin says. "Were you rewarded later for your intervention?"

"No, because we were no longer available. After finishing the job, we formed three parallel columns to increase our speed for the retreat, broke through the German lines, and drove out onto the steppes."

"And the Germans? Did they open fire behind you?"

"Heavy fire, but our water tanks were already empty."

"And then?" Podol asks.

"It was our intention to maintain our usefulness as a fire brigade once our three columns rejoined."

"And why were you no longer available?"

"Because we no longer had any real function! Out on the open steppes we had no task to fulfill. No village fire could ever be a match for our capabilities for extinguishing it! We wanted to stay together, but then we could go no farther."

"So you had run out of gas?"

"Oh no, the depots were glad to be rid of their supplies, but we had lost our collective will to extinguish fires. Our vehicles simply didn't want to function out on the steppes. If we had had tractors, something slower, we could have become an agricultural column and saved the harvest. But as it was, we simply despaired and then dispersed."

"What?" Nordanc asks—the story sounds familiar somehow.

"Two by two, our vehicles were attached to retreating Soviet divisions. That was the end of our column. From then on, we all just extinguished minor fires. We scattered across the steppes and were no longer available for any honors." Morosov grins.

And your Order of Lenin?—but Orten manages to squelch his question. The Kiev Fire Department surely had its share of conflagrations to put out. "When are you leaving?" he asks instead.

"In two days," Morosov says. "Would you like to join me? We could travel together for a good part of the trip."

Podol wonders if it might not be better to go back with Morosov rather than be led around by the nose here any longer. Kiev—you're almost in Prague. "We're going in the other direction, unfortunately. And we're in a hurry!" He glares angrily at Dobrodin, who smiles and waves.

"What a shame," Morosov says. "But if you ever do get to Kiev, you are welcome at our brigade anytime. You have shown us your art today, next time we shall show you ours."

"Yes, they like it, they're impressed, but now they want to know what we think about sports," Maltzahn says a week later. In the meantime, temperatures have fallen to twenty-five below. Ever since the entrance to their dorm has been snowed shut, their exhaustion and apathy have grown. They leave the building only rarely. The sporadic contact between Maltzahn and Dobrodin is like the slow sway of a pendulum. They no longer ask if they can leave, they don't know what they are doing wrong, and it apparently makes no difference, anything can be taken the wrong way. At one point Orten suddenly thinks of Kyoto and is seized with a fit of laughter, but it passes quickly.

Podol spends his days on his bed, with his shoes on, smoking, playing solitaire, whistling to himself, a bottle of vodka propped in the folds of his blankets. Sometimes, if he forgets to take off his gloves, it slips out of his hands, and the spilled contents mingle with the other odors in their room—until Nordanc or Qvietone comes in, still flushed from their winter sports, and flings open the windows, but in five minutes or so they capitulate before Podol's curses and the cold rushing in from outside. The heating arrangements remind them of their quarters in the castle in Friedland, the one difference being that the temperatures on autumn nights there seldom fall below freezing.

"Sports?" Despite his stiff fingers, Podol is sketching a sgraffiti triptych: in the middle, Dobrodin as a leering faun; on the right, Plotkin kneeling before his cock; on the left, Nyetchayev is doing him *a tergo;* the background, a red star. He gives some thought to which gable would work best for this trio. Next to the Allegory of Chance, if there's still room enough.

"It was a mistake, Stanislav, not to take Dobrodin up on his suggestion. You would already have been done with the second fresco by now."

"I regret that now, too." Podol shows him the sketch.

Maltzahn starts to splutter, "Don't leave that thing lying around in here! Maybe it would be better if we all participated in the athletic competitions at the gym."

"Don't tell me—pole vaulting."

"No, not that. But the broad jump, or the discus . . ."

"I haven't touched a discus since the time I banged up my knee with one of the things. The only discipline that I would be interested in is cross-country running—from here to Chabarovsk!" Podol gives Dobrodin a long red tongue.

"Even better, the biathlon; that way we could shoot our way through the militia at the borders of town," Qvietone adds.

"We could set up a boxing match," Nordanc muses.

"No, that could be misinterpreted," Maltzahn replies. "They asked about winter sports."

"Fine, Andy and Erik can ski and have their runs timed," Podol says. "If they want to see us in collective format, we can stand off to one side and cheer them on. They can't expect more concessions from us than that."

"How about ice-skating?" Maltzahn proposes tentatively.

"Bull," Orten says.

"When I was a kid I had the kind you had to screw on. Age has its advantages." Podol grins.

"I can still stay on my feet," Maltzahn broods. "And you two aren't bad." Nordanc and Qvietone shrug.

"Okay, well then, just run along and sled with the kids in the park. And bring us back something to eat." Podol pulls his blanket up over his shoulders.

"No, it's not that simple. We have to sign up."

"What are you talking about?"

"I've been thinking it over—now don't hit me." Maltzahn is sticking close to the door. "We have to play hockey with them. They expect that of Czechs. A kind of Izvestiya Cup. We were the ones who taught them how, you know."

"Until they started wiping up the ice with us," Orten says.

"Not always!"—Podol.

"That's right. And they know the names of all the Czech players; they're really crazy about them!"

Podol stares distrustfully at Maltzahn. "I know that joke." (In a reporter's voice): "Nedomanský has the puck! now Golonka! Jaroslav Holík! Golonka! Jiří Holík! . . . [softly] goal, Firsov!"

Maltzahn: "At any rate, I've already agreed, and I'm glad that you all see it that way too!"

"What are you talking about!" Podol sits up again. "I'm not going to break a leg just because you're so deep in sleaze that you're willing to double-cross us and sell us out, just so you can look like a well-behaved asshole!"

"Lower your voice! I'm only trying to make up for your gaffes! Who beat up the taxidermist? Who's constantly picking a fight? Just look at you! Bloated, fat! A little exercise wouldn't hurt! Even if it doesn't get us anywhere—at least we tried! Belching and bellowing is all you're good for!" Maltzahn slams the door.

They start training that afternoon.

Orten refuses to wear ice skates, he's never even tried it. They give him shoes with two low, broad blades, but even then he has trouble sliding around the ice. After a couple of falls, Podol decides in favor of the same solution. But Maltzahn ignores their advice and insists on wearing skates, even tries a few turns, with all the kids gathered at the edge of the rink looking on.

After just one day, to judge from their bruises, it looks as if they have succeeded in eliminating themselves from the match. But the next morning, there a beaming Dobrodin stands on the threshold. "My little doves, today we've got to work on goal shooting."

Orten loses the stick issued to him, but is given a second. Using it for support, he makes it out onto the rink, when a ten-year-old boy arrives with the first one; he had been "shooting a few goals with Stepka and Lyosha," and then vanishes among the skaters further out on the ice. Orten watches him whiz away; good thing they don't have to play the kids.

"Jan, you're the goalie." Orten exchanges his two sticks for a goalie's stick, which is twice as heavy and wide and easier for him to grip.

Their academic opponents are all apparently A-league players, although Plotkin assures them that none has ever played with the Aka-demgorodok Hockey Club.

"That's even more depressing." Podol can barely follow the puck amid the flurry of sticks. Nothing blocks them from scoring one goal after the other, unless the shot is wide or hits the cage. After twenty minutes, no one is counting. Dobrodin blows his whistle. Podol coasts shakily toward the bench and uses the back to catch himself. "Thank God that's over."

"That was only the first period," Dobrodin says warily.

Podol stares at him and flings his stick away. "Not for us."

"Wait, Stanislav Karlich, we'll change the length of the periods. Twenty minutes really is too long. And the sizes of the teams are unfair, too. There are only five of you, so you can't substitute. That is, unless you'd want some of our kids to . . ."

"So they can shoot our goals for us?"

"However you like. But now you should rest up and then practice a little more. Tomorrow is the big day!" Dobrodin smiles—whether in encouragement or mockery is not clear.

"What's the real point of all this?" Podol asks wearily. "You can have your laugh at our expense without it."

Dobrodin says nothing at first. "Do you know the fairy tale about the czar of the seas? The one where Ivan has three tasks to accomplish. The first night he must chop down a dense forest, plow the earth, sow wheat, harvest it, and bake piroshki from the flour. The second night he must tend bees, collect the wax, and build a castle from it. He can already see his head on a pike beside the gate, but Yelena the Wisewoman comforts him, 'That is no task, only a light chore; the true task is yet to come.' And she helps him with both. But the third night Ivan lets out a merry whistle: he is supposed to ride an unsaddled horse—that will be a pleasant adventure. But Yelena turns pale: 'That is no light chore, but a terrible labor. The unsaddled horse is my father.' "

Podol stares into the distance, his responses come slower here now. "So you think that the dove of peace was easy for us?"

"It's your job. Like putting out fires is Morosov's." Dobrodin chuckles.

Podol just looks at him. "But Ivan and Yelena do get away?"

Dobrodin shrugs. "Maybe they like it there and stay on."

"I doubt that." Podol skates back out onto the ice.

"I know another story," says Orten, who has stumbled toward them.

"Older than your tale about the czar of the seas. Even if you have closed the Ussuri border. From China. Flash was emperor of the south seas, Wink was emperor of the north seas. Deepdark was emperor of middle earth. Flash and Wink would meet from time to time in Deepdark's realm and were always treated most cordially. Flash and Wink discussed how best to repay Deepdark for his hospitality, and decided: Humans have seven openings—to see, to hear, to eat, and to breathe. The emperor has none. Let us try to bore them for him! Each day they bored one hole. On the seventh day, Deepdark was dead."

Dobrodin ponders this. "Our hospitality has never killed anyone."

"But perhaps your attachment has." Orten sees Podol take a fall and flounders out to him.

"How long have we been here?"

"Six weeks, two months? I'm not counting anymore."

They know today's game is absurd, but it is better than sitting around here at the end of a noose. Podol wants to keep his stick after the game so he can use it in their pointless, endless conversations with Dobrodin. He now knows how the fairy tale about the czar of the seas turns out—he borrowed a copy from Plotkin's daughter. The old man in the form of a horse has to be beaten until the flesh falls from his bones. Maybe that would get them sent somewhere else in Siberia—murder in self-defense. He has read *The House of the Dead*.

"I haven't been able to find my gloves for two days now," Maltzahn says as they head down Tourist Street. "I'm going to buy some new ones; wait here. Do you want some ice cream, Stanislav?"

"No, I've about had it with frozen stuff. Make it quick."

Maltzahn returns with his new gloves and a postcard.

"We should write Václav Patera a note."

"You mean as long as we can still move our fingers?" Podol writes one sentence and signs his name. The card is passed around. Nordanc is the last to sign it, just below the mushroom Qvietone has drawn. Orten sketches a hockey stick and a puck in the net. "I suppose they're waiting for us." Maltzahn is feeling queasy.

Walking down Pearl Street, they try to take their minds off things by making fun of the gaudy, flaking façades. Nordanc discovers a mailbox. Maltzahn pulls out the postcard, takes a last look at the Moscow Cinema on the front, the stamp, the drawings.

" 'The deportees send their greetings'?" he reads. "I didn't see that before!"

"Stanislav, you're getting ahead of yourself," Orten remarks.

Podol grins.

Podol takes the card from Maltzahn's hand and slips it into the mailbox. "Did you want to send Václav our greetings or not? Who knows if we'll get around to it later. This goddamn hockey wingding has finally put an end to my patience!"

In Golden Valley they run into several people they've become acquainted with during their visits to various institutes. Vitaly I. Goldansky tunnels his way through deep snow and eager groups of scientists are standing about. He shakes their hands. "We are thrilled by your interest in sports."

"It is more a matter of conformable substructures," Podol says wearily.

Nyetchayev compares what they will achieve today to the symbolic value of Podol's dove of peace. "And do you know, Comrade Podolský, your willingness to fight the good fight on the ice is almost more impressive than your art, which I do so admire."

"Just wait and see." This obsession with sports is giving Podol the creeps.

Login and Logoff/Ptolemenko, Vasya, and the entire work team from the computer center press in around them to wish them luck. "You don't look quite so green around the gills today, my dear." Login laughs, clapping Maltzahn on the shoulder. "Your stay with us has hardened you. And that's as it should be."

"Keep an eye out, they're perfectly capable of planting a bug in your stolen gloves," Podol notes—and Maltzahn's big grin freezes.

Qvietone is smothered by hugs from the biologists, as if today's game, which they are so looking forward to, could make up for his bilharzia project. Nordanc is surrounded by his friends from the ski slopes, who all have some final tips for him. A couple of young mathematicians from the Indeterminate Integral shake Podol's hand. "If you play your roles as well today as you did in *The Inspector General* . . ."

Emerging from this corridor of friendship, they come out onto the ice, where Dobrodin and Plotkin's team await them. One slant-eyed figure muffled in furs is leaning on the fence, Roger Snafu. This time he is chewing pine nuts—they supply their scientists well here. His eyes are glassy, he is singing to himself: "Speak your secret alphabet, light another cigarette, learn to forget." Orten holds out to him a pack of Bulgarian cigarettes he bought in Prague. Snafu stares at them. "I don't smoke anymore. Here"—he offers some nuts from his sack—"but not too many, there are rules against doping." He grins wanly. "I've got my fingers crossed for you."

They have agreed that the game will consist of three periods of seven minutes each, with two five-minute rests. Podol's suggestion of ten-minute breaks was rejected—the rests couldn't last longer than the playing times. He shakes the hand of the captain of the Russian team. The whistle blows. Plotkin wins the face-off against Nordanc, gracefully swerves around both Qvietone and Maltzahn, and taps the puck into Orten's goal. The crowd roars. They score three more goals in the first minute.

Orten is spending most of his time clinging to the cage frame, dodging flying pucks. His face mask bothers him; he frequently grabs for the frame and misses; one such maneuver blocks a goal. Podol hugs him and the others ecstatically bang their sticks on his head, the way they've seen it done on television, with the result that his helmet slips so far down over his eyes that he can't see anything for the rest of the period. He gives illegal body checks, shoots the puck too far—icing—but the referee, who apparently has his fingers crossed for the guests as well, seldom blows his whistle. He also decides several penalty shots in their favor, but they are unable to take advantage of them. The low score of 6 to 0 after the first period is due primarily to the selfless defensive efforts of Podol and Maltzahn, who throw their sticks between the attackers' legs, hang on to their arms, and use Orten's goal to push themselves off.

There are some nasty fouls, too. Maltzahn gives a kick in the shins to Vyacheslav Smyslov, doctoral candidate in physics. The up-and-coming young star in organic chemistry, Matvey Dobrodin, who thus far has been remarkable only for his absent-minded smile, pounces on Qvietone for no reason.

"I'll knock the hooliganism out of you!" his father shouts. Dobrodin is angry, because up until now the Russians have been playing a clean game.

He wants to ban Matvey to the penalty box for the rest of the game,

putting the home team at a disadvantage. But Qvietone fights back—
out of jealousy: all the *psilocybky* are under three feet of snow now,
and he suspects Dobrodin Junior is keeping himself supplied with syn-
thetic little scamps. Dobrodin Junior hops about, groaning and holding his shin. Boos and whistles from the fans.

Dobrodin, as referee, considers sending them both to the penalty
box for two—wait, everything's shorter here—for one minute, but then
they could hardly continue play, so he just gives them a warning. Nordanc suddenly bangs his stick on a Russian head—Lisputin, who has
thrown him an elbow when no one was looking. The crowd protests.

Icing, Dobrodin decides, and whistles for a face-off. Given the current score of 8 to 0, there is no real reason for the Russians to play
dirty. But Podol is determined to keep them below ten. At times he
suspects the Russians are intentionally holding back; the relatively low
score certainly can't be credited to Orten, who is still having trouble
with both his balance and his eyesight. Podol is now capable of slowly
reversing direction without taking a header. Maltzahn keeps his feet
by holding on to passing skaters, mostly Russians, who shake him off
angrily, mistakenly assuming he is charging or elbowing. Dobrodin
affably admonishes him to stop it—this is a warning, comrade. Podol
occasionally throws his stick in front of the advancing skaters and
delights in watching them fall, although he would gladly be put in the
penalty box instead of just being issued warnings. He also has the
impression that the Russians are only too glad to exaggerate each tumble so that they can incite the noisy fans with every foul. Maltzahn,
who insisted on wearing real skates, is paying for his vanity now. The
Russians shake him off violently every time he tries to hold on to them,
and he often loses his balance. One fall is so ugly that he comes up
spitting blood, and for the rest of the game he keeps running his tongue
over the lost filling in his tooth. Qvietone and Nordanc are holding up
well, they have mastered turnabouts now and generally make a good
impression. They even win several face-offs, but immediately lose the
puck to the next Russian who makes a play for it; they pursue him to
the middle of the ice, but haven't a prayer behind the blue line. At
least they manage to make it look like a contest.

6:0, 3:0.

Third period, five minutes to go.

The fans want ten goals and shout *"Shaibu! Shaibu!"* The Czechs feel all is lost until they hear a hoarse voice from behind the barrier: *"Do toho! Do toho!"* Podol looks up in surprise and realizes it is Snafu—no doubt about it, the Indian has a gift for languages. With thirty seconds to go, amid the ear-splitting *"desyat', desyat' "* of the fans, Modest Tretyak—Akademgorodok's idle goalie until now—is taken from the ice and replaced by the athletic hydrophysicist Prokhor Aspirin? (Had they heard that right?) Power play! Despite Podol's protests, the whistle blows. Maltzahn, Nordanc, and Qvietone place themselves in front of the goal alongside Orten, who has at least got the knack of keeping his visor from falling in his eyes, although the kneepads still get in his way.

Podol loses the last face-off with Aspirin, but trips over Aspirin's stick, kicking the puck aside. The puck slowly glides the length of the rink toward the Akadem goal—with Podol in pursuit, skidding on his chin as far as the blue line. But the puck reaches the goal. There it is, hanging in the net! The game is over. o to 1—the Czechs have won the third period!

The crowd goes wild, for some reason they are jubilant. They carry Podol off on their shoulders. Lisputin, Smyslov, Plotkin, Tretyak, Aspirin, and Matvey Dobrodin, followed by his father—one after the other they hug them. *"Druzhba, druzhba!"* They can leave tomorrow, but it is hard to let them go, everyone will miss them!

Qvietone rides with them to the airport in the minivan that Dobrodin has arranged for them. But once they reach Novosibirsk and are heading down Red Prospect toward Tolmatchyevo, he can no longer help himself. He pulls out his Intourist map and starts calling their attention to the same sights they hadn't wanted to see two months ago. "The largest opera house in the Soviet Union. De Gaulle attended a performance here."

"That doesn't improve it, either," Podol growls.

"Originally called Gusevka, or Goosetown, a peasant village on the banks of the Ob, it was first named Novo-Nikolayevsk in the nineties, and following the revolution, it was renamed Novosibirsk in 1925." Qvietone goes on reading. "At that time it had 120,000 inhabitants, today there are 1.3 million." He casts them a quizzical look. They say nothing.

The Park of Revolutionary Heroes—a monumental hand with a torch towers up out of a boulder. Gneiss or granite? Orten turns to look, but a trolley blocks his view. Podol points to a line of people waiting at a newspaper stand. "They even queue up for *Pravda!*"

A vacant lot, and the hand is again visible.

"They make saying goodbye easy," Orten says.

A guard in the aerodrome lobby holds Qvietone back. "What are you going to do now? Head home?" Nordanc asks.

"I originally intended to go to Ulan Ude, maybe that'll work out yet—seeing as I'm already here. I'm on an unpaid vacation. I still want to go to the local circus, they have Siberian tigers that ride on the backs of polar bears."

"I thought it was the other way around." Podol wonders if, given Erik's talent for complicating things, it wouldn't be better for him to return home as soon as possible. "Did you know that the bite of a single horse can be fatal to a wasp?"

"And tomorrow I'm going to the museum." Qvietone is not to be deterred. "They have a mammoth here."

FOURTEEN

"Comrade passengers, please fasten your seat belts."

Podol looks around. No one seems to be paying any attention to the instructions, and the stewardesses aren't checking either. He looks for his seat belt—one half has been ripped off, Maltzahn is sitting on the other. Maltzahn pulls out a bundle of striped plastic ribbons from behind him and spends the next ten minutes trying to connect them with Podol's half. The plane lurches as it climbs, as if stumbling through the air—eliciting amused faces from the locals. They have left Novosibirsk behind them. Podol leans across Maltzahn to look out the window, sees the belching chimneys of people-owned factories, blocks of apartments on the outskirts, and under a rigid, gray, lusterless layer of ice, the river that divides the city. Once they are higher, he can see Lake Ob among the snow-covered pine forests to the south. He searches for Akademgorodok, but the plane banks away in the opposite direction.

Closer at hand, Maltzahn is making a pouch of his cheek with his tongue, the bulges wander.

"Did you see a dentist?"

"Early this morning."

"It took that long?"

"He went to a lot of trouble with it. Because of the filling. Needed a total replacement, he told me. It feels so odd . . ." Maltzahn starts probing with his tongue again.

Podol leans back. "My whole body aches from yesterday." He tries to stretch his legs under the seat ahead of him and ends up kicking Orten in the ankle; Orten quickly pulls his foot away.

"Don't confuse me with Lisputin. We're not playing hockey anymore."

Nordanc, who is sitting next to Orten, grins. Through a break in the clouds he can see the industrial areas north of the city enveloped in smoke and haze. He doubts it can be worth staying on there just for a mammoth.

Orten recalls Dobrodin's fairy tale. Their production of *The Inspector General* got them nowhere, Podol's fresco got them nowhere—"That was no task, only a light chore; the true task is yet to come." They hadn't been allowed to leave until they had made asses of themselves, bruised their bones, got people laughing at them. There must be a way to get back at Dobrodin. Invite him to Japan, drag him off to an opium den or a teahouse, and then send compromising photographs to his local soviet. But his little scamps probably made him even more drug resistant than the Japanese. And he would dismiss the visit to the teahouse as people-to-people contact. Dobrodin was the sort who would be busy preserving world peace in the middle of a soap-down by two geishas.

The clouds are below them now, and they fly into fog. The plane rattles, the inside panels of the windows clatter, there is a draft. Orten is amazed that most of the passengers have taken off their coats, the red-faced stewardesses look as if they are about to break into a sweat. They pass out tea and *morozhennoye* (ice cream), which is devoured in great quantities. Orten says he doesn't want any; neither do Nordanc and Podol. With a determined look on his face, Maltzahn accepts some and packs it into his swollen cheek. He hisses in pain, then gulps it down all at once.

"What are you doing?" Podol asks.

"My tooth . . . is throbbing. My whole head is ringing."

"That's the change in pressure. Do you want a drink?" Podol rummages for his vodka bottle.

Orten motions to the stewardess and asks for some brandy. At first she hesitates—no alcoholic beverages are served in flight—but then retrieves a carafe of Georgian brandy and pours out a hundred grams for the frozen foreigner. Orten takes a sip and passes the glass back to Maltzahn who sips and makes a face. "I'm getting sick."

"Then give it to me." Podol empties the glass and orders another. They can't seem to get in the right mood. The strain on Maltzahn's face and the pressure in their ears don't help.

"How much longer?"

"Five hours," Nordanc says. Podol pulls his hood up over his head.

278

He is awakened by crackling and hissing on the loudspeaker. The pilot says a few unintelligible sentences, followed by a loud pop as he turns off the mike. "What did he say?"

"I didn't understand any of it." Orten is watching a stewardess hurrying forward. "I suppose he gave our altitude, or said he was thirsty."

"Why are they all so fidgety then?"

The drowsy passengers are all talking at once, getting their things down out of the baggage nets and fastening their seat belts.

They are only halfway into the flight, but the plane is now lunging toward a landing. "It must be some stopover," Nordanc says. "We're probably in Irkutsk."

They look out the window, but can't make out anything. As they emerge from the clouds, the plane is tossed by a violent gust of wind and enveloped in a blast of driving snow. The plane shudders in the gale, the toilet door bangs open, carry-on items tumble out of the baggage nets, but without hurting anyone, since the larger items have already been taken down. Podol can taste his brandy again. Nordanc bends forward, he has spotted a dull, shimmering riverbed as the plane takes another sudden turn. "That must be the Angara, maybe we'll be able to see Lake Baikal, too!"

Podol leans across Maltzahn—eyes closed, face white, hands clenched to the arms of his seat. "I don't see anything."

"That is not the Angara, comrades." The young stewardess is standing over them now, smiling and steadying herself on the baggage rack at each lurch. "That is the Nizhnyaya Tunguska. Are your seat belts fastened?"

"Comrades, we will be landing in Tura in a few minutes," the other stewardess says over the microphone. "Please remain seated. There is a snowstorm in progress."

With wobbly stomachs and legs, they emerge from the plane and are greeted by lashing snow that pushes them back against the stairway railing. They clumsily grope their way down the glassy-edged treads. The passengers flee into the airport and pile their luggage beside the entrance. There are no passport checks. By now Maltzahn is so apathetic that Podol helps prop him up and Nordanc takes charge of his bag, while Orten tries to locate someone who can tell them when the next flight leaves for Chabarovsk. A young man in overalls closes the inner door leading to the ramp and then slides another iron door into place.

"Chabarovsk? Why? There won't be any more flights today. Tomorrow? Citizen, we are in the middle of a *purga,* do you know what that is? Just look outside. You can be thankful you were able to land at all. There won't be any planes landing here for another week."

Orten returns to find Maltzahn still preoccupied with his throbbing new filling and Podol obsessed with one question: "Is today an even or odd day?" They can't agree. Nordanc is the only one who looks fairly normal, and he's better equipped, too. He gave his suitcase to Plotkin and bought himself a backpack in Akademgorodok. Next to him, the others feel like aging traveling salesmen.

A truck with snow chains has pulled up. The passengers and the crew get in—there is no point in waiting for a bus or a taxi. They scramble up without asking many questions. Just ahead of them is a snowplow that clears the way for the truck. Apparently accustomed to disasters, the people make no fuss as they squeeze together on the benches, even the children are quiet. The first buildings appear, two women get out and immediately vanish in the swirling snow. A hundred yards farther on, a group of airport employees climb out after an exchange of happy, shouted goodbyes; the men help the overweight, bundled-up women over the tailgate. The laughter quickly fades, those still left inside huddle closer together on the benches. The passengers drift away, there are no central pickup points, no stations—just a rap on the cab window and the truck stops. Orten tries to make out some sort of town center; to judge by the few feeble lights they do pass it is more like a diffuse, deserted periphery. He stops one of the women getting off and asks, *"Gostinitsa?"* She shakes her head, points into the dusk ahead and climbs down. Fewer and fewer lights blink from an occasional pole. The truck has emptied out. Only one young man is left, sitting there with skis and a heavy backpack with a tripod sticking up out of it. "And where are you gentlemen from?"

"Czechoslovakia."

"An expedition?" Curious, he checks over their equipment.

"No, we are trying to get to Chabarovsk," Orten replies wearily.

"By way of Yakutsk? But you came in from Novosibirsk; I saw your plane land."

"Is today an even- or odd-numbered day?" Podol suddenly thinks to ask.

The man apparently doesn't understand. "Oh, the date? It's the end of November." He mulls it over. "The twenty-ninth or the thirtieth. Around here we say that a *purga* can get your days and nights mixed up. One day more or less doesn't matter." He laughs.

"It does to us," Podol says. He turns to Orten. "Now I've forgotten if the flights on even days are in the afternoon or the morning."

"What?"

"Tura or Chabarovsk?"

"Forget it," Orten says, exhausted. "It could just as easily be Chita or Alma-Ata."

"Chita wouldn't be so bad," says the geologist. "It's in Transbaikal, so it's on your way."

Podol stares at him. "That's not going to help us much, unfortunately."

"Not at the moment. You're going to have to wait out the *purga*. That may be ten days. Or longer. Then you can continue your flight, by way of Chita if you like. If the storm doesn't abate, we'll all just have to put up with being snowed in for a few days. Have you ever been in a real *purga*? This is just the beginning!"

Orten notes the pride with which he says this—it reminds him unpleasantly of Akademgorodok.

"And where do you plan to sleep tonight?"

"In town. In a hotel maybe."

The man laughs. "Then you should have got out before this. There's no way you can do that now. The driver will be heading home. And the snowplow won't be going back, either." He looks at them, thinking it over. "I could put you up. But it's no hotel." He laughs again.

It has grown dark in the meantime, every light has vanished. The snowplow turns off at a fork in the road, the truck lumbers more slowly. After a while the driver stops without anyone's having rapped. "We're here."

They would prefer to wait and try to persuade the driver to turn back, but the young man has already jumped out of the truck and is busy buckling on his skis. "Shall we go?" Stiff with cold, they climb down after him. He waves to the driver, who honks his horn. Podol jumps up on the running board. "Are you going to Tura?"

"No!" The driver laughs. He puts the truck through a complicated turn and rumbles away.

"This way," the geologist says. "Keep close behind me. My name is Oleg," he says, shaking Nordanc's hand.

"André."

"Great. Andrei, you're right behind me. You're the pathfinder, our *molodets!*" He claps him on the shoulder.

They move out into the taiga. Oleg flattens the snow ahead of them. His spirits revived, Nordanc makes the first footprints. But the march soon gets bogged down—their bulky suitcases bang against tree trunks and boughs, get caught in branches that dump snow, great loads of it, down their necks. Soon there's not a dry spot left on their bodies. If they wander off the path, they sink in up to their waists or get wedged in between trees—both of which are enticing prospects—but their young Communist with his ideology of progress won't let them stop and rest; he screams at them until he is hoarse and drags them back onto their feet. Nordanc helps. Maltzahn in particular takes umbrage at this. Now Podol has joined forces with the others, and takes on the job of dragging Maltzahn across the snow. Orten and Nordanc carry his baggage. He cannot stand this Russian.

An hour and a half later—Oleg tells them it's normally only a thirty-minute walk—they arrive at a cabin in a clearing. The door is barred with a wedge of wood that has to be hammered out.

"Wait here." Oleg takes out his flashlight and walks around the cabin. "Good, no sign of them. We can go in."

"No sign of who? The people who live here?"

Oleg laughs. "These fellows were here before this cabin was ever built. We can only hope the *purga* will keep them at a good distance. That is unless they're starving."

You can spare us the suspense, Podol thinks. "Do you mean some sort of animals?" he asks.

"I mean wolves," Oleg says, and bars the door.

The middle of the room is occupied by a cast-iron stove and a woodpile. Old newspapers lie scattered about. On the left, a table with a kerosene lamp and a few cooking utensils. On the right, straw mattresses and felt blankets. Cold, musty air. Maltzahn trips over a saw propped against the door, setting off an avalanche of tools and utensils along the wall. Some of the logs roll off the woodpile and bump against their numbed feet. They are too exhausted to get out of the way. The noise brings Maltzahn to, and he looks around in astonishment. "Is this Chabarovsk?"

They wrap themselves in blankets and lie around the crackling stove, drinking tea. Their clothes are spread out to dry over chairs and beams. Podol picks up one of the newspapers and thumbs through it, then another. "These are all from last year. Hasn't anyone been here since then?" He stuffs paper into his wet shoes.

"Oh sure, but probably no one who reads *Pravda.*" Oleg fetches an empty sardine can for an ashtray. He takes a deep drag on the Camel that Nordanc has given him.

"Who does this cabin actually belong to?" Podol lights one of his own Bulgarian cigarettes.

"Everyone. Hunters used to stash their supplies here, and fishermen did the same in summer, until the cooperative built a blockhouse for them down by the river. Young Pioneers can use the place to rest when they're out hiking. And it's a way station for the *oderzhimye.*"

"For the 'possessed'?" Orten pictures a procession of lunatics wading through the deep snow; they used to deport political prisoners to Siberia.

"Yes, but no one stays for long. We don't take vacations around here," Oleg says solemnly.

Orten hesitates. "Are you one of the 'possessed'?"

Oleg laughs. "That's what people call us. But there used to be real madmen, the ones who came looking for gold. They usually died out in the taiga—drowned, froze to death, starved, got eaten by wolves or murdered by *varnaks.* Escaped prisoners can be more vicious than wolves, at least wolves only eat their fill. The few who did strike it rich usually went on a binge and lost it all again overnight. You don't see any real hell-on-wheels sprees like those anymore. They could shake the foundations of an *ostrog*—hell, not just of a jail, of a medium-sized town. There wasn't a man in the territory who wasn't a drunk. They'd get into brawls that ended in murder, or set fires—whole sections of towns went up in flames; there's something grand about a raging fire in the snow. Sometimes they were so delirious that they hacked off their own feet—they barely felt it in this cold. Witches filled the air."

"And what about you, what are you looking for?"

"We haven't made any big finds." Oleg offers an embarrassed smile. "Last spring we thought we were onto something, but except for a few 'indicators' there was nothing there. Now we want to move on up the Tunguska and along the Vilyuj, there's gold there."

"And if you don't find anything?"

"We always find something. There's coal everywhere here, and non-ferrous metals, too. The state can't even work all the ores that are found every day. They get registered. That's what we've done with the lodes we've found, but our objective is a gold mine of all-Soviet importance, like the Kolyma Basin."

Orten looks him over. He has seen films about young geologists who tap mineral resources for the state. One starred Tatyana Zamolyova; they all freeze to death at the end.

"Where are your friends?"

"They're waiting at the base camp, twenty miles east of here on the river, about a day's march. I was in Novosibirsk buying tools—something is always getting busted in these temperatures. And the necessary supplies—bandages, medicines, the item a woman needs most. . . . And this is for Shura." Oleg pulls his backpack over and extracts a bright green bottle of *dukhi*, shaped like a Kremlin steeple: cut-glass stopper, trimmed with tin. The florid script on the label reads: SKAZKA—Fairy Tale.

"You may well ask what's the point out here in the taiga. But a gift like this can make someone happy. A delight to the eye, and the nose as well." Oleg shakes a little onto his hair. "Here"—he tries to splash some on Orten, but he dodges just in time and also prevents Oleg from tagging the other three, who are already asleep.

"The name fits, I think." Oleg gives his present a last delighted look and carefully stashes it away.

"So you have women there, too?" Orten asks drowsily, no longer surprised by much of anything.

"We're three couples altogether. The latest pair made it official here in Tura."

"They got married?"

"It's better that way, simpler. There are problems otherwise, stirs up trouble. The women say they're being harassed, and they're always believed. Just makes things difficult. So the best thing is to go to the nearest Soviet town and make it official. Besides, it's too cold to sleep alone."

He gropes for his backpack again. "Here, this is our daughter, Vye-rotchka; she's three. She'll join us in the taiga this summer. By that time we'll all have gone in together to buy a *vezdekhod,* a snowmo-bile—'Riding to the Great Somewhere.' I always loved that fairy tale as a child: 'I shall go I know not where. I shall bring I know not what.' . . ."

As Orten falls asleep he listens to Maltzahn beside him, whistling through his half-open mouth, and to the snowstorm outside.

The next morning the door won't open. All five of them put their shoulders to it, but it moves only a handbreadth. Following Oleg's example, they urinate through the crack, then close it immediately—the wind is icy. So much snow has blown in through the roof that they can use it for tea. After a while, the shutters on the two windows opposite the door can be opened as well. The light reveals cheesy faces and a few objects they hadn't bumped into last night. Boards nailed to the wall, a couple of greasy rags hanging from them—"This was once a *kitaika,*" Oleg says as he rips the stiff blue material into strips. A can of motor oil that can't be opened because the lid has rusted shut. Two cans of *Zokra*—a brand of sardines that they know from Prague, with an expired date. *"Nichevo,"* Oleg says with some relief.

Their most important find is two bags of rice and a box of salt, all hard as stone. Oleg laughs and picks some black stuff out of one of the sacks and throws it in the fire. Maltzahn then pokes around in the sack of rice, too, and removes a few shriveled lumps of mouse dung. "What's this?"

"Fine, we'll use the other sack first." Oleg grins. He seems not to object to Maltzahn's watching his every move. "The most important thing is to get something warm in our bellies." He adds some logs to the fire, then inspects the woodpile. "It seemed like more last night, didn't it, little brothers?"

Here we go again, Orten thinks. These Russians all talk as if they had stepped out of their *byliny.* How many *puds* did Ilya Muromez's stone cudgel weigh?

"Three days at most. Then we'll have to go outside. To fetch more wood."

And when we have to take a shit? Won't we have to go outside for that? Orten can bet they were all thinking the same thing this morning.

They are unfamiliar with this herbal tea. Bittersweet, with a sour aftertaste. Oleg heaps sugar into his cup, then gets up and folds his blanket, stacks wood, throws himself to the floor and does push-ups. Nordanc, feeling a little stiff himself, does knee bends. The other three just stand there. Maltzahn, at a loss, walks over to the rice pot.

"Please, little uncle, no more until this evening."

Podol and Orten stare at one another. "It looks as if we need to prepare ourselves for a somewhat longer stay?"

Oleg shrugs. "Eight days, ten days, who knows. The *purga* has just started. Can't you hear it? It's already worse than yesterday." He flings open the window. "There she is, my roaring *purga,* may the pox take her!"

Orten closes the window again.

"Not too tight, friend, a little air is even more important than warm food. Do you know what? We shall all be brothers!" Oleg rummages in his backpack and pulls out a bottle of Stolichnaya. "Didn't expect this, did you? I'll bet you don't have any left!"

They become brothers, except for Maltzahn.

"Doesn't matter," Oleg declares. "If not a brother today, then a brother tomorrow. The days are long in the taiga!"

By the third day, Maltzahn also becomes a brother before he knows what is happening. He takes a drink from Oleg's bottle, and is given two smacking kisses on the cheeks—he retreats in confusion. Otherwise, they hardly notice him. Most of the time he lies on his bed, his head wrapped in his blanket, and whenever the storm abates briefly, they can hear him groaning softly. Oleg's home remedies make him sleepy, but don't relieve the throbbing in his head. He will allow no one but Podol or Orten to give him the tea containing the pulverized tablets. Sometimes he stares at Oleg for minutes on end before drinking it. Whenever Nordanc tries to find a station on his portable radio, Maltzahn goes into a frenzy. They have to be content with the cassette recorder, and then wait until he is asleep to tune in Radio Ust'-Ilimsk, very low.

Among the newly discovered objects are a pair of skis with no bindings and a concertina with a tattered bellows. Oleg spends the evenings trying to play it, humming along in *dumki* fashion wherever notes are missing. They try to distract him.

"Is this where the meteor landed?"

"The explosion in 1908? That was on the Podkamennaya Tunguska, two hundred miles south of here. They found debris scattered five hundred miles away, but no real crater, no indentations. The object had an irregular trajectory. No meteor falls like that."

"What was it then?"

"It's not clear. It was bright, like a 'million suns.' People saw the glow in Irkutsk, eight hundred miles away. Perhaps a comet that exploded and melted as it fell to earth. Or a satellite from some other planet." Oleg pokes the fire, musing. "We wanted to have a look ourselves, but they need us here." He stands up. "I'm going to have to leave soon. Shura and the others will be waiting for me."

"In the middle of a *purga*?"

"It's letting up, haven't you noticed? The sun will be out in three days." They stare mutely at the window.

"Once I'm gone, you should wait another day or two, until the weather has stabilized. Then you can start out. Down across the clearing there, then on through the woods, about a mile, till you reach the river. Keep to your left until you get to Tura. There's no way you can get lost really, just stick together. But the taiga is tricky, even for such short distances. You can end up going in circles. . . . Don't let anyone get separated."

They say nothing.

"I have to go in the other direction. I'll leave word at the next station that you're here."

"Isn't there somebody there who could come get us?" Podol asks. "I'm thinking of Olbram. . . ."

"Mostly they're just dead mailboxes. Sometimes there's a piece of dried meat in them. But I'll get some fresh meat from the Evenks."

"You're going to meet them then?"

"I know how to find them."

Podol hesitates. "Well then, how about us? Couldn't they maybe . . ."

"They're very shy. I can barter with them for meat, but they won't talk with me. I'll tell them that you're here and need help, but I can't force them to do anything about it. They're peaceable, but they just want to be left alone." Oleg falls silent. "Tura isn't far, you'll make it."

The next day he and Nordanc go out into the abating storm and gather brushwood for the stove and pine needles for tea. They also drag a pine into the cabin and saw it up, but refuse help from the others. When they stop for a rest, they fortify themselves with Oleg's vodka and Nordanc's cigarettes, holding the others at bay with their own efficiency. A whole week of being cooped up, and never once have they been over the threshold—except for their naked rear ends. Each of them recognizes his own frozen pile. They save the soiled pages of *Pravda* to feed the fire. (Podol doesn't make a second attempt at using the same method to dispose of his actual droppings.) They are all irascible. For Nordanc, it's the pores on Orten's nose—they're a nightmare. Oleg despises Podol for his flatulence. The two of them have another go at the saw, and Maltzhan's face wrenches with pain, which only fires them on; they have had enough of his pissing and moaning. They cap it off by hammering away at the old skis. Podol, who has been scribbling at a sketch of a witches' sabbath for two days now— "The Roaring Purga" as a throng of women, all of them his wife, her billowing hair, her naked legs, and his notion of lust in her eye—hardly looks up. Even Orten pretends he can just go on reading. Their work done, Oleg and Nordanc retreat to one corner and rummage in their backpacks. Oleg succeeds in brushing Nordanc's brow with his Fairy Tale perfume, and then, after some practice, learns how to play the Rolling Stones on the tape recorder at full volume. "Damn, you've got them, too? Will Lyosha ever be impressed!"

Soviet-Luxembourgian friendship is strengthened by an exchange of goods. Nordanc stuffs a can of meat into his backpack and pulls out two reserve batteries. "When I get home I'll send you some new ones. Do you have a permanent address?"

"University of Leningrad, Geological Institute. Nizhnyaya Tunguska 3, Oleg Ogarzev. Put a couple of extra stamps on it. I don't have any from Luxembourg. And the rest of you, too!" Oleg pours them all some of his Stolichnaya. "Write me once you're there. Either from Japan or Prague. Mail is more important than meat. Last year they dumped it in the wrong place, the pilot was new. We found the food, but the mailbag was gone. We searched the swamps for three days, we would rather have gone without the supplies. Four months' worth of mail!"

"What was in it?"

"What's in a sack like that?—letters, books, recent newspapers, packages from home with apples, hard sausage, cookies, cigarettes. Last Easter my grandmother put in an icon blessed by the metropolitan . . . but what do you know about that?" Oleg seems saddened. "My friends are waiting for me. Write us the minute you get to Chabarovsk, and send a postcard from Nachodka, too, none of us has ever been there."

Podol stares at him, then out the window, where the storm is still blowing. "I'd be glad to send you one from Tura."

Oleg swallows hard. "You'll make it. Andrei has a can of pork now, for the march. I can't give you more than that. But don't eat it before you leave. The rice will be gone in two days. So don't sit around here, otherwise you'll never get out. You get stiff, sluggish—cold and monotony do that. Keep moving, fetch wood for the next guy. Leave him some salt, too. And don't forget to put out the fire. Don't wait here for help; that would be pure dumb luck!"

The vodka has worked quickly on empty stomachs. Podol turns red. "Since you think we're such idiots anyway, why waste a can of meat on us? A postcard from Nachodka? From Japan? And we're supposed to put out the fire! You don't even trust us to get our asses in gear! You and your comrades can eat your pork yourselves!"

Oleg is slow to catch on. And the others are having some difficulty, too. But when Podol strides over to Nordanc's backpack and starts hunting for the can of meat, Orten pulls him away. "You don't have to eat it!"

Nordanc yanks the backpack out of his hand. "You can bet your ass he won't!"

In the skirmish, they bang into the stovepipe. They spend the evening airing the cabin and trying to fit the pipe back into place. Podol's fingers are numb and semiscorched by the time he gets the seal tight. "Come on, Oleg, let's make up. You really have helped us. Play us a farewell song."

With a mistrustful look, Oleg silently picks up the battered concertina, places his fingers on the keys, and presses air through the bellows—asthmatic creakings with an infiltration of whistles, which after a while are reminiscent of *"Podmoskovniye vechera."* Podol hums affably along.

"Do you know *'Put' dorozhka'*?"

Oleg grins. "The frontline song of the old men. And the dirge for fallen revolutionaries. We have so many models to emulate! It doesn't matter if we freeze to death in the taiga, get eaten alive by mosquitoes in the summer—the revolutionaries did time in prison, too! And then there's our Great Patriotic War! Marshal Konev, Budenny, Stalin! Then you learn that Stalin imprisoned thousands. Sat in the Kremlin drinking champagne and watching Westerns while the movie houses showed party propaganda films. And then later they tell you he wasn't all that bad." Oleg lowers his voice. "I think he was a gangster."

Podol stares at him. "You're allowed to know that, too? And Brezhnev?"

"What do you mean?"

"Have you ever heard of the 'intervention' in Czechoslovakia in '68?" Oleg doesn't reply.

"What did they tell you?"

"I don't know anything about politics. The newspapers said the Germans had already opened banks in Prague, and that American tanks were at the border."

"Did they also say that we called you in to help us?" Podol edges closer.

"Stop it," Orten says.

"Did you know that your comrades gunned a woman down on the street? She was opening an umbrella! A collapsible, they'd never seen one before. They thought it was a machine gun. A memorial stone was erected at the spot—'under tragic circumstances' was all they were allowed to write on it. Then even the stone disappeared. She was twenty-three. And Jan Palach . . . do you know the name?" Oleg shakes his head; his eyes are set hard, his eyelids half closed.

"Back off!" Orten pulls Podol away.

"Who is Jan Palach?" Oleg follows them.

"He was a student, about your age, who set himself on fire to protest your help! And there were others, Jan Zajíc . . ."

"I didn't know any of this! I swear. No one did! Ask Shura, Lyosha . . ." Oleg dashes to the radio, fiddles with the knobs. '*Shiroka strana moya rodnaya.*' Don't you hear—they don't tell us anything! Here"—he fumbles in his backpack and pulls out another bottle of vodka—"take it!" He goes on searching blindly, adds two onions. "We didn't have any idea! We were fifteen years old!"

"They sent soldiers that age, too," Podol replies. He simply can't let it go.

"I swear! Not one word!" Oleg throws his arm across his eyes and runs out the door.

They stand there at the open door, in the wind-driven snow. No one moves. "You picked the wrong man," Orten says angrily.

"Should I tell some old cynic like Dobrodin about it, who knows it all anyway?" Podol stuffs the bottle and onions back into Oleg's pack. "Because he is so young and doesn't have any idea, that's why!"

Nordanc grabs the flashlight and goes outside.

The next morning, Oleg is gone. The wind has let up, the sky is getting wider. They sit around drinking tea and jettisoned vodka. Podol stares at Oleg's note of farewell, then at Nordanc. "What did you two talk about later on last night?"

"He wanted to give me back my radio."

"What did you say to him?"

"That I'm from Luxembourg, that he could accept it from me."

Podol makes a face. "That's certainly some comfort!"

"After your clarification of things, nothing much could have fazed him," Orten remarks.

"Oh, yes it could." Nordanc picks up Oleg's note. "He asked me if people know about Jan Palach in Luxembourg. I told him that we'd named a town square after him. The Czechs weren't allowed to do that in their own country. He was the one who used the word 'occupation.' And he didn't even say goodbye this morning."

They fall silent.

"Do you think he'll make it back to camp?" Podol asks.

"Sure; they're expecting him. He asked if he could keep the fairy-tale drawings you did for his daughter. I told him, sure."

"Well, of course he can! What are we doing staring at this bottle? Let's drink to his making it back!" Podol unscrews the cap.

"And to our doing the same," Orten adds.

"Give me a little more," Maltzahn says, holding out his tin cup.

Podol fills it halfway. "Are you still in pain?"

"It's not pain, it's a roaring sound. Plus whistles today, high-pitched. I'm going crazy!"

"Haven't you got any tablets left?"

"I've had enough of tablets!" Maltzahn empties his cup, pours himself some more and creeps off to bed.

"How about you, Andy?" Podol nods toward the bottle.

Nordanc shakes his head. He reads Oleg's note again. "He took us in here," he says softly to himself.

Maltzahn chokes on that one. "It would have been a lot nicer of him to have told us when to get out in Tura! We wouldn't have been cooped up here the whole time, eating mouse shit!"

"Shut your mouth. You're drinking his last bottle of vodka!" Nordanc explodes.

"Well then, just run along after him!" Maltzahn lurches to the door, splashing vodka from his cup. "He was a pretty young thing! What are you doing here with us old fogies?"

Nordanc looks first at Maltzahn's dilapidated grin, then at the stuffy dark room where they've been glued to one another for days now. "I've asked myself the same question." He picks up his backpack and skis, pulls on his cap.

"Stay here," Podol says, grabbing him by the shoulder. "We'll all leave together tomorrow. Olbram is sick; he didn't mean it that way."

"If you ask me, we're all sick!" Nordanc pushes the door open, kicks aside a frozen pile of shit, and buckles on the skis. "If I run into anybody, I'll give them the word."

He follows Oleg's tracks across the clearing. They watch him go, until he disappears into the woods. "He turned off to the right," Podol says. "Weren't we supposed to keep to the left? . . . Andy!"

"Maybe he doesn't want to go to Tura," Orten suggests.

"And of course he took the can of pork with him!"—Maltzahn.

They are startled awake that night by pounding and kicking at the door.

"Who's there?" Podol gropes for the axe in the dark.

"Don't open it!" Maltzahn warns.

Orten sleepily picks up the poker and makes his way to the door, he unbolts it. In the flickering lamplight he recognizes Nordanc, who staggers forward, gasping, and collapses onto the chair. "Close the door!" He drinks the dregs of the pine-needle tea from the kettle and then falls into bed. "Put more wood on!" The next morning he cannot explain why he has come back.

"You were lost," Podol says. "You went off in the wrong direction."

"I wanted to make sure Oleg wasn't stuck in the snow somewhere. Then I must have started going in circles. But I'll make it today."

"You're not going off alone again?"

Nordanc doesn't reply, just unpacks the can of pork. "I forgot this yesterday—just something more to schlepp along. And watch out for wolves."

"Aren't you going to wait for us? We'll be leaving, too. Tomorrow at the latest."

"See you in Tura. I'm heading out on my own!" Nordanc slams the door.

"Well, he's got it bad," Maltzahn says. The can of pork has placated him.

"What are you talking about?"

"Unrequited love."

"More like 'taigamania.' " Orten drops the armful of wood he was outside collecting. "You can't find your way, you wander around in circles, nothing but trees everywhere. Did he say something about wolves? There are some tracks down by the woods."

"Holy shit!" Podol hurls the empty rice sack into the fire.

When they wake up the next morning, Nordanc is lying on the mattress.

"What's this now? When he did come in?" Podol whispers.

"During the night," Orten says in muffled tones. "He was lucky. That greasy meat last night didn't sit well with me. I was just dangling my butt over the threshold."

"He's starting to give me the willies. Actually, you were the lucky one—he came home alone. Do you know the joke about the Siberian toilet? The latest model? It consists of two sticks: you ram the shorter one in the ground in front of you, that's for your *čapka*. And you hold on to the longer one with your right hand. That's to drive the wolves off." They giggle in the twilight. "Look, the sun!"

Framed by the window, pink stripes appear along the horizon. When they open the door—cautiously, to keep it from creaking—the snow is glistening in the first rays of sunlight. "We'll move out today."

Podol is putting water on for tea when Maltzahn wakes up. Squelching all sarcasm, he looks right past Nordanc, as if he didn't even recognize him. Podol casts him an anxious glance. Maltzahn is sitting there with his mouth open and listening—they have gradually become accustomed to this semimoronic pose. But today there's a nervous smile besides, which doesn't improve matters.

"Everything okay, Olbram?"

"Psst!" Maltzahn is listening. "I hear voices."

"Where, outside?" Podol looks out the window.

"No, in my head."

Podol and Orten exchange glances.

"No, really. You guys don't believe me. I've been hearing them the whole time, but up till now it was more just a roaring sound. I didn't want to say anything in front of that Russian. Now it's ticking. Ouch! A gong!"

"Get hold of yourself!" Podol shakes him.

"Wait!" Maltzahn is listening again, staring wide-eyed. "They're giving the time."

"And what time is it?"

"Four o'clock."

Orten looks at his watch. "It's nine."

"Quiet! News is next." Maltzahn's eyes are growing wider and wider. "Disarmament talks have deadlocked, the General Secretary, Comrade . . ."

"Turn it off! Where's that coming from? Our radio is gone."

"It's in my tooth! If I press my tongue against it, it just hums. Now it's clear again. A band concert. Good God, is that ever loud!"

"It's that goddamn filling!" Podol shouts. "That's why you've been so strange all along. The replacement! Went to such a lot of trouble—damn right they did! Those assholes put a transmitter in there!"

"No, they didn't," Nordanc says. He is no longer asleep.

"What?"

"It's not a transmitter, it's a receiver."

"So what?" Podol is confused.

"Apparently they were trying an experiment and used the wrong material. Maybe it's only the porcelain cement acting as a kind of commutator. False galvanism . . ."

"What does false galvanism have to do with Olbram's tooth?" Podol snaps.

"Normally, nothing." Nordanc is miffed. "Besides, it's none of my business. I'm leaving!"

"If you think you can go get high on the taiga again and then wake us up in the middle of the night, you're sadly mistaken. We need those skis for Olbram! You're staying here. We don't need two crazies on our hands."

"André is right, it was supposed to have been a transmitter," Orten suddenly remarks. "Or do you think they just wanted to add some variety to our Siberian excursion by making sure we could listen to their radio program?"

"I haven't got around to thinking about anything yet!" Podol blusters. "One guy goes on about galvanism, the other one about disarmament talks, and has the time all mixed up. . . ."

"He's tuned to Radio Moscow," Orten says. "It's at least sixty degrees of longitude, and every fifteen degrees is one hour of time difference. In splendid weather like this, he's getting especially good reception."

Podol picks up the bottle, but there is so little in it that he sets it down again. "What you mean is that they intended to fit Olbram out with a transmitter, so that they could home in on us anytime they liked? Or that they were experimenting with some new material? If we foreigners can get ourselves this lost, dragging our idiot asses around in this crazy snow and falling into every trap—hell, we must be good for something, right?"

"You keep talking about 'us'! It's my tooth!" Maltzahn presses a fist against his cheek. "Let them lock us up and interrogate us, but first turn off the Khachaturian! His *Gayané* is driving me nuts! Saber dance!"

"We have to do something! Open your mouth!" Podol probes his cheek pockets.

"Ouch!"

"I didn't even touch you! Besides, I can't see anything. You have to open wider. Jan, haven't you got a screwdriver or a little chisel?"

"What are you going to do?" Maltzahn asks nervously.

"I'm going to try to get that filling out. Sit still."

"I don't have anything," Orten says.

"A sculptor, and no tools!" Podol picks up the can opener from the table and throws it back down. "Andy, don't you have something?"

"Here." Nordanc lays his Swiss army knife down beside the Czech can opener.

"Let's see that," Podol says, intrigued. He pulls the blades out. "Even a toothpick! But it's plastic, too soft. It shouldn't be too sharp and pointy." He tries various manicure utensils and decides for a blunt hook, even though he has no idea what it might be good for. "Jan, hold his head!" He scratches at the filling, and doesn't leave a mark on it. Maltzahn drools, digs his fingernails into Podol's arm, and emits full-throated screams.

"There's no point in that," Orten says. "You have to try to get under the filling, pry under one side, so that it pops out. Use that little knife. André, can you hold Olbram's hands?"

"I won't do this," Maltzahn says.

In the tussle that follows, Orten pulls Maltzahn's hands away from Podol, and Nordanc gets a lock on his head, so that Podol can go to work with the knife. Maltzahn involuntarily rolls his eyes, but as Nordanc comes into view above him, he wrenches himself free from the grip—and the knife slips on his gum. First blood is drawn, but there's not a scratch on the filling.

"This isn't going to work," Podol concludes. "File it down with a nail file, maybe?"

"Don't you get near me with that thing!" Maltzahn wipes the blood away. "What is this?" Spitting little slivers, he gropes with his tongue along a sharp-edged crater in the adjacent tooth.

"Let me see." Podol knows his way around Maltzahn's mouth by now.

"A cavity in the molars?" Orten bends down with interest.

"Unfortunately in the wrong one." Podol has paid his share of visits to dentists himself. "But we're in luck—just amalgam, very tiny. First one tooth during the hockey game, and now its neighbor. That doesn't say all that much for Czech fillings."

"Cut the jokes! I'm not going to let you skin me alive, that's for damn sure!" Maltzahn creeps into his corner, but is driven away again by Radio Azerbaijan coming in much too clearly. He takes a sip of tea, burns his mouth, and bolts from the cabin to cool his tongue with snow. For the first time since they arrived eight days ago, he looks at the landscape, at its menacing beauty: the dense, enveloping taiga, the snow's bluish sheen in the shade, its blinding glare in the sun. He takes four steps and sinks into a snowdrift—how are they ever going to get out of here? Another jolt of radio signals, even fiercer and louder than before, chases him back into the cabin. The stations change each time he turns his head; the native languages of autonomous Soviet republics cut through the broadcasts of Radio Moscow with unbearable clarity, they drown out Ust'-Ilimsk and merge to form an acoustic alpha inside his head.

He wants to lie down again, but they are playing another suite from *Gayané* there on his bed. He wanders through the room, his hands pressed against his ears, so tight that he can't even hear his own groans. At the window, the Red Army Chorus blasts him with a *chastushka*, a satirical song mocking a spoiled recruit who is having trouble adjusting:

> *That won't do, Vanya, this constant whining,*
> *sniveling every time you get a scratch.*
> *A soldier never thinks of just himself,*
> *a soldier must defend his native land.*
> *It's off to battle with you tomorrow ohoho,*
> *we'll make a man of you tomorrow ohoho!*

The ear-splitting scorn of the veterans pursues him through the room. His eyes are glassy and feverish; he barely misses running into the oven, bangs his head against the beams, gets his feet tangled in blankets and open suitcases, until at last he crawls under the table, tucks his head under, and crouches there quivering:

> *That won't do, Vanya. . . .*

"I can't watch this any longer!" Podol says. "That tooth has to go!"

> *. . . sniveling every time you get a scratch . . .*

"Do whatever you have to do, but make it snappy!"

The thread method would be no use. They don't have any pliers. Podol runs the poker through the flames, wraps it in a clean handkerchief, and sets it against the tooth—the axe in his other hand. At the first blow, Maltzahn's eyes bug out, he lets out a death rattle. The tooth doesn't budge.

Podol tosses both tools aside and buckles on the skis.

"Where are you going?" Nordanc asks.

"I have to get some help. There must be human beings here somewhere!"

"Give me the skis. You can't even stand up on them."

"Going for another of your excursions?"

Without replying, Nordanc takes the skis from him. He checks the sun's position. "I don't know how long this will take."

Maltzahn, his lip bloodied, finishes off the rest of the vodka and takes up his dazed wandering about the cabin again, searching for some spot where the radio waves of All-Union entertainment, the menacing guttural tones of Russian women's choruses, cannot reach him. Just behind the door, where the draft is worst, he lowers himself into the scoop of the snow shovel.

"Is it gone?" Podol brings him his blanket and tries to stuff it in the chinks.

Maltzahn holds his head to one side, turns it slowly. "It is softer, seems to be fading. . . ."

Orten goes out to collect wood. The clearing is full of tracks; he is used to the large ones by now. It's the smaller ones that interest him more; he wonders if he might be able to kill a rabbit or a snow grouse.

The afternoon passes in collective torpor. Now and then an animal scurries across the clearing—little spry shadows that grow larger and slower as dusk comes on. Crows fly low, cawing among the treetops, and a larger bird passes overhead two or three times, soundlessly.

Whenever Maltzahn has to go relieve himself, a new station provides some variety. At one point he hears the chimes for midnight, even though it is just turning dark—Radio Kamchatka with final news for the day, which is first lost in wheezes, then in whistles, then the signal breaks off. In the midst of this far-eastern fading effect, Vladivostok begins broadcasting the movement of ships in the Sea of Okhotsk: "The icebreaker *Lenin,* the battleships *Ushakov, Admiral Nakhimov* . . ." Maltzahn repeats the names in a tone of voice that sounds as if he has been waiting for them.

"Well, you're a bearer of secrets at last—you're listening in on military broadcasts," Podol says.

"*Borodin* the composer, *Mukhina* the sculptor . . ."

"Aren't there any painters?"

"No, but there's a *Taras Shevchenko.*"

"All of them battleships?"

"The *Shevchenko* is a tanker, the other two are passenger ships that ferry between Nachodka and Japan."

"At least we know their names now," Orten says.

"Now I've lost them." Maltzahn listens intently.

"Wait! Icebreaker *Krassin* . . . nice and clear. Icebreaker *Krassin* calling the *Italy!* It must be somewhere close by."

"They're a little late," Podol remarks. "That broadcast message is fifty years old. Or are they looking for Nobile's grandson now? They found the old man back then, too, in great shape. Weighed more than before the start of the expedition. Then they found the gnawed bones of his frozen crew. The whole Soviet polar fleet under sail for a cannibal! I can almost understand why he did it," he says, looking around the cabin—they've eaten the cupboard bare. "Shall we toss a coin, like Poe's castaways? I have a twenty-kopek piece . . ."

"In *A. G. Pym* they drew straws," Orten says.

"It sounds like a radio play." Maltzahn is engrossed in a new station. "From Ust'-Ilimsk, it's the strongest. Exciting. The icy wind . . . is that from outside?" He falls into a stupor, which they take to be sleep. They can't do anything for him at the moment anyway.

His dreams are troubled. He wakes up toward morning.

"Midnight!"

"You said that already," Podol grumbles, roused from a deep sleep.

"But now I can hear the Spassky Tower, and the national anthem!"

"So you've got Moscow again," Orten mutters. "Couldn't you find a position where you hear just lullabies, soft and tender, in Orok? About a hundred degrees farther east . . ."

In the gray of dawn Podol gets up. The pork took twenty-four hours longer to get to him than it did with Orten—different peristalses, about twice the time difference between Minsk and Kamchatka.

Once outside—he's glad they have stopped having to relieve their bowels at the threshold—he takes a few steps out into the clearing. The first birds are calling in the trees and shaking snow from the boughs, otherwise all is quiet. He thinks about the wolf tracks from the day before yesterday. If they were to surround him now, attracted by the odor—pork, after all, the first in a long time—they probably wouldn't wait until he had used his *Pravda*. Running through the snow with your pants down? And what if just by chance their bellies were full? What had Qvietone said about their hierarchy? He would have to prove to them that he is the alpha wolf. A little difficult with a naked ass. And kidnapping? What if they carried him off? He'd be too fat to play Mowgli. How did the joke go about the Siberian toilet? Your cap goes on the shorter stick, and you use the longer one to drive off . . .

Podol freezes. Granted those aren't yellow wolf eyes fixed on him, but they'll do. Three crouching Eskimos—Tungus, Evenks, whatever—all muffled up, squat, bow-legged, broad beardless faces. Most persuasive are the guns in their hands. His sphincter reacts immediately.

They creep closer.

He just manages to rebutton his fly and cover the traces of his business with snow—as if the most important thing was to show them how clean they were keeping the taiga. Instinctively, he tries to bury *Pravda* considerably deeper than his own pile. They are standing around him now in a semicircle, sniffing (why hadn't he just stuck to rice?). They break into grins. "You vodka?"

It's just like with Indians, he thinks. Buy up the whole Nizhnyaya Tunguska with firewater. "Sorry, no."

"But we have!" They beam and offer him some from a bottle. He doesn't recognize the brand.

The follow-up party arrives a half hour later, with sleds and reindeer. Half the village has come to have a look at them. Nordanc is sitting atop the first sled, surrounded by laughing Evenk children, and crows: "Higgy tiggy tuggy, we're riding in a buggy, we're riding in a pullman car, higgy tiggy tuggy!" He has apparently regressed to childhood, where language plays a less significant role.

"Higgy tiggy tuggy," the children repeat exuberantly. "Higgy tiggy tuggy," the men say, greeting Orten and Podol and pounding Nordanc on the back. He has become a local hero overnight. Podol and Orten, fuddled by the unusually strong vodka, can't figure out if this display of affection and trust is the result of his lonely trek through the taiga or of his artless and faulty Russian.

The reindeer spread out over the clearing and start pawing in the snow and eating moss and lichens from the trees. Orten, who has disappeared behind the cabin, finds himself surrounded by calves that press in on him to lick his steamy, salty urine. On several occasions that morning, he notices that the herdsmen have no objection to this form of symbiosis.

No doubt about it—Nordanc's alien tongue is a great success. He remembers games and rhymes that his new-found friends have no problem whatever understanding, and not just the children. Encircled by an enthusiastic audience, he takes hold of an old man's chin, the only face with a few hairs on it, and lets him tug at his own beard:

> *Je te tiens,*
> *tu me tiens*
> *par la barbichette,*
> *le premier*
> *qui rira*
> *aura une tapette.*

The slap at the end—and everyone laughs. The children make a rush for Orten and Podol's beards. "Andy, call them off!" Podol fights off three little Evenks trying to climb up him.

"Don't you know any other games?" Orten's chin is being plucked by two little girls, who apparently are afraid to risk attacking Podol's thick beard.

"A little variety never hurts!" Nordanc laughs, romping with the other kids.

"And he's supposed to be a historian with a Ph.D.!" Podol fingers the bare spots on his chin.

"You'd like more elevated entertainments? They're yours!" Nordanc calls the children over and counts off:

> *D'Alembert and La Mettrie*
> *hadn't any symmetry,*
> *everywhere they went, to whit:*
> *was a third, good Diderit!*

"Diderit! Diderit!" the kids shout, and the last one counted has to step out. Podol and Orten are enjoying a little peace now. "I'd love to know where he's getting all that," Podol says. "More than likely some more of those little scamps. These guys probably know their mushrooms."

By the end of the day "higgy tiggy" and "diderit" have become firmly embedded in the Evenk language. "Higgy tiggy" means: sled, ride, fast, Nordanc. "Diderit" means: fun, run, tease, Podol, Orten.

No one pays much notice to Maltzahn, who lies in his blanket behind the door, barely moving, eyes closed, lost in All-Soviet whistles and roars. They let him sleep. When they come to check on him, he lifts his head and declaims solemnly:

> *Though slow our pace, we travel every clime.*
> *You see, my son, that space itself is time.*

They look at each other. "Did we miss the start of the lyric-poetry contest?" Podol asks.

"He didn't write that," Nordanc quickly replies. "It's from *Parsifal.*"

"Channel Two, Riga, recorded in Bayreuth." Maltzahn lies back down.

"How long is this going to go on?" Podol asks Nordanc.

"They want to take him to see their medicine man."

"A shaman? Couldn't they just take him to a dentist in Tura? Surely that's closer. There are Evenks there, too."

"There's a difference. These here are hunters and herdsmen. They won't go into town."

"But they have to go into town at some point, to trade furs and meat."

"Once or twice a year. But they don't like to. They won't go there now. I've already asked."

"Then we'll go with them!"

When Maltzahn steps outside the cabin, he is surrounded by children—they haven't had a chance to pluck his beard yet. Nordanc holds them back. Maltzahn looks around in bewilderment: sleds, reindeer, Evenks, plus these voices in his head. The world is much too thickly settled. They pack him in furs, Nordanc takes the reins. The first sleds pull away.

Podol and Orten straighten up the cabin, fold blankets, put out the fire. They haven't any more rice, but to replace it they wrap a piece of dried reindeer meat in an issue of *Pravda* and lay it on the table. Podol packs up his drawings: the roaring *purga;* wolves in the taiga, bellies dragging in the snow; the five of them squatting, trying to keep their balance while hanging their naked asses over the threshold. Oleg is the most elegant, hovering there without holding on—he has had the most practice. Nordanc tries to imitate him. Defying the saber dance in his tooth, Maltzahn keeps both hands on the doorposts and squeezes. Orten's ridiculous attempt to use a shaky stool for a proper European shit—the attempt culminates in a brown sausage hardly any different from the others. Podol's own red buttocks, half frozen in the *purga.* He carefully folds up the collection and bolts the door. Orten is waiting in the sled packed with their luggage.

After two hours of traveling east along the Nizhnyaya Tunguska, they arrive: large yurts or *balagans,* made of two layers of leather sewn together, with an opening in the roof to let out the smoke. More children and women, a few old people who prefer a nomadic life in the taiga to the care in a municipal nursing home. The herd comes trotting home toward evening.

"To keep houses from rotting, you must tear them down and move on," explains an old woman, who greets them with a serving of raw reindeer liver. "Eat, my little sons, there is nothing healthier." She adds a bowl of fresh marrow. Her language sounds like stifled giggles, but the lad who translates for her is a serious sort. Even her wrinkled face makes her look as if she is laughing, but Orten's stomach revolts, he can't get a bite of it down, despite Nordanc's warning that she will be offended. Luckily, vodka is passed around as well—so potent that they can't even taste the liver.

"Our water of life!" Their host laughs, a fifty-year-old man in wolf pelts, with slanting eyes and a snout that matches his outfit. He is Suruy, the chief, also known as Comrade Chairman when he negotiates in Tura. They learn that up here vodka has a proof equal to about twice the latitude. What they've been drinking is about 120 proof. This particular batch comes from one of the countless bootleg stills in the taiga.

The celebration is in full swing. Suddenly, the girls performing the "crane dance" are interrupted by Oronka Tagir, a scrawny old man with a thin beard and shining eyes, who bursts in upon them swinging a bloody tooth on a thread. The tribe cheers. Podol makes a dash for the exit, followed by Orten and Nordanc—Oronka had not allowed them to be present in his tent.

"With a thread, that's no art. I could do that myself! It's probably the first time he's ever done it, to judge by how he is carrying on." Podol throws back the tent flap.

Maltzahn is lying on a chaise longue that looks like a summer version of Podol's barber chair—his face smeared with blood, but beaming. This is one of the few moments in his life when he has felt love for all humankind, even for Nordanc. He embraces them, one after the other, and executes a dance with Oronka, who has come to check on him, stumbles over the beam that was used to anesthetize him, sings a Moravian folksong ("I'll not be a soldier boy!"), listens to his tooth, which Oronka has hung around his own neck—in recompense for an almost toothless mouth.

"You have to take that with you," Podol says.

"As long as we're here, Oronka can wear it. You don't know what a relief it is to hear nothing at all!" Maltzahn runs his tongue across the bloody hole in his mouth.

"Did it hurt?"

"There's no comparison! Let's celebrate!"

Maltzahn enters Suruy's *balagan,* where the assembled Evenks greet him with wild enthusiasm.

Holidays are drawing near. The tribe is getting ready for New Year's. The kids begin decorating the pines encircling their camp; the men shoot mistletoe from the trees—they dare not pick it by hand. Later, after the solstice, it will be used as a medicine for children's ailments and gall-bladder attacks. A bundle of mistletoe and ptarmigan feathers passed over a patient's head drives away the symptoms of epilepsy—because "mistletoe never falls out of trees," Oronka explains. He lays a spray of it against Maltzahn's cheek, and the swelling goes down in two days.

"Would have done that anyway," Podol remarks.

The free-ranging herds are lured in with salt licks; the yearling calves are counted, so that they can be taken to market in Tura before the holidays. The Czechs want to come along: there is still a tiny chance they may make it to Japan by way of Chabarovsk and Nachodka before year's end.

They exchange souvenirs. Maltzahn gives Oronka his watch and is solemnly presented his own tooth in return. To show his thanks, Nordanc gives Suruy his camera and now runs around with a necklace of wolves' teeth. Maltzahn holds on to his and uses it to take the last pictures: Podol on a reindeer, steadied by two herdsmen; Orten with a group of kids beside a decorated pine tree; Nordanc playing blindman's buff; several self-portraits with laughing young girls. The rest of the photographs are of the locals: Suruy among his hunters, pipe and camera dangling from his neck—the women barely visible behind the men; the "snow-hare race," where children jump around in the snow with sacks on their feet; Oronka's mistletoe dance, his head decorated with feathers—he calls it "flying."

Much to their hosts' joy, they leave their square-edged suitcases behind, along with a few shirts and some underwear, in exchange for three supple backpacks of reindeer hide. The potlatch ends with supplies of meat and vodka provided by the Evenks, plus a beaverskin blanket for their journey by sled.

They have to tell about their families and their work. Nordanc is a general object of pity because he has not yet found a wife. Suruy suggests he have a look around for one in the village. They all laugh— the girls and Maltzahn laugh the loudest. The hardest thing to explain is why they must labor for years on end to keep an old house in repair.

While the herdsmen are rounding up the reindeer in the taiga, other villagers are busy clearing wood left behind by the *purga*—broken branches and saplings, tree trunks ripped up by the root and blocking the paths. A few tents have to be repaired as well. Children play hide-and-seek in the brushwood debris.

Orten is some distance from the others; he is bending down to pick up a fallen birch, when he sees a wolf sitting in a trough of fresh snow. At first he thinks it is a village dog, until he sees the yellow gleam in its eyes. The wolf is almost white; it lifts its muzzle to the wind and blinks at Orten. Then it jumps up, not all that quickly, and runs off, turning around to look at Orten just once, then vanishes among the

trees. Orten watches it go, stands there frozen, but more out of amazement than fear—he is almost certain it was a she-wolf.

Podol has joined a group gathering driftwood frozen fast in the river.
"At this place we caught beavers," an old man explains to him, laying
the palm of one hand beside the other to represent the tail. His grandson translates the rest—a ten-year-old who does not see that much
difference between Russian and Evenk, except that "grandfather knows
more words for snow."

"There were once sable here, too," the old man says in a low voice.
"But that was long ago. It is the Russians' fault. They began to anger
the sable. First they caught some and sent them back to Moscow alive.
There people gawked at them as if they were *animals*. They cannot
bear that. And they cannot stand people gossiping about them either.
They can hear it all the way out here if people talk about them in
Moscow. They have been hiding ever since. There are too many Rus-
sians everywhere."

"That's true," Podol says. "And what about beavers? Are there any
left here?"

"Hardly any. The water is no longer so clear as it used to be. Human
beings make great noise in the taiga and leave the bones lying everywhere, so that the dogs can gnaw on them. The beaver know very well
what has happened to them. If you do not give them a proper burial,
no beaver will show its face. You must throw the bones in the fire or,
even better, cast them back to the others in the water."

"You mean dead beavers know what becomes of their bones?"

"Why do you grin? Have you ever caught a beaver? Then be silent!
Even if there could be a cold-hearted beaver who did not care if its
bones are returned to the river—at least it would please the net that
caught the beaver."

Podol thinks of the Indian with the chopped-off arm on the façade
in Friedland, of Roger Snafu's stubborn search for his own tribe—
maybe he would feel at home here.

Two snowmobiles come around the bend in the river—*vezdekhods,*
like the one Oleg Ogarzev wanted for his group. They are still far
enough away so that the Evenks can stand there unseen among the
trees. The old man picks up his bundle of wood and calls to the children.

Podol watches, intrigued. "I would like to talk with them."

"You are our guest. You cannot go to them now."

. . .

For the past two days, Oronka has been sitting motionless in his tent on a bed of mistletoe. "What is wrong?" Podol asks.

The old man—Podol will never learn his name, because Death might be listening—throws his hands in the air. "We have not found what he has dreamed about. We must keep searching."

"And if you don't find it?"

"That will mean calamity and sickness. But we have until the full moon."

"We will have left by then."

"If we have not found it, you cannot depart. No calves may leave the herd."

Podol, Orten, Nordanc, and Maltzahn now join the others in the search for the object Oronka saw in his dream.

On the morning of the third day, Oronka leaps to his feet and begins a dance outside his tent. Maltzahn smiles—how flattering: Suruy has dragged his suitcase over and spread his pajamas out in front of Oronka. But Oronka is dancing out into the taiga, where two village hunters have appeared. And on the sled they are pulling lies a dead bear. The whole village comes running, and everyone joins in pulling the kill ahead of the hunters across the last few yards of snow. Oronka has found his dream.

The day is spent in preparing for the Great Feast of Welcoming the Bear. That evening the hide, stuffed now with branches and straw, is brought to the campfire, where the villagers have gathered to celebrate. First they congratulate Oronka on his dream. Then they begin to spit and laugh at the bear, to kick it. After they have humiliated it sufficiently, they set it up on its hind legs, decorate it with branches and ornaments and praise it for its strength and courage. The children offer it their toys, the women dance, the hunters whisper in its ear that it was the Russians, that they should be the object of its anger. They comfort and caress the bear, they make broad, menacing gestures. Then they cut off its head and lay it in the snow among the steaming pots. They invite the bear to join in their banquet. Along with pieces of roast meat, it is given apples, sweetmeats, more ornaments, and, finally, a spray of mistletoe between its teeth—for good health. It is told to inform the other bears how well it has been treated and to invite them to come, too.

"It reminds me of Russian policy in Central Europe," Podol remarks. "Except that the Czechs have to join in the cheers, and the bear doesn't have to say a thing."

"Do you think they really believe all that?" Orten wonders.

"Just watch Suruy," Podol replies with a shrug. "He does it to make the old people happy. Have you seen the books of statistics in his tent? Animal husbandry in Central Siberia, maps showing where natural resources have been found along the Nizhnyaya Tunguska, so he'll know where to drive his herd next year. A socialist farm for raising reindeer—these people aren't all that much wilder than our collective farmers from Stadice or those Young Communists out prospecting for gold. A little more imagination, maybe. Take Oronka, for example: he can use his own name, even though he is an old man, because as shaman he can alter the books that Death keeps anytime he pleases. He just has to keep his nose to the grindstone. Think of Goldansky's tunnel effect, or Dobrodin's plate tectonics—what makes them more credible or more true than the bill of goods the Evenks are selling this bear here? Well, look there—we have visitors."

Attracted by the noise and fire, a group of snowmobile Russians have emerged from the edge of the taiga to watch the Evenks' exploits. Their leader, a sturdy young fellow with a pink face and pale pink eyelashes, comes closer, grinning and waving a bottle in one hand. "Well, telling lies about us again, are you? Good thing the bears aren't that dumb. They know we leave them in peace. We do our duty around here. We'd never attack a hibernating bear. We respect life in the taiga!"

"I'm almost moved to tears, my little doves!" Suruy has had it up to here with their propaganda. "Ask the bears who disturbs them more!" He makes an obscene gesture that would also be understood in Prague. The Evenks laugh.

The Young Communist turns red, pulls out of the grip of a comrade who is trying to calm him down and, bottle still in hand, walks up to Suruy. "No Tungu is going to insult me!"

Suruy is no longer laughing. He grabs the Russian, who is a good head taller than he, and pulls his face down to within easy earshot. "We're Evenks, remember that!" Suruy pushes the Russian down into the snow—so hard that he is left with half a university badge in his hand. Outraged at having lost both part of the inscription on his chest and his cap, the young geologist now lies there next to the bear's head.

The Evenks, for whom an albino is a rarity, burst into laughter at the sight: two monsters lying at their feet in the snow!

The Komsomols, including one young woman, come running to help their comrade as if he were in great danger. The Evenks, determined to continue their festivities, pay them no attention—until one Russian suddenly spots Nordanc, and stops in his tracks. Now he sees Podol and Orten, too. And behind his back the female Komsomol has discovered Maltzahn as well.

Conflicts with indigenous nationalities can mean only trouble, but a smirking European is always a welcome provocation. Nordanc gets a fist pasted in one eye, but can still use the other to take a better look at the Russian—after such a long time, finally someone who can box. The rowdy who started it all jumps in again now, swinging his bottle. When Podol pushes him away, he turns, with arms flailing, to Maltzahn. The third Russian, who has kept out of it until now, takes on Orten. The Evenks are showing some interest again now, too, and the fight looks as if it may get out of hand, when the girl steps in: "Comrade Ragulin, pull yourself together!" She drags the albino off Podol, then separates the boxer and Nordanc. Ragulin picks up his cap, spits some blood, and staggers away, following his comrades. At the edge of the woods he turns around and shouts: "You haven't seen the last of us!"

"It's always the same old thing," Suruy says, scratching his shoulder and pouring Podol some more 120-proof. "They're always telling us what to do. They just can't lay off. Come in here drunk—they're only kids, they can't hold their liquor—and make a ruckus, disturbing the animals. Our herds get all scrambled up. That's the only reason we still haven't got all the calves counted yet! But we're leaving tomorrow, I can't wait around here until after New Year's."

The celebration is growing increasingly frenzied. The defeat of the Russians has inspired the Evenks. They leap over the fire, faster and faster, pile the wood, higher and higher. They dance with the bear's head. One of them puts on the hide, still sticky with blood, and whirls through the frightened women, searching for his she-bear, who must follow him into the row of dancers. Finally, what is left of the bear is mutilated, too: the paws are hacked off, the teeth broken out. Nordanc, Podol, and Orten are each given a tooth as a farewell gift, but Maltzahn gets two—to make up for the one he has lost. They give a man strength, they are told.

As they fall asleep, they can hear a lonely voice singing beside the campfire. It is Oronka Tagir the Venerable, who squats there, staring into the dying embers and chanting in a language long since forgotten. He is calling the Great She-Bear.

They start out around noon. Suruy leads them down the path to the river, where farther upstream they will run into herdsmen with sleds. They trudge along in his footprints—at least with backpacks the going is easier than with the suitcases they used to carry. Suddenly he stops among the trees, on the lookout for his animals. "We should be able to hear them by now. Don't you notice anything?" They look around blindly: trees in every direction, all buried under snow. Nordanc remembers his repeated attempts at escape. If Prague has little claws, the taiga has talons.

The view from the riverbank is of a wide, frozen swamp on the far side, lined by bare, leafless trees that mix with pines and firs again out along the horizon. The bank on their side falls steeply to the river at some points. There are open, barren tracts where felled trees still lie beside stumps. No reindeer in sight. "We'll see more at the next bend." Suruy moves on ahead.

Although his backpack is twice as large as their own, he travels across the snow so quickly that they have trouble keeping him in sight. A couple of times he turns around, waits. Like Dersu Utsala, Orten thinks, only more powerful. When they catch up, he is tapping on his pocket calculator, adding up profits from the calves he has already counted. "This way they can't cheat us!" he says laughing. "Damn fine gadget, isn't it? Got it from the government delegation last summer. A personal gift from the deputy chairman of the planning committee. You can do percentages on it, too." Suruy passes his calculator around: *Pioner. Zdelano v SSSR.* "In recognition for our having almost fulfilled our quota. I told him, Comrade Chairman Foma Fomich, we could breed more calves, and more splendid animals, if we had a little more peace and quiet. This constant grubbing and digging . . ."

Two earsplitting *vezdekhods* come around the bend, Ragulin is driving the one in front, and the moment he sees them he heads for the shore to cut them off. The second rattling snowmobile moves toward them now, but somewhat more slowly.

"You guys thought you could slip away, didn't you?" The albino plants himself in front of them. They suddenly find themselves surrounded by twelve Komsomols, four of them women, who give them all a hopeful once-over.

"We know who you are. Dead mailboxes. Need help! Like hell! Capitalists! Right, you?"—this last to Podol.

Suruy gives him a push. "Cut the gab! We need to be on our way."

"Ah, my Tungu again! You looking for your animals? You'll look a long time. We've moved the salt licks, haha!" Suruy slaps him so hard he loses his balance, but stays on his feet because right behind him is his boxer friend, who immediately doubles up his fists and goes for Nordanc—another round of the match begun yesterday. Ragulin is out of action for the moment, but the others move in on Orten and Podol. Suruy is able to divert two of them, but the Russians are in the majority, particularly since the women go on the attack now, too. "Don't hit them, Volodya, we just want their passports, so we can have them checked in town! Search them for their papers. No foreigners are allowed clear out here without an escort!" The stocky girl from yesterday, who looks for all the world like the shot-putter Tamara Press, grabs Maltzahn by the shoulder. She is actually the brigade leader, Galina T., who has already lost one husband in the process of opening up Siberia and is currently running her scrawny younger colleague, Volodya Kupryin, ragged. Maltzahn, it seems, offers a refreshing change of pace—he needn't be afraid, she will stand up for him and his friends, she whispers as she drags him to the snowmobile. He tears himself out of her grip, but she hangs on to his backpack. She tosses it into the sled.

Orten and Podol are doing no more than warding off the Komsomols who are trying to take their passports away, but Suruy and Nordanc are engaged in serious battle. Suruy is furious that his reindeer have been led astray. He has not yet quite shaken off Ragulin, who has attacked him from the rear again, when a second Russian, apparently Ragulin's pal, joins in. Nordanc is fighting for the sport of it; his opponent appears to be a decent fellow with no interest whatever in his passport, although he does hit a little hard.

One of his final blows loosens the blue gemstone in Nordanc's ring, the one with the engraved dedication from his fickle Czech lover. It disappears in the snow—a small recompense for next summer's diamond hunters. As he bends down for it, Nordanc takes an uppercut to the chin, but is able to counter with three quick blows to the Russian's solar plexus.

"That's enough!" Podol pulls him off. "Come on!"

Orten and Maltzahn are already waiting beside the snowmobiles. Maltzahn sees his chance (Galina has turned to her three girlfriends and is deeply involved in a loud conversation—they are apparently arguing about "the foreigners"), and he leaps into the sled and starts it. The *vezdekhod* lurches forward, pulling Orten with it; he manages to scramble on and make room for Podol and Nordanc, who likewise jump aboard just ahead of the ladies' clutches.

The women first try to hang on to the snowmobile, but then make a run for the second one.

Maltzahn makes an abrupt U-turn, the *vezdekhod* draws a loop in the ice and skids up onto the bank. "Jump on, Suruy."

"Just get out of here, you guys!" Suruy is holding back two Young Communists who are trying to run after them.

"Thanks for everything!" They are still waving as they take the curve and lose sight of him.

The second howling, clattering snowmobile suddenly appears behind them—Orten is reminded of the final scene in *Taras Bulba*. Despite a double load of passengers, the Russian vehicle appears to be picking up speed.

"Hooligans! Thieves! Foreigners!" The Komsomols are in hot pursuit.

FIFTEEN

"Have we got everything?" Podol is looking for his other glove. "Olbram, where's your backpack?"

"Under the seat." Maltzahn is concentrating on the route. The ice is rough, with lots of bumps that make the *vezdekhod* bounce wildly and that can be avoided only if he slows down and drives carefully.

"Step on it," Podol says.

The distance between them and their pursuers grows. They take a look around at the landscape—the river's banks open into broad, snow-covered marshes with swarms of squawking crows that take wing as the snowmobile approaches. The sun breaks through the overcast sky.

They stare at the taiga in silence.

"We're not heading toward Tura," Orten says after a while. They look around—their pursuers are now about three hundred yards behind them.

"They've got the way blocked," Podol says. "Should we turn around and run right into their waiting arms? Actually, we didn't want to go to Tura, but to Chabarovsk, so we're headed in the right direction." They laugh nervously.

"We don't have enough gas for two thousand miles," Orten remarks.

"That's the least of the problems in Siberia." Podol pulls his hood up and holds it tight against the wind. "Gas would be cheaper here than in Prague, that's for sure. Just think what we pay to tap a few gallons of their Ropovod Druzhba. And after '48, for uranium and coal, for machines—our Tatra Works were retooled for tractors overnight, and any engineer who refused was lined up against the wall. Clothes—we were once a major producer of shoes! Bata hired unemployed Germans—nowadays we import our shoes from Hungary, or

313

from the Jeedy Arses, nothing but plastic and German bad taste. Just watch GDR customs agents at the border sometime, the way they swagger around in their sleazy people-produced duds! Everyone enslaved, everyone hating everyone else, everyone bled dry. The only ones who impress me are the Poles, who've got the Russians dipping into their own pockets."

"Mostly it's the pockets of their brothers in the other socialist states," Maltzahn says. "The last time I was in Wroclaw, even the gallery owners were laughing at how dumb we are!"

"Those bigots should keep their traps shut!"

"And Cuba?"

"Cuba's even worse! Of late they've been exporting soldiers to Africa, while they eat our cupboards bare. How did that go? Why are there still sleds in Czechoslovakia? Because it doesn't snow in Cuba."

"That's not true," Orten says. "I haven't seen a sled for ages, at least not one made of wood. Only those pressed plastic dishes."

"From the GDR," Maltzahn adds.

"Czech sleds are exported to the Alps, for the price of the wood, with no labels, and are marketed there as Naether or Davos sleds," Nordanc says.

While they have been taking glum stock of Central Europe, the Russians have moved closer. *"My yedim, yedim, yedim, v dalyëkiye kraya . . .* We're traveling, traveling, traveling to distant lands. Good neighbors, happy friends . . ."

"I'd love to stop right here and beat the tar out of them," Podol says.

"Anytime you like, but I'm not sure just how it would turn out." Maltzahn steps on the gas.

"Where are we headed actually? Wouldn't it make more sense to stop and straighten things out, so we can get back to Tura and take a flight out of here as soon as possible?" Nordanc wonders aloud.

"They're already waiting for us in Tura!" Podol shouts above the noise of the motor. "Just picture an interrogation session that would last long enough for you to miss several flights. And then it's not even certain they'd let us go."

"But what have we done?"

"Nothing." Orten shrugs. "But how are you going to explain to them that we can't even keep our directions straight! That we have an annoying tendency always to board the wrong plane, the wrong truck, the wrong sled. Somebody else's at that! So if these Komsomols were to claim . . ."

"They better keep it to themselves!" Podol fumes. "If the local soviet were to find out that they delayed the meat deliveries to Tura before New Year's and offended their fellow citizens, the Evenks—that's sabotage and discrimination right there. They'd be lucky to get out of it with just a disciplinary hearing!"

"We could write them!" Nordanc suggests. "Throw a note back to them, a signal that we're prepared to negotiate. That would slow them down besides. They let us head for the airport, without any military escort, and we give them back their sled and don't say a word."

"We're so badly outnumbered that we'd have to keep our mouths shut in any case."—Orten.

"And what about the reindeer herds? Suruy can back us up."

"Don't depend on an indigenous 'national' getting involved in a hearing with sworn testimony. And considering the All-Soviet danger that we present as foreign spies . . ." Podol grins.

"Don't be absurd!" Maltzahn is getting nervous.

"Me? Absurd? Just keep driving straight ahead."

The Komsomols report in with verse two: "Our lives are happy, we sing a happy song . . ."

"Ditch 'em!"

"Easy for you to say! It's not all that simple." Maltzahn is having trouble steering; his "straight ahead" veers to one side, but he manages to pull it out again.

"*My za mir!* We are for peace!" the Komsomols thunder behind them and ball their fists, eager for battle. "And we shall carry this song, friends, out into the world, where it will echo in the hearts of men!"

Maltzahn's *vezdekhod* takes a leap, but then glides forward again over the smooth surface. "Our will is harder than granite!" They hear that much, but then there is only the distant rumble of pursuit.

"Couldn't we just get out and hide, leave the sled for them?" Maltzahn is trying to flex his right hand inside his glove.

"Bullshit!" Podol scoops up some snow in his gloved hand and throws a snowball in the direction of the singing Russians. "How do you plan to get out of here? There's not a soul for miles! And even if the Komsomols didn't track us down and beat the crap out of us, we still wouldn't get very far. We have to find a village, there must be one somewhere along this river."

"My fingers are absolutely stiff, and besides I have to go. Can somebody take over for me?"

"You're the one who knows how to ride a motorcycle! When we're far enough ahead, you can do what you have to do. But only number one. Where's that bottle? Does anyone have a piece of meat?" Podol tries to cut the pemmican, but to no avail. "It's a little windy for a picnic. We'll take a break later—I hope." He looks back at the second *vezdekhod*. Although their pursuers get lost from view in a curve from time to time, they don't let that deceive them. Up ahead lies the wide, frozen river, no sign of human life, no smoke on the horizon, only the slanting red rays of a sun that does not warm. All is quiet behind them, until a dark spot appears on the ice and moves in their direction. Nordanc has taken over for Maltzahn; they drive on without a word, each convinced for reasons of his own just how absurd the whole enterprise really is—the impulse to keep going is solely the result of pursuit.

The dark spot vanished a while back, they no longer hear a motor. Snow grouse nesting in the underbrush along the bank take flight, their beating wings leave ornamental fans in the snow. No footprints. They get out and try to walk on the ice. Their first steps are like those of shuffling old men, and Orten knows that if he slips he won't be able to stand up on his own. The stiffness eases a little, but only enough for them to feel the cold as pain—even the Evenks' beaver pelts are no match for the cold of their ride. They fear night. They drink Nordanc's lukewarm tea, but the flask is soon empty, and all they have left is the high-power vodka, and even that they can hardly taste. The same goes for the tough pieces of meat Podol forces on them. It hurts their facial muscles to chew.

It is getting dark. They wonder if they ought to spread branches and reeds over the sled, creep in under their pelts, and wait, but Podol urges them to go on—there has to be a cabin or a settlement somewhere along the river, and it's too early to sleep yet.

Before they can come to any agreement, the pursuing *vezdekhod* roars around the bend and speeds toward them, its headlights beaming down on them. They jump in and take off, without even considering that the Komsomols have spared them having to make a decision.

"Our will is harder than granite!" The second sled comes closer in the dusk. By the last light of day, Orten can see Galina's Gorgon head in the light of the setting sun, the eyes and mouth gaping wide—we'll soon be turned to stone in any case, my lovely falcon, just be patient. Darkness is falling rapidly, but their pursuers are so close now that they can see the glow of Ragulin's pale pink skin. "Faster, Olbram!"

Maltzahn floors it, but the Russians force him from midriver toward the bank. They can feel their pursuers breathing down their necks, can hear the women shriek as they reach out to clutch them. As they round the next curve, the Russians cut them off. Maltzahn veers onto shore at full speed, and cutting a short parabolic curve that shakes the very rivets in the runners, he shoots past the Komsomols, already hooting for victory.

See you later, accelerator, much much later—Orten watches bands of color come tumbling down from the sky, ending in the smudged purple hues of the sunset on the horizon, which he had lost sight of from the sled just now. For one fleeting moment he realizes that he is flying, that he has been flung from the sled in a high arc—now the soft depths of a snowdrift, burning snow on his cheeks, on his brow, in his mouth, in his nose, in his eyes. Night.

Stars glistening in the frosty sky, pulsating vestiges of suns that have burst in the cold of space. Caught up in night's murmurs and roars, hurtling toward the Horsehead Nebula, where Michelangelo is chiseling at the solitary shape of its dark cloud, Orten flies across the taiga, pursuing the Bohemian dream he dreamed in Friedland.

Hollow men. They approach soundlessly. Air bubbles, so light of foot, dancing in the ice under a full moon—touch them, and your fingers are tinkling icicles. Orten watches his fingers jut from his hand, brittle coral—they slowly retract and grow limp.

A figure emerges from one wall of the yurt, a woman—she reminds him of a statue of the highest level—erect, her head touches the ceiling, where Suruy and his men would have had room to stretch their arms high over their heads. Orten is lying in a tent, a double-walled, roomy *yaranga,* on a thick bed of reindeer hides beside an open fire, whose warmth he has begun to feel now in his hips, he is naked. The woman watches him, her face static, he reaches for a blanket, she comes closer, but does not help him in his search.

She gives him something to drink. It is warm reindeer milk with a bitter aftertaste, one sip and the roar returns, but without the icy cold of his flight. He closes his eyes, feels dizzy, and opens them again. While she holds his head up, he hangs on to her braid and stares at the symbols on her forehead: a white bird whose wings are her dark brows, above her right eye a labyrinth that extends down her cheek to her mouth; the thin lines are a maze of complex patterns, some of which he knows in a simpler form from the frieze of the façade.

She could be forty, or older—fifty or thirty. A jolt, and his eyes meet hers: the iris is so dark that it is indistinguishable from the pupil, until it takes on an amber glow in the reflection of the fire, like a she-wolf; her prominent cheekbones, the skin taut, a golden brown—he would use bronze.

"I am Elueneh, the Great River. Who are you?"

Orten ponders who he is. He says his name. That apparently isn't enough; he explains where Prague is. She asks him to what element he belongs; he does not understand.

"Cloud, tree?"

He is silent. "A stone," he says, recalling the Tungus' meteor. "I don't know how I got here." He looks around.

"My reindeer scratched you out of the snow. There was not much left of you." Her gaze passes down his body.

He pulls a hide up over him, but without shame. "Elea . . .?" He tries to pronounce her name.

"Elueneh. You may call me Lena, like the river."

He is still unable to say much, and yet he understands everything, although he could not say what language it is she speaks. It might be Moravian.

"What were you doing in the taiga?"

He gathers up words, names cities, the stops along their erratic journey across Russia. She makes a face, asks about Prague. Shivering with a sudden chill, he tells her about Strahov Garden, the Famine Wall in Petřín Park and about the towers on the bridges.

"So many walls. Here, take another sip." She holds the bowl to his lips.

"Why is it so bitter?"

"Those are spices, herbs to allay your fever. Soon you will do more than walk; you will fly. What can you do?"

"I am a sculptor." He explains to her what that means.

"We are that, too. But we draw more. The children stamp pictures in the snow. Do you wish to see them?" She tosses him some deerskin clothes and leads him outside the tent, where little girls are building a snowman, but not the usual sort—it is a snowwoman, with breasts and a carefully sculpted opening between her legs. Orten gazes at this ice-cold slit and realizes, much to his embarrassment, that he is getting an erection. He turns away.

"Come." Elueneh takes his hand and leads him back to his bed in the tent.

"What was in the milk?"

"Dried fly mushrooms and shredded *panty,* you must become a man." She lies beside him with naked legs, bare breasts, he wants never to get up again.

"What is *panty?*"

"The velvet from antlers of the Manchurian spotted deer, it is hard to get. *Orkhoda* is even more difficult—ginseng, you know what that is. The deer are very delicate. Not like our reindeer, though we value them highly as well." She pushes away an animal that is nudging her. "That's enough, Fyodor."

"Do your reindeer have names?"

"Certainly, they are not deaf. They know what we think of them. Some are lazy, some are hard-working. The affectionate ones are almost always lazy. But they learn." She pushes the animal outside. It turns its head to look at her, its eyes are almost *lovesick,* or so it seems to Orten. It throws him a sidelong glance, too. Can the animal be jealous?

Lena's drink makes him feel light. He rises and flies.

He flies above the settlement, gazing down on the *yarangas* from the air; the women lift their heads and smile at him, but go on tending their herds. The children are having snowball fights, building tunnels, making sculptures in the snow; the figures all remind him of Elueneh.

That night, once she has fallen asleep after quenching his unexpected eruptions of desire several times, Orten slinks outside to cool off in the snowwoman's slit. Her breasts thaw beneath his kneading hands— until his attention is distracted by several other women lying awake in their tents.

"You spare them a long trip," Elueneh explains the next morning. "Besides, it is a duty owed one's guests."

Orten's only problem is that he is essentially monogamous. To him, she is Marie and his wife in one—she reminds him most of Alina Szaposznikov, his Polish sculptress, but without her destructiveness.

When, after a week's convalescence, he rises from his bed without the help of *panty* or muscarine, they all know him. As he passes, the women ask him how he is feeling, they offer him koumiss, rabbit soup, boiled reindeer tongue, or bear fat to oil his body. From inside furry hoods, the eyes of the younger girls follow him with curiosity. He whittles dolls and little sleds of birchwood, then leaves them lying in the snow at their feet. After some hesitation, they pick the toys up, they giggle and whisper, until one of them reveals to him that real sleds are made of larchwood.

He makes sled runs and builds igloos so that they can play hide-and-seek with their tame squirrels and woolly, dun-colored dogs that never bark. A jackdaw hops along behind them.

There are no boys. The girls live in a semicircle of twenty *yarangas* around Lena's tent, with their mothers, sisters, and grandmothers— there is no other camp in the vicinity. Orten doesn't dare ask where their fathers are. He is not sure if they would even know the word. He watches them at play. The same slanted eyes, the same plump chestnut cheeks and pouting lips—little Genghis Khanettes who look like Elueneh. There seems to be no need of a father here.

One day a hunter passes, but no one pays him any attention, apart from a certain restlessness among the reindeer. Another hunter who approaches too near is chased away by the children's snowballs and shouts.

"They never stop trying," Lena says. "They startle the herd, often an animal disappears, or a child, we have to keep an eye out."
"A child?"
"Yes, they take their daughters with them."
Orten stares at her.
"Even though they cannot know if it is their child or not. They grab

the first one they happen to run across, mostly older girls, but sometimes very small ones, too."

"And what do they do with them?"

"Turn them into slaves. Make them cook, wash—work for them, just like the Russians. 'I am your father,' they jabber, 'you must obey!'—as if my daughters care about that! But usually we catch them in time. One day, two girls disappeared at once, the scoundrels had planned it together and used a snowmobile, you know what that is." She looks at him. "One child was able to escape, but we found the other with a mangled foot—so she couldn't run away from her 'father.' We kill no one, but we did make him jump. In those days I was inexperienced, but furious beyond words. He was the first. Since then my herds have grown ever larger!" Elueneh laughs wickedly.

Orten looks about him in confusion. The animals are scraping nervously at the snow. She cracks her whip in the air, the herd scatters a few yards, but the dogs circle around them. "This is only a small group, most of the animals are out in the taiga. They won't let strangers catch them. They can bite. Besides, my sisters are with them."

Orten understands none of this. "But how are they their fathers?"

"Do you see Yelena there, or Ushé? Both will give birth to girls this spring."

"Girls? Is it some sort of parthenogenesis?"

"No, but we don't want boys. It doesn't happen often, either."

"And if it does, what becomes of them?"

"We return them. There are enough simpletons who prefer sons."

"And where do the fathers come from?"

"The neighboring village. My girls go there occasionally for two days or so, and find themselves a man. Then they come home."

"Don't any of them ever want to stay?"

"Never!" Elueneh laughs. "All too often it's the other way around—the males follow them. We try to drive them off, but if they simply refuse, then they stay on, only in a different fashion." She points to her prolific herd.

"You cast a spell over them?" Since his first flight, nothing surprises Orten much.

"We make them run a race to catch their bride. And they have to leap over the fire."

"And they are burned?"

"No. There are herbs and charms that . . . change them."

"Can all of you do that?"

"It's better if I am present. There have been accidents." Elueneh chuckles. "I am for neat, standard forms."

Orten looks back at the herd. "So your reindeer are all rejected lovers? That's why they watch me so peevishly."

"Those are more likely the political types. They can smell that you're a foreigner, who is not allowed so far upcountry without permission. But most of them are of natural origin. And normally the lovers can be reasoned with—there aren't more than a dozen or so. The politicians are much more bothersome. They're lazy, good-for-nothing, no stamina, can't pull anything. They're too old for slaughter, the meat is tough. Some can still be taught, but it takes a great deal of patience." Elueneh flicks her whip across the back of a fat animal close by. "This gawker is the director of the last census committee. I warned him— Comrade, there's nothing here for you to count. He even brought bread and salt—the Slavs love the spare, official style, but they always have an eye out for vodka and a joint of bear meat—but he wouldn't loosen up. Even asked where our men were, he had heard various stories. His main concern was that there should be more pretty children like this, and he gave one of my little girls a pat. That was too much for me. He was too heavy for leaping, but a little *mukhomor* in his fermented milk got him up and moving. When he started after me, clucking and gushing about how all nationalities are equal, and how an East Yakut was just his thing, I made my leap, with him hot on my heels—he was going to get his money's worth!" She lifts the animal's head with the shaft of her whip. "Looks quite docile now, doesn't he? You should have seen him before. But he's been doing a good job of pulling sleds of late." She raps the reindeer's haunch, and sends it on its way.

"And the others? Did they see all this going on?"

"They were drunk. And even if they had seen it, they wouldn't have believed it. The story was that their comrade director had already headed back, or was still out hunting—they all love to take potshots! They were just lucky I didn't want any more fat reindeer that night. Although they kept blustering about how they were going to make the rivers flow backward, the Irtysh and the Ob. But not the Lena—so I let them go. I wouldn't put it past them. They were plastered, yes, but even drunker on technology and the things it would allow them to do

here. Before I let those louts turn our rivers around, or fell more trees
and kill more animals, I'll increase the size of my herds. Give these
apparatchiki a little time, and they can learn to work!" She laughs.
"The Russians are a miserable lot, don't you agree? They multiply
faster than reindeer, the idiots—and then sell out to the Japanese, who
have always been the enemy. My sister from Yukaghirya told me what
the coast looks like there now. They are gouging out the earth for the
Japanese, who wasted their own land long ago. They are felling whole
forests and mining great masses of coal and metals. And what do they
get for it? Machines, so they can destroy everything that much faster!
A great nation, and greater slaves! Of late they've been providing hunting tours for foreigners, for dollars. You see that fat mongrel there,
the reddish-gray draggle-tail, with the mange? He said his name was
Fischer, but he was a hunter. A professor, who spied on animals from
cages he built for himself, he slit lizards open. He was down by the
river with his binocs and saw a woman being attacked by a drunkard,
and he just laughed—told us how clumsy she'd been at defending herself, beating him on the back, like a fat doe. Instead of helping her!
Now he follows us around, a stray, whimpering cur that can't stand
to be alone. And always soused besides!"

"The question I'm asking myself right now is what you're going to
turn me into," Orten says. "Maybe just one of your fuzzy dogs to keep
you warm."

Lena looks at him. "Men are beautiful creatures, sometimes, but
they're even better as reindeer. And more useful for the most part. You
could have stayed on just as you are, you're not the worst of the lot.
I've noticed for some time now how you've been watching the sky, as
if you're waiting for the birds to return. It is too early, another six
weeks at least. Can't you wait to go back to your city of stone? To
shoulder your way through wet, warm Europe, to sweat in the crowds?
You can leave tomorrow, I'll give you two reindeer. Yegor is good at
pulling a sled, Fomich still has to learn. He's been with us since last
summer. Wanted to count heads as well, the idiot. You can't beat him
hard enough. Use this willow whip, and when you whack him under
the tail with a bone hammer, he ought to fly—but he just bucks, the
bureaucrat! Never did a lick of work in his life. Don't go easy on him."

"Foma Fomich, the deputy chairman of the planning commission?"
Orten asks.

"I think so, yes. Do you know him?"

Orten remembers Suruy, and the pocket calculator that this reindeer had given him. He pictures Lena decimating the entire Supreme Soviet, one by one.

"We have a Nikita and a Leonid, too," she says, "but that doesn't mean anything. They were just flunkies. I'll be slaughtering Leonid today for your farewell banquet."

"Let him be. I wouldn't be able to swallow a bite."

As Orten takes his seat on the sled, he turns around to look at the sculpture he has created beside the snowwoman in front of Lena's tent, her silent sister. A statue of the highest level, the only one he has ever managed—probably because it is impermanent, not a trace will be left come spring.

It occurs to him that by next autumn he may well be a father several times over. But where will they be then? He looks at Lena, standing at his side, but she is already all Elueneh again, the great female shaman.

"Our city is called Ulbus, its name is always the same, but it is always somewhere else. Do not look for us."

SIXTEEN

"Jan! I'll be damned! Where were you the whole time? We've spent weeks searching for you, we thought you were out there somewhere buried under the snow, and here you come walking in fat and sassy!" Podol hugs Orten so hard he can't get his breath. Nordanc and Maltzahn are no less enthusiastic.

"I didn't think we'd ever see you again!" Maltzahn is close to sobs.

"Who were those two guys that brought you here? Why didn't they come in?" Nordanc is looking out the window.

Orten looks around in a daze. "Where are we actually?"

"Other side of Kurya, a crawler tractor picked us up. We would have kept going, but a hunter here told us he had seen an *inorodets* in the taiga. The description could have fit you. We thought we'd better stay here. Andy was just about to go out looking for you again. And here you are on our doorstep! Sit down. What do you want to drink?"

The taste of high-power vodka jogs Orten's memory: "And what about the Komsomols?"

"What Komsomols? Oh, our *vezdekhod* friends? We soon came to terms with them. We stopped right away to search for you, but it got so damned dark so fast. We could hear a herd of reindeer, even saw their shadows, and figured Suruy would be a long time rounding up his animals, and then here came the Komsomols."

"And you had it out, huh?"

Podol looks at him in surprise. "No, they helped us search, of course. We spent three days on the shores of the Tunguska looking for you. Where were you hiding? Did our good fairies, the Evenks, dig you out of the snow?"

"Not exactly," Orten stammers. He knows that they won't believe him anyway. "Right, locals," he says.

325

"For six weeks?" Podol says doubtfully. "Couldn't you get away any sooner than that? Or at least send us some word?"

"Where to?" Orten is confused. Six weeks? It was hardly six days.

"The main thing is that you're here. How did you find us? You must have followed us the whole time!"

"The reindeer brought me."

"All on their own, under some magic spell, right? Haha! I know what you mean. When the vodka runs out, there are always mushrooms to chew, and they work faster. You see all sorts of things flying in the air, that's if you don't start flying yourself. I could swear the animals can speak and look at you with human eyes. I'm on good terms with wolves myself already."

Just keep talking, Orten thinks. "When do we leave?"

"With the next shipment. But that may be a while yet. This camp is a fishing cooperative, that's why it stinks so bad. But we won't starve. The boys will be here this evening, you'll see. For a real blowout! You're back among civilized soviets!"

Orten wonders if several fathers of Elueneh's children may not be among them. He would rather not meet them. "And our Komsomols, have they left?"

"They brought us as far as Inarigda, but they wanted to move on to the Vilyuj. They gave us Ragulin's skis as a farewell present."

"They kicked him out," Maltzahn says. "For boozing."

"Ragulin? Might as well all pack their bags in that case," Orten replies.

"Of course they all drink," Podol says. "But it all depends on what kind of drunk you are. If you're a fun drunk and sing *dumki* and dance the *kazachok,* then everything's okay. Even the whiny ones who hang all over you are tolerated. But if you're a mean drunk, you'd better stop and think who you're being mean to. As long as it's just your wife and kids you beat up, or even your in-laws, that's hooliganism, but private hooliganism. But if you're a member of a collective and offend ethnic minorities, in front of witnesses, the others can't keep silent! Moving those reindeer salt licks was the end of Ragulin's career as a geo-prospector."

"Then he can try becoming a hockey player," Orten says. "Slugging Czechs ought to help relieve his itch to beat up on other nationalities, they always start it at any rate."

"Well, at least you're here," Podol says.

"Not quite." Orten would love to call the reindeer and head back.

That night, after the fishermen have left, they lie awake under blankets and tarps drenched in fish-liver oil.

"If we're lucky, we'll be in Irkutsk within a week," Maltzahn says.

"What do you mean lucky?" Orten is not yet used to the stench of fish. "Irkutsk isn't Kyoto, and it isn't Prague, it's just one more town where we don't want to be."

"Don't exaggerate now, Jan." Podol gets up and rummages in the cupboard. "Even if you've been lying in delirium somewhere for weeks—which you won't or can't tell us about—you must at least have some sense of reality left. You can forget about Japan. It will soon be March, and your agreement with Kyoto was for New Year's. We can be happy just to make it to Irkutsk and catch the next train back to Prague."

"Like the Czech Legion, huh?" Nordanc crawls out from under his blankets and walks to the door, which is slightly ajar. "All they could think of was heading home on the Trans-Siberian the minute they captured it. You Czechs always give up too easy. Just like your Charles IV. Instead of taking care of things at home in Luxembourg, he hands it over to his half-brother, who promptly loses it to Burgundy. And then you're amazed that every bastard comes marching in with his troops!" Nordanc is still tipsy from their evening with the fishermen.

"To Burgundy?" Podol stares at his bottle. "Well, you're the historian and you ought to know. But don't be under any illusions. You're fond of Czechs precisely because they've never fought back, the assholes! Look at the Russians—generous, hospitable, warm-hearted— the Czechs ought to just slink away and hide. And their politicians? The softer the people, the harder the government. Enough to make you vomit!"

Orten thinks of Lena's solution. A world full of reindeer? The worst thing is that he's already terribly sober again.

Not for long. Even in this rancid shed, a man can fly. In addition to the large supply of dried fish, which hang from the low ceiling and get in the way (and the half-eaten remains of which are piled with the rat shit in dark, icy corners), there are other items in the brighter part

of the room: tea, sugar, tobacco, vodka, fish pâtés, and canned meats—
all of it contributed by their fishermen friends, who barter with passing
truck drivers, trading their lox for these small treasures, which they
then bring to their wards at the weekly Feast of Hospitality. Like all
Siberians, they find any change in routine exciting, even if it is only
four lost foreigners, who have no business here and whose survival
depends on the silence and helpfulness of the locals. And the locals
love nothing better. These supplies have cost Nordanc his digital
watch, Maltzahn a necklace he made for himself and all the ballpoint
pens he could come up with, Orten his electric shaver (worthless here
in any case—although their bearded faces are a source of some confusion among the Siberians, because, as they learn later, adult Buryats
pluck all body hair as a sign of dignity and consider beards decadent)—
all out of a concern not to be obligated, and besides it seems the right
thing to do. And the fishermen are happy, indeed eager, to accept,
although somewhat surprised as well.

More exciting than the great feasts, however, are the visits of Cerbin
Yesungge, a freelancer in the cooperative, who years before found his
way to Tungusiya from Kamchatka and whom the local fishermen are
willing to tolerate. Since the day he arrived, he has walked around
with his pockets full of dried *mukhomors*—an atavism deriving from
his homeland and a time when fly agaric was bartered for reindeer and
horses were held to be strange dogs that dared not be used as beasts
of burden.

There is something enigmatic about Cerbin. His relation to mushrooms is as intense as that of his ancestors, but he is much more at
home with horses, as if his friendly Koryak blood, and its memory of
volcanoes, were mixed with the genes of some race from the steppes
or the impassable thickets along the Ussuri. In the transports of a high,
he calls himself Temüjin and raves about a world empire. At other
times he is Geser Khan and battles with a black-spotted leopard—in
serial episodes, groaning and slobbering. The unsaddled rats, which
he is continually trying to mount, are his horses. These battles are
exhausting and protracted.

The result is a hard core of muscarine users—Cerbin and Podol;
whereas the psilocybin friends—Maltzahn and, after several vomiting
incidents resulting from fly agarics, Nordanc as well—are sold on their
little brown scamps, which cause a lighter euphoria and also help one
locate lost items. Orten is the golden mean, who recognizes musca-

rine's superiority but does not admit it—it isn't half as interesting without *panty*.

The fishermen gradually weary of their guests' fixed stares and antisocial lethargy, and of the stench—they now avoid the cabin. At first they still stopped by and gawked at them, smiling in embarrassment at Cerbin's struggles and Podol's arguments with the walls and other objects. But in time, these strangers strike them as bizarre. The Russians can see the point in vodka and sociability, but not in the exhausting alkaloid excesses of egotistic recluses.

But, as Podol remarks on those rare occasions when he is sober, better diarrhea and vomiting and hallucinations than the deadly boredom of waiting to get out of here.

Finally, at the end of March, they are picked up by a convoy of logging trucks heading down the Nizhnyaya Tunguska in the direction of Kirensk and Ust'-Kut. The drivers find their fishy clothes hard to take at first, but slowly they absorb the heavy odor of cheap chewing tobacco, schnapps, and resin—350 miles of *druzhba*. The drivers trade off at the wheel, their guests sleep in the rear of the cabs. There are two kinds of trucks, Czech and Japanese. At first, out of patriotism, they crawl into the Tatras, but the Toyotas are larger and more comfortable. After three days of taiga and snow, they at last see a train again in Ust'-Kut.

In Irkutsk they learn that they will have to wait another week before four seats are available on a flight to Moscow. A train, however, will be leaving in the morning; until then they should inquire at the Intourist, which handles all foreigners; the other hotels in town are only for Soviet citizens.

They walk past the old wooden houses with their carved gables and blue and green window frames, a few façades are red. "It could be a beautiful town without the modern buildings," Podol remarks.

"And with a few more taxis."—Maltzahn.

Someone has built a snowman out in front of the House of Young Pioneers. Orten regards it with curiosity, but it is the usual oaf with coal for eyes and a broom under one arm. The carrot stuck in the lower half doesn't make it any more alluring—these Young Pioneers! Orten casts a sidelong glance at Nordanc, who doesn't seem interested either.

The heavily made-up receptionist at the Intourist Hotel thumbs through their passports very carefully before pulling out the registration forms. She lays Orten's badly frayed passport to one side, as if it must be checked further. At first Nordanc absent-mindedly lays his Luxembourgian passport on the counter, but manages just in time to replace it with Svoboda's Czech version. It has been a while since they were subject to any official checks. He thinks back to Oleg and the Evenks, to the snowmobile they captured from the Komsomols, to the fishermen's capacity for vodka, to Cerbin Yesungge's pupils after each victory, and to the truck drivers on the way to Ust'-Kut. It's a country a man could live in. At least out in the taiga.

The woman has trouble establishing any similarity between him and Svoboda, but likewise between Orten and Orten, Podol and Podol. Maltzahn tries to imitate his expression in his passport photo, but all she sees is his odious beard.

"You'll be paying in dollars?" Only Westerners can be guilty of such slovenliness.

"We're from Czechoslovakia, as you have perhaps noticed by now." Podol gets himself under control. "Our currency is the koruna. Or you can have rubles if you would prefer. We should have enough for one night."

"Where is your group card?"

They learn that as foreigners they must either be a delegation or a tourist group. In either case, they would have a tour guide, a *provodnik,* whose responsibility it was to enter their names on a group card and reserve their rooms months in advance. Private persons could only be business people, scientists, engineers, or journalists in transit, who could produce the appropriate invitations or documents and pay in hard currency. Visitors from fraternal socialist countries either have a *provodnik* or a group card.

"Not us," Podol says.

"But you do have your tickets?"

Podol wonders if he should show her his expired airplane ticket. She would probably then ask what they were doing in Irkutsk if they were on their way to Chabarovsk. Why did all Intourist employees have to be spies?

"The ticket window was closed at the train station," Orten says, enunciating as if speaking to a deaf mute. "On their noon break, at ten in the morning! We're going to pick up our tickets now. We only want to leave our baggage here."

The woman glances at their backpacks, then at Orten. A speech-impeded Czech, with a beard and a penetrant odor, without a *provodnik*. The others look no better. "I'll have to see if an exception can be made." She goes to the phone.

"Don't bother." Podol gathers up the passports. "We're leaving today!"

"But the only train to Moscow has already left," Maltzahn says once they are outside.

"So what? Then we'll take the one to Baku or Astrakhan. I don't want to have anything to do with those KGB types she just called."

"You think she did?" Maltzahn turns around as if expecting a Cheka squad to come pouring out of the Intourist.

"Of course!" Podol kicks an empty Pepsi can into the bushes by the hotel driveway. "It's the same shit here, too. She can't help it; like all fellow travelers she has to report every suspicious person." He looks around in rage at the bundled-up pedestrians. Most are Asians—Buryats, Mongols—placid sorts, nothing hectic about them.

"Can I help you?" A broad-shouldered man has stopped in the middle of the sidewalk. Podol spots the fish floundering in his shopping net.

"No!" They walk back to the train station.

Posted in front of the House of Young Pioneers now is a grim-looking militia guard, who gives them a stern once-over as they pass. The carrot is now back in the snowman's face.

Changing of the guard at the war memorial by the banks of the Angara. The loudspeakers strike up a dirge, two Young Pioneers play drums and goose-step past the new guards in the direction of the eternal flame honoring the victims of fascism. Moving parallel with the honor guard, an old woman shuffles along the edge of the onlookers and waves furtively to one of the Pioneers. "Petya, your gloves!" The boy manages a skewed glance to one side, blushes, and keeps on goose-stepping, eyes fixed ahead. "It's our Petya." The woman has stopped beside a group of tourists from Uzbekistan. "He forgot his gloves."

"Pssst!"

"The little one, that's our Petya," she whispers. "They take only the best."

"Same with us," an Uzbek woman whispers back. "How long do they stand guard?"

"Fifteen minutes. At forty below." Grandma shrugs in apology. "But from April on, a full hour. Petya . . . !"

"He'll never forgive her for that," Podol says. "And neither will his father, the district deputy director of indoctrination at the municipal funeral agency."

"No jokes," Maltzahn whispers. "People are looking at us!"

"They should keep their eyes on the brave ol' lady stalking her distinguished grandson, mistress of the tactics of encirclement learned in the Great Patriotic War, when as a partisan she . . ." They drag Podol away. Orten wonders if some kind of urban fever has infected Podol after his having survived the taiga.

The next building, with a red façade, is a museum for local history. Orten suggests they should at least inform themselves about the region before leaving it. They have to deposit their backpacks at the checkroom.

As they wander the dark rooms they are followed by an old man, an administrator with nothing to do of a morning. He tries to explain the chronology of the exhibits, in Russian, then in German, but only Nordanc bothers to listen. Orten and Podol stop to look at the Decembrist Revolution, pictures from the penal colonies: the deportees, their feet bound in chains, outside their barracks; the women who followed them into exile, waiting behind the fence with a piece of bread, tobacco, a couple of onions; the guards, rifles at their sides, pose for the camera. The work gangs slaving in the salt and gold mines of the Baikal region, or laying railroads—graves along the embankment.

"That was almost humane." Podol examines the pictures. "Have you ever read Solzhenitsyn? Wives with onions—not likely! Stalin escaped from his czarist *katorga* every time, the same with Trotsky and Lenin. After that, they knew how it had to be done! Dogs, machine guns, sliding traps for grub, latrine buckets—the barracks crammed full,double the capacity; while one half work the other half sleep, change shifts every twelve hours. The guards may shoot you on the way to the mines—out of boredom! Where do you see all that here?"

Orten looks over at the old man who is standing beside one of the display cases explaining to Nordanc the history of the founding of Irkutsk. He is immersed in his documents, recognizing them even in the dark, explaining them in a stately language reminiscent of Russian fairy tales, salted with archaic bits of German, as if he had taken part in one of the expeditions of Pallas or Erman: ". . . at the crossing of the roads, the Sable Road, which bore our soft gold, and the Tea Road, bales of it from China. Pokhabov and his Cossacks chose well! Before the gates of the Baikal, with its fur-bearing animals, fishes, cedars, its seals—*lachtaki,* the only freshwater species—its ladybirds. They had to withstand storms, and wild beasts that lay in ambush in mountain ravines. Had to beat back Tartars and Mongols. Many fortresses were razed to the ground; Irkutsk resisted. Do you know *Mikhail Strogoff* by Zhil Vern? It is set here in our Irkutsk! And we have books still more beautiful!" The old man lowers his voice. "The indigenous peoples were versed in the *kamlanye,* were shamans and spies, but the *ostrog* held, became the capital of the General Government of East Siberia, a region larger than all Europe! Our *kupchiny* were headstrong fellows, had their laundry done in London. One such merchant bought the world's largest mirror at an exposition in Paris, no wagon was big enough to hold it and it had to be carried all the way here. When they arrived four years later, it was not right for his house, did not match the carpets, I believe. He broke it into a thousand pieces and cast it into the Angara. That is why she glitters so, our little mother river."

He goes on and on. Orten counts the Homeric epithets: the merry river Irkut, the incomparable Angara, stalwart Ostrog Irkutsk at the river's mouth; the brave Cossacks against the cunning Tartars, headstrong heads rolled (not those of the merchants). The Baikal region is inexhaustible: Great, Mighty, Unique, Holy Baikal. . . . "Soft gold" was a kenning for sable. But Russian apparently lacks one term: "delusions of grandeur." What are ladybirds?

Maltzahn stands looking at photographs and maps of the Trans-Siberian Railroad. The section Irkutsk-Harbin is shown as completed in 1904; nowadays you cannot reach Vladivostok directly, but are shunted around by way of Nachodka. The little red flags of the newly opened stations mark their success at cordoning-off the region.

Twentieth-century history in the next room, the Civil War battles of the Reds and the Whites. In December 1917, the governor's palace, the seat of Soviet power, is besieged by rebels for eight days, until armed miners from Cheremchovo, eighty miles away, come to the Bolsheviks' aid.

"I don't see any mention of Hašek," Podol says.

"In the winter of 1903–1904, however, Josef Dzhugashvili was in town." Nordanc points to a list of prominent prisoners, Stalin's name is listed next to that of Prince Trubetzkoi.

"Of course, a writer who published only his own work will always come off second best compared to him," Orten says.

Podol leaves the history collection and comes upon an old wooden house from the region around Zabaikalsk, with black weathered walls and tiny rhombic windows made of pieces of mica sewn together with horsehair. It is the former posthouse of Tarakanova; outside the door is a milepost that gives the distances to Petersburg and Moscow in the old script: 5963 and 5450 *versts*. Across from it, a reconstructed Buryat settlement: the cone-shaped tent is the same as the Evenks', but is covered with felt instead of leather. The woman squats by the fire; the daughter is busy making an ornate headdress; the father, musket in hand, stands beside his short, dun-colored pony, a thick tuft of mane over its brow. The flap of the tent is thrown back and inside you can see a cradle of quilted scraps of cloth hanging from the roof. The man's pipe is small and exquisite, silver with inlaid coral. "Buryat metalwork was much in demand even beyond the borders of China and Russia, their matchboxes in particular were preferred to the best European wares and very costly." The horse's harness is ornately worked in the same fashion, and the man's musket is elaborately embellished. Photographs of daily life in the display cases: the family's horses grazing inside an enclosure around the tent, their small herds visible out on the open steppe—cows, sheep, goats, camels. "The Buryats are of Mongolian origin and were once nomads who have been given permanent settlements by the Soviet government. They now attend school and have their own autonomous region in Transbaikal." The administrator has caught up with them.

"Only the very poorest were placed in permanent settlements and forced to take up farming." Podol is reading aloud from the text below one photo.

"That was before the Revolution," the Russian says.

They move on. "What is that?" Podol stumbles over a pile of pressed blocks that look like dark briquettes of peat.

"Money," the old man says, laughing. "Bricks of tea, mixed with oxblood, the daily drink of the Mongols. They were converted to squirrel skins, and those, then, into rubles as you moved farther west. But the bricks were the hard cash."

In the adjoining room is a piano from New York and a music box made in Geneva; it plays Rossini while they look around for more Buryats.

As they descend the stairs, Uzbeks throng up from the street below, happy and excited to be coming out of the cold.

"Well? Parade over?" Podol shouts. "Now they'll spread their embroidered caps out for those stuffed Buryats and prove that they're the older culture."

"Come on." Orten grabs Podol by his backpack and pulls him along. It is snowing.

At the train station they learn they cannot take a train to Moscow for the next three days, because on weekends only the more comfortable Chinese cars are used, and for those they need hard currency.

"What sort of bullshit is this? I don't believe it!" Podol turns around to the line of people waiting behind him—they shrug, somewhat impatiently.

"Complaints can be made to the stationmaster, comrade, but please do not obstruct the window." The woman is already selling a ticket to the next person in line, a sport fisherman who wants to go to Slyudyanka. Behind him are twenty skiers and others looking forward to a weekend outing.

"It's pointless." Orten stops Podol from going to look for the stationmaster.

Two militiamen patrolling the station are looking their way with considerable interest. "We shouldn't make such a racket," Maltzahn says.

"How much is it?" Nordanc pulls out his dollars and starts to count.

"Are you crazy? Not here in front of everyone! Don't forget you're traveling with a Czech passport." Maltzahn pulls him into a waiting room, where they pool their hard cash, to the amazement of families and day workers.

"Enough for two and a half tickets," Orten states. "Standa can buy a children's ticket, considering how he's behaving, and one of us stays here." The look he gives Maltzahn is unambiguous.

"What do you mean?" Podol has temporarily lost his sense of humor. "Either we all go or we all stay."

"Where?"

"Why, here, in Irkutsk."

"Then we shouldn't have visited the museum already."

"Don't be a wet blanket, Jan, there're sure to be other possibilities. Pubs, for instance. And Lake Baikal is only a few miles away."

"Forty," Nordanc says.

"That's really no great distance."

"About as far as from Friedland to Prague."

"That far?" This has set Podol thinking. "I'm hungry."

They walk back into town, they know several streets by now. "I don't see any pubs." Orten gazes fretfully at the façades. "We should have had some borscht at the train station."

"They had hot kolbasi, too." Nordanc looks back.

"Don't turn around, I think we're being followed," Maltzahn suddenly whispers.

"Where?" They all turn around—no militiamen anywhere in the vicinity.

"Come on, let's duck around this corner." Maltzahn picks up the pace, his eyes fixed straight ahead.

"Olbram, I'm hungry, too. But you're overreacting. Who do you mean?" Podol stops in his tracks.

"Come on, come on! It's the little guy behind us; he's Chinese or Mongol."

"They're all Mongols, and none of them are little."

"The old man in the blue quilted jacket," Maltzahn whispers. "He was listening to us at the station and followed us into the waiting room, right after Jan came in."

"I didn't notice him," says Orten.

"I don't know . . ." Nordanc turns around to look at the man, who is now standing in front of a grocery, staring at the cans in the window.

"Maybe he wants to do a black-market money deal," Podol says.

"A guy that old?"

"Why not? Wants to get on his kids' good side maybe. Shall I ask him?"

"Come on!"

They turn into a passageway that leads to a back courtyard. They squeeze through beds of frozen Brussels sprouts and sheets hard as boards hanging from washlines. Urged on by Maltzahn, they climb over a wooden fence and find themselves in more vegetable gardens and ash heaps, one street over.

"That's the last time I do that!" Podol scrapes his shoe on a street-lamp. An old woman watching from behind a window raises a finger in warning, then a young man joins her. They both stare at the street.

"Now we've got people gawking at us!" Podol makes a gesture that has nothing to do with *druzhba*.

"There's a *restoran*." Orten points to a sign catercorner from them— the Turnip Inn. "Standa, you could paint one of your signs here."

"Did we ever do a turnip in Friedland?" Podol pulls up short.

"I did," Maltzahn says. "And Brussels sprouts, too." He looks up and down the street before entering.

It is a smoky, loud tavern, full of truckers and workers from nearby factories who eat their lunch here. Most of them are sitting in front of glasses of vodka, waiting. A waitress named Ninotchka, who bears no resemblance to Greta Garbo, bulldozes with large, red arms through the room and sets down big steaming bowls of soup, without anyone's asking. Lubitsch hadn't the vaguest. Orten wonders where it was he saw the movie.

Along the wall above the bar, a series of panels tells the fairy tale about the grandfather and the turnip that no one can pull up. A favorite story in beginning Russian courses because of its repetitious sentence construction: the dog behind the grandmother, the grand-mother behind the grandfather, the grandfather behind the turnip, and they pull and pull. And the turnip—no go. They call the cat. The cat behind the dog, the dog behind the grandmother . . .

The young Buryat girl tending bar is wearing an embroidered *kitaika* and has glass beads in her braided hair. She glides across the floor as if dancing to folk music—or like the inventive lad in his homemade car in Akademgorodok. She sets glasses of vodka down in front of Podol and Nordanc. Maltzahn gets tomato juice, Orten gets kefir. When he tries to call her attention to the error, she laughs and vanishes into the kitchen.

The kefir tastes bitter. One of Elueneh's runaway daughters?

Whether it's real fly agaric or the memory of Lena, Orten feels light-headed, carefree. He walks to the bar and bends over the bottles; no one is watching. The dog behind the grandmother . . . The drawings are soot-covered, the place needs some whitewash. In addition to the turnip story, there is also the fairy tale about the grandfather's lost glove, in which various animals find a home, and the one about Koblishek, the glorious carp "roasted in butter, baked over the fire," who runs away from the grandmother and rolls through the great, wide world, boasting to all the animals in the village, until he comes to a forest, where the hungry wolf lies in wait for him. . . . The compulsion to count everything—and grandparents, the most important factor in Soviet family life. Orten's head is spinning. The grandmother behind the grandfather, the grandfather behind the turnip. . . . Freud would have shown that it was really the other way around. And would have interpreted Koblishek as a death wish: a depressed Berliner wandering through Russian forests, where all their fairy tales are set. Russian songs, however, lead down to the river, their *byliny,* the heroic sagas, lead out into open fields, to battle. What was in that kefir? Orten sees Freud and an infantile Churila Plenkovich wandering across the landscape—the *bogatyr'* on horseback, Freud on foot. While their fellow countryman from Příbor moves through dense forests, Churila keeps an eye out for open steppes, where he will meet Ilya Muromez and the Thieving Nightingale. Long live Russian literature and alkaloids!

"Have you found something?" Podol is standing at his side, examining the paintings behind the bottles. "Why don't you do a stencil. It's the same crap as those animated films of the Japanese. And as your punishment, I'll splash a Lenin on the wall!"

"Don't spoil our appetite. It's one of the few walls he's not hanging on."

Their soup arrives.

Podol angles roe, pieces of fish, vegetables, bay leaf, and juniper berries from the milky broth in his bowl and savors them one by one—the spices only with his eyes. "Just like my Christmas carp soup! I pick out the head meat first, too. Olbram, you've got some there, from just behind the gills." He points to some darker flesh in Maltzahn's bowl. "With roasted bread crumbs, if you like. Have you ever tried the eyes?"

Maltzahn swallows hard and shoves the dark stuff to the edge of his bowl.

"Suruy told me that reindeer eyes are a delicacy," Nordanc says. "And that the Kamchadals eat . . ."

"Stop it!" Maltzahn shoves his soup away and reaches for Podol's vodka.

"Don't you want the rest, Olbram?" Podol pulls Maltzahn's bowl over to him. "What a shame Patera isn't here."

The Buryat maiden brings the main course, fish for everyone. "Did you like the *ukha?*"

"The soup? Excellent. What kind of fish was that in it?"

"That's *omul*. The 'live gold' of Lake Baikal, as we Russians say. The only fish that has a voice. They scream when you pull them out of the water. He's wailing like an *omul* is what we always say."

"I'm not hungry," Orten remarks.

"Well, I am!" Podol takes a cautious taste. "Better than my Christmas carp. Jan, you have to try this. Or better yet, give me yours."

"It tastes like salmon," Nordanc comments.

"It is salmon," the girl says. "They spawn in the tributaries. The ones from the Selenga are especially good." She clears away the soup bowls.

"And I thought I could never eat another fish." Podol spreads herb butter over his *omul*. "Is something wrong?"

Maltzahn is staring at the table across from them, where four young Sibiriaks are wolfing down double orders and joking with the imposing Nina. In one corner a small man in a blue quilted jacket sits drinking tea.

"You don't think that's the same old man we saw on the street, do you? We shook him off."

"Stop treating me like an idiot!" Maltzahn says. "I know you're just trying to calm me down, but anyone can see that it's the same guy. Where is your painter's eye?"

"It's not all that obvious. They all wear those jackets, and distinguishing between Mongols and Chinese is . . ."

"Don't give me that bullshit! We've been here long enough. You think I'm overreacting again, don't you?"

"Okay, fine." Podol looks hard at the man. "It could be him. So what? Actually they don't look all that much alike. Do you know the one about the two Chinese? 'I can't tell them apart,' a European tells his friend. 'We're twins, sir.' "

He is still laughing as the man approaches their table. "Excuse me. You're from Czechoslovakia? I happened to overhear you in the train station. . . ." A face like thin, crumpled paper, blackened teeth.

Maltzahn looks at them in triumph.

"Would you like to learn Czech?" Podol is still laughing. It occurs to Nordanc that they have been here much too long already.

"I know a few phrases." The old man laughs, bowing. *"Dobrý den! Ahoj!"*

"Ahoj ahoj!" Podol simply beams. "Sit down. Would you like a drink?"

"I already have one." The old man holds out his tea glass. *"Na zdraví!"*

Podol is more and more charmed. *"Na zdraví.* Bonzai! I mean . . . damnit, are you a Buryat or a Mongol? What do you say in your language?"

"I am Chinese," the man replies politely. "In our family we say: May you die with dignity."

"Alright then, may you . . . no. May you live a long life!"

"A relative of mine lived to be a hundred and four."

It is not clear if this is an argument for or against the toast. The conversation seems to have died.

"Do you live in China?" Orten asks guardedly.

"A man can live to a hundred and four here as well." Since the man doesn't laugh, they don't risk it, either. Podol recalls that it was easier to communicate with the Evenks. He has no idea what this man wants from them.

"You're not eating?" Podol asks.

"I shall have some stewed fruit." The man bows. "Other than tea, rhubarb was once China's most prized export. And pornographic porcelains." He laughs.

Maltzahn wonders if he may be an agent provocateur.

"On the cheap cups there were only birds and branches. There was an extra charge for human forms. The higher the price, the more intertwined they were. The Chinese enjoyed such jests. Things today are much more uniform." The man turns more serious. "You were talking just now about those pictures there. Are you painters?"

"I'm a painter," Podol says. "And they are sculptors."

Orten and Maltzahn introduce themselves. Maltzahn still has his guard up.

"And you?"

"I'm a historian," Nordanc says.

"That's wonderful!" The Chinese is delighted. "I was a librarian. I no longer work, at least not in the library. But at home." He lowers his voice. His teeth are visible again. *"Na zdraví!"*

Orten has had enough of Podol's giggles. He has drunk the rest of his kefir and clearly senses Maltzahn's nervousness, and Nordanc's distanced caution as well. All this fuzzy camaraderie just because of a few Czech phrases is getting on his nerves. And the joke is getting stale.

"Excuse me. You mentioned something about dignity."

The old man looks at them attentively.

"How do you reconcile your personal desire for dignity with Chinese philosophy, with Confucianism for instance, which does not even concern itself with the idea?"

Podol and Nordanc stare at him in amazement. Maltzahn's uneasiness increases.

"You are mistaken. K'ung Fu-tzu ascribes dignity to all living creatures," the man replies with a weary smile. "Besides, I am an atheist. And should it interest you, a Communist until ten years ago. But at eighty a man may permit himself some peace and quiet. My name is Liu Chu Ts'sai."

"What does dignity mean to you?" Orten can't let it be, despite Podol's kicks under the table.

"To me dignity means finishing my *Secret History of the Mongols.*"

They stare at him.

"You see," he says, laughing, "the Chinese have ruled the Mongols for almost six hundred years. And that has meant the death of a whole culture and language that once influenced all of Asia. From one day to the next, the Mongols suddenly no longer had a past. Then Chinese manuscripts were found, but they were only fragmentary. I am reconstructing and comparing these old texts. By giving back to the Mongols a piece of their history, I gain my own. If that sounds all too noble to you, I can assure you that the work proceeds very slowly. I started late in life and do not know many things I should. But in that particular regard I am eastern, or Chinese, if you will. The path itself, the tao, is goal enough."

The waitress brings another round of vodka, the old man drinks his tea.

341

"But I have joined you for another reason," he says. "Until recently I worked helping to inventory the local library. And books are always being weeded out. I find it difficult to discard them in the trash. And I have no more room for them at home." He laughs again. "Perhaps these would give you some pleasure." He pulls a stack of old newspapers from his jacket and lays them in front of Podol—two issues of the Čechoslovan, from 1916 to 1917, published in Kiev; one issue of a trilingual newspaper Sturm-Roham, "World Revolution," in German, Hungarian, and Russian; some tattered pages of a soldier's magazine, . . . Put'. And finally, wrapped in a Mongolian newspaper—Ör—an octavo volume, and Podol, who has already made out the name Hašek several times, is willing to bet that he knows what his fingers can feel inside The Dawn. But it is not the first part of Švejk in Prison nor the second, but a Czech translation of Voltaire's Candide.

"This is all there is." Liu apologizes with a smile. "I quickly ran home to get them when I saw you coming into the Turnip here."

Orten picks up the book. "With notes penciled in the margins . . ."

Nordanc pages through the German articles. "These are incredibly rare!"

Maltzahn opens up the Čechoslovan. "Look at those folk costumes!"

Podol embraces the old Chinese. "Where did you get these?"

"A friend of mine lived with him. We did not know one another at the time. The little house on the Angara no longer exists. There was a German there, too, and Gašek's Russian wife. My friend Chin Zhan Chai told me she married Gašek because the Whites would have shot him otherwise. Gašek, he said, was a very friendly man. When he was sent back to Czechoslovakia, other people took over the house, and my friend was ordered to Nerchinsk. The rest of his things were lost. I found these in the library cellar after the war. I have been keeping them ever since."

"Why do you want to give them to us?" Podol carefully restacks the papers.

Liu looks at Podol. "I overheard you at the train station, how angry you were . . ."

Maltzahn gives Podol an I-told-you-so look.

"While the others just stood there and apparently found it perfectly alright that because it was a weekend you could not buy a train ticket to their capital with their own currency."

Liu pauses. "I saw Gašek once. I was sixteen. We had been fighting Zemenov near Chita, I was wounded and sent to the military hospital in Irkutsk—the *Znamenskoye* here in town. About a week later, I heard that Comrade Gašek would be speaking at a *mítink*. I knew the name. Several of us went, although I wasn't supposed to get out of bed. But they let us into the hall with the trade unionists, while other people had to crowd around outside." Liu laughs, then falls silent again.

"He looked shabby and sad, not a ramrod commissar at all. I had the impression, no, it only comes to me now—as if he had always had his doubts about the Revolution, but knew no other, better way.

"Then he started to speak—in Russian, Chinese, Mongolian, German, Czech—and we listened and applauded and laughed, and there was no officer or commissar, whether White or Red, who could ever frighten us again."

SEVENTEEN

They walk back to the train station in silence. "The biggest surprise is the *Candide,*" Orten says.

"The biggest surprise is the Chinese guy," Podol replies. "Now I'm going to stretch out on the floor in the waiting room and sleep till dawn, without a grumble."

Half an hour later, weary as they are, they are booted out of the waiting room because they do not have valid tickets. Shortly thereafter, they are discovered in the empty room reserved for mothers with children, and someone goes to fetch the militia. In the middle of the general ruckus, Podol's eye falls on the posted schedule and he lets go of the stubborn dispatcher with the Lenin pin on his lapel.

"Come on! There's a train for Ulan-Ude in seven minutes!" He buys four tickets and they run to the track, without anyone's seriously trying to stop them—except for Maltzahn, who suddenly comes to a halt. "We need to go in the other direction! What are we going to Ulan-Ude for?"

Two guys in uniform, very young and obviously freezing, appear at the entrance and start down the tracks toward the train as it pulls out. "Nothing!" Podol hauls Maltzahn on board. "I just want a good night's sleep while we're getting there."

They spend the next three nights in trains of the Soviet National Railway, and along with Ulan-Ude, are introduced to Novoselenginsk, Kyachta, and Naushki. The last stop is Ulan Bator, a crowded jumble of hundreds of yurts, interspersed with concrete apartment blocks draped with uplift banners and touched-up portraits of politicians. There is a large Stalin monument in the center of town. Outside the tents are a horse or a motorcycle, a few Czech Jawas, latrines behind plank fences. The local museum has a rare collection of dinosaurs, including a nondescript slab of limestone on which are the skeletons of a plant eater and a meat eater, locked in a struggle to the death some seventy-five million years ago. The city has no trees, but the sky is a dark blue, and the velvet-brown mountains on the horizon hint at the size of the land beyond and the barren beauty of its steppes.

No monument to the half-orphan Temüjin, who united the Manghol peoples and founded an empire stretching from northern China to the Volga—instead of Genghis Khan, Sühbaatar.

That evening they leave the city. The train moves very slowly past the expanse of tents that forms the suburbs, as if it were going to stop again, this time at the real capital—"with a palace of black sable and ten thousand white camels." By the light of the setting sun, they see women in buttoned-up *deels,* carrying buckets and canisters, and standing in line beside water wagons. Little children press tightly to them and watch the train with serious, suspicious faces. Orten waves, and a few small faces brighten.

They come around a curve and the Stalin monument emerges in the distance one last time. "They could have put one up for Ungern-Sternberg, too," Nordanc says.

"For who?"

"Don't you remember? Liu was talking about how he was wounded at Chita in the battle against Zemenov. The whole time I kept wondering where I'd heard that name. Ataman Zemenov was an ally of Kolchak's. After the Whites were defeated, one of his followers, a Baltic baron, retreated to Mongolia. He had the notion of founding a new Mongolian empire. He gathered Mongols around him and drove the Chinese out. Then he married a Chinese princess from some exhausted royal line and declared himself heir to the Chinese throne and a Living Buddha. His reign was so cruel that his Mongolian troops mutinied, chained him up, and left him behind in the desert, where he was captured by the Red Army and later executed. It is thanks to the Mad Baron that Mongolia is independent of China today." Nordanc lights one of his Mongolian Papirossis and coughs away as he continues. "There were other private initiatives during the revolution, too. In Ulan-Ude a poet named Sorokin proclaimed himself king and minted his own money. It was worthless no doubt, but he was so revered by the peasants that they accepted it and gave him whatever he needed.

Maybe what pleased them most was the way he ran around wearing Manchu robes and a W-shaped beard that he sometimes dyed orange. He wrote a fervent antimilitaristic novel and sent handwritten copies to kings and heads of government. Only the king of Siam had the courtesy to reply. He thanked Sorokin for the gift, but apologized for not knowing enough Russian to read the book. The same night that Kolchak marched into Omsk, Sorokin had his own posters pasted over those of the Whites, proclaiming he would make his ceremonial entry into the city the next day. At twelve on the dot, he appeared in a brocade robe, riding an aged camel, the saddlebags stuffed with his own manuscripts, which he sold to the cheering throngs—but only to one side of the street."

"That's the solution," Podol says, waking from his Ulan Bator torpor. "That's how you sell art to the common man! Jan, I'll take my pictures and you get your plaster sculptures, and Olbram his bimetallic and cement objects, just the smaller items of course, and we'll ride through Žižkov and Podolí and sell them to the cheering population."

"Where will you get the camel?" Orten asks.

"We'll use giraffes from the animal park near Pardubice. I like this Sorokin of yours!"

"That's not all," Nordanc says. "They say there's a monument in Moscow that reads: 'For Anton Sorokin, the great national poet of Siberia.' I would love to see it."

"If we ever get there," Maltzahn says.

The steppes roll by outside the window—pale frozen grass bent beneath the wind, scraps of snow in the hollows. Here and there out on the plains are large quadratic blocks of yellow stone tinged with pink, once part of a vast massif, erratics from Mongolian prehistory, witnesses to an erosion that has continued uninterrupted since the Silurian period. Orten gazes at the dusky landscape and the strange forms silhouetted against the horizon. In the Mongolian night he rediscovers the old, almost forgotten itch to handle stone.

When they arrive in Ulan-Ude the next morning, their nocturnal railroad roamings are over, but neither will they be able to leave the train by day now. It is Monday, and their Russian money is valid in its own country again—for the trip to Moscow. They don't have that much of it left, however, just enough for the "open" second class, where passengers crowd the cars for shorter trips and the crew changes frequently. But no one seems to have less than a three-day trip in mind, given the provisions of vodka and piroshki. They are treated to large quantities of Russian and Buryat delicacies in exchange for chitchat about Prague and their work. Since foreigners normally don't travel in this class, there are many questions. But it is cheap, and they owe these savings to Maltzahn's deceptively Russian looks and accent—at least they deceived the woman at the ticket window in Ulan-Ude.

A folklorist from Perm is interested in the older motifs of the Friedland sgraffiti, and when Podol sketches a few birds and ornaments, she discovers to her delight a similarity between them and the patterns of left-handed carpets woven by the Oghuz Turks, her current research project. This is celebrated with Georgian brandy.

For some time they have been following a river, notable for sand flats coated with glassy green ice and flocks of magpies in the frozen silt of its banks—the Selenga, Lake Baikal's largest feeder, a friendly Buryat informs them.

"That's where the *omuli* come from," Podol recalls, winning over two more passengers sitting in the aisle. The compartment has no doors, passengers come and go, stand and talk, the whole car is one big family. While glasses of kvass, *chai,* and pickles are being passed around, one Russian opens the window and leans out:

> *Venerable Baikal, thou glorious sea,*
> *A barrel with sails is my beautiful vessel.*
> *O winds of the Barguzin show me your grace,*
> *Help me to flee from the terrors of prison. . . .*

The whole compartment sings along. Several kinds of home brew help to wash down the pickles and salute the great lake. Podol elbows his way to the window and catches a glimpse of Lake Baikal: beyond the shore and its barrier of jagged ice floes and wintry debris, a glittering mirrorlike surface stretches to the horizon; in the foreground, snowdrifts and islands of rusty reeds; deserted bird nests in the sedge.

The view on the other side of the tracks is blocked by cliffs. The locals are delighted to have found someone with no real conception of

Lake Baikal. They start right in with all the record-breaking data: the oldest large lake on earth, and the deepest, the only one in which seals live. And the hundreds of species of fish and crustaceans, including the translucent oilfish, the *golomyanka,* which lives at great depths but bursts and melts at the surface. *"Comephorus baikalensis vivipara,"* says a limnologist from Listvyanka, then adds, pointlessly, "endemic." But he soon gets off, and the others can continue to talk about the mirages on *her* surface, the dangerous storms that rage down from the gorges of her tributaries, the most treacherous of which is the hurri-canelike *zarma,* about her islands and currents, about victims of drowning whose bodies are never found because the mineral content is so low that the bones quickly dissolve. The old people can remember the Barguzin sable and the sturgeon, waterspouts that dumped thou-sands of *omuli* onto the shore. They tell of the rumblings of the Angry Spirit and of how at one time the lake sang.

Ladybirds, *baba ptitsa,* are pelicans.

The Angara has its own story: according to Buryat legend she was the beautiful daughter of the old widower Baikal, who was in love with her and held her prisoner behind impenetrable mountains, until one day she learned from the birds that far to the north lived a beau-tiful giant, the Yenisey. One stormy night, breaking through the walls of rock, she fled in search of him. Her father hurled a huge boulder after her, but he could not stop her. And that is how old miser Baikal, who has 336 tributaries, finally got an outlet.

They hear this story, with further embellishments from other pas-sengers, for the next six hundred miles, as far as Krasnoyarsk.

Once they are beyond the basin of the Yenisey, tales of the Ob begin. A wag boards the train in Achinsk. Unlike the other passengers, he wants to shock them. Instead of stories about the heroic miners in Kuzbas, they hear about noses dropping off from frostbite and bedbugs that no cold can drive out.

"That was in the old days," an outraged grandmother says.

The man scratches himself, however, much to the displeasure of the whole compartment, and laughs. "But that is the view you would like to have of us, is it not?"

"Not really," says Podol, who has been disturbed in his reading. The community that has formed in the compartment, to which they now belong as well, closes ranks. The man spends the rest of his trip out in the corridor.

Just beyond Bolotnoye, the toilet paper runs out for good.

"What do we do now?" Podol asks.

Three newspapers are stuck under his nose: *Pravda, Izvestiya,* and *Red Star*—the majority swear by the army's paper. "The best thing is reindeer moss," a Yakut named Sergey says, guffawing. But, unlike their reaction to the bedbug gag, the others laugh along. The jokes now begin.

"Why did one eighteen-year-old girl marry an eighty-year-old American and the other one marry an eighty-year-old Russian?" Podol asks, aware that his jokes about rabbits and bears are probably not appropriate here.

"The American because of his money," the passengers guess.

"Right. A millionaire. And the Russian?"

A long pause.

"He can still remember Lenin!"

Collective laughter shakes the whole compartment—except for Orten and Maltzahn. They have all heard it.

"Marusya is swimming in the brook, naked," Sergey begins.

"I know that one," says his friend Kolya, a soldier.

"I don't."—Podol, Nordanc.

"Suddenly Volodya, who is hiding in the willows, leaps out at her."

"In the willows?" Kolya asks, mistrustful now.

"Yes, in the willows," Sergey replies. "Marusya flees."

"Naked."—Podol.

"Sure," Sergey says. "Volodya catches up with her, grabs her . . ."

"Comrade passengers," shouts the conductress, who has been in charge of the car for two days now, "please get your luggage ready if you are leaving the train in Novosibirsk."

"Always ready!" Kolya salutes and runs to his compartment. Sergey likewise recalls that he was sitting somewhere else and goes to look for his baggage.

"What about the joke?" Podol shouts.

The rest of the way to Novosibirsk, they invent various punch lines, and reject them all. "There's not much you can do with just the beginning," Nordanc remarks.

. . .

During the twenty-minute stopover, while they buy warm piroshki and grog on the platform (the quality and size of the servings of borscht on the train fluctuates with the state of the strained relations between the young conductress and the head cook), they look nervously around the station, as if at any minute someone from Akademgorodok— Dobrodin, Login, Goldansky—may pop out to deliver a lecture on the latest theoretical discoveries of the last six months. Given the current thaw, they would not be able to rescue themselves with a game of hockey. And if Qvietone were to show up, they wouldn't get out of here for at least another three months. They breathe a sigh of relief as the train pulls out—although Nordanc feels a certain wistful longing for Plotkin and the young mathematicians, and he would love to know if Roger Snafu ever got back his complete set of Pogo comic books.

He wanders through the train that night, peering into compartments: sleeping families, open doors barricaded with baggage and chicken cages, mothers eyeing the prowling stranger suspiciously, children fast asleep even in the most contorted positions, babies strapped into the baggage nets, soft, whimpering bundles. As he walks back, he notices two of them being nursed.

Next to the toilet at the far end of the car, an old woman is sitting in the aisle and scaling a large fish. "That's not an *omul*," he says, trying not to startle her.

She looks up. "What a numbskull! Trying to tease an old lady," she hisses through the stumps of her teeth. "Anyone can see that!"

"Beg your pardon."

She gives him a quick once-over. "Sit down. You're a good boy, but a numbskull. This is a *chir,* the king of all Arctic fish."

"Arctic fish?" Nordanc folds a seat down.

"My grandson sent it to me as a present from Chukotka."

"From Chukotka?" Nordanc doesn't find himself all that intelligent, either.

She laughs. "He is a soldier, stationed on assignment there." The military jargon makes her grow serious again. "They can weigh up to fifty pounds. This one here is only fifteen. Do you want to try it?" She cuts a piece off the side she has already scaled.

"No, thanks." Nordanc stands up.

"What did I say. Numbskull!" She laughs again. "Come tomorrow when the *ukha* is ready. Then you can have a piece of it cooked, too!"

On the other side of Tatarsk, there is less snow. "Do you notice how mild it's getting?" Podol holds out his hand against the wind. "Plaster would even set."

The nights are still below freezing. At the small stations where the train makes brief stops, bundled-up babushkas sell hot drinks, kolbasi, roasted apples. They stomp their feet to keep warm. But if someone asks, they reply that spring is in the air, and some of them even sing.

They've started to feel the long trip in their joints. Podol reads standing up, leaning against the window in the corridor. At the smaller stations, Nordanc runs to one end of the train and back, the way he's seen Russians do—most of them in sweatsuits, some in pajamas, which they use as a kind of training outfit over their shirts and long underwear. Orten and Maltzahn run with him sometimes. Podol less often—he is deep in his book now.

Maltzahn spends a lot of time flirting at the other end of their car, where he has struck up an acquaintance with two art students from Semipalatinsk. Sometimes they can hear the laughter all the way to their compartment. Maltzahn is a favorite with the other passengers. It's those charming little mistakes he makes in Russian, intentionally inserted to elicit peals of laughter and well-meaning corrections—and to encourage the view that Czechs are a manageable lot.

Nordanc is interested in four sailors on leave, whom he often sees in the corridor. But when he follows them, checking out their narrow hips—the waist should never be larger than the head—he has a sheepish look about him, which does not pass unnoticed, given the casual atmosphere in the car. The four cadets are curious, but cautious as well. It takes five hundred miles for him to learn that they are from Vladivostok, which was no secret to anyone else in the compartment. But slowly they thaw out. They ask him slightly patronizing questions about the Czech navy. He tries to explain a little about shipping on the Elbe and Oder, and when they grin, he comes up with twelve seagoing vessels—though there are certainly more than that, he assures them.

"Battleships?" they ask.

"No, I think they're merchant marine." He decides to ask the Czechs, although as usual they won't know anything about it.

"It doesn't matter," the blue-eyed navigator assures him—the one whose arrogance and military starch make him especially attractive. "We'll defend you."

"That's what I'm afraid of," he says, suddenly a Luxembourger, and for the first time his attention is diverted from those narrow hips. They let it pass as the typical awkwardness of a foreigner.

The taiga receded two days ago, giving way to steppes. There are still sporadic patches of snow, and slush everywhere. They can no longer tell one station from the next. For miles along some stretches, the landscape is hidden behind rows of poplars. Birds are returning north above the treetops. Orten recalls Dostoyevsky's *House of the Dead* and the wounded eagle that the prisoners return to the steppes after three months of torment in the prison yard. "Look at him! He is not even looking back! That is freedom, he has smelled freedom. . . ."

He keeps an eye out for some trace of Dostoyevsky, who spent four years at hard labor here, but only Lenin adorns the façade of the train station in Omsk—it is best to let "Russia's stricken conscience" rest, or at least not make itself all too obvious.

Ishim, Tyumen, Kamyshlov—*Bystro lechu ya po rel'sam chugunnym, Dumayu dumu svoyu* . . . "And gliding along on endless tracks, I give myself over to my thoughts."

Orten looks out into the night. This embankment has been heaped up atop the bones of thousands of men who died in accidents or froze to death; the abolition of serfdom came just in time to build the railroads; there were not enough men in the prisons for the job, not at that rate of attrition. He thinks of the end of a poem by Nekrasov that unites the rhythms of railroad ties and language: The *muzhiki* have finished work on the embankment, and payday has come. But they are all in debt to the management—too often sick, too many baths. The owner cancels the debts and even pays for a barrel of beer. With a cry of "Hurrah!" they unharness their horses and pull the huckster down the tracks.

Slavic prisoners of war, who were inspired by the idea of Pan-Slavism and deserted to the Russians, were considered "very dependable material" by czarist officers and were set to work building the most dangerous and terrifying stretches of railroad. The 28th Infantry Regiment of Prague built the Murmansk line without winter clothes, and with their bare hands. "The Russians are unmerciful, systematic realists. They use ideas solely for catching men, the way flypaper is used to catch flies. We were no more than slaves for them. . . ." Orten folds up the old *Čechoslovan*. Stalin followed the same principle in employing European Communists, who were not prominent enough to be handed over to the fascists, to build his dams and railroads.

> *Great is the burden our people have borne,*
> *And not just this railway here!*
> *To despair of the future—that is pure scorn,*
> *A sin against yesteryear!*

"COMMUNISM—THE GLORIOUS FUTURE OF MANKIND!"—lit by a weak spotlight, the banner is draped across a small station west of Beloyarsky and flutters in the wind. The radioactive landscape of Kyshtym is not far. "Stanislav, have we got anything left to drink?"

Podol is reading, a grim smile on his face, and refuses to be diverted. "Baron Thundertentronkh was one of the greatest landowners in Westphalia, his castle even had a door and windows."

Some of the notes penciled in the margin are illegible: . . . *Argument with Braun, because I said that I'd even drink German beer out here. . . . Chin smokes too much . . . write Franta Sauer, write Kuděj . . . Šura is nagging again for a new jacket, . . . wanted to iron, but I said we need the coal for heat . . . her mother . . . thinking of Jarmila, wonder what Říša is doing . . . better to just hole up somewhere!*

"*U popa byla sobaka, i on yeyo lyubil* . . . The pope had a dog, and he loved it. The dog stole a piece of meat, the pope had him destroyed"—it's coming from the sailors' compartment, they are bawling the chorus a fourth time now. Nordanc's hoarse voice gets hung up each time at the stupid word *unichtozhil.* Laughter. ". . . and the gravestone read: The pope had a dog . . ." Shaggy-dog songs are the hard drugs of all group trips.

Sverdlovsk.

O che sciagura d'essere senza coglioni! . . .

". . . Now tell me, my dear Pangloss, when they hanged you, when they quartered you, beat you to a pulp, when you had to row in the galleys, did you still believe that this was the best of all possible worlds?—I am of the same opinion as ever, for after all I am a philosopher . . . and besides, the most beautiful thing in the world is its preestablished harmony . . . !"—*cut this! Philosophy in literature has always been crap!*

Candide here in Irkutsk? in the middle of the Russian Civil War?
Went fishing in Devil's Lake this afternoon . . .

On the back cover: "Political Commissar Jaroslav Hašek's recipe for sailor's grog, the effect of which will allow any man to cross the English Channel:

"Boil one pint of water with 2–3 allspice berries, 6–8 peppercorns, and 10 cloves, plus 1 stick of cinnamon and the juice and rind of a lemon. Add 1 pound of sugar. After it comes to a boil, add 1¹/₂ quarts of white wine and strain. Add 1 quart of brandy, and bring to a boil again. Be careful not to let it boil over! Bring it to the table (be sure it's nearby), remove the lid, and ignite the fumes, re-cover immediately. This concludes the solemn act of preparation. And if anybody tells you to add vanilla, punch him in the nose!"

Podol rises in Hašek's honor and stretches after sitting so long.

"What's up?" Orten, wrapped in his coat, gazes sleepily at him.

Dawn. The Obelisk of Pervouralsk, the border between Asia and Europe, rises against the slowly brightening sky of a rainy morning.

"Look," Podol says, "we're almost home."

Part Three

NEVER-ENDING

EIGHTEEN

"GREATER FRIEDLAND HAILS MAY DAY!"

"They've put on some weight while we were gone," Podol says.

"Half of Moravia has been annexed." Orten looks around. The square in front of the bus station is decorated with uplift banners, the street is lined with posters proclaiming the pledges of various enterprises, march music and slogans chanted by parade monitors can be heard coming from the center of town. Bedraggled scraps of cloth flutter from streetlamps in imitation of Czech and Russian flags.

My mother always washed and ironed our big flag so that my father could make a fool of himself and scramble onto our weather-beaten roof to display it. He would tie it down at the attic windows with twine and let it fall over the front of the house—leaving us with a temporarily darkened and sullen household. Although she agreed with the neighbors, she simply could not bring herself to let him hang a dusty, wrinkled flag.

"I'm wondering if coming back today of all days was the smart thing to do." There is an edge to Maltzahn's voice.

"We're behind schedule!" Podol grins and points to the picture of a steelworker in the drugstore window across the street—"WE WILL FULFILL OUR QUOTA!" "You see? You can't bank the fire. Critical segments of the economy must work round the clock, without regard to any silly holidays."

"You mean we've been called up for emergency service—the façade is in danger and has been surrounded by the enemy. Zeroing in on the target. Roger, over?"

"On target?" Podol stops in front of the travel agent—a papier-mâché Friedland Castle atop a pedestal. The town's hallmark has been decked

357

out with the trappings of May: a large 1; a 5, the Prague Uprising, four days before the end of the war; and a 9, the country is liberated (after Berlin had already fallen)—all spread in gilt splendor across the sgraffiti. Upon closer examination, the motifs in the coffers prove to be stenciled hammers, sickles, sheaves, and military emblems.

"I had an uneasy feeling all the way home!" Podol rips off one of the golden laurel leaves and takes a pull on his Stolichnaya—he still isn't used to this low-proof stuff. "Who's responsible for this mess? Even restorers should have some legal protections. People can't go around making copies of anything they like. In Florence they're even selling pictures of David's cock, I've seen them, or of just his pubic hair, or thighs, or stomach, his navel, one eye . . . grave robbers, that's what they are!"

"You're just jealous because they haven't used your fauns and fat-assed Leda for postcards." Maltzahn pulls out *his* bottle. Siberia has left its mark on them all. "It could have been Svoboda, trying to better his cadre image."

"Don't slam him all the time, Olbram," Podol says. "You can't stand him because his 'polychromes' and your 'bimetallics' are so damn much alike. Don't interrupt me! This could be the work of anybody, some window decorator or whatever—got his wall-postering job done and they let him have a go at art."

"He had no artistic ambitions whatever." Orten examines the papier-mâché model. "And didn't know much about the basics, either."

"Besides, Svoboda doesn't do representational work anymore," Nordanc adds—they stare blankly at him. "I'm amazed that a bus was even running today." He wants to change the topic. The noise from town is growing louder.

"The driver wanted to get out of having to be in the parade," Podol says. "The cadre leader checks off the roll every morning out in front of the depot—lines them all up, gives them the exact time, and tells them when they're supposed to be back at Wenceslaus Square—and away they all trot to spend the next six hours in a traffic jam. You can cover the same distance in an hour on foot as you can using public transportation. And the whole time he's brooding about the pledges he's made: 'Our department no longer drinks!' "

"I tried to get hold of Patera yesterday." Orten lights a cigarette. "His wife said he's been in Friedland for two weeks now."

"That surprised me, too," Maltzahn says.

"What is Václav doing here by himself? He can't do any real work." Podol gives the castle model another glance. "He should have left us some word."

"Where? In Naushki?" Maltzahn asks. "Or in Ulan Bator? I felt like an idiot when I got home, as if I'm supposed to know what it's like in Kyoto."

"Same thing happened to me. My daughter was expecting a Godzilla sweatshirt. They simply wouldn't believe that we got waylaid in Russia for six months." Podol laughs.

"My sons have decided that I've finally become senile," Orten says. "The only part that amazed them was that they ever let me out of Siberia. Were glad to see me leave again, too."

"Three days in Prague weren't enough!" Maltzahn says again. "So much stuff is piled up at home that I'll have to spend my weekends taking care of it."

"Things have piled up for all of us!" Podol is getting impatient.

"I had some mail, too," Nordanc says. "From Canada, a New Year's card." Orten stares at him. "But it didn't bother me. When I first read it, I thought it said Oleg instead of Zdeněk."

"Ogarzev?" Podol asks. "We ought to send him a postcard."

"I already sent him one from Prague," Nordanc remarks.

"Then we'll send him one from Friedland now, with the castle on it, so he'll know what it is we do here."

"I wonder if we couldn't invite him for a visit." Nordanc seems doubtful.

Podol grins. "We could at least try. He's still a couple of bottles up on us. I'll cook for him!"

He crosses the street, moving stiffly—he has jumped the gun by donning his work clothes, and they slow him down. He lifts his legs as if he were still wading through snow, and is almost caught up in the May Day parade unit of the municipal gas and electric works, which has unexpectedly emerged from a side street, bearing portraits of honored miners and slogans: "WE BELIEVE IN THE STAKHANOVS OF TOMORROW!" "LET US ALL SAVE ON ENERGY!"

A brass band strikes up close by. "And on through burned-out cities, across the rivers of blood, revenging troops roll unrelenting on. . . ."

They are swept along down the narrow street and are unable to escape until they reach Townhall Square, where they grab hold of the trees outside the Four Knights, a building from the Renaissance. The Friedlanders march by: slogans, caricatures of warmongers, false noses, flags.

"Don't stand there under the trees, join the parade!" the demonstrators shout. "Rolling stones gather no moss!"

"We have to get back to the façade!" Podol waves his bottle.

"Better 'higgy tiggy tuggy' than this," Orten mutters.

Elbowing his way out of the crowd on the sidewalk, Svoboda comes toward them. "There you are! And nice tans, too." He gazes enviously at their weathered faces.

"What's new, Antonín?" Podol gives him a hug.

"Same old crap, trouble getting stipends, no shows. But you're the ones with something to talk about! How were things in Nippon?" Svoboda pulls them back under the shade of the trees. "You can give me my passport back this evening, Andy." He looks around. "What's this? Yen?" A brown banknote is stuck to the cover.

"No, Mongolian tugriks."

"Put that away!" Maltzahn whispers.

"Weren't you guys in Japan?"—Svoboda.

"We almost made it to the Gobi," Nordanc says proudly. "I simply can't understand why you Czechs are always moaning about how you can't travel anywhere. On my own passport I never would have . . ." Maltzahn jabs him with an elbow.

"So you never got to Kyoto?" Svoboda is beaming.

"Well, almost," Maltzahn mutters.

"We didn't even make it to Chabarovsk!" Podol laughs. "Here, have a drink. But we were in Ulan Bator! Cheers! Ör!"

"No thanks, it's a little early." Svoboda is no longer smiling. "What were you doing in Ulan Bator?"

"You'd be surprised. Absolutely nothing."

Svoboda looks at them, more with disappointment than *schadenfreude.* "So you simply up and left for six months?"

"It wasn't all that simple," Orten says.

"Qvietone mentioned something about that." Svoboda lowers his voice. "Said you guys put on a play somewhere in Siberia, and did an ad-lib dove for some academics, but not in Mongolia. I didn't believe the part about a hockey game!"

"Is he here?" Podol asks.

"Been back for a month now, and moving fast up the ladder. Almost has the final hurdles behind him at the university—got his professor all perturbed with his talk about his 'friends in the Soviet Union.' Breaks into Russian pop songs every now and then—and who really speaks Russian around here? Besides, he's made a significant contribution to the culture of the town."

"I find that hard to believe," Maltzahn remarks.

"Wait, there they are! You see the director of the museum there? He's especially proud." A banner flutters above the director's head: "OUR GIFT TO SOCIALIST RESEARCH!" and beside it three large papier-mâché objects, which are greeted by spontaneous cheers from the crowd.

"What's that?" Maltzahn is puzzled. "Looks like a Henry Moore, in triplicate."

"Three stools?" Nordanc guesses.

"Reminds me of your tooth, Olbram," Podol says. "Three molars!"

"Lukewarm, but getting warmer." Svoboda is keeping up the suspense. "What do you say, Jan?"

Orten is engrossed in one of the shop windows along the arcade, where Lenin is peering out from among the pink girdles and bras. A fetishist would not have an easy time of it with this underwear. "What?" He turns around, still preoccupied. "Those gnawed bones there?"

"That's it!" Svoboda is delighted. "They're mammoth vertebrae. Qvietone brought them back from Siberia."

They stare at him.

"You don't believe me."

"But of course we do," Podol assures him.

"They were laying a pipeline somewhere out in the tundra and ran across this mammoth. His story is that the construction workers disposed of the whole carcass so that scientists couldn't cordon off the area and jeopardize their bonuses. They fed the meat to the dogs and scattered the bones for miles around. No outsiders were allowed to get even near the site. He was able to stuff three vertebrae into his backpack, that was all that would fit. He almost cried when he talked about the skull, completely undamaged, and whole ribs intact! Meanwhile a bear had wandered into the pipeline and couldn't find its way back out. It ran through five miles of pipe, roaring the whole way because it couldn't see anything or turn around, until it finally came out the other end, and demolished a completed pumping station, which delayed their work for the same amount of time it would have taken to excavate the mammoth."

"And what happened to the bear?"

"Nothing. It ran off. It was still mad enough to bang up a truck as it left, but everybody was able to take cover in time."

"If I know Qvietone, he didn't take cover," Maltzahn says.

"He gathered up his vertebrae, was glad to have their attention diverted. But then the real tug-of-war started. He wanted to bring the bones to Friedland, but the national museum in Prague laid claim to them. So it was agreed that they'd divide them, but Prague wanted at least two. That wasn't the agreement. That got Qvietone angry, and with the help of the local department of orthopedics"—Svoboda grins and looks at Orten—"he carried the day and all three vertebrae of the *Mastodontus sibiricus*—sounds great, doesn't it?—were given to the Friedland Municipal Museum. The *Friedland Echo* has provided us all with new and exciting details every day. These bones are forty times older than those of Cyril and Metoděj! Rumor has it he won't be spared a nomination to the Party."

"Poor kid." Podol laughs. "He was always a little too eager. There he is now, marching with his vertebrae! My, but he's grown big and strong, quite a handsome man! That he got orthopedic support doesn't surprise me. Your doctor always had a good nose for these things, Jan!"

Orten is about to say something, but Maltzahn pulls him under an arch. "It's time we took cover ourselves." Qvietone is about even with them now.

"I want to say hello to him," Nordanc says.

"You can do that later, otherwise we'll never get out of here." Podol observes Qvietone's confident smile. "The future belongs to those guys," he says gloomily. "Have you seen Patera?" He is already thinking of work.

"Once, briefly," Svoboda stammers.

"And where's Max?" Nordanc inquires.

"Who? Your cat? Up at the castle; it wouldn't leave." Svoboda is suddenly in a hurry to rejoin his marching unit. "I'll see you guys later at the Ram."

. . .

The noise reaches its climax, the parade oozes in among the trees. They are showered with confetti, pulled along into the lines of dancers, honked at.

The more people drink and the longer the parade goes on, the more peculiar the slogans. The work pledges are becoming increasingly forthright.

Podol leans against the arch and spells out the banner of the municipal sanitation workers: "MORE BANANAS—FEWER SKINS!" "MORE PUBLIC TOILETS!"

"Pretty brave of them."

"DRY CRIMEAN CHAMPAGNE!" "PILSNER PRAZDROJ!"—the gastronomic branch is greeted with considerable applause. The waiter from the Oriole bows discreetly to Orten. No one seems to understand his poster—"HELP THE EAGLE: ENDANGERED SPECIES!"

"The crowd's getting picky," Podol remarks.

The manager of the Ram has spotted them now and waves with her papier-mâché (roasted) squab. "Mr. Podolský! Back from Japan already? You'll have to tell us all about it this evening!"

The librarian marching with the "cultural workers" likewise sends hopeful glances their way.

"We're going to disappoint a whole lot of folks this evening," Podol says. "Jan, do you still have those Japanese stamps?"

"LET THE MASSES PARTICIPATE, SET NEW RECORDS!" "TOGETHER TO THE SPARTACUS GAMES!"—fourteen-year-old girls, gymnasts in outfits so brief that they distract from their slogans. The Red Star Athletic Club marches in a formation that might have built some sort of figure if it had not been for the uncouth members of Spartak Friedland, second runners-up in the hockey league, who jostle them from behind and shout their demand that Golonka be brought back home—to the enthusiastic cheers of the crowd. "JOINING THE GERMANS WON'T BEAT THE RUSSIANS!" "WE NEED NEW HOLÍKS!" "TENNIS IS CRAP!"

"FEWER PATIENTS—BETTER SERVICE!" "MORE EFFECTIVE ANESTHESIA!"—the municipal hospital marches by in white. Hardy convalescing patients wave their crutches as they roll by in well-oiled wheelchairs and sing songs of uplift—living legends. Wasn't that Marie? Orten tries to plunge into the throng, but is pushed back by a crowd that has gathered around a truck carrying two brown bears beating drums: "WORK FOR PEACE, WARS WILL CEASE!"

"All we need now is an ad for Ropovod Druzhba," Podol says.

The Artists' Union marches past carrying paintings they have not been allowed to exhibit. Their banners read: "SUBSIDIES FOR MATERIALS!" "THE JURY WAS A DISAPPOINTMENT, BUT NOT A SURPRISE!" "ART CRITICISM BY PROFESSIONALS!" Svoboda has joined their ranks and defiantly waves one of his polychromes.

"WHERE ARE THE COLLECTED WORKS OF LADISLAV KLÍMA?"

"DOWN WITH THE NEW HRABAL!" "DOWN WITH BEERY BON-HOMIE!"

"READ MORE!"

"DOLL COLLECTORS, DUMPLING EATERS, ŠVEJKS—KEEP IT UP, CZECHS!"

"BOOK CLUBS FOR 'PUBLIC SECURITY AGENTS'—POLICEMEN HAVE A RIGHT TO AN EDUCATION, TOO!"—the group of teenagers carrying this banner are keeping a sharp eye out, but the spectators applaud and wave.

"They'd do better not to wish for that," Orten says. "Otherwise some cop just might figure out their slogan."

"How did that go? Two policemen find a murdered man outside the library, and write up a report." Podol's voice is rather loud now. " 'How do you spell "library"?' the first one asks. 'I don't know. Come on, let's drag him over to the butcher shop!' " People on the sidewalk laugh.

"The way I heard it, it was the cinema," Nordanc says.

"FORWARD LEFT, FORWARD LEFT, AND NEVER A RETREAT!"

"DON'T JUST STAND THERE UNDER THE ARCADE . . . !"

"ANYONE DRIVING TO PRAGUE ON MAY 3RD?"

"ROOM WANTED!"

"Now they're getting down to business." Podol picks up his brief-case.

Their legs are heavy as they climb the hill to the castle. Podol pulls off his mason's jacket and rolls up his sleeves, as if he can't wait to get to work; he isn't used to this warm weather. Orten looks down the steep side streets, where the crumbling plaster on the houses is even more apparent after the long winter and their long absence. The town is smaller and shabbier than he remembers it, and at the same time more a town like every other town he has seen these last six months.

They turn up the driveway. Behind the portal, the gables of the west side come into view—Podol's hovering giantesses, horseflesh, water snakes, cupids, and Medusa heads. The tulip chimney on the adjacent roof tilts badly to one side. Orten has the feeling that it all should be ripped away, even before the weather can obliterate their work. He wants to keep going, to the top of the hill, then turn back down into town, to check out what is playing at the film club, to find Marie. . . . He wants to go back to Prague, to his stone from the Charles Bridge, lying now under a tarp, to those first rough cuts he has made in it.

Where might Ulbus be now?

What he doesn't want to do is stare at this façade, year in, year out, to waste the warmest months of the year on a bleak wall, alien dust in his eyes and mouth, scratching mindless ornaments in the plaster. Not when he could be chiseling at stone out in the open air, relaxing.

"We're here!" Podol apparently is delighted, and even Maltzahn is looking at the sgraffiti with curious and excited eyes, no longer in such a hurry to get back to Prague. He spots his pears and apples and decides that they don't look all that bad there.

"This wall is done." Podol walks on ahead, without once looking back.

The south side, the one they were working on last, has taken some damage. The façade has cracked, one fissure runs through several sgraffiti: Josef K.'s bicycle license is unrecognizable, likewise the ugly mug of the prison chaplain and the naked butt of Chance, a variation on a theme by Podol.

"Wouldn't you know, the new wall!" Podol runs his hand over the surface. "Someone has been scratching these off!"

"Maybe it was a hard winter," Nordanc says.

"It doesn't happen that fast. Winter was hard on the Tunguska, too." Podol looks up. "What's that scaffold doing over there? We're not done here yet."

Apparently someone is working on the chapel. They move in that direction.

From around the corner Patera emerges with a wheelbarrow of sand. "Václav, so you are here!"

"Standa! When did you guys arrive?" Patera is so dumbfounded that he is not sure if he's really happy to see them.

A large German shepherd appears, a shovel in its mouth. It drops the shovel and starts barking at Podol.

"Hasso, heel!" Jirse, in overalls and a mason's cap, comes stomping up behind him, commands the dog to let him have the shovel, and limps back to a cement mixer on the east side of the chapel. Director Horský is just pouring a bucket of water into it.

"Ah, our artists have returned!" Horský, in an elegant jeans leisure suit, stops what he is doing and gazes at them in curiosity. "Been marching in the May Day parade, too, huh? You've still got some confetti there, Mr. Podolský." He plucks a few red bits of paper from Podol's shoulder.

Maltzahn peers through the arcade into the courtyard and the windows on the first floor.

"In case it's my wife you're looking for, she's gone on a trip, with the children." Horský smiles stiffly.

"I've just about had it up to here with this window dummy," Podol says. "What's going on here, Václav?"

"You must admit we've got quite a bit done in just ten days." Patera is trying to imitate Horský's nonchalant tone of voice.

Podol looks around. "I'd say! Who's that?"

A little man with thinning hair, a silk scarf around his neck and a spatula in his hand, is carefully drawing a loop in fresh plaster at the base of the wall. From there to the corner of the building run two rows of newly decorated coffers—dainty, delicate, monotonous tendrils and festoons. This section is done.

A buxom woman drags over a sack of lime from the carriage house and begins to mix the plaster, while the man fondles her rear end and Jirse looks on, smiling a cheap, obsequious smile.

Before the man can put spatula to plaster, Podol pulls him away from the wall. He stares first at him, then at the wall. "Towers! I should have known! Our pig baron! Didn't you get enough mortar thrown in that degenerate physiognomy of yours?"

"I beg your pardon, when I still had legal claim to a title I was a count." Thurn dusts off the spot where Podol has touched him. "May

I introduce—my dear, this is Mr. Podolský, I believe I told you about him." He squints his eyes. "Countess Erzsébet Báthory, my fiancée."

The woman looks up indolently from her mortar and makes some comment in Hungarian. Podol blinks in disbelief: he is seeing double now. And he is panicked about his façade.

"We shall be married in our family chapel come St. John's Day," Thurn continues, "thanks in large part to the comrade director's kindness." He makes a slight bow in Horský's direction. "But first the façade must be finished. Unfortunately preference was given to plastering the other walls. One cannot in fact call it 'restoring' them," he snorts. "I have taken an unpaid vacation in order to arrange for final preparations here, and my fiancée was so unselfish as to come along as well—even though her own estates in Čachtice are currently being laid waste by socialist economics. And since Master Patera was ready to begin work and our good Jirse was also willing to put his hand to it, I hope that we shall be ready in time. Our work would certainly be in line with the intentions of my uncle, the last legal . . ."

"And you've gone along with this?" Podol glares at Patera, who grins in embarrassment.

"There is a quite pragmatic reason for that," Thurn says with a smile. "Certain relatives of mine . . . exactly who is not important, at any rate a lateral branch—they were here at Christmas and were as horrified as I at the current state of affairs—and for that reason, they have placed a certain sum of money at my disposal. A not inconsiderable sum. Not alms, mind you, the money belongs to me. And since, as you know, one may not officially be in the possession of hard currency . . ."

"Jesus, a thousand marks," Patera whispers.

"What, for the whole wall!" Podol explodes.

"It's only a couple of rows."

"That's extortion," Nordanc says.

"For each of us!"—Patera.

"So that's why that joker is here." Podol nods at Horský, who sidesteps the dog on his way back with the next bucket of water.

"If he converts it on the black market, that's fifteen thousand!" Maltzahn is busy calculating.

"I have a family of five to worry about!" Horský replies with suppressed anger.

"We all have families."—Podol. "What do you mean five . . . ?"

"And Jirse, is he getting a thousand marks, too?" Maltzahn wants to know.

Jirse spits contemptuously in the mixer, his dog barks.

"Jirse is loyal," Orten says.

"Yes indeed, even if you do crack jokes about it! You don't know what loyalty is!" Jirse glowers hatefully at them, his scornful gaze wandering from the director to Maltzahn. "Quite some surprises around here, haha!"

"Pull yourself together!" Thurn casts him a quick glance.

"Ain't none of my business." Jirse slinks over behind the mixer; his dog follows him.

Orten briefly considers keeping Thurn here to ride herd on Jirse, but he wouldn't be allowed to show his face anywhere near the façade.

"But let us not dwell on bagatelles." Thurn waves all this aside. "There is still a certain amount left in reserve, gentlemen. You could begin work right away, and we'd be done that much sooner. And I could share with you, then, something of my ideas . . . or should you wish not to be disturbed, you can begin on the east side, from which one can also have a view of the chapel, and not a stroke of work has been done there. At the very least one could begin with the plastering."

Podol moves closer.

"I do hope that we shall all have an interesting time here together." Thurn laughs. "I hear you were on a trip. A little fresh breeze from the outside would do no harm here. People like myself seldom travel as far as from Stadice to Friedland. What's the news from out there in the world? Japan is still the leading economic power, they say. Their second sword, so to speak . . . At any rate, gentlemen, *konnichiva*, welcome back to your workplace!"

"*Konnichiva*, sayst thou, thou knave!" Podol picks Thurn up and looks around, trying to decide whether to stuff him in the mixer or the wheelbarrow. "I greatly long to see that asshole cadre leader of yours, you pustule! So, you're going to get down on those old knees and marry? And an Erzsébet Báthory at that, a lard-ass that can't even speak Czech? You two can screw wherever you like, in the family crypt for all I care, but you are not going to touch this wall with your filthy, perfumed hands. We beat the tar out of you once already. Where are the sgraffiti we did last year? Why did you scratch off my drawings?"

Incipient death rattles are coming from Thurn.

Jirse unfastens his leg and hobbles over on crutches. "Sic!" Jaws spread wide, the German shepherd leaps at Podol, who gets a good grip and shakes the dog off. It attacks again, and Podol, who has dealt with Siberian wolves, grabs it by the tail and sends it spinning through the air. The pedigreed beast hits the ground with a smack and creeps away with a whimper. Neither Jirse's blows nor commands can rouse it to another attack.

"Too fat and lazy, the poor son of a bitch!" Podol is disgusted, but still manages to parry the whacks from Jirse's prosthesis.

Erzsébet Báthory scoops up a trowelful of mortar and aims it at Podol. She hits Horský, who is resolute in his denunciation of such a squandering of materials. "Not today," Podol tells the countess. "Not with me. A waste of lime. Get out of here right now, otherwise I'll put you all through the mixer and you'll end up on the wall!"

"Like Max and Moritz!" Nordanc remarks, inappropriately, and sticks his leg out to trip Jirse.

"Damn foreigner! Pervert!" Jirse is drooling now as he points at Nordanc.

"Just put your leg back on and ask this bimbo here if she has decorated Čachtice with the same furnishings old lady Báthory used for her torture chamber. How many young maidens was it, three hundred? She needed fresh blood for her bath! Compared to her, de Sade was a repressed duffer! The finest nobility—go ahead and snivel for them, Jirse."

"Erömy!" The woman has found a pitchfork and goes for Podol.

"Don't overtax yourself, sweetheart." Podol ducks, snatches the tool out of her hands and flings it in a wide arc across the lawn. He is surprised at what good condition he is in.

"How dare you behave with such impudence to my fiancée!" Thurn rears back with his spatula and stabs away at Podol, until the handle breaks. Podol is a man steeled by Siberia, and he first watches in amusement, then grabs Thurn by the green acorns on his lapel and shoves him up against the wet plaster. "Your new coat of arms, you bootlicker!"

For one brief moment, flanked by the fresh plaster of his towers, Thurn adorns the façade of Friedland Castle. On his left are the clearly etched lines of wolves' teeth, emblem of the Báthorys. Podol the plebe is not impressed by the grandeur of this anachronistic composition. "We'll make immediate inquiries in Stadice if they are missing a run-away flunky or two—and ask the National Council how it reconciles a church wedding with our workaday socialist world. What a waste of good money the state has spent resocializing you, you kulak! Where did you get this lime, from the shed?" He turns his back on Thurn.

"I bought it myself!" Thurn angrily shouts after him. He looks down at his fancy loden jacket, which is quickly turning stiff, then at the façade, where between the emblems of their two ancient houses—the Báthorys go back to the eleventh century—the texture of quality fabric imported from Germany is clearly imprinted. Madness, madness everywhere.

"We shall inform your cadre leader posthaste that you are working on May Day, the ultimate profanation of the workers' holiday," Orten says. "There are in fact several offenses here—sabotage and iconoclasm."

At this last word, Jirse clings all the tighter to his shovel. The threats of these non-Party members may be no more than bad jokes, but for his master to be subjected to such abuse is worse than his experience with the partisans at the end of the war, when he had to hide in sewers for weeks. He lets out a roar—Thurn holds him back. "Let them be, Jirse, they're rabble."

"Stick your D-marks up your ass and get out of here," Orten says clearly, he has not stammered for quite some time now. "And take Jirse with you. There's no opportunity here for him to show his loyalty."

"Are you really taking all this seriously?" Maltzahn asks with a smirk—and with a little disappointment, too, when he notices that Thurn is packing to leave. "I thought you didn't care about the façade."

Orten looks up at the scratches on the wall. "We've been working at this for years now. We can't let some bungler arbitrarily come in here and destroy it all."

Podol emerges from the carriage house, his neck and shoulder crooked to one side, and right behind him a boy in the same malformed position, as if a polio epidemic had broken out in the shed. Podol is grinning foolishly. "Andy, you're a father!" Nordanc winces; he doesn't like jokes of this sort, and for the last half hour Podol has been sober, or so he thought.

The boy turns out to be Pepi, and the deformity is revealed as four scrambling kittens that have set their claws in Podol's neck and Pepi's shoulder. Max trails out behind Pepi, in the best of health, her fur shining.

"Don't worry, Mr. Podolský is being careful." Pepi picks her up; Max sniffs at Podol's shirt, gives three maternal licks, including one to Podol's chin.

"Here, get her off me!" Podol feels as helpless as he did when he first met the Evenks, but at least he could talk with them.

"Can they really be . . . ?" Nordanc stares incredulously at the colors. One red, two red-white-black, and one black, almost invisible against Pepi's sweater. "This one too?" He hesitantly gathers them up and claps them awkwardly to him as they climb up, purring each time he instinctively reaches out to hold on to them. "They're really very pretty," he says after an embarrassed pause.

"Mendel would've been beside himself with delight." Orten strokes the back of the red one.

"One for each of you!" Nordanc gushes.

"You don't have to," Orten quickly replies.

"I wouldn't mind," mutters Patera, who has been keeping his distance behind Maltzahn.

"Mr. Patera helped me look after them," Pepi says.

"And what are you doing here?" Podol asks. "I thought you weren't supposed to be here until June, with Hanna and the others."

"The rest of them won't be. I'm here for my agricultural fieldwork, it's a graduation requirement. But I'm not staying with grandpa," Pepi adds proudly. She slips Maltzahn a letter. "From Marcela Horská. I decided it was better to carry it around with me. The new address is in it," she whispers.

"Why did you have to look after the kittens, wasn't their 'mother' doing her job?" Nordanc looks suspiciously at Max.

"She's been taking care of them, but she's gone a lot, out catching mice and such. She really tore into the dog once, scratched his nose bloody. He's never risked getting close since then, but you never know." Pepi pets Max, who purrs and brushes against Nordanc's legs. "She's prettier than ever."

Nordanc puts the kittens on the ground. "Which tom was it?"

"There were several." Pepi laughs. "Definitely Fousek from the brewery, but he wasn't alone."

371

"Maxine, we need to talk," Nordanc says.

The cat turns around and marches off to the carriage house; her kittens make a beeline after her, their little tails jutting up at an angle.

Sacks are piled high around Jirse's lawn mower, from which the hood is missing, much to their elation. There are more than their normal allotment at the start of the season—as if the Landmarks Office had always wanted to test their stamina and endurance each year before coughing up the rest of the lime and sand. With hard currency in hand, you don't have to dun them.

Thurn crosses the courtyard with his fiancée and peers into the carriage house at his sacks, but walks on without a word.

"Barely two hundred years after the French Revolution, and he understands that the historic role of the aristocracy in Bohemia is passé," Podol remarks.

"I wouldn't be so sure," Orten says.

Horský has packed his bags and is decamping as well. Jirse is right behind him, with his dog. It growls when it picks up the scent of Podol and the cats.

"Heel!" Jirse hobbles away, and never looks back.

They are all struck by the same thought. "It's too beautiful to be true," says Podol.

"If it comes to that, Qvietone can always retrain that mutt. He only has to spot Jirse, and he starts drooling and breaks out in herpes," Orten says.

"Who? Jirse?"

"No. Jirse just gets the shakes."

Nordanc watches Thurn go. "Who was that really?"

Maltzahn suddenly leans back against one of the beams in the carriage house. They know that expression on his face.

"Olbram, do you have a toothache?" Podol bends anxiously his way. Maltzahn stares right through him, as if radio waves bearing All-Union entertainment have caught up with him again.

They exchange glances.

"She's a very pretty baby, looks just like our Pavlína did," Patera says in a steady voice—he has been staying in the background until now.

"I have to leave right away!" Maltzahn rouses himself from his cataleptic state.

"That's why Horský was so sour!" Podol laughs. "Now you have a family of five to feed, they've been talking about separating for years. Well, let's get to it! There won't be any buses until this evening. And what about you, Václav, can you work without hard currency?"

"Maybe I'd better explain. . . ." Patera searches for something in his pockets.

"Just in case you need it." Podol hands him the bottle. "I won't, not for the rest of the day." He climbs the scaffold. "Andy, say hello for us to old Patočka in the archives, and if you happen to brew a pot of strong coffee, think of us, too. I'm not used to these heights anymore."

"I'm coming along," Pepi says.

They spread out over the scaffold and examine the damage. Repairs will take several weeks, but then they can move on to the new wall.

Horský drives up into the courtyard and loads Thurn's belongings into the car. Jirse and the dog are nowhere to be seen. Thurn looks up at the façade. Podol waits until he gets in the car, he wants to be sure that they are not disturbed in their work again today.

Another dreamer.

They begin, trying to find the rhythm of their routine. They are still isolated islands, each wrapped up in his own pictures and cares, and hopes. Orten draws a yurt and an igloo, sketches a figure that could have stood outside Lena's tent. The façade may be crumbling, but it is too solid for his fleeting vision. The woman looks more and more like Marie. Podol has drawn a Chinese man, but he can't quite capture Liu's smile. He looks up. Above him on the wall are rows of shrubs, flowers, vegetables, and fruits, intermingled with birds, fish, monsters.

We must tend our own gardens.

Maltzahn has sketched a dirigible and a bearskin, he remembers what an *omul* looks like and a *chir,* he draws pelicans and wolves and a railroad car, he is amazed that he can work this fast. He cannot yet bring himself to draw a baby. Patera tries to give more shape and body to the flimsy tendrils and ornaments that he started with. When he notices how the others are scratching away with such furious, greedy energy, he starts spreading the plaster for them so that they won't be slowed down.

They soon discover strange lines that remind them of Chinese characters—along the frieze and in the spaces between the sgraffiti. Podol picks up the story, writes the secret history of the Mongols on the façade.

It is hot. They can hear the "Internationale" being sung down in town, the rally in the square is coming to an end.

Their final battle has been won for today.

Now shines a sun never-ending.

A NOTE ON THE TYPE

The text of this book was set in a Compugraphic version of Sabon,
a type face designed by Jan Tschichold (1902–1974),
the well-known German typographer.
Because it was designed in Frankfurt, Sabon was named for the famous
Frankfurt type founder Jacques Sabon, who died in 1580
while manager of the Egenolff foundry.
Based loosely on the original designs of
Claude Garamond (c. 1480–1561), Sabon is unique in that
it was explicitly designed for hot-metal composition on both the
Monotype and Linotype machines as well
as for film composition.

Composed by Creative Graphics, Inc., Allentown, Pennsylvania
Printed and bound by R. R. Donnelley & Sons, Harrisonburg, Virginia
Designed by Mia Vander Els